THE
MISSING

ALSO BY DAISY PEARCE

The Silence

THE MISSING

MISSING

DAISY

PEARCE

THOMAS & MERCER

Published by Thomas & Mercer, Seattle

www.apub.com

Amazon, the Amazon logo, and Thomas & Mercer are trademarks of Amazon.com, Inc., or its affiliates.

ISBN-13: 9781542018920
ISBN-10: 1542018927

Cover design by Tom Sanderson

Printed in the United States of America

For Poppy, my North Star

'One, two, three, four,
Rattlesnake hunters knocking at your door.
Give them meat and give them bone,
And pray that they leave you alone.'

Samantha – Now

Start with a joke, they'd told him, and so he did. It was the only joke he knew.

'Why is a woman like a vet's finger? Because they're both stuck up bitches.'

The wedding speech went downhill from there. Six months later I gave birth to our daughter, and three days after that he left, moving back to his parents' in Northampton. I never heard from him again. So for a time it was just me and Elizabeth, and now it is just me.

Her name was Elizabeth but I always called her Edie. *Ee-dee*, like the percussion of a heartbeat. The drum of her feet on the stairs that led to her bedroom. *Ee-dee*. It was a fanciful, wistful name, conjuring up images of beatniks and poetry and dappled sunlight on skin. My girl, my Edie, she was not like that. She was a dagger, a thorn, the upturned tack embedded in your heel. Never still, a loose-limbed nail-biter with thick dark hair and round eyes, permanently worried.

After Edie first went missing, I shook for days. I lay in bed, curled on my side with my knees tucked up to my chest, and I trembled so much it looked like a seizure. The doctor told me it was adrenaline, the body's way of coping with the shock. As a kid I'd once witnessed a storm take out the power line of our house. The cable had crackled and snapped and twisted like a snake. My daddy had told me that if I touched it, I'd be barbecued meat. Lying there in my bed, the covers pooled around my feet, body jerking with shock, I felt that same frantic current pass through me.

I still have something from that time: a shopping list that I keep in a drawer. My handwriting's a spidery crawl across the page, almost without cohesion, sliding on a downward tilt. There is nothing steady about it, and it frightens me a little. That's why I keep it. To remind me of how bad it was, those first days after she'd gone. My hands are still shaking now.

My pregnancy was a nine-month-long dash to the toilet, me bilious and woozy, barely able to hold anything down. Try ginger, they told me in the baby group, which I attended alone. Try peppermint. Try yoga. *Try going and fucking yourselves*, I thought, feeling the slow burn of bile rising in my throat.

When Edie was born, I was terrified. It wasn't the blood or the way it seemed to coat everything with its coppery odour. I wasn't afraid of the pain either, not even when it felt as though my spine were filled with crushed glass.

I was afraid of her. The baby.

The midwife who passed her to me whispered, 'She's beautiful', told me she was a perfect little girl, but I wasn't able to see it. I was terrified of Edie; the weight of her, glossy and slick as a baby seal, coated in a waxy vernix. She opened her mouth and instead of the primal howl I had been expecting, she began to mewl like a kitten, tiny fingers clenching and unclenching, her plump face crimson and crushed-looking, irritable. I lay back on the pillows feeling hollowed out. In that moment I wished I could go back in time and undo everything, starting with Mark Hudson and his stupid promises to pull out of me, delivered with his fuggy, alcohol-laced breath. To a time before then even, to ever meeting him, to ever going to the bus stop on that rainy Tuesday, trying to hide behind my *Just Seventeen* magazine and risking sly peeks at him over the pages. Imagine how I feel now, looking back at myself, at the young woman in the past, this new mother, thinking that I wished I could undo it all.

Talk about a life sentence.

Frances – Now

I'm trying not to look at him, but his tears compel me. He has been on the phone for so long our food has grown cold and hardened on our plates. Outside, a car alarm starts bleating *waa, waa, waa*, desperate for attention. William cries silently, wiping his face with the back of his hand. I clench my fists beneath the table hard enough to leave crescent moon imprints in my palms.

'What is it?'

'Mum.' His voice is heavy, like tar. 'She's had a fall. It sounds bad. Alex said she's been taken to hospital. Thank God he was there.'

He's *always* there. William's younger brother, Alex. The little boy who never grew up and left home. What is he now? Thirty?

'William, I—'

'I'm sorry, Frances. Can we just – I need to. . .'

He stands up, runs his fingers through his dark hair. In the candlelight his features soften, eyes glittering, heavy brows drawn together. 'Have we got any brandy?'

'Top shelf,' I tell him. I pick up my phone, put it down again. I'm impatient, sparking with nervous energy. My phone is an unexploded bomb.

I found you out, I want to say. *Rattlesnake*.

But I don't say these things. I can hear William sobbing hoarsely in the kitchen. She's not even dead yet! I don't say that either. Of course not. Instead I go through and sit with him on the cold tiles of the kitchen floor and drink a brandy and carefully I tease the story out of him. We're talking in whispers, even though the little box room above us – the one I've been tentatively referring to as our 'future nursery' since we moved in – remains resolutely empty, except for the teetering files and William's weights in there, gathering dust. He cups his brandy in his hand, holds it close to his chest.

'Alex found her at the bottom of the stairs. He said there was so much blood he was sure she was dead.'

'What have the doctors said?'

'They're still there, running tests. God love the NHS.' He groans. 'Ah, Jesus. It's so hard, Frances. She's only in her seventies. It's too soon for – for all this shit.'

'I know, I know. Will you go down there, do you think?'

'Not sure.'

He tugs at his hair, a habit I've seen before. My stomach curls a little. It's a micro-gesture, and he's unaware of it. Deceit. I've come to know it well.

'You don't have to decide yet. Get some sleep tonight if you can, speak to Alex in the morning. Things might not look so bad once you've got the right information.'

'Knowledge is power.'

It certainly is, I think, venomously. Then, out loud, 'Do you want to come to bed?'

'Nah. I won't sleep now. My brain's rushing all over the place. Think I'll get some work done. Do you mind?'

'Of course not.'

One of the other things in the box room is William's desk and computer, used mainly for his accountancy work and occasional game of online poker. It was the poker I was concerned about, initially. I'd discovered the slow-burning hole in our finances completely by accident, and even though he told me it was just a bad month for expenses I saw that little gesture again – one hand reaching to pull the ends of his hair – and I knew different.

After we sold our three-bedroomed house last year and moved to this one – smaller, cheaper, more comfortable – I started to put aside a little nest egg, carefully curated for 'when the baby comes'. Once a month I add a bit more to the pot, and William does the same, so that when the day comes it'll be one aspect we won't need to worry about. Because that day *has* to be soon, right? Married two years, together for six. I'm thirty-three this year. *It's not a race*, William keeps saying, *we've still got time.* Meanwhile the box room exists as an outlier, dust motes spinning in empty afternoon sunlight.

Thing is, I've started to notice that the nest egg is shrinking. First by a little, then a little more, and a little more. I've rarely checked the balance – as far as we've been concerned, it's off-limits until the day my waters break and, besides, we have other money. It's a saving, right? So, where's it going?

Outwardly nothing has changed – mostly Will is still himself; a little dour, clumsy, shaky from too much coffee – and we've been talking about booking a holiday when my redundancy pay comes through, maybe to India or Thailand. But still, there's that germ, the one that infects my whole nervous system. *Something's wrong.*

The first day I went searching I hadn't known what I was looking for, only that the sour, uneasy feeling in my stomach had got worse those last few days. His computer was switched off, the box files full of random paperwork labelled with his neat, blocky handwriting: *Bills, Mortgage, Warranties.* On his desk, beneath the piece of coral he uses as a paperweight, was a small stack of documents. I slid the top one aside with my finger, then the next and the next. Halfway down the pile I found something that caught my attention: a handwritten bill of sale for seven hundred and fifty pounds. The descriptor read only *SSB (MM)*. The headed paper read *Porters of Mayfair*, the date written in heavy ink in the top left corner. Nineteenth of March. My eyes stung, and a pain blossomed in my stomach. I sat down in his chair, staring at the piece of paper as though I could somehow decode it. *Something to do with the car, maybe? A repair?* No, no. He would have told me. William told me everything. It used to drive me mad to hear the long, detailed litany of his day, particularly when I'd first left work and was bored stiff, but I wouldn't have missed this, would I? No. I was scrupulous about our assets, particularly when we were more reliant on our savings than ever. I thought about the online poker again as I slid the bill of sale back into the stack of papers. *SSB (MM)*.

Later that night, I curled into William on the sofa, my feet tucked beneath me, my head on his chest so that his heartbeat drummed against my cheek. He had a half-drunk bottle of beer in his hand. He smelled good, comfortable. I tilted my head up to catch his eye. He smiled down at me.

'All right, babe?' he said.

'Sure,' I told him.

And for a while, it was.

I didn't want to know. Sealed myself in ignorance, cocooned by my defences. Easier that way. Safer.

But two weeks later my eyes rolled open as the alarm went off and I knew what was going to happen. Even as I scraped my knife against the toast and took a mouthful of too-hot tea, my head foggy and dense with tiredness, I knew. I showered and dressed and dried my hair, taking my time. I kissed William goodbye and then I sat at my laptop and listlessly browsed the job sites, one eye on the clock. When it reached nine, I took a deep breath and opened the door of the study again. The rain pattered softly against the narrow window. It felt as if it had been raining for days, a shimmering veil of grey silk. The sky was the colour of worn stone.

At the top of the receipt I'd found during my first search was a phone number and I dialled it quickly, feeling my heart pick up as a voice at the other end said, 'Porters of Mayfair, good morning.'

I explained, in a voice that was running just a fraction too fast, that I was trying to do my tax return and had discovered a receipt among a pile of others, although I couldn't for the life of me remember what the item I'd purchased was and would she be able to help me, please?

There was a pause and then the voice answered, 'I'll try.'

'It just says "SSB" with "MM" in brackets. The price was seven hundred and fifty pounds.'

'It's a bag,' she said almost immediately. 'Sequin Shoulder Bag by Miu Miu. Your husband paid cash.' There was a silence and then her voice came again. 'Are you still there?'

'I'm still here. Thank you, you've been very helpful.'

That evening Will called me. It was nearly seven o'clock, and I'd offered to pick him up from the station because the rain had grown heavy, sluicing against the windows in gusts. His commute, uncomfortable and expensive and nearly two hours long, had been part of his reluctance to move house when I'd first started pressing him about it. He'd told me he didn't want to live in suburbia and I'd told him Swindon wasn't suburbia, and he'd said did I know that an anagram of 'Swindon' was 'disown' and that maybe he'd disown me if I kept on about it, and that had made me laugh and then everything had been good again.

'Babe, I'm going to be late home.'

A coldness, spreading in my chest. In the background I could hear the faint rumble of conversation and music, a pub perhaps.

'Why?'

'Huh? Sorry, it's so noisy in here. I'm in the pub, the one by Paddington, you know? I came for a drink with Matt and Olly and I've only just seen the time. I'm only staying for one more, though.'

Silence. I let it float, like dark clouds.

'Babe? Frances? You mad at me? It's only a couple of pints.'

'No, it's not. It's not that. Who did you say you were with?'

The noise faded a little. Perhaps he'd moved outside. I could picture him with his overcoat unbuttoned and the phone pressed against his ear, stubble shading his jaw. Maybe he was playing with his hair, tugging at it the way he does when he's lying. My hand gripped the phone tighter.

'Matt and Olly.'

'Which Matt?'

'The one from – sorry, mate – I'm in someone's way. The one who used to live by us.'

'The courier?'

'No, the other one. The Arsenal supporter. Are you okay? You sound weird.'

'Put him on.'

Silence. My heart quickened.

'What?'

'Matt. Put him on the phone to me. I want to say hi.'

Will laughed uneasily. 'You barely know him, Frances.'

'Just do it, would you?'

He sighed; the line bristled with static. I waited, holding my phone so tightly that my knuckles were turning white. I had forgotten how to breathe. There was some rustling, and then a surprised voice, male, cheerful-sounding.

'Frances? Long time no speak! How are you?'

'Matt?'

'Yeah! From Turnham Road. I bumped into Will as I was heading to Paddington. You all right, yeah? You staying dry? It's miserable up here. Hang on, hang on, he wants the phone back – we promise we won't keep him out too late!'

William's voice sounded heavier when he took back his phone and asked me again if everything really *was* all right.

'You need to be working,' he told me. 'All this time at home alone, it's not good for you.'

By the time I hung up, tears were building behind my eyes and I blinked them away before they could spill, annoyed at myself. *If William was having an affair, you would know*, I told myself sternly, opening a bottle of wine. Besides, when would he find the time? He's on a train for four hours a day and in an all-male office the rest of the time.

One of a team of only three, Will's computer consultancy business had nearly been called The Three Amigos before I pointed out that there were copyright laws against that sort of thing. They'd settled on Three Squares because, as they told me, they were the most boring nerds they knew. Straight down the line. Dependable. Prosaic to the point of banality. It was one of the things I'd loved about William the most, in the beginning. My polar star, guiding me away from the wreckage of my twenties, sane and modest and easy to read, so unlike the other men and women I'd had relationships with.

Not long after we'd first got together I'd gone out alone one night and ended up drinking in a basement bar in Camberwell before finding myself at a party in Vauxhall in the early hours. Some woman had pressed a pill on to my tongue and I'd swallowed it without thinking, washing it down with warm cider and a kiss that smeared my lipstick. 'I don't normally take MDMA,' I'd told her, and she'd smiled and said, 'It isn't MDMA, sweetie.'

For the next three hours my body had turned to liquid, something hot and molten beneath the strobing lights. Shadows swam at me, and I kept finding myself in the same spot where I'd begun, sitting on gritty concrete behind a speaker which rattled my poor prone body with each beat. I don't remember doing it, but somehow I'd called William and he'd driven to collect me with only the vaguest of directions, searching the Vauxhall arches for me with his sweater on over a pair of cotton pyjamas as people around him ground their teeth to powder, eyes rolling, sweat sour and ripe. He'd taken me back to his house even though I'd vomited down my front and my legs wouldn't work, and he'd had to put an arm around my waist to guide me. He'd put me to bed in his spare room, crisp cotton sheets with the creases still in from the packaging and a bowl beside the bed. I'd slept for nine hours straight, only waking up once to see him putting a cup of tea next to me, brushing stray hairs from my face.

My man. Even his name, William, meant 'resolute protector'. That was how he was. But still, as I sat in front of the television that night, waiting to hear his key in the lock, my heartbeat fluttering wings against my ribcage, I kept thinking. Over and over, until the wine washed the thoughts away.

I'm not proud of what I did next, but I was getting desperate and needed to get on to his computer, just for peace of mind. God, 'peace of mind', what a lovely phrase. My mind was in perpetual motion, even in sleep, like a snake eating its own tail.

Because many of 'Three Squares' clients were in other time zones, William spent a proportion of his time making phone calls in the middle of the night from the box room. Some nights when I couldn't sleep, I would lie awake and listen to the soothing rhythm of Will's voice asking, 'How's the weather out there in Kyoto?', 'How's Seattle treating you today?' and '*Ni hao*, Mr Ling, I hear you need our help.' It was a balm, his voice, in the dark.

About three days after I'd called Porters of Mayfair, I sat awake, back pressed against the wooden headboard of the bed. I'd been trying to read a book, but the words had slid about on the page like grease in a pan. In the end I just gave up and sat there, hands folded on my lap, listening to the metronomic tick-tock of William's muffled voice. The clock read three-oh-seven as I slid out from under the covers and padded to the box room. The door was ajar and William was leaning back in his chair, talking on the phone. When I silently pushed the door open he looked over at me, his eyes widening as he covered the mouthpiece with his hand.

'You're naked!' he whispered, smiling, trying not to laugh. 'What are you even doing awake?'

'I'm horny,' I said. 'Come back to bed.'

He laughed, but I could see how dark his eyes had turned. That was the thing with Will. I always turned him on. Still, I remember how he shook his head, saying uh-huh, sure, sure into the mouthpiece while frantically waving me away. I didn't go. I walked on tiptoe into the room and bent over his desk so my nipples brushed against the keyboard. I hissed between my teeth as they immediately hardened into small, pink peaks. I let my free hand slide down my stomach, in between my legs, shifting my position a little so he could see. He'd stopped shaking his head now. Poor William was frozen to the spot. I pulled my hand away after only a moment so he could see my fingers glistening, before sliding them between my lips and closing my eyes, tasting myself. I heard his voice, strangled-sounding, telling his client he would check in with him tomorrow and not even waiting for a reply. He put his hands in my hair and pulled me towards him so that when our lips met they were crushed against my teeth.

His breath tasted of coffee and the antacids he chewed. I felt it against my cheek as I led him into the bedroom, shedding his clothes with a speed I rarely saw in Will, pressing his erection against me and tangling his hands in my hair. When he came he arched his back and his hands were claws on the curves of my shoulders, digging into the flesh to the point of pain, a sharpness that thrilled me. However much he loved me I could never get him to agree to hurt me, even consensually. This would have to do.

Another thing I know of Will is that he always, always, sleeps after sex. It's a perverse narcolepsy, a form of sexual concussion. I lay still, waited for his breathing to soften and lengthen, watching the rise of his belly in the darkness. I looked back at the clock. Three thirty.

William's computer has a timeout setting of thirty minutes before you need to re-enter the password to gain access again, and even though only twenty-three minutes had elapsed since I'd left the bedroom I had no idea how long he'd left his computer idle before I'd gone in there in my birthday suit, smiling wickedly. Perhaps I was already too late, I thought as I sat in his chair. I pulled the keyboard towards me, alert to any movement from the bedroom, the rustle of the bedcovers, a hand scratching at his chest. *I should have closed the bedroom door*, I thought; *at least then I'd hear him coming.* Too late now. The screen lit up. It was unlocked.

Carefully, I minimised every tab he had open until I reached the desktop. I didn't really know what I was looking for. I opened his emails and scrolled quickly through, looking for anything unfamiliar, a name I didn't recognise. One thing I've learned about myself from leaving home aged just sixteen is that I know instinctively when something is amiss, and trust me, living like that, it's fucking exhausting.

Nothing jumped out at me. In fact, his most recent emails had been *to* me, sending me a link to a new gym that was opening near our home and suggesting jobs I could apply for. His search history was a combination of media sites and clients, with a handful looking at Airbnbs in southern Thailand and flights to Indonesia (third choice on our list). Nothing for Porters of Mayfair, and his last visit to a poker site had been nearly three months ago. I even discovered a news alert set up for the small town he grew up in. In fact, I was so caught up that I barely noticed when the sky started to lighten outside. I stretched, hearing the muscles of my spine click noisily. I wanted a shower, to get warm somehow. The rain hushed against the glass as I closed down the browser windows and stood up, careful to leave his desktop as he'd left it. He couldn't know I'd been snooping.

That's when I found it.

A memory stick, taped behind the screen of his computer. I reached down for it carefully, using my fingers like tweezers. My hands shook as I pushed it into the port, and just for a moment I had that same sour taste rising in the back of my mouth, fear tasting like spoiled apple juice.

My stomach clenched as I opened up the folder and peered at the single file there. The name of it was numeric: 16032015. *Secret bank account*, I thought as I clicked on the folder. *He's hiding money from you. You knew it all along, you felt it in your gut and he—*

I caught my breath. Snatched it, holding it hot and shivering in my throat.

She was young, although beneath the carefully applied make-up and coy, doe-eyed poses it was hard to tell. She knew her angles, I can tell you that much. Her skin was as golden as Egyptian silk. Her nose was long and straight with a noticeable bump on the bridge that only surgery could iron out. There was a piercing in her nose, a tiny silver stud, barely there. She had a curtain of straight dark hair, glossy and slick. I touched my hand to my own messy blonde waves, half grown out from a blunt bob I'd given myself last autumn. I felt something in my chest, a singular shard of glassy pain. Envy, maybe.

I quickly flicked through the handful of photographs. She wasn't naked, but her underwear was revealing: the hard little bumps of her nipples beneath peach-coloured lace, the soft creases of her upper thighs as she sat on the edge of a bed, toes pointed, delicate and ballerina-like, to elongate and define her calf muscles. Like I said, the girl knew her angles. In one she was bent over a dressing table, ass towards the camera, pink satin and the long road of her spine just visible where her hair fell. She was looking back at the lens with an eyebrow arched, slight smile on her glossy lips, and in her hand was a bag. I stared at it for what felt like a long time, even as outside the birds began to sing. A pink sequin shoulder bag with a chain strap, and on it, the Miu Miu logo in silver. Distantly, I heard the alarm going off in the bedroom, the grunting noise Will made as he reached for it, his voice furred with sleep.

'Frances? Where are you, babe?'

'I'm just here,' I said, struggling to keep my voice straight. I hurriedly pulled the USB out and taped it back behind the screen. I'd barely had time to close everything down when I heard his feet shuffling out into the hallway, the long, elastic sound of him yawning. I was swept with a fierce chill that flushed my skin with goosebumps and rattled my teeth.

In all the years we'd been together I'd never ached for him as much as I did right then.

After that, I waited each morning for Will to leave, his bag slung crooked over his shoulder, hair still damp from the shower, and I would watch him walk up the tree-lined avenue towards the train station in the pearly morning light. I'd watch him until he was out of sight, letting my forehead lean against the glass until my breath misted my vision. Then I would take the USB from its hiding place behind the computer and look through the photographs over and over again, searching for clues in her poses, in the background of her small, messy flat, until acid burned the back of my throat. Her mirror, smudged with fingerprints; the unmade bed, the tattoo snaking up her outer thigh, the catalogue flatpack furniture – nothing gave me any idea about the type of person she was or how she knew my husband so intimately.

I studied the faces of every dark-haired woman on the street, on the train, looking for the familiar lines of her features; almond-shaped eyes heavy with kohl, narrow lips, that thin, angular chin. Since I'd first seen her photographs I'd felt there was something familiar about her, and it was only after a week or so that it came to me. Samira.

When I'd first told William about my previous relationships with women, we'd both been drunk on wine and Pernod and he'd struggled to conceal his interest.

'Is it better or worse than with men?' he'd asked, picking up the knife and cutting a chunk of brie from the cheeseboard on the table. The candlelight had carved shadows in his features, sharp glaciers of bone. 'Like, is it, uh, softer?'

'Softer?' I'd laughed. 'How do you mean?'

He'd shrugged awkwardly, and I'd decided to make it easier for him. 'Do you mean hornier? Is that what you mean? You want to hear about me with women, is that it?'

'God, yes. Fuck. I thought you'd never offer.'

We'd both laughed. Then, he'd leaned in closer. 'Was there ever anyone serious?'

'Sure.'

'Who?'

'She was beautiful. Let me just get that out the way. As you know, I'm incredibly shallow' – we'd both laughed, because it's true – 'and Samira was just – you ever meet someone so good-looking you almost forget to breathe? Like that. She had long hair almost to her waist and the darkest, blackest eyes I've ever seen. She knew all these great bars and clubs and just dazzled everyone she met, and I can honestly say that it's the only time I've been happy to be in someone else's shadow. She had tattoos and a piercing in her nose and another in her labia and she made me feel – I don't know – *vital.*'

'You're so pretentious.' William had laughed, but his voice was heavy and when he kissed me I could tell by his urgency how turned on he was. It had been funny, at the time.

Samira. That was who she looked like, William's mystery girl. The piercing, the long curtain of hair, that golden skin. At least, I thought more reasonably, she looked like my *description* of her: the one I'd given him all that time ago on a humid night in Avignon, our sweat glistening and scented with aniseed.

If you'd asked me any time over the last six years how I'd react to William's infidelity, I would have laughed and told you William was no more capable of infidelity than he was of alchemy. Finding the photos had shaken me, but not in the way I would have expected. I felt energised, curious. That same feeling of elemental *wrongness* persisted, and I couldn't put my finger on why, and until I could I didn't feel like I could confront him. I felt like I needed to know more. Knowledge is power, after all.

That night I cooked tarragon chicken (a memory of Avignon still lingering, perhaps) and Will noticed as soon as he came through the door. He put his bag on the sofa slowly, telling me how good I looked. I'd tidied my hair and put on the simplest thing I owned – a mid-length black dress with spaghetti straps – because William liked things simple. Or so he'd told me. Now, though, who knew?

We ate sitting close to each other, not opposite one another but side by side on the floor, our backs against the sofa, legs stretched out in front of us. I'd lit candles, and the dreamy scent of next door's roses washed in through the open window. The rain of the last couple of weeks had given way to a clear, bright warmth.

'I noticed you're not sleeping very well at the moment,' he said, spearing a piece of chicken with his fork. 'You having those bad dreams again?'

It's happened before. Me, running through my dream, heavy and ugly and slow-moving as molasses, chased by a man with a hammer raised over his head. I don't know where this image has come from. A film maybe, or a story told to me as a kid by my older sister. The finer details of the dream change from time to time; sometimes I'm a kid with scabby knees and a bowl haircut, sometimes I'm in the jungle, sometimes I'm underwater, but it's always a hammer and it's always the kind with two hooks on the back, a claw-head. When I have these dreams William tells me I start to twitch and then cry out, clawing at the air. I wake in a panic, close to tears. It wasn't the dreams, though. Not this time.

'Do you love me, Will?'

He paused, fork halfway to his mouth. I watched him carefully and sipped my wine. Waited.

'Of course. What kind of question is that?'

'You don't sometimes wish things were different?'

'No!'

'Ever miss being single?'

'Jesus, Frances.' He picked up his own glass and drained it. 'What's brought this on?'

'Sometimes I feel like you're not really here.'

'I have to work, babe. It's all I do. We're living off one wage right now until you get another job.' He held up a hand to ward off a verbal attack. 'I know, I know. Employment is tough to find at the moment. I'm not blaming you. It's just tiring, that's all. And now you're having a go at me for not being present—' His phone vibrated in his pocket, just once. A message. He put his plate to one side and reached for it. 'It feels a little unfair.'

'I suppose I've just been thinking about the old times recently. Before.'

'Before what?'

But he wasn't listening. He was looking at his phone. Whatever that message was, it was holding his attention. He stood up, still staring at the screen.

'Where are you going?' I asked him, my heart beating too fast. I wanted him to stay, I wanted to claw at him and drag him back towards me so I could bite the soft sides of his neck until he gasped with pain. He flicked his eyes up to me, just once, then back to the phone, scrolling.

'Email from Phil at work. I need to go upstairs and get some information for him. I'll be two seconds.'

His hand strayed to his hair and tugged at the curl there, just once. *You lying bastard*, I thought.

That night I waited until I heard his breathing soften and then I slid out of the bed and into the box room, swiping the USB stick from its usual place at the back of his computer. I loaded it into my own laptop and locked myself in the dark bathroom. There were more photos. I thought of that message he'd received earlier and a bitterness rolled through me. I clicked on them all the same. She was in a different room this time, and it was daylight, but the poses were the same, the looks she was casting towards the camera hazy-eyed, glassy almost. Stoned or bored, it was hard to tell. She wore sheer black knickers and no bra, holding her breasts in her hands as if she couldn't contain them. I was fascinated with her; the sparse rooms with the peeling wallpaper, ashtrays balanced on the arms of sofas, even the small bruise flowering at the top of her hip. I was fuelled with a slow, throbbing anger that made my muscles clench. I enlarged the picture, taking in her false eyelashes, the mole on her elbow, the thinning places on her scalp where her hair extensions needed refitting. Then, in the background, through the window overlooking the street, a sign. Sandwiched between a bookmaker and a Turkish restaurant – *Tufnell Park Food & Wine*. I stared at it for a long time. *Found you*, I thought.

I didn't tell William I was planning to go to London. I forced myself to wait an hour after he'd left the house the following morning before picking up my bag and heading out the door. I was dizzy with a reckless, headstrong sensation I hadn't felt in years. I wore a bright lipstick and winged eyeliner as sharp as a knife and when a man smiled at me on the Bakerloo line I returned it with feeling. By the time I got to Tufnell Park I was fizzing with adrenaline. My mother used to say I was *spoiling for trouble* when I got like this as a kid. She'd tell my sister not to come near me. She was right.

I found Tufnell Park Food & Wine quicker than I expected. Outside the tube station I handed a couple of pounds to a young woman with damp, grey skin sitting with a cardboard sign in front of her reading *Need WORK, Need MONEY.*

There but for the grace of God, I thought as I pulled my phone from my pocket and opened up the picture I'd transferred to it. I lifted the screen so I could find the angle seen through the window, moving it slightly left and right until I discovered a match. I looked up towards the building above the phone shop I was standing outside, the windows reflecting the cobalt sky like still water.

There were three buzzers at the entrance to the flat and as I pressed the first one I felt the first tremblings of anxiety. *What the hell are you doing?* a voice in my head asked me, and I answered in a whisper, raking my fingers through my hair: 'Spoiling for trouble.'

There was no answer at the first buzzer and after ringing it a second time I moved on to the one above it. This one had a name label attached but the writing had rubbed off. After a minute a voice blared out, fuzzy with distortion.

'Yes?'

'I'm looking for – uh, a girl, a woman who lives here—'

'Oh yeah? Which one?'

Shit. *Shit.* I hadn't thought this through.

'She has dark hair. Very pretty.'

I waited. The voice, young-sounding, female, seemed to consider for a moment.

'Probably Kim. Wait there.'

I waited, digging my hands into my pockets. Behind me a car horn blared and a cyclist responded crisply: 'Go fuck yourself!' When the door opened there was a young woman standing there, dark hair cut into a sharp bob, round blue eyes looking down at her phone. I felt a spike of disappointment.

'You're not Kim.'

'Nope.' She looked up at me once, scanning my face. I could almost see her interest drop off. I'm old, I'm plain. I'm a hausfrau. 'Kim's at work.'

She extended her hand, still tapping on her phone. 'You've got a package, have you?' When I told her no, she rolled her eyes. 'Give me your name, I'll tell Kim you were here.'

'Wait, hang on. Where does she work?'

'Today she's in Arlo's. You might still catch her.'

'Where's that?'

'God,' she huffed. 'Mate, you want me to draw you a map as well? It's down on the high street.' She pointed to the left, and without looking up from her phone, slowly closed the door in my face. I stared at it for a moment before turning and walking away.

Arlo's was a cafe with steamed-up windows and a radio playing too loud. The dance music jarred, given the mainly geriatric clientele mopping up fried egg with slabs of white bread. I picked up a laminated menu but barely looked at it. She was here: behind the counter, that sweep of glossy hair held back from her face in a bun. I recognised the jut of her chin, the slim line of her neck, her expression giving her an air of sweeping contempt. Not William's type *at all*. *Oh, she is,* a sneaky little voice in my head interjected; *you just didn't know it.*

'What are you after?' she asked me. Like her friend at the door, her eyes slid away from me with disinterest. She peeled a page of her notebook back and picked up her pen.

'Tea,' I told her, unsmiling. I took a seat at a table near the window and swept the crumbs from it on to the floor. I watched her approach, skinny hips and ankle boots and studs in the curves of her ears. I waited, predatory. My heart raced and I liked the feel of it, that edge. When she put the cup on the table I grabbed at her hand and pinned it there, pulling her towards me in a quick, jerking motion.

'Hey, what the fu—' she cried out, trying to pull away, but I was too strong, too angry. Her mouth formed a neat, pink 'o' of surprise.

'I know you,' I whispered, and gave her hand a brisk squeeze that made her eyes snap up towards me. They were round and shocked. *Good.*

'Let go of me!'

'You've been fucking my husband.' I said it as quietly as I could beneath the music, spitting the words into hard little bullets.

To my surprise she let out a bark of laughter. 'What would I want with your dusty old husband?' She clucked her tongue. 'You better let go of my hand, yeah?'

I didn't. I scrabbled for my phone. She watched me with nothing more than mild interest and pointed good humour.

'This is you. Isn't it?'

She looked over the picture I was showing her. 'Yeah. I wasn't well that day. Allergies. You can see my eyes are still red.'

'Why does he have these photos?' I spat. Her apathy was frustrating. She lifted those dewy brown eyes back to the counter and signalled to someone standing there. Just a finger raised. *One minute.* Then she sat in the chair opposite me, her back to the glass.

'You want this tea or not?'

I shook my head. She pulled it towards her and tipped in packet after packet of sugar, lifting spilled grains from the table with the damp pad of her thumb and transferring them to her mouth. She examined me carefully.

'Where you from?'

'That's not your business.'

'I feel like you've come a long way just to confront me. Why aren't you sitting your husband down and asking him these questions?'

It was a good point. None of this was going the way I'd thought it would. I felt myself beginning to deflate, anger hissing from me like a punctured tyre.

'You been married a long time?'

'Two years. But we've been together for six.'

She drew breath through her teeth, vexed. 'Christ. That's a third of my life.'

'You didn't answer my question. Why does he have these photos of you?'

'He paid for them.'

'What?'

'He paid for them. That's what they do. That's the whole point.'

'I don't – I'm not sure—'

'Here. Give me your husband's name.'

I stared at her in frank disbelief. 'You don't know his name?'

She laughed again, but gentler this time. 'Listen. Half these men, I don't even know what they look like. Including your husband, probably. You know what this is, right? This arrangement?'

I shook my head, heart sinking. She sighed.

'There's a website. "Secret Sugar". You heard of it?' When she saw my blank expression she shrugged. 'Never mind. It's for men who like to give their money to girls like me who need it.'

'What do you give in exchange?'

She nodded towards my phone. 'Pictures. Nudes, if they earn it. You've heard of sugar daddies, yes? Paypigs? Men with spare cash and us girls needing to pay our bills and university fees – makes sense if you think about it. If you think me working in this cafe is paying enough for me to live in London, you're wrong.'

'How much?'

'Like I said, depends. I've got a couple of regulars who give me a monthly allowance for photos and stuff. Sometimes I let them take me on dates. Others just drop in and out, send gifts, ask for underwear pics, you know?'

'He – my husband, Will – he bought you a bag. A Miu Miu one.'

She smiled. It was so genuine it broke my heart. 'Oh yeah. "Rattlesnake80". That's his username. He's nice. Kind. Always very polite. He helped me with my credit card bills a few months ago. I like him.' She looked at me with concern. 'You're not going to leave him over this, are you? It's just pictures, that's all. It's not real life. None of it's real life.'

On the train home I sat stiffly, bag on my lap, fingers pinching the top of it so hard the tips turned white. I kept thinking of the way Kim had looked at me, a mixture of pity and agitation. *Why aren't you sitting your husband down and asking him these questions?* she'd said, and I hadn't been able to answer. I hadn't known how to tell her about my fear of losing him, his stability and humbleness and all of it, all of it; the velvet sofas and the granite worktops and the even keel, holding steady, not drowning in debt and waking up bilious and raw with self-loathing in the shadow of a three-day hangover – he is the weight that pins me to the earth. I can't lose him. I'd float away.

Still, I thought as I got off the train at Swindon on legs that weren't quite steady, *still. We can't have this secret between us.* My mother had told me that these sorts of secrets were like a worm in an apple, destroying it from the heart out. She'd been drunk, of course. In the days before I'd moved out, one or both of my parents had been drunk, clumsily stroking my hair and pouring their twisted wisdom into me, how love was blind, was sour, was a lie. Their breath had been wine and cigarettes and rot.

◆ ◆ ◆

That evening I made a lasagne with a brown and bubbling crust, and opened a bottle of Merlot as William walked through the door. I heard his coat and bag slither to the floor, his keys jangle into the dish. I knew exactly how it would feel to kiss him – the coldness on his lips from the outside air, the smell of the trains and all those other people, cigarette smoke and pollution. I waited until he was sitting opposite me before I spoke, passing him his plate.

'I went into town today. London, I mean.'

'Oh yeah? This looks great, babe. Did you get up to much?'

'I went shopping.'

'Uh-huh.'

I was watching him eat. I was slow. Deliberate. 'I went to a place in Mayfair. Porters. It's very fancy. Long way out of our price range.'

He looked up at me, chewing slowly. Something passed over his features in that moment, a ripple. Annoyance, maybe. Fear. 'Did you buy something?'

'No. Like I said, we don't have the money to be shopping in places like that. They had handbags in there that cost nearly eight hundred pounds!'

His hand, straying to his hair, pulled at it gently. He drank some wine, leaned back in his chair. He was smiling. 'And what would *you* do with an eight-hundred-pound handbag, beside trash it and lose it?'

It was a joke, I knew that. I'm forever losing things – leaving them on buses, dropping them in puddles and in the road. William used to call me an urchin because I dirtied everything up. But I wasn't laughing, not this time. I picked up my phone, jabbing in the code so I could open up the photo I'd saved on there of Kim, the one she'd sent him with her back arched and her lips just parted, looking suggestively over her shoulder. *Spoiling for trouble.* At that moment William's own phone rang. He looked at it briefly, then stood up, apologising.

'Sorry, it's my brother, I'd better take it.'

When he left the room I shoved my plate away from me and drained my wine. I massaged my temples, tried to steady my breathing. My pulse was ticking like a clockwork motor in my neck and outside, the car alarm, demanding, *waa, waa, waa.*

I know what you've been doing, Rattlesnake80. I'm so angry. It's a bitter, acidic feeling that ulcerates me on the inside, the sting of deception. I can't ignore it. It won't go away. It will keep me awake at night, the poison of it infecting my sleep, making it toxic. Then the dreams will start again, that faceless figure with the claw hammer raised, drawing ever closer until their footsteps pound and their shadow spills over me like ink.

But, of course, then he comes back through the door with his shoulders hunched as though against a great wind and I can see the tears that are shivering in his eyes, ready to fall.

'What is it?' I ask.

'Mum.' His voice is heavy, like tar. 'She's had a fall. It sounds bad. Alex said she's been taken to hospital. Thank God he was there.'

I pick up my phone. I have to do this. It's going to eat me up if I don't.

'William, I—'

'I'm sorry, Frances. Can we just – I need to . . .'

Inside me a coldness blooms, like a bite of snow.

Samantha – Now

There's a new man working in the shop today. I like him. He smiles and charms and calls me 'madam'. He doesn't know me, so there is none of the bottomless sympathy that I often see in the eyes of people who know about what happened. I'm so used to seeing it I notice when it is absent. Like gravity.

This man is pleasant, although you can tell he's bored already. He's young, and this is just a job to cruise on, to get by. Just enough to pay his rent and get him out at the weekend maybe. Parties with his friends, some booze and some cigarettes, maybe some – I don't know, what is it now? Ecstasy? Is that still popular? I don't think anyone takes speed any more, do they? Whatever it is now. I never have to go through this with Edie – I suppose in a way that's lucky. She's frozen, isn't she? She'll never come home in the back of one of her friends' parents' cars, stinking of alcohol with sick in her hair. She'll never fall pregnant at school, get mugged or get raped. She won't settle for less than she's worth or marry someone who likes the fear on her face when he hits her. I won't ever have to smile and pretend I like her new tattoo, her life choices or her baby names. Is that meant to make me feel lucky? I don't know.

◆ ◆ ◆

Today my skin feels heavy and cold like clay. I'm a golem, conjured to life. I leave the shop and walk alongside the river, which is peaty-brown and fast-moving. Overhead are drifts of white clouds, as fine as lace.

I cried this morning, for the first time in a long time. A boy, up in Manchester. Eleven years old. He'd been missing over a week, his body eventually discovered weighted and dropped like an anchor in the canal. They had arrested the boy's uncle. The news footage showed him driven into court in one of those vans with the blacked-out windows. People were throwing things at it, shouting. One man had a placard that said *Burn In Hell*. The crowd were chanting, 'Die, scum, die.' I found tears on my cheeks and wiped them away with the back of my hand.

In the days when Edie first went missing I was raw with a kind of undernourished grief, like the throb of a toothache. Back then I cried the same way, with a frequency and desperation I was only half aware of. Some days I would find myself in a queue at the supermarket or bent over a crossword and be surprised to discover my face wet with tears.

I had a grief counsellor, for a while. Some sessions my GP had organised for me. A leaflet and a cup of tea in a polystyrene cup in a small beige room that smelled of yeast and damp cloth. She didn't last long. I've visited several on and off over the years, when finances will allow. They fill a need in me to be heard. To say Edie's name in the stillness of the room. Right now, though, I am quite calm, feeling a strange sense of disintegrating, as though I'm floating apart. 'Dissociation', my last counsellor called it. She was worried that I wasn't confronting my feelings, but I've had nearly eighteen years to confront my feelings – because that's how long it's been now since my little girl walked out of the door. A Thursday, October the ninth in the year 1997. Spice Girls and *Titanic* and Princess Diana dying in a dark Parisian tunnel and Tony Blair and Pokémon and my daughter, Edie.

I take the path across the large playing field, away from the river. From here I leave the town behind. Straight ahead past the industrial estate upon which squat concrete blocks: housing offices, carpet warehouses, depots. A thicket of brambles and nettles grows through the diamond-shaped fencing adjacent to the road, pushing through the gaps hungrily, with purpose. Serrated edges and spikes and bristles, fine white hairs that make your skin itch. The dust eddies and rises in the low breeze. Even the weeds here are virulent, rooted in the cracks of the pavement and along the side of the road in thick handfuls. I marvel at their tenacity.

I heard about the ambulance at Thorn House last night. My friend Theresa phoned me. It's a small town, you see, and news is passed on the old way, on a grapevine. She told me its lights had been on but the sirens had not, and it had moved slowly, like a hearse.

'Do you think she's dead?' Theresa asked me and I answered, 'I hope not. I like Mimi. She taught at Edie's school. She was the only teacher there who—' *Could stand her*, I thought. I left the space empty, and Theresa glided smoothly over it, and the conversation moved on.

Still, later I found myself thinking of Mimi's son for the first time in years. Back then he was a young man with a mess of dark hair he had a habit of pulling at, a boy who looked me right in the eye and said, 'I swear on my mother's life, Mrs Hudson, I don't know anything about your daughter', as I pressed the knife against his neck.

◆ ◆ ◆

I walk until the road narrows and rises up, up away from the fields that cloak the valley and form the edge of the Sussex Downs. The church of St Mary de Castro is near the top of the hill at the back of a terrace of cottages. While the church is small, the grounds surrounding it are broad and ancient, with some of the yews and oaks that grow densely on the edges over five hundred years old. In parts, some of the graves are little more than hummocks in the earth, lumpen headstones marking victims of cholera and consumption and the plague.

I enter the graveyard through the old iron gates and walk through the grounds to where the trees start to thicken and crowd in overhead, freckling the pathway with sunlight. Above, a magpie barks in its harsh, staccato way. Below my feet the ground is spongy and soft with decay.

I find the place the same way I always find it. Back here the grounds aren't maintained like the rest of the churchyard and the ferns and long grass tangle around my ankles. The large yew tree is many-limbed and sinuous, broad as a bus, trunk mottled with age. A few graves huddle in front of it, thrown crooked by the questing roots ploughing into the earth. I am not interested in graves. I come here because it was the last place Edie was seen the night she disappeared. Her friends told of how she walked into this dark grove of trees and never came out again.

I put my hand on the yew. It is smooth and warm and strong. Here at the base is a patch of bare earth no bigger than a dinner plate. It is the only spot that is free of weeds. I clear it as often as I can, which isn't as often as I'd like. Today there is a cluster of dandelions, which I pull up and discard. They drift away like little ghosts. I've buried things here, in the absence of a body, of a coffin or a grave. Little things.

When she was younger Edie would dig in the garden, shallow graves for strange treasures she'd collected. I would find them half-buried, sometimes months later. Little china animals, tiny pipe-cleaner dolls, coins, a hairbrush. I found something eleven years after she vanished, while I was digging manure into the roses: a pink-and-red plastic bracelet, the elastic turned to grey, the beads cracked and faded. The shock, like being winded, was as great as if she'd walked back through the door again. I saw stars and sat down abruptly into the freshly turned flower bed. I sat with the bracelet pressed against my lips until the shadows had lengthened and the Siamese cat from next door began coiling about my calves, crying plaintively.

I bring things up here now to bury them, but not discard them. *More dissociation*, I think.

I sit down beneath the tree, tucking the folds of my skirt around me. I am all alone, the sound of rustling leaves like whispering voices, the sky a soaring, polished blue. On what would have been Edie's eighteenth birthday I carried a bottle of wine up here, drinking it too fast and getting woozy and disoriented. Last year she would have been thirty-two, and I buried a beautiful hair clip decorated with pearls. I wasn't able to decide if it was the kind of thing a woman in her thirties would wear, but had bought it at the last minute anyway. This is my grief, lying beneath the earth. Long years of mourning unspooling like a bright red thread, running through the ground to meet the roots of trees.

But I'm wary of being maudlin. I have to measure it – ration it almost. Edie was a beautiful toddler but a difficult child. Obstinate, wilful, impossible to please. I caught her stealing money from my purse at age ten. When I asked her why, she answered simply, 'Because I want it.' In the months before her disappearance she was suspended from school for a week for getting into a fight and biting another girl's ear.

No, wait. That sounds worse than it was, makes her sound like Mike Tyson. It's true that there was a fight and it's true that Edie, quick to provoke, got this girl into a headlock. At some point a small chunk of flesh was taken from the top of the girl's ear, the part where it curves sweetly like an oyster shell – a tiny crescent, the slightest disruption of the curve. Edie didn't know what happened to it, thought she may have swallowed it. Apparently, the sight of her blood-smeared mouth cleared the classroom and the headmistress found all thirty-odd children standing silently in the corridor as she raced towards them. Then I got a phone call. There had been an incident, they said. She was becoming feral, they said. Impossible to manage. They told me I was lucky the other parents weren't pressing charges. Edie was there in the office, stony-faced in the hard-backed chair, her jaw rigid. There were scratches on her neck where the other girl had clawed at her. She'd cleaned the blood off her teeth but there was still more on the collar of her shirt, her cardigan.

Afterwards, the newspapers had asked me if I'd given up on her. Given up on her? What the fuck do you think?

I've read that there are creatures below the surface of the sea in the dark, uncharted parts of the ocean that have evolved to survive the crushing pressure the water exerts on them. I envy them. Some mornings I wake to a weight of such intensity pinning me to the bed that I feel like my bones will liquefy. It's a sickness, a blight, a thorny plant crawling towards sunlight through my guts. It's her. I miss her. She is my trigger.

I talk about triggers a lot. I've been in a lot of behavioural therapy where the search to find your trigger is as inexorable and precise as conception. My trigger is Edie, always and always, but sometimes I find myself wondering what her trigger was. I think I know, and like all important things it began very small, and grew like a seedling.

◆ ◆ ◆

We were slipping into the summer of 1997 and his name was Dylan. Such a waifish, dreamy name. I was expecting a golden-haired hippy who carried a guitar painted with flowers, so I was surprised when Edie brought home a tall stocky boy who could easily have passed for nineteen. He was a rugby player and had been on family holidays to places that Edie could only dream about: Florida, the Gold Coast, San Tropez. She was fifteen and absolutely in awe of him. Dylan smiled easily and referred to me as 'Sammy'. He wore his school tie to one side and had a rangy, hungry look in his eyes. *Fuck the pleasantries*, it said, *and show me your tits*.

I tried to give them room. I tried to show Edie that I trusted her. I was told that this was important. Personal space, you see.

The problem was that Edie, while funny and bright and often deep-thinking, had her father's narrow, suspicious gaze, thin lips and ruddy cheeks like fillets of meat. She'd inherited my wild hair and short, rounded torso. Added to that, the previous winter she'd started hanging round with a group of girls who dressed all in black; thick, heavy eyeliner, lace and velvet and silks, chipped nail varnish on bitten nails. They called themselves the Rattlesnakes and drew tattoos on to each other's arms in thick felt-tip. That winter I'd watched her morph into something vampiric, all funeral pallor and choking, Victorian clothes. In the evenings she would leave the house to meet her friends, trailing black scarves like kite ribbons, her perfume a suffocating mixture of patchouli and nag champa, and I would watch her from the upstairs window, arms folded over her chest, her back stooped as though trying to diminish herself, to turn to smoke and fade away.

♦ ♦ ♦

One muggy July night, just before the summer storms had come, Edie and I sat outside in the yard, chairs pushed close together, her bare feet hanging in my lap. Some days we barely spoke, such were her moods. But today was not one of those days.

'It's too hot,' she moaned, peeling her T-shirt (black, full of holes) away from her chest and fanning herself with it.

'The weather's about to break,' I told her. 'They're forecasting big storms all the way up to the weekend.'

'Oh, great. I'm meant to be meeting everyone tomorrow.'

'In town?'

'I don't know.'

'In the park?'

She shrugged.

I let a moment or two pass. In the distance, thunder.

'Will Dylan be there?'

'Yeah. He plays football in the mornings but he'll be finished by lunchtime. He's making something for me.'

'Is he?'

'Yeah. Nancy reckons it's a mixtape, but he gave me one of those last week, so I don't know, maybe a painting or something. It'll be cool, whatever it is.'

'Because he's cool, right?'

'Right. Only don't say it like that.'

'Why?'

'Because you sound like Nonno.' Nonno was her grandfather – my father – in Italy. She poked me with her long toes to indicate that she was teasing. 'Dylan speaks Italian. French too.'

'Does he?'

'*Oui. Il est bon à French.*' She laughed again. I always remember her laughter, slow-moving and heavy as honey.

'I used to speak French. *Un petite.*'

'It's *un peu.*' She rolled her eyes. 'Please don't do this around him.'

'You wouldn't give me the chance. I've barely said more than two words to him.'

I waited. The air was cooling noticeably now, and I wanted to say something else before the moment was washed away.

'What else does he do?'

'What do you mean?'

'Well, football, mixtapes, French. Anything else?'

'He's into everything.'

I bet he is.

'I mean,' she added, 'he's not, like, totally into music but he listens to it. He doesn't really like science, but he knows about stuff, you know?'

'Ah. He dabbles, you mean?'

'I guess.'

'Are you two serious?'

A pause. It was a question designed to trick her, to elicit the answer I wanted. *No,* I wanted her to say – *it's only been two weeks, Mum, don't be crazy!* But I could never catch her out. She shrugged to show her indifference, but I was her mother. I knew she wanted it to be serious. That was the danger.

'Because if you are – serious about each other, that is – then we need to talk about getting you some protection.'

'Oh, Mum, come on.' She covered her face with her hands. The backs of them were scrawled with her spiky writing.

'No, listen, listen. It's important. I know this is about as much fun for you as a poke in the eye but my mother never had this conversation with me and look how I turned out.'

'Oh, thanks.'

'I didn't mean you,' I said, instantly agonised because of course I had meant her. 'I meant that I had a baby young with no clue, no money, no support.'

'Apart from Nonno—'

'Yes, and he was great, but he disapproved and it showed. It still does sometimes. I'd hate for that to happen to you. You have such a bright future.'

'So I can't have a bright future with Dylan in it? Is that what you're saying? You do realise that your idea of a bright future and my idea of a bright future are very different, don't you? I don't want to end up like you, in a crappy job.'

I ignored her cheap dig, her rising voice. I hadn't taken my A levels because my morning sickness meant I hadn't been able to move further than a few inches without vomiting. When I'd finally returned to work I had a handful of scrappy qualifications and no experience. I don't mind the clerical work, but, as Edie often pointed out, what little girl grew up dreaming of data entry? Still, I'd hurt her feelings and I felt bad about it. I tried to divert her.

'I think Dylan is a nice boy, I do, but I just want you to be aware of how much you're giving away.'

'Mum, seriously, please shut up.'

'I think we'll go to the doctor after the weekend and speak with him about contraception, because if you're going to do it—'

I heard her starting to wail – it was a frustrated, angry sound, primal – but I spoke over her just as the first fat drops of rain began to fall.

'Because if you're going to do it then I am going to make sure you are both as safe as possible. It's ridiculous to think otherwise. What on earth would you do if you got pregnant?'

'We'd manage, okay?'

I laughed. 'Oh, brilliant. Where would you live? Where would all the money come from? You're aware babies need someone there all the time, aren't you? You can't just leave it in the cot while you go and hang out with your mates.'

'Fucking hell, Mum! Why are you talking about babies? We haven't even had sex yet!'

Ah. *Yet.* There it was. I let the word hang in the air. She was glaring at me, her cheeks flushed, her eyes glittering.

'Monday,' I told her. 'We'll go on Monday.'

She stormed off, slamming the door so hard the glass shivered. I dragged both the chairs in just as the rain became a downpour. Dark clouds the colour of charcoal. For a moment I stood, letting the water trickle over me. The curls of my hair plastered themselves to my skin. I hadn't handled that very well.

Three days later it was all over with Dylan. I caught Edie, eyes streaming, make-up running like black ink, at the bus stop in town. She wouldn't tell me what had happened, just that she hated him. He was a bastard; a sketchy, horrible bastard. That was fine by me. Boys, young boys, are mostly fickle. I bought her a pot of tea in a nearby cafe and let her cry on my shoulder for a bit, her head turned towards the wall so that no one could see her. I kissed her and smoothed her hair. In that moment I wanted to hurt that young man. I wanted to gut him and leave him lying in the road. Ropes of bloodied entrails, leaking sacs of testosterone and the smell of Lynx deodorant. That would be all that would remain of Dylan, breaker of my daughter's heart.

Of course, my anger burnt itself out by that evening, and over the next few days Edie regained some of her buoyancy. A week later she was even smiling and singing along to the little radio on the kitchen windowsill. I watched her making herself a peanut-butter sandwich and swinging her hips to the music, all glands and tall hair and hormones. And I knew.

'Who is he?'

She smiled at me secretly, but she could never stay quiet for long. 'I met him at the youth club. He doesn't go to our school.'

'The youth club at St Mary's? I didn't think you still went there. Thought you all thought it was for losers.'

She made an 'L' shape with her left hand and held it to her forehead, laughing. 'Yeah, sometimes it is. There's nowhere else to go, though.'

She was right. God save any fifteen-year-old in a small town with no money. I felt for her.

'What about Dylan?'

She frowned as though she genuinely had to think about who he was. Maybe she did. 'Oh yeah, no, sure. He's got a new girl-friend now.'

Ah.

'But he's history, he really is. Truly.' She took a bite of her sandwich and smiled at me. 'He goes to St Andrew's.'

For a moment I can't work out who she means. Then I remember. The new boy. Not Dylan. He's *history.*

'The private school? Really?'

'Yup. He's gorgeous. Very intense.'

Uh-oh.

'Is he coming over tonight?'

Tonight was my night out at my women's group. I would be out for a few hours. I narrowed my eyes at her, watching a pink blush stain her cheeks.

'He might do,' she sang coyly, and I rolled my eyes.

'You stay downstairs. You leave all the lights on. Your body. Your decision.'

'Yeah, yeah.' She was walking up the stairs.

'I mean it, Edie.'

I heard her bedroom door slam and a moment later her music started. I sighed, considered having a cigarette and thought better of it. I was meant to be giving up. I'd even taped an image of a blackened, diseased lung to the fridge in an effort to quit smoking and eat less. It hadn't worked in either case.

I still wonder how things could have been different. If I had arrived home later, or earlier, or hadn't gone to my group at all. If it hadn't been raining, maybe. I still think about the little things – the way my foot slipped on the wet pavement as I got off the bus, the way I allowed a man on crutches to use the cashpoint in front of me. If I hadn't done these things, how much would have been different? How many triggers could I have avoided? But you can't think like that. It'll kill you.

So here's how it happened. I took the bus to my women's group – which was really no more than a handful of us sipping instant coffee in a church hall and talking about the lack of good, meaningful, fulfilling sex – and got off at the high street. I waited in line for the man on his crutches to negotiate the cashpoint. It was not raining yet but it would start soon, the forecast said.

I headed down Eastleigh Avenue and took a right at St Mary's church. Here, on the eastern side, the high stone wall was choked with ivy and star jasmine. The perfume cloaked the evening air, so thick I could almost touch it.

Round at the back of the old church an ugly, flat-roofed prefab building had been tacked on, used for the youth club and neighbourhood meetings. The spaces beneath the windows were stained with rust, which ran like teardrops down the pale walls. Inside it smelt like damp towels and sour milk, the hot metal of the tea urn. It's a smell I find at once repulsive and comforting. When I reached the door, however, the first thing I noticed was the sign, handwritten and covered with clear plastic so the ink did not run in the rain.

Below that was drawn a smiley face in a large, irregular circle. The smile had been formed out of the word 'sisterhood'.

'Bollocks,' I said, turning up the collar of my denim jacket as the rain fell harder. The sky had darkened to a dull chrome. It felt like winter had arrived already and it was only August. I turned to leave and that's when I saw him. Standing beneath the towering gingko in the middle of the churchyard. He was wearing a dark overcoat and wellington boots and was staring right at me, his face as pale and round as the moon. I felt a shiver of discomfort. The man was holding a bag in his hands, swinging it as he started to walk towards me, his expression as still as a stopped clock. I lifted my hand.

'Hi, I'm here for th—'

'It's closed.'

'I know. I just saw the sign.'

He looked me up and down. There was a smell coming off him, like old clothes in a trunk, mothballs. He had pink scar tissue stretched thin across his neck, fine lines cobwebbing his eyes.

'I got the keys here. You come in, out the rain.'

I stared at him. His eyes were silvery blank pennies. 'No thanks. I have to get back.'

'I'd better draw the curtains. Getting dark. More storms rolling in.'

'Yes.'

We stood there silently as he rifled through the ring of keys he'd produced from his pocket. The keyring had a little pink plastic bird attached to it, rubbed almost smooth with age. It was the kind of trinket you'd find in a Christmas cracker and it was so incongruous, given the man holding it – broad and stooped with only a clutch

41

of brown teeth still left in his mouth – that I almost burst out laughing. The caretaker pulled at the handle and the door wheezed open. I took a step back, calculating the distance between me and the iron gates. I couldn't tell you why I was so nervous, but the one thing I'd learned from my women's group had been written on a T-shirt Kath had worn one evening: 'Trust your gut – that bitch knows what's up.'

I looked over at the gates again. They were a long way away but I could make it, if I sprinted. If I needed to. If he reached for me with his big, callused hand.

'The graves'll flood.' He was looking up at the sky. 'Sink right into the ground.'

I was looking at the white plastic bag he was holding, the handles stretching with the weight of what was inside. *And what is inside?* I thought, with a feeling of creeping horror. My stomach somersaulted as I caught a glimpse of dark wet fur and a glassy, staring eye. There was a smear of blood on the wall of the bag like a streak of brown paint on canvas. He looked down at it, then up at me.

'We've got a rabbit problem,' he said, 'but they're too clever for traps. Don't like the poison, though, no sir. They come out the ground to die, because they want to see the stars.'

'Do you have to poison them? Can't you find a more humane way?'

It was as if he hadn't heard me. He had a strange, faraway expression, looking past me, back towards the trees. 'You'd want to see the stars too, wouldn't you? In your last moments. Better than down there, in the earth. In the dark.'

My eye was drawn again to that bag, bulging with small leporine corpses. There was the faint smell of blood, a coppery tang, and something else too, carried on the wind. Sweet and awful at the same time, a rot like overripe fruit. Fear tasted glassy and metallic in my mouth. I pulsed with it, feeling his shadow creep over me like a cold wind. There was something wrong with this man. I knew this as simply as I did my own name.

'Bagged a whole warren,' he continued, as I started moving away, walking backward through the long grass. 'You know rabbits scream when they know they're close to death? It's like they see it coming. Sends all the others into a fr-fr-frenzy.' He was starting to stutter. There was spittle collecting on his lips. 'First time I heard it I screamed right back.'

'I have to go.' I started to jog over the damp spongy grass. My heart was hammering in my chest, that smell of decay thick and gluey in my sinuses. My hand reached for my back pocket, instinctively. I was as jumpy as a hare in spring. He still wasn't done, still talking to my retreating back.

'Told 'em to stop coming here. All of 'em, but it don't make a difference.'

By the time I got home, I'd been gone for about an hour and a half. Thunder rumbled in the distance, a warning. I entered the house quietly, put my keys on the side and walked into the living room, switching on the light on the wall with the heel of my hand.

And there was Edie, frozen to the couch, her jeans around her thighs, her eyes comically round with shock. On top of her a boy, athletic, good-looking, his hand shoved into her knickers, moving as though searching for something. He had thick curly hair and dark, blank eyes. When he saw me he lowered his head on to Edie's chest. I could hear his muffled swearing, could see Edie's hands in the crotch of his trousers. His T-shirt was pulled up to reveal the skin of his torso, the muscles there clearly defined. I'd remember this scene for a long time. Every moment of it.

'Edie, get dressed now.'

'Mum!' She was angry, embarrassed, her face turning a vivid red.

I turned to the boy. 'Who the fuck are you?'

'Mum, stop it.'

The boy looked up at me. He pulled his hands out of Edie's knickers, wiped them discreetly on his trousers. I could feel the pulse in my throat stutter. He didn't respond to me. He talked to Edie. 'I thought you said she was going to be out for hours.'

'Mum, what the hell?'

'Right. You, upstairs. You, out.' I pointed at him.

He smiled slantwise. It wasn't a very nice smile and there was no humour in it. 'Sure.' He raised his hands. 'I'm going, I'm going.'

'I'm coming with you,' Edie said, rising from her seat.

I laughed. 'Are you joking? Get upstairs. Now.'

'All you do is embarrass me. I hate it here. I can't wait to live by myself.'

'But you don't, do you? You live with me, in my house, under my rules. So get dressed and go upstairs before I do something to really embarrass you.'

There was a brief silence. I tapped my nails on the sideboard. *Click, click, click.*

The boy looked shifty and caught-out. He ran his hand over his face. 'Edie, maybe I should go.'

'Then I'm coming too.'

'Your mum says – uh—'

'That bitch doesn't tell me what to do.'

I grabbed her. I grabbed her by the arm and I knew I was squeezing too hard because she looked shocked, horrified, and I was glad because that is how I wanted her to look. Later I would think about the marks I left there, red stripes on her pale skin.

'Upstairs, Edie. Now. Now!'

I heard her start to cry as she walked through the kitchen and then clattered up the stairs. I just wanted the best for her, and these boys, these eager, narcissistic boys, were not the best. I stared at him. He stared back, defiant. He sat like a man, his legs spread almost the length of the two-seater couch. His hands dangled in the gap between them.

'What's your name?'

He mumbled.

I made him say it louder. 'Speak up.'

'William, I said.'

'So you like my daughter, do you, William?'

'Yeah.' He lifted his hand and tugged at his hair where it hung over his ears.

'Well, then, you need to have some respect for her—'

I stopped and looked at his face and I remembered that he was just a kid, and that he was just as humiliated as me, and that all he wanted was to get out of here and go home.

'Get out of my house. Stay away from Edie.'

He rose, left, closed the front door quietly. I composed myself, lit a cigarette. I had thought I was liberated, easy with my daughter's burgeoning sexual desires. I tried to remember myself at that age but it was like catching water in a sieve. Edie had turned her music up to screaming pitch.

We didn't speak for a few weeks or so after that, kept our distance from each other. In September, Edie went back to school and I hoped she would forget about him, this William with the shifty eyes and fleeting, half-felt smile. Then, one bright morning barely a month later, she left for school and I never saw her again.

Don't talk to me about triggers. I know all about triggers.

Frances – Now

William's mother has forgotten who I am. At least, that's how it seems. Alex has told us we are to expect some mental 'hiccups' caused by the brain injury. They're temporary, the doctor has reassured him, but it doesn't make it any less difficult.

She peers at me with watery, Arctic eyes. 'Which one are you married to?'

'The handsome one,' William cuts in, and his brother groans in the background.

I'm sitting beside her bed, my hand on hers, the skin paper-thin and stitched with blue veins. She is propped up on pillows, facing the French windows which lead into the walled garden. Alex has moved her into the study, setting up a bed among the polished teak and musty old books.

'She likes to watch the birds,' he said, filling her hot-water bottle from the kettle, steaming up his glasses. 'They've always given her so much joy.'

His voice cracked then, and William stood awkwardly while I held him, running my palm up and down his back. It's okay, I told him, it's all right.

◆　◆　◆

Later we are together in Mimi's room, Alex, William and I. The television plays in the corner. Her respiration is wet and noisy.

'You want me to brush your hair, Mum?' Alex has her hairbrush in his hands; old-fashioned, silver-handled, porcelain-backed and decorated with roses. It's an oddly intimate moment, his hand so large on her bony shoulder, turning her towards him. As she turns her head I catch sight of the bruising she suffered in the fall. It's a livid inkblot crawling over her temple. Along the side of her skull, about seven inches or so, there is a row of ugly black stitching, raw-looking.

I wince, and Alex nods. 'Beat yourself up pretty good, didn't you, Ma? You want me to get the photos back out?'

She doesn't respond, and William asks, 'What photos?'

'The doctor said she's going to have some short-term memory issues. I thought it might help her to look through some photos so I got some out the attic.'

'Which ones?'

'The whole box. You don't know what'll get through to her so I thought I'd cast a wide net.' He turns back to Mimi, who stares vacantly ahead, mouth hanging slightly open. 'I'll go and get them, shall I, Mum? You stay here with Will and Frances.'

'Where's your father? Is he in the greenhouse?'

William and Alex exchange a concerned glance. The silence drips, drips, drips into the space until William turns away from Mimi to look out the window as he says, 'That's right, Mum. He's just checking the tomatoes.'

Mimi says nothing. Her eyes are sunk deep into her narrow skull. She is wearing a dressing gown over her nightdress but she still seems to be shivering and when I touch her arm it is as cold as marble.

'Maybe get another blanket for her, Alex?' I say, and he calls back, okay, sure.

William and I drove the three hundred or so miles from Swindon beneath a gleaming cerulean sky laced with clouds as thick as whipped cream. Lewes is a small market town surrounded by the richly rolling Sussex Downs and backboned by the River Ouse. Sculpted white cliffs rise up over the tile-hung cottages and flint walls, while the smell of hops from the brewery permeates the air. Thorn House is set a couple of miles outside town, a large Georgian building of oak floors and draughty casement windows surrounded by overgrown allotment gardens and clipped hedges. Just beyond those is a meadow of wild clover and yarrow and the broad sweep of woodland descending into a valley thick with shadow. William once told me that when they were boys they'd discovered an old dry well in the forest there, partially concealed with ferns and nettles and brambles heavy with fruit. The two boys had taken their torches and shone them inside, and at the bottom, lying in the dark and the dirt, they'd found a dead sheep, partially rotted away. Twelve-year-old William had nightmares about their grisly discovery for months afterwards, but Alex, then only seven years old, had visited again and again, fascinated by the decomposition, the slow revealing of dark, spoiled flesh and yellowed bone, the low droning buzz of flies. When Mimi had found out she'd been horrified and had immediately instructed their father, Edward, to board the old well up. Her words, according to William, had been, 'A fall like that will snap their necks.' Edward had done as his wife requested, despite Alex's weeping protests, but that night he had presented Alex with a souvenir he had excavated from inside the well itself – the sheep's skull, bleached and cleaned to a bright white. Alex had put it in pride of place on his bookshelf over his bed, and William would avoid its dread, blank-eyed gaze for years afterwards. As far as I know, it's still there.

◆ ◆ ◆

William takes his phone from his pocket and examines it, frowning. One of the advantages of being down here is the limited phone reception. If you need to make a call you have to walk to the top end of the garden where the bench sits beneath the old apple trees, arthritic boughs bent and heavily knuckled. An old rope swing still hangs there, the rope grey and frayed, moving gently in the ghosts of a breeze.

'I need to call work,' William tells me. 'Stay here with Mum, I'll be back in a minute.'

I watch him leave the room, ducking his head beneath the small doorway. My anger curls and uncurls inside me, burrowing deep into my chest, glowing ember-bright between my ribs. I still haven't told him I know about Kim, the photos, the payments, the transactions making the erotic beige and mundane. He will know something's wrong, though. Sooner or later. It comes from me in waves of cold, like a hoar frost.

'Which one are you?'

I look up at Mimi. Her head is turned towards me again. White hair floats about her patched skull in wisps of cobweb. Her skin is thin and as creased as crêpe paper.

'I'm Frances, Mimi. William's wife. Remember?'

'Are you off the telly?'

I shake my head. It's frightening how vulnerable she looks in the big white day bed.

'I'm afraid not,' I say.

'Are you dead?'

'I hope not!' I laugh and after a moment she reaches up and touches my face. I try hard not to recoil from her cold fingers.

'Are you real?'

'Yes.'

She lowers her voice to a whisper. 'Don't let him hurt me.'

I stare at her, fear tracing a cold finger down my spine. Her eyes are watery and pale and she looks at me with utter conviction. I think of that twisted line of stitching running up the side of her skull, the way her thoughts seem tangled in each other. Alex told us to expect confusion, but it's still jarring to hear her talking about her husband, Edward, a man a long time dead, or for her to whisper to me with her nails digging into my cheek. I'm opening my mouth to respond when Alex walks back into the room, a box held beneath his arm.

'You saying hello to Frances, Mum? We've got some pictures in here of their wedding. You'll like to look at those again, won't you?'

Mimi's hand drops away from my cheek. She turns back to the window and says, 'Where's that robin?'

I'm making tea when Alex comes into the kitchen an hour or so later. William is upstairs setting up his laptop, turning his dad's old study into a temporary office. I wonder if he has brought the memory stick with him. Maybe I'll find a way to make it disappear. Maybe I'll find the old well and toss it down.

'Don't worry about Mum,' Alex says. 'The doctor said this is normal after a knock to the head.'

'What's the deal with Edward? She thinks he's still here?'

'Yeah.' He sighs, scratching the back of his head. 'I was hoping she'd have got past that by now. She doesn't seem to remember that Dad's dead. That's, like, the ninth time she's mentioned him. Sometimes she talks like he's just walked out the room.'

He takes a seat at the breakfast bar, the box of photos in front of him. He starts flicking through them, still talking. 'I'm just glad it isn't more serious than it is. Head wounds bleed *a lot*. It's a good job I wa— Hey, look at this! I knew I'd find it in here somewhere.'

He holds up a photo. It's William and me stood with our arms around each other in front of our first car. It was taken right outside Thorn House in the spring of 2010. We'd been together just a year, and bought ourselves an old Volkswagen to drive through Europe in. That's where William would propose, four months later, outside a restaurant in Lisbon surrounded by orange blossoms. I take the picture from Alex and feel a lump in my throat as the room blurs and wavers through a prism of tears.

'Oh! Oh no, Frances, what is it?'

His arm around me, I wipe my face with my hands but still the tears come. I'm shaking with them, choking. I can't believe how happy we look there. It crushes me, our wide-open faces, our anticipation. It turns me to stone.

'I'm sorry. Oh God. This is embarrassing. It's okay, Alex, I'm okay.'

He squeezes my arm and releases me almost immediately. I've always liked Alex, with his faded old shirts and ripped jeans, round face beneath his crown of curly black hair. He looks so young, even now, still chubby, dumpling-shaped. Where William is dependable and sturdy, Alex flickers like a flame in a draught, unable to keep focus. It's why he's still here, living with his elderly mother in this big, rambling house at the age of thirty.

'Let me do that. I'll get the tea. You sit down.'

'I'm not an invalid.' I laugh, but my legs feel watery and I'm relieved to slide on to one of the stools. I put the photo back into the box and pick up the one beneath it, blotting my eyes with my T-shirt.

'Is this your dad?'

Alex comes and looks over my shoulder. 'Yeah. Campaigning. It did his heart no good, that.'

The picture is taken in front of the stile leading to Thorn Woods from the access road. Edward Thorn has his jaw set, his arms crossed, his mouth drawn down into a frown. Propped beside him is a placard reading *It's MY way, not the BY way.*

'I'd better take that one,' Alex says, easing it out of my hands. 'If Mum sees it and remembers, she'll have a fit. She hated him doing all that stuff.'

'Was this about the public access to his land?'

Alex rolls his eyes. 'Yes, but don't ask for details, it's too boring to tell you. Just know that he got his way in the end because we Thorns are tenacious motherfuckers.'

I smile, flicking through the rest of the pile. Something catches my attention. It's a photo I've never seen before. A group of people – teens, I suppose, although the ages are difficult to judge. They are standing in front of a low wall and squinting into bright sunshine. There are long shadows at their feet and their smiles are tight and self-conscious. All the girls – I count four of them – are wearing black. Not in a stylish, minimalist way, but wild and gothic: dark shaded eyes with slices of black liner, long lace veils. One of them has hair so black it appears to shine inky blue. When I see William on the end in his skinny black jeans and low-slung studded belt I actually gasp aloud.

'Is that – it's Will, isn't it? Oh my God. He was a goth?'

Alex peers over, laughing. 'Nah, not really. We just hung out with a bunch of people who were for a while. We all went through weird phases. You should see the photos of us from when William and I were going out raving.'

'I can't believe it. His fringe! He's wearing nail varnish! Look at this! This is amazing, I'm going to have to get a picture.'

I take out my phone and snap a quick photo of the picture, still smiling.

'Brilliant!' I say, and then I notice the girl William has his arm around in the photograph. I have a strange feeling then – like the way it feels to miss a step; that lurch in the stomach, a moment of bright and fleeting anxiety. I hold the photo closer to my face. She's shorter than William by quite a way, her hair dark and wild, eyes tilted slightly upward like those of a cat. She is looking into the camera with such stubbornness it is almost aggression. There is a tight, hungry expression on her face. *I've got all I asked for*, it seems to be saying, *but I want more.* It's William who has put his arm around her but it's her that's clinging to him; both her hands are tightly gripping the one he has draped casually over her shoulder. Her hip is pressed against his leg, leaning into him almost, like she is trying to fuse herself to him. Even in this snapshot, this captured moment, her expression is so familiar to me it makes me catch my breath. I've seen it before, in Samira laughing in that throaty, dirty way she had, pupils wide and inky, cheekbones jutting. I've seen it in Kim, in the photographs hidden on the memory stick, looking back at the lens of the camera with an arch, knowing smile. *Pay me. Pay me.* My hand is shaking slightly but I'm pleased that when I finally manage to speak my voice is not.

'Who's that girl he's got his arm around? The one with the lace gloves?'

'Ah, shit. You found it.' Alex laughs slightly uncomfortably as he takes the picture and studies it carefully. 'That's her. That's Edie Hudson.'

'Who?'

'Edie. Elizabeth, really. But she hated that name.'

I stare at the girl in the picture. It's funny, all the times William has spoken with me about the past it's always *my* stories he ends up unspooling, my past. All the loose ends and burned bridges, what he describes as my 'murky history'. He gets a kick out of it. I touch a finger to the photograph. Edie Hudson.

'Was she his girlfriend?'

'I don't think it was ever that serious. This one' – he points to the girl in the middle with a scowl on her face and her middle finger pointed up to the camera – 'that's Charlie. I gave her a Valentine once when I was ten years old and she broke my heart. And that one, on the end, looking like she doesn't really belong there, that's Nancy Renard. I still see her around occasionally. She was nice. I don't know why she hung around with that lot of bitches.'

I take the photo back from him and he brings me my tea. 'Where was this? Round here?'

'Yup. At the church in town. St Mary de Castro, at the top of Eastleigh Avenue. Back then we called it "St Scary de Castro" because of the caretaker there. He used to poison the rats and rabbits that lived in the graveyard and the whole place was just littered with the corpses of slowly decomposing animals.'

'Ugh.'

'Yeah. It *reeked* in the summer.'

'So why did you hang out there?'

'It was where the youth club was, in the hall that we used to go to on Fridays, back in the days before we could get served alcohol and go and drink in parks like normal teenagers. Of course, Dad was involved in the church too – he wanted a protection order put into place for the old trees that grew there. He said some of them were centuries old. He and the caretaker used to cross swords about it all the time. Us kids, we didn't give a shit about a few old trees or the bad smell or the dead animals. I mean, look at us there' – he taps the photograph of the black-clad teens – 'all doom and gloom. William loved that stuff. He'd take me along to the youth club with him but we always used to sneak off into the churchyard and play dare and spin the bottle. Dad would be out the front with his placards and his petitions and me and Will would be round the back trying to get off with the girls.'

'Oh, *those* kind of dares?'

He winks at me. 'Yeah. Kissing mostly. Sometimes we'd dare each other to go into the old Prevett family tomb and touch the wall. I didn't like doing that. It smelled really bad in there, and it was always cold. This girl here, with the ponytail?' He points to a girl in the photo to the other side of William. Her dark hair is piled high on her head and her skin is coffee-coloured, in striking contrast to William's unhealthy pallor. 'Her name was Moya. She would do the craziest dares. It got so we were just thinking of the stupidest stuff – dangerous stuff – just to see if there was anything she'd say no to.'

'And was there?'

'Nope. One time we dared her to go into the caretaker's cottage and bring something out, a souvenir or something. We watched her over the wall as she climbed in through the back window and came out again with a gas mask. Horrible thing, it was. From the war. I don't know why the caretaker had it in there – he was always an oddball – but I know that none of us wanted to touch it. We stopped playing dares after that.'

We're silent for a moment and then he slides the photo to one side, putting his hand over mine. His skin is soft and slightly damp.

'*Is* everything all right, Frances? With you two?'

I think of Kim, her back arched in see-through knickers just so she can afford the rent on her Tufnell Park flat, her expensive handbag and her scuffed ankle boots, the way her hair darkens where her roots need doing. I think of William setting up a separate bank account, hiding money from me, hiding the photos of her squeezing her tits together and lifting her leg a little so you can see the creases inside. *It's just photos*, she told me. *It's not real life.*

'Yeah,' I tell Alex. 'It's fine.'

◆ ◆ ◆

The next few mornings I am up early, watching a bright dawn mist curl into the valley, slithering between the trees like a living thing. The dewy hedgerows glitter in the sunlight, all nodding meadowsweet, campion and snarls of bramble. I walk into town one morning, with a shopping list in my back pocket and the weight of my dreams upon me. Since we've arrived at Thorn House my sleep has been fitful, dreams stuttering like a blown engine. I've been waking up with a jerk and a gasp, eyes snapping open, one hand reaching as if to grasp something – or to ward it away. The dreams are always of Mimi and me sitting in front of the French windows, her thin body propped up by her pillows. It's a sunny day, and we're watching the birds. The old box of photos is on her lap but when she opens it the pictures inside aren't old family portraits. They're of me, in the past. I try to snatch them back but I can't seem to move my hands and William's mother's saying, *Is this you, dear, you don't look well*, and there I am aged nineteen with a nosebleed and pupils dilated to wide black saucers from the ketamine, the MDMA. There's me in the years before I met her son, slumped in the corner of a squat party in Ilford, calling my parents crying because I couldn't make my rent, cleaning my neighbour's car while he sits inside and watches me and jerks off his stubby penis and when he pays me it's five pounds short so I don't eat that night. I'm trying to take the photos away but she has seen them all, and the bruise is spreading over her face, black threads working their way over the bridge of her nose, even into the whites of her eyes, down her neck and shoulders like the diseased roots of a plant. There's me trying to kiss Gary Webster at the bus stop aged fifteen and he recoils and calls me a stupid bitch, there's me thrown out of a pub for selling wraps of speed, there's me, there's me, there's me. *Don't look*, I tell her, *don't look at them*, and when she finally turns her head towards me she says, *No wonder he wants to leave you, Frances.*

◆ ◆ ◆

I walk the long way to town, past the river, which gleams like polished brass in the sun. I arrive at the chemist's just after nine o'clock and hand over Mimi's prescriptions to the woman behind the counter. She looks up at me, smiling. 'Will you be waiting for these?'

'Sure.'

She turns away from me and I find myself looking at the display of baby products: soft blankets and dummies and smooth wooden rattles. I pick up a brightly coloured octopus designed to rustle and squeak under tiny, seeking hands. I press it to my chest and hold it there, eyes closed. I think of the box room back in our Swindon home, the way it seems to hold the mellow afternoon light like spun honey. The day we moved in I sat in there on the bare floor and William came in and saw me, and he smiled.

'I've never seen you so quiet,' he said, crouching beside me. 'What are you thinking about?'

'Where the cot could go. And the toy box. It would be so beautiful in here.'

He kissed me, slow and hard, with his hand cupping the back of my skull. But he didn't say anything. I suppose, even then, I should have known. He didn't want this.

The bell over the door rings and a woman walks into the pharmacy. She has shoulder-length hair that falls in amber waves, thick and bouncy. Everything about her is long and almost perfectly straight: her figure, her nose, her long, lean legs. She walks right past me as if I'm not there, trailing a cloud of floral perfume so sweet it makes my teeth hurt.

The woman behind the counter looks up and gives her a perfunctory smile. 'Miss Renard, I'll get your prescription. One second.'

I slide my eyes over to her from beneath my fringe. She's tall, slender, tapping her manicured fingernails on the counter impatiently. The pharmacist comes out from behind the counter, her glasses lowered on her nose, a prescription in hand.

'Mrs Thorn?'

'That's me,' I say, stuffing the octopus back on the shelf. I've been feeling absurdly close to tears just holding it.

'You've got a medication here that reduces intracranial pressure. I'm going to need to know if she's taking any other medication before I can prescribe.'

'Oh, yeah. I've been given a list.'

I pass it to her and she notes something on her prescription pad, making a noise under her breath. 'Goodness. There's a lot going on here. Was it a bad injury?'

'She had a fall. Some stitches in her scalp but we were told it's superficial. She's having memory problems, though, and struggling with her speech. It looks like she'll need to see a specialist in the next few months.'

'Well, that's a real shame to hear. I'll see what we've got here – anything else can be ordered in.'

She turns to the woman with the auburn hair who came in after me and nods towards her. 'Someone taking care of you, Nancy?'

'Apparently,' the woman says. She's smiling as if she's making a joke, but the words seem cold and unfunny. She looks at her gold watch. 'Good job I paid for parking.'

'I'm sure she'll be with you soon.' The pharmacist smiles, then turns back to me. 'It'll take us a little while to get this lot ready. Do you want to come back? There's a cafe over the road. Shouldn't be longer than fifteen minutes.'

Okay, I tell her. Fine. I risk another glance at the woman waiting at the counter. There it is again, that strange familiarity, like the prick of a needle. Close up I realise she's not as old as I'd first thought; her pale skin and hooded blue eyes are only finely lined, the irises the colour of old porcelain Wedgwood plates.

Miss Renard. Nancy. I take my phone from my pocket, remembering. Alex pointed to the photo and said, 'That's Nancy Renard . . . She was nice. I don't know why she hung around with that lot of bitches.'

'Excuse me,' I say to her. She looks at me, smiling that taut, cold smile. 'I know this will seem strange, but – are you Nancy Renard?'

She nods. Still smiling. Still cold. *Oh God, leave me alone*, that smile says. I open my phone and scroll to the photograph, turning it around to face her.

'That's you, isn't it? Right there on the end! Wow. *So* weird!'

Nancy takes the phone from me and studies the picture. There's no light of recognition in her face, but a crease appears between her eyebrows and she smiles tightly. 'Goodness, that's a blast from the past.'

She hands it back to me coldly, her smile rigid. Her eyes are suddenly hard, glazed marbles. There is an iciness coming from her in waves. I feel a blush building in my cheeks, a growing swell of embarrassment as I slide the phone back into my bag, muttering an apology. Nancy turns her back to me in one swift movement, walking towards the desk, hair swishing in a long shimmering curtain behind her, leaving me standing in her Arctic wake.

The bell rings over my head as I open the door and scurry out, heading to the cafe over the road, dizzy with awkwardness. I don't know what response I was expecting but it wasn't that flat, dusty stare, nor that coldness, brisk as winter. My ears buzz, blood rising high.

In the cafe the young man behind the counter is good-looking in that sunken-cheeked Brat Pack way I loved in my teens. It makes me think again of William in the photo, thin and moody, that pout, the way his head was cocked like a pistol. I order a pot of tea and take a seat at an empty table towards the back of the room. The cafe smells of pastry and a light sweetness of honey, making my stomach rumble. I skipped breakfast. Bad dreams shrink my appetite. I watch as Nancy Renard leaves the pharmacy and heads directly for the cafe, a white paper bag in her hand. She approaches the counter and talks with the young man there before walking over to my table in the corner.

'You're not going to put that on Facebook, are you?'

I'm surprised by her tone, abrupt and almost accusatory. I've become good at reading faces over the years – the years I spent working as a counsellor will teach you that, right off the bat – and hers is anxious and tight, close to tears.

'The photo?'

'Yes. I don't want it on there. On anywhere.'

'Of course not. I just – it was just a coincidence, that's all. I found it a few days ago and then, boom, there you are in the same shop. I wouldn't dream of putting your picture online.'

She relaxes but only for a second. As a counsellor I specialised in post-traumatic stress disorder and anxiety, and I can see the way a person holds trauma – for some it is in the set of the shoulders or the way it compresses their face into a tight knot. Others can't keep their hands still or stop their leg jittering. It's how I noticed the way William tugs at his hair when he's lying. Nancy Renard is uptight, sure, but there's something else there, something she maybe isn't even aware of. She licks her thin lips and conjures up another cold smile.

'Where did you find it?'

'Do you want to join me, Nancy?'

She hesitates, and I don't think she does, not really. That coldness is a shield, a way to keep people at a distance. But also there's that element of curiosity, isn't there? *All this worry over a photograph,*

I think, and then immediately I remember Kim saying, *It's just pictures, that's all. It's not real life.*

'Fine,' she says eventually, making a show of checking her watch and jingling her car keys.

I catch a glimpse of the gold crucifix she is wearing over her polo neck, the small pearl earrings, iridescent in the overhead lights. Nancy rubs at her arms as if she is cold.

'I got a shock when I saw that picture, too,' I tell her. 'I had no idea William went through a goth phase.'

'Oh, you know William?'

I lift my hand so she can see my wedding band. 'I married him.'

'Well.' Her eyes sweep me then, up and down. Sizing me up. She doesn't try to hide it. 'Good for you. I'm at the tail end of a nasty divorce.'

'I'm sorry to hear that.'

'Don't be. You know why divorces are expensive? Because they're worth it.'

I laugh politely but she isn't laughing. Just that same, tight smile. A sweep of the eyes, up, down, before she asks, 'Any children?'

That pang, like elastic snapping somewhere inside my chest. I shake my head.

'I've got three. They keep me busy. My oldest is nearly the same age as I was in that photograph. I hope she keeps better company. Did William give you that picture?'

I tell her about Mimi's fall and Thorn House and the box of photos. When I mention Alex her eyes light up. She clasps her hands together. It's almost sweet.

'Alex Thorn? He was a sweetheart. I think he had a bit of a crush on me. Is he married?'

'He's still single, as far as I know. He spoke highly of you.'

'Really? What did he say?'

61

I don't know why she hung around with that lot of bitches.

'Just that you were the nicest of all of them.'

'Well, that wasn't hard. None of us were particularly likeable. Teen girls, you know? Think they rule the world. Ah, Alex. Such a sweetheart, he was. Shy. William was always a handsome devil. I used to feel intimidated by him, and Edie of course. He was whip-thin *and* he had a Dead Kennedys T-shirt with the sleeves cut off. Everyone thought he was the greatest.'

I laugh. 'It's a side of him that's completely new to me,' I admit, pulling up the photo and enlarging it. 'He doesn't talk about his life down here much.'

'Well, he wouldn't, would he? Not after everything that happened.'

I lower my cup into the saucer. Nancy sniffs and presses a tissue to her nose. Everything about her is dainty and bone-white, like a china tea set.

'What do you mean?'

'Sorry?'

'Just now. You said "after everything that happened".'

'Oh, just. You know. The stuff we did as kids, all of us. Messing around.'

'Like what?'

She looks at me with a trace of a smile. Her cupid's bow is a sharp inversion, an arrowhead. 'You know what we called ourselves? A coven. We used to write poetry and light red candles and let the wax burn our skin. At the weekends we used to head down to Brighton and go to the car boot sale there, looking for leather jackets and bullet belts and old top hats. My mum must've aged ten years every time I walked out the door.' She points at my phone. 'That picture you've got there was taken in St Mary's churchyard. It was where we all gravitated to with our preoccupation with' – she flutters her fingers to indicate something fanciful – 'death and rituals. Saint Mary de Castro. We used to hang dead roses from the branches of the trees. That was where we met William and Alex too, at the youth club there. And it was William who told us about Quiet Mary.'

'Who?'

The man behind the counter brings Nancy a cup of black coffee. Nancy thanks him, and turns back to me. 'Mary Sayers. Died in 1897, of drowning. That's what it says on her gravestone. It was William who first took us to see it, hidden away near the back of the churchyard. It was covered in ivy and moss, and very, very old. And it was William who told us the story about her.'

'What story?' I'm fascinated, despite myself. I lean forward in my chair, arms folded on the table. I'm aware of someone standing by the counter, the itching feeling of a gaze having fixed on us. It's there in my peripheral vision like a swelling blot of ink, but I dismiss it.

'Ah, God. You'll have heard versions of it over the years. These sorts of stories always end up that way. The way William told it, every winter a girl – this "Quiet Mary" – is seen hitchhiking on the road from Newhaven into Lewes. She only appears on nights when it's raining, along the stretch of road by the river as you come into town. Drivers who stop to pick her up have spoken of a chill that seems to come into the car with her, and that even if it's not raining she's always dripping wet, like she's just climbed out of the Ouse. You can smell the river on her. She doesn't speak, and as they enter Cuilfail Tunnel some people have said they can see movement out the corner of their eye, frantic, like she's clawing at the window to get out. When they turn around she's disappeared.'

I laugh uneasily. Nancy straightens up, brushing her hair away from her face, finishing her coffee.

'We all got caught up in it. Took it too far. The romance, the drowned girl, the haunted road. When I look at that photo I don't see four girls on the cusp of the rest of their lives. I see frightened young women who didn't fit in and couldn't find a valve to release the pressure. That picture is probably one of the last ones of us all together.'

'How come?'

Nancy is silent for a moment, her pale eyes grazing me, the table, the window. Her fingernails tap against her cup. They are highly polished, a delicate shade of coral.

'A couple of days after that photo was taken, Edie Hudson disappeared right in front of us.'

I open up the picture again. There's Edie, William's arms draped around her. She isn't smiling, and her pretty kohl-ringed eyes look defiant.

'What happened to her?'

Nancy shrugs. 'Don't know. They never found her. One minute she was there, the next? Gone.'

Shock is a detonation, a hollow boom in the chest. I stare at the girl in the picture, so like Kim, so like Samira. That attitude. That sneer. It unsettled me at first, how similar she was to both women, but now there's something else. The girl who is not there. My mouth is dry and dusty. I reach for my tea, sip it. It's gone cold.

Nancy sees my disorientation, smiles a little. 'You didn't know?'

'Like I said, he doesn't often mention his old life down here.'

But that's not quite true, is it? I've heard stories from his childhood, from both William and Alex. About the time William tried to make his mother breakfast in bed and nearly burned the house down. How they both nearly got arrested for climbing scaffolding in the town centre. How William once put his hand through a window, leaving a small, pale scar on his right palm. Kids' stuff. But still. This – this is something else. How could he not have told me this?

'It was the worst day of my life,' Nancy continues, her voice softer. 'Everything changed after that. Everything.'

She looks at me and smiles briskly, and just like that she seems to shrug back into the frosty, uptight woman who walked in through the door of the chemist. She grabs the white paper bag and stands, putting a five-pound note on the table.

'This is for the drinks. Tell Alex I said hi.'

Then she turns and leaves, tall and thin as a reed nodding in the breeze. As the door closes behind her I become aware of that movement again at the corner of my vision. There's a woman sitting at the counter, partially hidden by a pillar. She's watching us in the mirror. I smile at her, but she doesn't smile back. Her expression is as cold and hard as rain-soaked stone. I can feel her gaze even as I wrap my coat around me and pick up the bag from the pharmacy, and it's not until I'm out the door and over the road that the feeling, like legions of ants crawling beneath my scalp, dissolves.

Samantha – Then

It was Nancy who interested me. Out of the three of them. She was so guarded: her folded arms, her legs wrapped around themselves, the way she stared at the floor. I wished I could talk to her alone.

The girls sat opposite me in the headmaster's office. His name was written in gold paint on the frosted glass of his door, like a hard-bitten detective in a film noir. *Mr Peterson, Head.* He sat with his fingers buckled together on his desk, thin grey hair webbing his skull. He must have been due for retirement soon. Maybe this would be the incident that finished him off. Edie.

Focus. Focus. I'd had too much coffee.

Behind me were two police officers, one of whom was distractingly good-looking. He was Asian, a few inches shorter than me, long, black eyelashes. He was sitting with a notepad on his lap while the other stood, arms folded. They'd introduced themselves by their first names – Nathan and Omar – I supposed so the girls wouldn't feel intimidated by their presence. But I *wanted* them to feel intimidated. I wanted them to feel so afraid they couldn't think straight, I wanted them to carry the same fear I was being forced to carry, like a raw and bleeding heart that grew heavier with every step.

Edie had now been missing for four days.

'One of you must have seen something,' I said. They looked like a group of crows – what's that called, the collective noun? *A murder.* How prescient. 'You were right there when she disappeared. Think back – is there anything at all?'

No one spoke. They'd given the barest nod towards school uniform, with white shirts and ties fatly knotted against their throats. Their make-up was thick and unguent; high, arching eyebrows, long spiked lashes and lipstick so dark it made slashes of their mouths. Collectively they wore so much jewellery they rattled when they walked. I turned to the headmaster, frustrated.

'Don't you have rules about what the kids wear to this school? Shouldn't you be enforcing something?'

Mr Peterson frowned, rubbed his glasses with his sleeve. 'We see it as – uh – a means of expression which they are entirely – ah – which is entirely valid. At this age.'

He put his glasses back on, blinking. He was a mealworm of a man. I stared at him and then turned back to the girls. Charlie, in the middle, her skirt only an inch below her gusset, slid her hands between her thighs. She was wearing frilly ankle socks and Mary-Jane shoes. Her lips were plump and wet, a deep berry brown. Her gaze drifted away from me, bored. She was looking at Omar, the police officer.

'Are we under arrest?' she asked. Nancy looked up from beneath her fringe, caught my eye, looked away again. 'Because if we are, you have to caution us.'

'I want my one phone call,' Moya added, twisting her curly hair around her finger. She had black ripped jeans on, rubbed her leg against Nancy.

'Who would *you* call?' Charlie asked her.

'Domino's,' replied Moya, and they both dissolved into giggles. I clenched my fists on my lap, looked back at the headmaster, exasperated. *My daughter is fucking missing*, I wanted to yell. I tried to stay calm.

Omar coughed. 'No one is under arrest, but we need to know what happened. You said you saw Edie walk towards the back of the graveyard?'

'That's right,' Moya said. She was tiny, maybe a little over five feet, and sinuously thin. She had a hard, flat chest and the big round eyes of a cartoon animal, almost liquid. 'She walked away from us into the dark.'

'Why did she do that?' the other officer, Nathan, asked. 'Had you fallen out?'

The girls shrugged, shook their heads, *no*. Earrings rattled like chains. Nancy lifted her head and for a moment I thought she would say something in her small, broken-bird voice. But it was Charlie again, with the chipped nail polish and ripped fishnet tights, turning to me this time, ignoring the question.

'Where did she go the last time she ran away, Mrs Hudson?'

We stared at each other, Charlie and I. My hands tightened and squeezed. I heard an intake of breath over my shoulder, Omar's tongue clicking.

'There's a history of this behaviour?' he began.

I cut him off. 'No. No, there's – it's not like that. Sometimes Edie plays up, goes off with a friend for the night.'

The girls stared at me. What was it they called themselves? Cobras? Pythons? It's written there on Moya's bag, scratched into the leather in jagged letters: *Rattlesnakes*.

'Well, that would have been useful to know,' he said, and I shrivelled inwardly.

Charlie smiled to herself, catching my eye. 'Maybe she went looking for her dad,' she said, sing-song, inspecting her nails. In that moment I hated her. I could cheerfully have shoved her through the wall. But the police had already asked me about the possibility of

Edie trying to find her father. Can you give us his contact details, they'd asked, and I'd laughed nastily, lighting another cigarette. He walked out when she was three days old, I told them. Some men should just chop it off, you know? They hadn't liked that. So far, I had not enamoured myself to these people. I was frightening them, too angry and shaken up, a wasp trapped in a bottle. I wasn't sad enough, not yet weeping and needy. *Give me time. I'll get there.*

'What about drugs?' I fired back. 'I know you were all taking them.'

It was a cheap shot and it didn't land the way I'd hoped. I wanted to shock them – *show me some fucking contrition!* – but Moya just smiled, displaying perfect white teeth, glossy enamel.

'Which ones?'

'What?'

'Which drugs?'

She leaned over her legs to look me right in the eye.

'I said, which drugs? MDMA? Speed? Meth?'

'Crack?' Charlie said, hiding her smile and widening her eyes, which were a deep subaqueous green.

'Angel dust? PCP?'

'I saw Edie snort a line of instant coffee once.'

They dissolved into laughter, looking at each other from the corners of their eyes. The headmaster straightened in his seat, adjusting his cuffs, saying girls, please, some decorum.

I heard the police officer – Nathan, I think, with his rough morning breath – sigh behind me, and Omar stood.

I turned to look at them. 'What? We're not done here! I thought you were questioning them?'

'Not officially, we're not. We can't force them to cooperate. It's wasting time.'

'What about Edie? They must know something! For God's sake—' I looked back at them imploringly, the Rattlesnakes, skins shed and shrivelled on the floor, mean girls with bright eyes and pouty, trembling mouths, fingers intertwined as they joined hands. Moya put her head on Charlie's shoulder. Nancy flicked me a quick glance.

'Are we free to go, officer?' Charlie said in a baby voice. She was looking at Omar over my head. He must have indicated that they were done because suddenly the girls stood, a black mass, floating chiffon and tight, pinching lace, secretive smiles waxy with lipstick. The smell of them was bruises and crushed violets, cheap tobacco.

'Mrs Hudson?' Omar asked, his hands toying with his belt. I looked up at him. 'How many times has Edie gone missing before?'

'Once or twice.'

'Which is it?'

'Do you count the time that she snuck off to her friend's house in the middle of the night?'

'I count that, yes.'

'Then three. No, four times. But this is different.'

'How so?'

He was being so patient with me. I could feel tears welling. I swallowed the hard rock in my throat.

'Because the last times there were—'

'Triggers?'

'Conflicts. Yes.' I nodded. I grasped the fabric of my skirt and bunched it in my hands.

'And there wasn't this time? A conflict? An argument of some kind?'

I hesitated, looking up at him. Tears hazed my eyes and rolled slowly down my cheeks, viscous as honey.

Omar smiled, revealing straight white teeth. 'We can't help you if you aren't prepared to tell us the truth, Samantha.'

'Yes. There was. She gets so angry,' I said quietly, sniffing.

'Okay, well. You see, in itself this is a good thing. It indicates a typical pattern of behaviour for Edie. There's a problem, she runs away. Gets her head straight. Comes home. The reason she disappeared is fairly academic. We're more interested in where she's disappeared *to*. Edie's a fifteen-year-old schoolgirl, not a master criminal. She didn't just vanish into thin air.'

He lowered himself into a crouch, putting his hand over mine. I hadn't realised how much I was shaking until he stilled it, his skin warm and brown. 'Whatever happens, we'll keep looking.'

'Thank you.' I sniffed. 'Thank you, Omar.'

I didn't see Nathan or Omar again. They were assigned to another case, more high-profile – a schoolteacher had run off with a pupil to Cornwall – and so I printed my own posters, taking them as far as Worthing and Bexhill, hanging them in shop windows and on cafe noticeboards. *MISSING*, they said in fat black font, and underneath, printed slightly smaller, *Can You Help Find Me?*

The photo I'd chosen did not show Edie favourably. Part of me hoped she'd see it, maybe behind the counter of a newsagent she was buying Rizlas or pints of milk in, paying with handfuls of change held out in grubby hands. I thought she'd laugh if she did. The 'Borstal photo', she and I had called it, because she looked like she was on prison day release; unsmiling, arms folded, dark hair with a lopsided fringe she'd hacked herself in the bathroom one Sunday night. I'd originally looked for a photo of the two of us in France, one I'd had pinned to the noticeboard in the kitchen. I hadn't been able to find it, even moving the sideboard away from the wall to see if it had slipped down behind. I grew more and more frustrated until I realised I wouldn't be able to use it anyway. In it, Edie was smiling and tanned – the healthiest I'd ever seen her – but the advice I'd received from the family liaison officer had been to choose a picture to help the public recognise her, and I couldn't remember the last time I'd seen her smiling.

◆　◆　◆

The morning Edie left for the last time was sunny and dry. I remember that. The sky was as blue as cornflowers, frosted with drifts of white cloud. I remember that too. The clarity of that moment is so rich I could reach out and run my fingers through it. The radio was playing 'Waterloo Sunset'. The garden smelled ripe, of tangled roots and the slow creep of autumn with its mists and moss and damp stones. High overhead, a lark trilled and twittered, sketching shapes against the sky. I can remember the sound of her feet on the stairs and the smell of toast and the incense she constantly burned in her room. Her carpet was pockmarked with burn holes like craters on a distant planet.

Afterwards I realised – all these small things; the brain can only take on so much. It hands it back to you in bite-sized pieces of grief. You simply cannot digest any more. The thought that she had disappeared seemed like a grand idea, something oblique and vast, and I couldn't get a handle on it. But the little things I remember, and they strip away my armour bit by bit. The way the thrush had sung in the garden. Edie's shoes in the hallway, lying aslant where they had been kicked off. Cotton-wool balls smeared with make-up at the bottom of the bathroom bin. The rich blue of her veins, her wet hair dripping on to her shoulders. This, it is a form of madness.

As I was getting ready for work that morning I discovered my necklace was missing. At one stage I'd almost grown accustomed to my make-up and clothes and jewellery disappearing, only to reappear in Edie's bomb site of a room a week later. Only then she'd gone and taken a pair of my gold earrings, ones I wore only on very special occasions, and they hadn't turned up in her room – or anywhere else, in fact. Edie had feigned ignorance, told me I was paranoid. I found them eventually, a month or so later, in the window of the jeweller's on the high street. She'd sold them for just sixty pounds. I thought back to all the other things that had gone missing over the years – my seventies records, my pearl pendant, the silver bracelet studded with lapis lazuli – and my heart sank.

I'd considered getting a lock on my bedroom door but hadn't got round to it. It had seemed excessive, and besides, I'd told myself, she'd grown out of it now. I lifted my jewellery box and tipped the contents over my bed, raking through them with my fingers. I checked the drawers and my handbag and even the pockets of my coat, getting more and more agitated. All the while Edie was in the bathroom. I'd heard the shower run briefly, and the rattle of the curtain rail. When she didn't come out after half an hour I banged on the door with the flat of my hand.

'Edie!'

'In a minute!'

'Not in a minute, *now*! What are you doing in there? Are you ill?'

'I'm fine!' The toilet flushed. 'I just need a minute!'

'You did this yesterday! Tied up the bathroom for nearly an hour! Other people live here too, you know!'

Silence. I paced outside the door, the small hallway closing in on me, twisting my anger tightly. Finally, the door opened a crack. Her face was pale-looking, with bright spots of colour high up on her cheeks. She'd pierced another hole in her ear, red and raw-looking, a scab of blood building up around the silver stud.

I held out my hand. 'Where is it?'

'What?'

'You know what. My necklace. My favourite one, the one my mum left me.'

'With the dragonfly on it?' She shrugged. 'I haven't seen it.'

'You're lying.'

She rolled her eyes and tried to close the door on me. I pushed back and for a second there was a tense stand-off.

She relented with a sneer. 'Ugh. I hate it when you're like this.'

'I left it in my jewellery box and now it's not there.'

'I said I haven't seen it! I hate it, I wouldn't wear it anyway!'

'It's not you wearing it I'm worried about, Edie, it's you selling it.'

'Oh, here we go—'

'I want it put back where you found it by the time I leave the house.'

'You need a hobby, Mum. You've started to imagine things.'

'I *said*, put it back!'

'I told you I don't fucking have it!'

I reached out and grabbed her. My nails sank into her damp skin. I saw the wince of pain that pinched her face, quickly replaced by something harder and meaner.

'Put it back or I'll call the police.'

'Do it. Go on! And I'll show them the black eye you've given me!'

'Wha—'

Edie lifted her hand and slapped at her own face. The air rang with the sound of it, sharp and brisk. I stared at her in horror as she did it again, her eyes watering. The right side of her face glowed brick-red.

'Edie, stop – what are you doing?'

'Let's see how you like it in prison, huh? You know what they do to women in there who beat up their kids?'

This time she drove her head against the wall, staggering for a moment at the impact. I was filled with a cold horror as a trickle of blood seeped from one nostril and there was a strange, distant look in her eye. I forgot the necklace and grabbed her with panicky tightness, hard enough to leave red imprints on her skin, pulled her towards me, wrapping my arms around her as tightly as I could so her hands were pinned against her sides. Although she didn't fight against me, she was filled with a stiffness, a rigidity that meant I had to lean her against me so that we didn't both fall down. It was like clinging on to a plank of wood.

'Don't, Edie. Don't,' I said, again and again. She started laughing and her spittle flecked my cheeks, settled in my hair like snowflakes. Something shrivelled in me, a withered rosehip turning black.

That day I didn't even see her leave, although the front door slammed so hard the house shook. I went to work and thought nothing, felt nothing. My ears seemed to ring all day with the shock of seeing her drive her head into the plaster. By the time I got home that evening it had started to rain. I can remember seeing her coat, the big winter one, still hanging on the hook, and I thought, *She'll be cold without that.* I wasn't surprised when she wasn't home before me. She often went to friends' houses after school, or down to the shops in town or the youth club. Later I would see my own words repeated over and over again in print: *I wasn't surprised when she didn't come home.* They had made me sound neglectful, careless. A half-mother.

I made pasta, had a glass of wine. I noticed I was checking my watch more frequently as it grew darker outside. Her dinner was cooling under a plate on the worktop. I felt the faintest stirrings of unease, like telepathy. Once the hands had crawled past nine o'clock I sat beside the phone. I went through my address book, old and falling apart on its binding. It was that tall boy I was thinking of, William, with his hard, shining eyes. I didn't know his number; I didn't even know where he lived. My heart quickened, just a little, as outside the darkness pressed against the windows. By half past I was speaking with a girl called Kate Robinson, who was in Edie's class at school. They had known each other for years – the soft pencil with which I'd written her details into my address book had faded to a very pale grey. Kate came to the phone after her mother had got her out of bed. I could sense that talking to me made her nervous. If I'd had more presence of mind I would have questioned why. I remember Kate as a sweet girl, with a slight lisp, short and friendly in plum-coloured corduroy. She and Edie had been inseparable all through primary.

No, she told me, she hadn't seen Edie. Not today.

'Did you not see her at school, love?'

Silence. She didn't want to answer me. At the time I thought she was worried she would get Edie into trouble. I know better now.

'Hello? Kate?'

'I'm here.'

Her breathing, soft and snuffly like she had a cold. She was holding the phone too close to her mouth.

'Kate, please, you have to tell me. Edie isn't in any trouble, I just need to know.'

Her mother speaking softly to her in the background. I pictured the two of them together in their softly lit kitchen, Kate in a long nightdress that drowned her small frame, her mother reassuring her with a hand on her shoulder, stroking her hair. I envied them.

'She wasn't at school today.'

'Perhaps she just had different classes to you?'

'No. We have all the same classes. Except history and science because I have history on Thursdays and she has it on a Monday.' She sniffed.

'What about at lunchtime or after school?'

'Nope. I didn't see her, anyhow. She's usually in the churchyard with her friends. That's where they go. But it started raining today so . . .' She tailed off.

'Thank you, Kate. You can get back to bed now.'

'You won't tell Edie you spoke with me, will you? I don't want her to know you spoke with me.'

'Absolutely not. But if you do see her then you tell her that I'm looking for her and that she is to come straight home. Tell her she isn't in trouble. Can you do that for me?'

She told me she could and hung up. I stared at the phone for a while, silent in its cradle. Something inside me had begun to fray.

I turned all the lights on in the house that night. Lit it up like Christmas. A beacon in the dark. *Find your way home, baby.* I wandered from room to room without thinking. I'd been here with Edie before, of course. Slammed doors and raised voices and her spiriting herself away for a day or two. But my mind kept circling back to the argument we'd had that morning, the way she'd driven her own head into the bathroom wall.

There was a dent there; I'd seen it earlier when I went to the loo. A tiny depression in the plaster like a crater, alien and somehow unreal. The way she'd laughed afterwards, even as the red mark on her forehead gave way to a darker and more livid bruise. She'd left me open-mouthed and silent, her eyes glittering with malice.

She's just punishing you, I tried to tell myself in a calm, rational voice, *she'll be back tomorrow morning just like the last time.* But still. The way she'd hurt herself, the energy she'd had, the way she'd been vibrating with it. That wasn't normal.

Edie isn't normal, a rogue, disloyal voice whispered, and I rummaged in the drawer for the cigarettes I kept there, the small box of matches. That first evening passed in a series of frozen images, like a slideshow. I watched a moth driving its plump body into the window pane over and over, mystified at its stupidity. That compulsion. Over and over, even when it hurt.

I stood in the garden and smoked beneath a thin rind of white moon. I slept fitfully on the sofa beneath an old blanket that smelled of mothballs and lavender. There were, mercifully, no dreams, but I woke cold and afraid in the pinkish light of dawn, her name jumping from my mouth. *Ee-dee.* That was the moment, that perfect pivot into helplessness, when I could do nothing but pitch forward into the longest day of my life.

When I was small, about five years old or so, I had an accident. I'd accompanied my older brothers into the woods to build a den near the stream there. The heat of the day had made the fields shimmer. My eldest brother, Rupert, had stripped to his waist and climbed the thick trunk of one of the trees which crowded about the water. There were the frayed remains of a rope swing and he tugged at it, testing his weight. Finally, he said, 'Pot' – 'Pot' was his nickname for me until I was fourteen, because of my little rounded belly – 'I think this will take your weight. In fact I'm sure of it. Want to give it a try?'

I looked across at my other brother, Danny, older than me by a year. His jeans were stained indigo from the knees down where he had waded into the stream to fetch a stick he'd seen floating there. We called him 'backward' and 'simple' but now he would have been referred to as having 'additional needs'. We didn't care, though. He was our brother. He was one of us.

'Okay,' I said. The heat made everything still. A cloud of gnats were dancing just above the surface of the water.

Rupert tied a long, thick stick to the bottom of the rope, something for me to sit on. The wood was warm from the sun. It felt nice against my skin. The rope creaked alarmingly as I settled against it, wrapping my legs about each other. Rupert pushed me away from the tree and I swung out over the glimmering water. I can remember seeing Danny, standing as he often did with that faraway look in his eyes. I swung out in an arc, seeing minnows scatter beneath my fast-moving shadow. I didn't feel the rope break, but I heard a snap beside my ear and became suddenly engulfed in icy water. My mouth was full of it, the sharp taste of the cold. All sound disappeared with the popping of bubbles and a vast roaring noise that sounded like the engine of a jet plane, *whooooosh*. I couldn't find the ground, couldn't find the surface. I could see sunlight flickering but didn't know which way was up and there were stones beneath my fingertips and my lungs were shrieking for breath, but there was nothing. I was being carried away, I thought, downriver. Because I was young, and shocked, I did not panic, and because I did not panic I did not die. I broke the surface, shouting, and Danny was there, waist-deep, reaching out a long skinny arm. Hands the colour of cream dipped into the water, pulling me roughly by the hair. The water filled my nose, thick as treacle. I did not know how long I was under for, only that when they pulled me out I felt like I was floating away from my body.

I must have blacked out because one moment I was lying on the bank staring up into the sunlight sifted through leaves, and the next I was on my knees throwing up gutfuls of bile and silty water, and Danny was crying in great honking brays. I started to feel scared when I saw Rupert's face, ghost-white, and the remains of my lunch about my feet. I realised I had lost a shoe in the water and that my mother would be cross with me. I was gripped with panic then – a huge, rumbling dread – and the taste in my mouth was the same bright taste that filled my mouth that endless, horrible day many years later. Fear, bright as neon.

◆　◆　◆

Detective Tony Marston introduced himself the way he did everything: slowly, and with great care. He took one of my hands and simply held it in both of his for a moment, catching my eye. His face was so deeply lined it appeared corrugated. Indentations were carved into his brow, his cheeks, a deep cleft in his chin. He had scruffy grey hair and blue eyes nested in creases, and what he said in his soft, coaxing voice was this: 'My name is Detective Tony Marston and I am here to help you find your daughter.'

I made him a cup of tea and he leaned against the doorway of my tiny kitchenette. Edie had been missing now for a week. Tony had a picture of her in his hand, a school photo, unsmiling. He was talking to me, voice lifting and falling like the sea. My head was low, stomach rumbling.

'Samantha, in cases like this what we usually find is that these kids come home when they're hungry or broke. A night or two on the streets is usually a good wake-up call. Makes them think, do you see?'

He lit a cigarette and took the tea from me. The female officer who had accompanied him was tall and thin with flat brown hair, like a reed. She sat silently, sipping milky tea. I don't recall her ever speaking.

'What do you mean, "cases like this"?' I asked. My ears were ringing; the shock, coming in waves.

'I've seen a lot of runaways, Samantha – is it Samantha or can I call you Sam? And I can tell you that they've all got one thing in common. They all discover that they can't run away from a problem. It catches up with them in the end. Now, the good news is that this is something they discover of their own accord, usually pretty quickly, and they come home with their tail between their legs. Not all of them, mind, but most. And you said there had been conflict, did you not?'

He looked to his colleague for confirmation. She gave him a quick nod.

'It was just a silly row,' I said. 'Over nothing, really. A missing necklace. I thought she'd taken it – she does that sometimes, without asking, it's just a little thing. I can't believe she'd leave over it.'

Tony smiled at me sympathetically, face crumpled like soft towels. 'I have a teenager. In fact, I have two of them. You don't need to explain this to me. But we need to know everything you can tell us because as far as we are concerned this is an open case. The more information we have, the better our chances of finding her.'

'Sure.'

'The other good news' – here he smiled as if he really were delivering good news – 'is that Elizabeth is what we class as a low-risk missing person. What that means is, from the information you've given us, there's no risk of harm either to the public or herself.' I thought of Edie thrashing in my arms, that bruise blooming in shades of yellow and deep violet. I stayed silent. I hadn't told them about that. I didn't want to look like a bad mother.

'What that also means is while abduction or kidnap are a possibility, it's minimal. As there has been a pattern of her – uh – "absconding", if you like, that gives us hope that this is another one of those times. Her age is the thing that makes her most vulnerable, but according to the notes I've got here you've told us she is "very streetwise".'

Had I? Those initial days after Edie had walked out were like stones dropping from my hands.

'Okay,' I said. 'But she's never been gone this long before.'

He leant forward, placed his hand on my forearm. His palm was warm. 'We'll find her, but in all honesty, Samantha, I think she'll be home before the end of the week.'

'I hope so.'

'End of the week,' he said, smiling. 'You'll see.'

◆ ◆ ◆

But she wasn't. She wasn't home that night, or the night after. Detective Marston returned two days later, alone this time. He had a folded-up newspaper under his arm and when he came into the house he wrinkled his nose as though it smelled bad.

'How are you bearing up?'

'Have you got any news?' I didn't have time for his pleasantries. My heart had started to stutter, little palpitations at odd hours of the night like rusty machinery, trembling beneath my skin.

'We haven't found your daughter yet. But we're making inroads, Samantha, I promise you. Can I get you some tea? Have you been sleeping?'

I lifted my head to meet his gaze. I'd been mistaken about Marston's eyes being blue. They were the grey of cold stone. He wasn't smiling.

'What is it? Tell me.'

'Come through to the kitchen. Let's talk in there.'

He led me through and filled the kettle while I cleared a space on the kitchen table, shoving the junk mail and newspapers and food packets to one side. I was living off cereal and instant noodles. I was too jittery to sit down. I lit a cigarette and when I offered one to Tony he took it gratefully.

'We've been up to your daughter's school. Spoken with some of her teachers there. It seems Edie has had some problems engaging with her education.'

'What does that mean?'

'Truancy. We know that, of course. The day she went missing she'd skipped school. Where did she go? We're still looking into that. But according to our timeline she was with her friends that same Thursday evening at the youth centre at St Mary de Castro. We know that because she was seen with them as late as 7 p.m., when the caretaker was locking up. What we want to establish is, where had she been that day and what bearing does it have on her disappearance?'

He made strong tea for us both, brown and tarry, the milk slightly turned. He handed me the sugar bowl.

'Stick a few spoonfuls of that in. It'll taste better.'

We sat opposite each other at the table. The pouches beneath his eyes were dark purple, lined with veins.

'We got the impression from Edie's teachers that she has something of a history with the school. Aside from the truancy, there were episodes of bullying – quite severe, by the sounds of it.'

'Edie never mentioned she was being bullied.'

'No, no.' He was talking softly. 'Edie was the bully.'

There was a pain behind my eyes like an iron band squeezing and squeezing my skull. A warning carved of stillness. In 373 BC historians recorded that all the animals deserted the Greek city of Helice just days before it was destroyed by an earthquake, alerted by some strange telepathy. Rats, snakes, weasels, running in silence. I had that same feeling now. The calm that precedes devastation.

'Edie wasn't a bully. She was difficult, but she wouldn't—'

'Samantha. You must have known.'

You did know, a voice said. *Remember that time you saw her coming in with bloodied knuckles? Or how about when she split her lip and she told you she fell over but you knew, didn't you, Samantha? You knew. You just couldn't confront her.*

That's not true.

It is true. Tell him. Tell him how much she frightened you. Her temper. Her rage.

I straightened in my seat, suddenly defensive of Edie, feeling disloyal. *You are her mother*: that same voice, calm, rational. *You should have been in charge.*

'She got in with a bad crowd. They're the ones you need to speak to. Those girls, the ones that look like witches. Speak to them. They've been poisoning her!'

'It's been going on a long time.' Tony spoke as if he hadn't heard me. 'Little incidents, but they build up. Jumping people in cloakrooms and toilets, theft, fist fights—'

'Fist fights?'

'It's all on her record.'

'It's not.' I shook my head vehemently. 'I would have known.'

'You know who Katie Robinson is?'

'Not Katie. Kate. I spoke with her the first night Edie didn't come home. They're old friends, have been since they were little. Why?'

He sighed, rubbing his temples. 'Kate was pushed down a flight of stairs in school this year. Back in March. She said Edie had done it.'

I laughed. I couldn't help it. If he just knew Edie, he wouldn't have said these things. She had her faults, sure. But she wouldn't *do* something like that. It was dangerous. She could have killed her.

'Well, that's bullshit.'

'Kate suffered a fractured wrist and multiple bruising to her shoulders, ribs and legs. There were witnesses.'

I sat quietly, thinking back to the conversation with Kate when Edie had first gone missing. *You won't tell Edie you spoke with me, will you?* she'd said quietly. *I don't want her to know you spoke with me.* How frightened she'd sounded.

'I know it's hard to hear—'

'It's not.' I shook my head so hard I saw stars for a moment. 'It's not hard at all because it's not true. You're blowing it out of proportion. She was a difficult girl, and she had a hard time growing up without her dad, me working all the time. The way she responds to things is sometimes . . . excessive. I think people forget how fucking hard it all was for her. And this girl, Kate – why are we just taking her word for it? Why is she going unchallenged and just allowed to blame my daughter?'

'You think she threw herself down the stairs?'

'I don't know what I think. I wasn't there! That's the point. No one was.'

'Edie was, Samantha. And like I said, we have witnesses.'

We stared at each other across the table. A grey pall hung in the air above us, hovering like a spirit. I glanced down at my cigarette and saw a long arc of ash, slightly drooping. I'd forgotten to smoke it. I stubbed it out.

'The school said they've tried to make contact with you in the past.'

'They have not!'

Haven't they? There it was again, an internal voice, so calm, so unlike my own. I tried to think. I recalled a phone call once, on a rainy evening when I'd just got in from work, later than usual. The trains had been running behind, packed with damp, heavy breathers and wet clothes. The teacher had asked me to make an appointment to go and speak with the head. Edie had been misbehaving.

'What kind of misbehaviour?'

'I really think it's better for you to come in and discuss it face to face.'

'Well, that's going to be difficult. I'm on my own, you see, and I work a lot. I'll talk to her.'

I didn't remember what had happened after that. I could remember thinking, *I must speak to Edie about this, it's gone too far.* But I hadn't, had I? I must have forgotten.

No.

I must have forgotten.

No. You didn't. You were afraid of her.

My memories of those days at the beginning of the year were thrown-together dinners on our laps in front of the television, stunted conversation, Edie trailing me like a shadow. That was in the days after she'd taken a bite out of Amanda Litton's ear – another time when she'd been provoked, Edie had said. Amanda had pushed and pushed until Edie had reacted. Any of us would. I felt like saying as much to Tony Marston now, his clear, hooded eyes watching me carefully. She was easily provoked, I'd say, people just didn't understand.

It's not me. I'm not a bad mother.

'So you had no inkling of any of this, Samantha? You never saw this kind of behaviour at home, she never mentioned it to you, not even in passing?'

I'd catch her standing quietly behind me in the kitchen or on the stairs, silent and lethal as a shark. She'd laugh when I'd jump, one hand fluttering to my chest. Her eyes round and gleaming. A coiled snake in the shadows. I used to think she liked the look of fear on my face, but then I would remind myself that this was my *daughter* we were talking about. Don't be silly, Samantha.

Tell him.

'No, nothing at all.'

'You don't remember the school contacting you? The messages they left? You never saw the letters?'

My hand lifted and started to rub at my temple. My face creased in concentration. 'Uh, maybe? There might have been a letter. I don't know, I've been so busy—'

He sighs. 'Okay, I see.'

'Anyway,' I told Tony firmly, 'what's her behaviour at school got to do with the fact that my daughter hasn't come home?'

'It fits a narrative.'

'What?'

He shrugged, flicked his ash into a saucer already littered with butts. 'Troubled teen runaway.'

'Listen, Tony. I know she's done this before once or twice, but she always came back within twenty-four hours. She hasn't even picked up the phone to call me! You don't think that's worrying? You don't think that's worth looking into?'

'What are you suggesting, Sam?'

He had his notebook out, scribbling things while I'd been talking. Now he stopped, pencil poised over the page. It was little more than a stub in his thick, blunt fingers. He looked up at me.

'I don't — I just – I don't think you're taking it seriously!'

'I can assure you we—'

'So why is it just you? Where's the team of officers out looking for her? Where's the helicopter and the dogs and the newsflashes? She's fifteen years old, she's got no money! What have you been doing this last week? Huh? Fuck!'

I swiped angrily at my eyes. There were tears there but they were hot and bitter, acidic.

Tony laid his pencil gently down beside his notebook. 'Sam, I've spoken to her teachers, her friends at school. The last people to see her – these girls, the ones you mentioned – said she'd been acting strangely the last couple of weeks. On edge. Crying. Flying off the handle.'

'Huh. You've just described an average teenage girl, for God's sake.'

'They all watched her walk into the copse of trees at the back of the churchyard. No one saw her come back out. What does that tell you?'

I shook my head.

'It's a deliberate act,' he said, rubbing his temple with his forefinger. 'Maybe not carefully planned, but what is when you're fifteen? She walked away and climbed over the wall, maybe, or snuck out through the side gate there.'

'That gate's always locked.'

'Well, the caretaker claims the keys went missing from his office back in June. He's reported several break-ins. Last one was the tenth of October.'

'You think Edie stole his keys?' I laughed, disbelievingly. *Ha!* 'You make out like she's some sort of demon.'

Tony finished his tea and nodded towards me. 'You want to put that down?'

I looked at my hand and saw I was holding a knife. Small, about the size of a palm. I was gripping it so hard the beds of my fingernails were white.

'What, you – you think I'm threatening you?' I laughed, letting the knife fall to the table. I hadn't even realised I'd picked it up.

He smiled without humour. 'You mind if I take another look in her bedroom?'

'They've already been up there.'

'Just – would you mind? A quick look around?'

'What are you looking for?'

'Something that might help us.'

'Is this about what the caretaker said? About a break-in? Tony?'

'Partly. It would certainly help us to know if Edie was responsible.'

He stood and so did I, too fast. The blood rushed in my ears, making me feel dizzy. 'You'll need a warrant.'

Unsmiling now, he looked at me levelly. 'And I'll get one, if that's how you want to do it. But Samantha, you could just let me and go and have a poke around now, and we'll get back to the business of finding your daughter all the quicker. Won't we?'

He left the room and I followed, calling after him up the stairs, aware that my voice was shrill and trembling. 'I know what you're looking for! And you won't find it! She isn't a thief! She's just a little girl with a lot of problems! She's my baby! Do you hear me, you old bastard?'

He didn't even turn around. Just the sound of his footsteps and the stairs creaking under his weight. There was a sob in my throat so loud it was going to choke me. I was going to suffocate beneath the weight of it, beneath my love for her, beneath the fear. I covered my mouth with my hands, holding it back. I was suddenly reminded of a time I'd walked into my bedroom just out of the bath, skin still beaded with water, towel clutched about me, and Edie had been standing there alone in the dark, waiting for me. She'd stepped out from behind the door and I'd screamed, throwing my hands out defensively in front of me to ward off an expected attack. Of course, in that moment, I hadn't known it was her, had I?

Had I?

I stood in the doorway to Edie's bedroom and watched Tony as he opened and closed her drawers. The floor was still littered with her worn clothes and shoes, black tights twisted into knotted ropes and left discarded among the T-shirts and lace. Tony picked his way across carefully.

'Find anything?'

'Not yet.' He looked back at me over his shoulder, his expression neutral. 'You say the police have already been up here?'

I nodded. 'The day I called them. They were trying to work out if she'd taken anything with her. You know, clothes, passport, money.'

'Uh-huh. And had she?'

'Not that we noticed. As you can see, it's hard to tell. She wasn't house-proud.'

'I can't make my daughters set the table for their own bloody dinner, let alone tidy their rooms,' he said gruffly. 'I know how it is.'

He used his pen to lift a scarf on the dressing table. 'They ask you about Edie's father?'

'What about him?'

'Is he local? Are they in contact? Could she have gone to live with him?'

'No, no and no. He wouldn't have her either way. Hasn't seen her since she was three months old and he barely noticed her even then.'

'Do you have contact details for him?'

I laughed nastily.

'Okay.' He straightened up with a grunt.

'When can I talk to the press? I feel so useless sitting here doing nothing.'

Tony glanced over at me. There was a low light that day, robbing us of shadows and depth. Everything was grey and flat, as though viewed through dirty water. 'I don't know if that's a great idea, although I can't stop you.'

'Why not? Surely any publicity is good publicity? I mean – I mean, Edie could be anywhere, with anyone! The more people looking out for her the better.'

'There's no evidence that anyone else is involved in your daughter's disappearance and we have no reason to believe any harm has come to her. Plus this isn't the first occasion the police have been involved when she's run away, is it?'

I looked at him flatly. 'You're joking, right? She was twelve years old. She hid in the neighbour's garden down the road, for God's sake. Came back once it got dark.'

It had been the first time she'd run away and the only time I'd called the police. They'd found her two doors down, hiding behind the hydrangea bush. She'd broken in by climbing on to a bin and jumping over the wall. The neighbours said they hadn't minded, but I noticed afterwards that they'd put a layer of concrete studded with jagged shards of broken glass along the top of the wall. They hadn't liked Edie much. I once overheard them call her 'feral' in the newsagent's. It had stung.

'Think about how it looks. From the outside.' He turned away, started opening the little drawers of her dressing table. 'This one's locked.'

'I don't have a key.'

'Okay, well – do you have a screwdriver?'

I walked down the hallway to the airing cupboard, where the toolbox was kept. We'd lived in this house over fourteen years, Edie and I, moving in after an ill-advised stint living with my parents in their cramped terraced cottage. In the winter it was cold, with patches of damp blooming on the walls, and in the summer stifling hot, the old bricks absorbing and retaining the heat of the day. I pulled the toolbox open and took the screwdriver out. As I fastened the latch I discovered something on the floor, in the warm and the dark. A small elastic hairband with plastic bobbles. It must've been lying there for years. I reached out with trembling hands and lifted it between my fingers, blowing off the dust that clung to it.

A memory.

'Mummy, will you plait my hair?'

I'd looked up to see Edie in my bedroom doorway. Six years old and cute as a button. She had dressed herself and one sock rode up to her knee, the other down to her ankle. She had a dress on, with a skirt beneath, legwarmers and a winter hat. Her woolly cardigan was too big and beginning to pill. And because she was mine, I thought she looked delightful. She climbed on to the bed next to me, plump hands holding my cheeks and studying my face.

'You've cried,' she'd said simply.

'Yes,' I'd told her. 'Sometimes grown-ups feel sad.'

'Your face is stripy black.'

I'd lifted my fingers to it and found mascara printed on to my cheeks.

'It's make-up,' I'd told her.

'Messy.'

'Very messy. Shall I do your hair, Edie?'

She'd turned so I could plait her curly, unruly locks. Glossy brown, like polished mahogany. The sun had been as warm and soft as butter.

'Sam?' It was Tony, from down the hallway. 'Sam? Don't worry about the screwdriver. I got in.'

I came to as if surfacing from a fitful sleep. I was hugging my knees to my chest as if I was trying to make myself as small as possible, down there on the floor in the dark of the cupboard, among the lint balls and folded towels and sheets that smelt soapy and old. The hairband was still in my palm. That memory, it was so acute, so painful, it was like subsidence beneath my feet. I could feel the slippage like an aftershock, making it hard to grasp reality. *Sometimes grown-ups feel sad*, I'd told her, and now I couldn't even remember why I'd cried, what trivial upset had reduced me to tears on that lucid summer day all those years ago. I remembered the feel of her hair, slippery and glossy in my fingers, how we'd giggled when I told her I'd once cut my brother's hair half off with the kitchen scissors when I was five years old, the way it had fallen to his feet in white curls like feathers. I put the hairband in my pocket where I could still touch it with the tips of my fingers, holding on to her as long as possible.

◆ ◆ ◆

'What did you find?' I said as I entered Edie's bedroom. Something crunched in the junk beneath my feet. One of her CDs, cracked down the middle. There were dents in the walls where she had frisbeed them across the room. Tony was holding up a small brown bottle between his thumb and index finger. He had driven the handle of a spoon from one of Edie's discarded cereal bowls into the edge of the drawer, pulling it open.

'Amyl nitrate,' he said, and looked over at me. 'Poppers.'

'Oh.' I folded my arms, clutching my elbows. 'Well. Add it to her charge sheet, I guess.' I laughed, but it came out like a mewl, soft and weak.

'It's not necessary.' Tony put the bottle back in the drawer. 'She's hardly Tony Montana. We already knew about the drug use. The girls I spoke with were refreshingly honest about it.'

'The Rattlesnakes?'

'Heh. Jesus. I know, right? The Rattlesnakes. You know, I asked one of them why they chose that name and she said, "Because it makes us sound cool." Can't argue with that logic.' He walked back towards me, hands in his pockets. 'This brings me back to the point about the press, Samantha. A young, single mother with a tearaway daughter she can't control who's taking drugs and beating up other kids? They'll tear you apart. I don't want that for you. I don't want that for Edie. It might scare her right off coming back at all.'

I squared my shoulders. It was a defensive move, as pure and instinctive as raising my fists. I opened my mouth to dispute with him: *You don't get it, Tony, it's not like that, you don't understand.* Only he *did* understand, didn't he? They'd take us apart bone by bone, Edie and me. The fights, the absent father, her grades, our home. It made my stomach hurt to think about it.

'Okay. What about the hospitals?'

'What about them, Sam?'

'Are you checking them? All of them? She might be lying in a coma somewhere.'

'Lucky her,' Tony said, and shook his head. 'I'd welcome a coma right now.'

Me too, I thought. A long sweet coma, like falling backward on to a cushion of velvet and black mink. My numbness was starting to give way. Soon the pain would come, like splinters dug deep into the softest parts of me, and with it the slow certainty that Edie was dead. Not missing, not absent, but dead.

A hand on my arm, gentle. Tony was looking at me earnestly. 'Sam? You going to get that?'

Distantly, I heard the phone ringing. I scrambled down the hallway and into my bedroom, no Edie waiting to jump out at me behind my bedroom door, and picked up the phone from its place on my bedside table.

'Hello?' I was breathless, desperate. I could hear the pleading in my voice even as I said it. 'Edie? Honey? Is that you?'

More silence. The line crackled.

'Say something. Please!' I said. Tony came into the room and peered out the window into the street.

'I know where she is,' a voice said. It was a woman's voice, but deep and bronchial-sounding, as though she had a bad cold.

'Oh my God. You do?'

'Yes.'

I clutched the phone and motioned to Tony. 'Tell me! Tell me what you know! Where is she?'

'Your daughter is in a house. It's rural. A lot of ground. Farmhouse, maybe? I can see dogs, but not sheepdogs. Big ones, guard dogs.'

Tony was looking at me, his hands on his hips.

'What do you mean, you see it? Are you looking at it now? Where is it? Hello?'

'You got someone in your family with a lost limb?'

'A what?'

'A missing arm? I'm getting a missing arm. A man with no arm. Does that sound familiar to you?'

'I don't – I don't think so.'

'She's been taken, but she's alive.'

The phone was snatched from me. It was Tony. His eyebrows were drawn together, mouth quivering in a bow of distaste.

He lifted the phone to his ear. 'Who is this?' He waited while she talked, smoothing down the front of his shirt with the palm of his hand. Finally he said, 'Piss off, pal.' And hung up.

I stared at him, open-mouthed. 'What are you doing?'

'It's a fucking psychic. You're going to get a lot of these calls. Fuck's sake. You need to go ex-directory.'

'She said she knew where Edie was.'

'Yeah, sure she does. They're touched in the head, these people. You start listening to them, you're going to tie yourself into knots.' He squatted in front of me, taking my hands in his. His knuckles bristled with dark hairs. 'You got an answerphone?'

I nodded, my heartbeat finally beginning to slow. That woman, she had sounded so sure.

'Use it to screen calls. You'll get plenty of weirdos calling you now that word's got out. They think they're helping, but they're parasites, so don't give them anything you can't afford to lose. That goes for your money, your energy or your time. Understand?'

His eyes drifted to the left, towards my bedside table. The drawer was half-open there, just a few inches, but enough to see inside. Tony leaned across me and pulled it open a little further. The object in there rolled forward and he picked it up, looking at me with interest.

'Where did you get this?' he asked me.

I shrugged awkwardly. 'A friend brought it back from the States for me.'

'Take Down Spray,' he read aloud. 'What is it, Mace?'

'Yeah. Pepper spray.'

'Why do you keep it there? You afraid of burglary?'

'Sure.'

He studied me carefully and I gave him a smile, folding my arms, elbows on my knees. *Your body language, Sam*, I told myself, *is going to give you away. He's a policeman; he must see people lie all the time.* I'd asked Theresa to get it for me when she went to New York last year. I'd told her it was because I was frightened, living alone, and partly that was true. *Partly.*

'You know this is illegal. You shouldn't have this. And Sam, if someone's going to break into your house, chances are you'd be better off hiding the pepper spray from them. And what if your daughter found it?'

My mouth was so dry it clicked when I swallowed. Finally I said, 'It makes me feel safe.'

'Jesus. Who'd be a woman?' he said, and slid it back into the drawer. But he was still looking at me strangely. Like he knew.

Edie got violent sometimes, I thought of telling him, but I didn't. Instead I said, 'That woman. The psychic. She said Edie was still alive. She said she knew where she was.'

Tony looked at me sympathetically. 'They all say that, sweetheart. We'll find her. We'll find your daughter. Girls like Edie will always find their way home.'

Frances – Now

There's something different about Mimi when I return from town. She is clear-eyed and lucid, sitting in her high-necked dressing gown watching the afternoon news.

She turns her head to me and smiles as I come into the sitting room. Through the fine gauze of her hair the gash on her scalp is still visible, clotted with dried blood as dark as ink.

'How are you feeling?' I ask her.

She brushes crumbs from her chest and smiles. 'A bit foggy. Better than yesterday, at any rate. Did you manage to get the paper?'

'Yes, I did.' I pull it out of my bag and her smile broadens. She was a great beauty in her younger days, according to William and Alex. It was a mystery to so many that she married Edward, a plain-thinking bureaucrat nine years her senior who liked to garden and play cribbage. There is a framed photo of the two of them on their wedding day on the mantelpiece, standing outside the town hall and smiling in a shower of confetti. Mimi was twenty-seven years old, her ash-blonde hair thrown over one shoulder like Brigitte Bardot. Edward, tall and thin beside her, unassuming, almost blends into the brickwork. He is the invisible man, dwarfed by his wife's brightness.

'You didn't have babies outside of marriage then,' she said once, slightly tipsy, her long fingers folding and unfolding a napkin on her lap. 'You just got married and got on with it.'

'Very romantic,' Alex said wryly, to which she replied, 'Darling, your father was one of the most romantic men I knew, in his own way. Here was a man who planted climbing roses outside all the windows so I could have flowers every day. Even without him, they still bloom, as he knew they would.'

Edward Thorn died one late November afternoon in 1997 when the car he was driving veered off a bank and into the chill waters of the River Ouse. It was three days before they managed to pull it out again, covered in pondweed and rushes and full of rusty-coloured water. His body was found still strapped into the front seat. He hadn't even tried to undo the seat belt. William said that was typical of his father, to not unbuckle even as the car filled with water. Safety first.

Now Mimi picks up the paper, reads the headline and drops it in disgust. 'Oh, how I hate politics. Bunch of bloody schoolchildren. I wish it would all go away.'

'I got your medicines, too. I think I'll need to talk to William about them, though, to make sure the dosage is accurate.'

'He's not here.' She lifts the remote control and changes the channel. Outside, the leaves flutter against the window, making the light flicker.

'Did he say where he was going?'

She thinks for a moment. 'Just into town, I think. Maybe we needed some milk?'

My heart is beating so fast I feel dizzy with it. It's her I'm thinking about, of course. Kim. Kim, with her thick glossy hair and sucked-in stomach; the tattoo, loaded with meaning, on her thigh. What's he paying off for her now? Student loan? Month's rent? What would that get him? I clench my fists. Anger furs my throat. I have to get out of here.

I stand up to leave, and Mimi looks up at me, surprised. 'Everything all right?'

'Yes, I just – I'm going to take this through to the kitchen. Can I get you anything? Have you eaten?'

'You're such a good girl.' She smiles again, reaching out for my hand. Hers is soft and warm, the bones there as fragile as a bird's. 'I wish we could get Alex to settle down with someone like you. He needs a good woman in his life.'

I smile tightly. Her youngest son's sexuality, while not a secret, has never been explicitly discussed in front of her. Alex explained it to William and me in a hushed voice in the kitchen one Christmas Eve. 'It's not that she's a homophobe,' he told us. 'I just can't bear to watch her try and hide her disappointment.'

'I'm sure Alex will find the right person in his own time,' I say carefully.

Mimi rearranges the cover over her legs. 'He never gave me any trouble when he was younger. Not like that husband of yours. Alex was always the apple of my eye.'

She's teasing, of course, smiling a little as she says it. It's a well-rehearsed script I've come to know by heart. I am the straight man in this particular routine.

'So what does that make William?'

'I suppose you'd call him a little plum!' she says, and claps her hands, delighted. Every time. Every single time.

I smile as I leave, taking the bag of medicines into the kitchen and spreading them on the counter there. Sedatives. Anticonvulsants. Painkillers; may cause drowsiness.

No wonder you're having funny turns, Mimi dear, I think as I pour myself a glass of water from the tap. *If we shook you, you'd rattle.*

A movement outside catches my eye. Through the kitchen window I can make out the old greenhouse towards the end of the garden where the high stone wall separates the house from the allotments on the other side. Through the windows of the greenhouse, filmy with grime and condensation, I can see someone inside, moving slowly and deliberately. My mind turns back to William telling his mother that Edward was out in the greenhouse and a shiver crawls up me as I put the glass down and head out the back door.

◆ ◆ ◆

The greenhouse is old, the whole structure slightly rickety-looking, as if a breath of wind could knock it askew. Leaves press up against the panes, making it difficult to see inside. The effect is almost like camouflage. I knock on the door.

'Hello?' I say, pushing against it. It's stiff, the rusted hinges squealing agonisingly. I am sure it will be William, his phone in one hand with his trousers around his ankles, breathless and red in the face. I almost hope it is. I want to catch him, want to see the look on his face as all his deception falls away.

'Frances?'

Not William.

'Alex?' A shard of disappointment.

He straightens up and looks at me. 'Everything all right? Is Mum okay?'

'She's fine.'

I squeeze into the crowded space and notice immediately the smell. It's bright and green like cut grass, almost sweet. It's hot, too, pressing against you like folds of velvet, slightly damp. Everywhere there is foliage: serrated leaves of deep, mossy emerald, slightly bristly to the touch. The tomato plants swarm into one another, tangling together like drunks, spilling out of pots and clambering

100

up bamboo-screen trellises, drooping beneath the weight of ripe, glossy fruit. There are also tomato plants hanging from the ceiling in baskets, and young plants, their leaves slightly curled at the edges, pale green, crawling out of old ceramic chamber pots balanced on a trestle table. I pick a small cherry tomato, bright red and shiny as a button, and look over at Alex.

'Someone really likes tomatoes,' I say.

'Yeah. Dad.' He wipes his forehead with the back of his hand. He's wearing old clothes – an old grey jumper fraying at the elbows and jeans splattered with paint – and in that moment I can see Edward Thorn, his father, in him. Stale and grey and sensible, obsessed with conjuring life from the earth. I put the tomato in my mouth and it pops beneath my tongue, as sweet as honey.

'It looks like a lot of work.'

'It is.'

'What do you do with them all?' I pick another. It's not like he's going to run out.

'Make stuff. Soup, ketchup, passata. We tend to get a glut in the summer and so we end up giving loads away. The season's tailing off now, though.'

'Your mum wants you to meet a good woman.'

'Ha! Is that what she said?'

'She seems clear-headed today.'

'I noticed. It's good. We're hoping for longer spells of clarity as she recovers.'

'What happened?'

'Huh?'

'When she fell. What happened?'

Alex looks at me steadily. He peels off his gloves and picks up a mug from somewhere among the plants in front of him, takes a long sip.

'It was late. I thought she was in bed. I didn't hear her on the stairs. The bulb had gone so the hallway was dark, and she didn't know where I was. I'd say she tripped over something – a cord maybe, or just the runner where it's frayed. Either way, by the time I got to her she was unconscious, and there was a lot of blood. Nearly stopped my heart, seeing her like that.'

'It must have been scary.'

'It was.' Alex pushes his hair away from his face. 'You sound like the policeman who spoke with me afterwards.'

'What do you mean?'

'In the hospital. "Where were you when your mother fell, sir?", "Is it just the two of you in the house?" I told him right there that if I was planning to kill my mother I wouldn't push her down the stairs.'

'Why not?'

'Too messy. Not sure enough.'

We're silent, staring at each other. The smell in the room is prickly, like the leaves. It makes me want to scratch at my skin. It's cold too, a creeping, sinister chill. I fold my arms. I'm thinking of the story William told me, of the little boy who found a dead sheep at the bottom of a well and who went back every day to mark its decomposition. Alex, who, even now, twenty years later, keeps the polished sheep skull over his bed. People think it odd, a man his age still living at home. They talk. How strange that he wears his late father's clothes, still sleeps in his childhood bedroom, is so close to his mother. William dismisses it as small-town gossip but I know that gossip can sometimes be the thorn on the briar that spikes the finger. Sometimes it can make you bleed.

'How would you do it?'

He looks up through the glass of the roof, thinking. His Adam's apple bobs in the column of his throat. 'Poison,' he says finally. 'A little bit in her food each day. You do it slowly enough, it's insidious and almost untraceable. I know enough about plants to know which ones can stop the heart or induce organ failure. You know foxgloves can kill you? Few years back a woman in Colorado was accused of attempted murder after she fed her husband a meal of spaghetti and salad that had foxglove leaves in.'

I take another tomato and put it in my mouth but this one is sharp, unripe. It floods my tongue with bitterness. Alex is pulling his gloves back on, bending over. He talks to me over his shoulder. 'Is that why you came in here, Frances? To find out my plans for matricide?'

'No! I – I was looking for William.'

'He's gone to the supermarket.'

'Okay. Okay, great.'

'Are you quite sure everything's all right with you two?'

He's talking more quietly now, not lifting his eyes. His voice is a purr; low, steady. I move closer to him, through the leaves. He is standing in front of a large earthenware pot full of black soil.

'Everything's fine.'

'Sure. You want to pass me that trowel beside you?'

I do so, watching him as he drags a large plastic sack across the floor towards him, digging inside and pulling out an ashy grey powder that he sifts into the turned soil.

'You know you have a tell, Frances?'

'A what?'

'A tic that gives you away. It's subconscious. You wouldn't even recognise it in yourself.'

'Like William?'

'How's that?'

'He pulls at his hair when he's lying.'

Alex laughs. 'Okay, yes. Like that. You've noticed him doing that, have you?'

'Yes. Lately it seems he's been lying a lot.'

Alex lifts his eyes to mine and then drops them again. He digs further into the bulging plastic sack. He moves with such stiffness, as if he has grown too big for his skin. His veneer is so highly polished, so constrained, you sense that at any moment it might crack. Like he is gritting his teeth against some inner flow of filth, some awful toxicity. It makes him hard to like, I'm told, but perversely, it is the reason I find myself warming to him. I like the discomfort I feel in his presence, the way it makes me alert and wary. I like the ripple of anxiety when his gaze lands on me and he does not smile, and his thoughts don't show on his face like they do in so many other people, all the time. I'll never look in Alex's face and see disappointment or regret reflected back at me. He is a man who doesn't care what I once was.

'Oh,' I say, twisting another tomato from the vine, 'I bumped into your old friend in town. Nancy.'

'Oh yeah? You talk to her?'

'I did, yes. Just for a little while. I showed her the photo I found in the shoebox.'

'Bet she loved that,' he deadpanned, sifting grey ash through his gloved fingers.

'Why didn't you tell me about Edie, Alex? About how she went missing?'

He is silent for a moment, looking up at the roof as if expecting the answer to be written there on the dusty glass. When he next speaks it is in a solemn, low voice, without looking at me, not once:

> *'One, two, three, four,*
> *rattlesnake hunters knocking at your door.*
> *Give them meat and give them bone,*
> *and pray that they leave you alone.'*

'Cute,' I say. 'What's that? Some old nursery rhyme?'

'It's the song we used to sing at the grave of Quiet Mary. Other kids were playing Knock Down Ginger and there we were trying to raise the dead. Isn't memory a funny thing? I can't remember the names of any of my old teachers, but I can remember that song, every word. How it used to make me feel like I was hot and cold at the same time, so scared I wanted to throw up. The song scared me and the rhyme scared me and those girls scared me. God, they scared me. Moya, Charlie, Nancy and Edie. Especially Edie. You never knew what she was going to do. She was unpredictable, but in a way that made her frightening to be around.'

'But you were just a kid.'

'Yup. And awkward as anything; you've seen the photos.' He sighs. 'But she – Edie, I mean – the way she behaved meant she got one of those reputations, you know? We could all see the way her life was going to go in this town. Mud sticks, doesn't it?'

I blink rapidly, my vision doubling as tears threaten. *Yes, I know.*

'I like to think she cleared out while she had the chance. Started somewhere new without all that hanging over her. It wouldn't have been hard, not back then. Train to London in an hour, Newhaven Harbour just down the road, then the ferry to France or beyond. She could have gone anywhere.'

'Is that what you think? That she ran away?'

He shrugs. 'I think they should have looked more closely at the caretaker for that church. That's what I think.'

'Who?'

'I don't remember his name. Liver, maybe? He was an oddball. Used to hide in the bushes and take pictures of us coming out the youth club they used to have there, although "youth club" might be selling it a bit high. Darts and warm orange squash and custard creams, sometimes table football if someone hadn't broken it.

When the police went to his house they found hundreds of pictures of us kids.'

'Oh my God. Why didn't they arrest him?'

'For what? It's not illegal. Weird, but not illegal. There was even a rumour going round that he'd kidnapped Edie on behalf of the Freemasons. Another that he was keeping her prisoner in the crypts beneath the church. Edie's mum got arrested once in that churchyard. She held a knife up to William's throat. I remember seeing her picture in the papers.'

'Jesus Christ.'

'Listen, Frances—' Alex begins, and then we're cut off by a cracking sound so sudden we both flinch and put our hands up over our heads as if the roof is coming in. I cry out, and when I finally peer upward I glimpse a smear of blood on one of the panes there.

'What the hell was that?' I'm saying, and Alex is laughing shakily, pressing his hands to his mouth. It's then that I see it. A bird, a blackbird maybe, or a crow. It's flown into the glass. Slumped body lying like a shadow against the pane. For a moment I think it has survived the impact but then I see it is just the wind stirring its feathers. I can just make out one small claw curled against the dirty glass.

'Bad omen,' Alex says sombrely, returning his hands to the earth. 'It foretells a death.'

'Oh, come on. It foretells a near-sighted crow. You've lived in the countryside too long.'

He doesn't say anything, but when he looks up at me he smiles. There is a faint dusting of the grey powder on one of his cheeks.

'You've got some of that stuff on you. Here, let me,' I tell him, wiping it away with my sleeve. My heart is still racing from the shock of the bird's swift and unexpected death. 'What is it, anyway?

'Bonemeal.'

'Ugh.'

He shrugs. 'My dad always said you're not feeding the plants, you're feeding the soil. Bonemeal is rich in the phosphorus and calcium that help the roses and tomatoes grow. He didn't trust his plants to anyone else so he always made his own.'

'His own bonemeal? How?'

'He made friends with the owner of a slaughterhouse, took away all that was left of the carcasses. In the nineties, when mad cow disease was endemic, he switched to sheep and game and road-kill. Boiled up big pots of bones in the shed. It drove Mum crazy. He told her it was recycling. She called him Reg Christie and made him wash the surfaces down with bleach.'

'You must miss him.'

Alex shrugs, taking a drink from his mug. I thought it was tea but I imagine I catch a whiff of whisky as he sighs. The heat in the room is growing stifling; I can feel it slowly sketching colour on my cheeks.

He looks at me with his head tilted, smiling. 'You're going to be all right, aren't you, Frances? You and William.'

'Sure.'

'There's that tell again.' He grins. 'Let me know when you work out what it is.'

I can't help but laugh. 'You're so full of shit.'

'Maybe,' he says, his smile broadening. 'In the meantime, do me a favour. Don't tell William you've seen that picture or spoken to Nancy, okay? In fact, don't bring up Edie Hudson at all.'

'Why not?'

'It was a bad time for him. Dad died not long after she went missing and Edie's mother came round to the house causing trouble. Mum was in bits.'

'But—'

'Look, Frances, she was just a kid. Kids go running off, they do stupid things. William probably barely remembers her. I doubt he'd even know her name. What he *will* remember is that feeling in the days after she'd disappeared, how people looked at him and talked behind his back. How it felt to come home to find the police car outside the house and Mum at the kitchen table saying, "Boys, there's been an accident", and her voice not quite steady. That's what he'll remember.'

'Okay,' I tell him, but it's not, not really. *There but for the grace of God go I*, I think again. That homeless woman outside the off-licence in Tufnell Park, Kim with her student debts and Miu Miu handbags posing in her underwear, Edie, the lost girl with the hard, unremitting stare right into the camera lens. They could have been me. They were, once upon a time. Something splits open inside the hard bedrock of my memories, the ones I've compressed over and over again until they turned black and solid and unreachable. *If you put enough weight on it you'll bury it forever.* Not true. Now one is escaping: a splatter of blue paint, bright blue, the scarred wood of the front door, the word that was daubed along the hallway. *Whore.*

I turn to leave, but as I'm opening the door I look back and see Alex looking upward, towards that bird lying on the glass beneath a sharp spray of blood like a constellation. He looks troubled by it, haunted almost. I think about the police questioning him over his mother's fall. It must be hard to live the way he does, so firmly in the closet, so desperate for her approval. No wonder he seems repressed.

◆　◆　◆

Back inside the house I find William's laptop and open it. Unlike our home computer there's no password on it, and the desktop opens up to a photo of William and me in Tenerife a few years ago. I'm drinking a pink cocktail decorated with glacé cherries. It tasted like cough syrup, but I had two more that afternoon, lying on a sun lounger while my shoulders burned.

I open up the browser and after some hesitation I type in 'Edie Hudson, Missing'. There are several matches, mainly in the smaller local papers – the *Argus*, the *Sussex Express*, the *Lewes & Ringmer Herald*. If Edie had gone missing today her face would've been all over social media in moments. A dedicated page on Facebook, a hashtag on Twitter and Instagram, a JustGiving page to fund the continued search. Back then, you relied on print media to get the story out there, and it looks as though Edie's story didn't circulate outside of East Sussex. I'm surprised. A vulnerable fifteen-year-old girl walks into a grove of trees and never comes out again? I would've thought the press would have been all over it.

All the articles have been digitised and catalogued from print, so the photographs are grainy and undefined. The first article is small, no more than two paragraphs. There's Edie. In this photograph she's unsmiling, almost aggressive-looking, with her arms folded in front of her. The headline reads: 'Mother's Plea to Missing Girl, Fifteen'.

Officers have been speaking to motorists and local residents this afternoon in the area where missing Edie Hudson was last seen. Her mother Samantha describes her as 'dark-haired, slim build, wearing black clothes and make-up'. She added that if anyone has any information regarding Edie's whereabouts they should contact the police.

'If you're reading this, Edie, please, please just come home. Come home.'

I clicked on the next article, dated a week or so later, from the *Lewes & Ringmer Herald*. This time the headline reads: 'Police Question Caretaker in Teen Disappearance'.

Fifty-six-year-old Peter Liverly has been taken in for questioning following new information received by police. Liverly, who helps run the St Mary de Castro youth centre in Lewes, has previous convictions for assault. Edie Hudson, fifteen, has been missing since Thursday 9th October. She was wearing a long black skirt, black high-necked shirt and a leather jacket. She has connections to Eastbourne and Shoreham and the Wood Green area of London. She has been described by her teachers as 'street-wise', with her headmaster adding, 'Despite everything, we are all very worried for Edie.' Her mother Samantha Hudson, thirty-three, a resident of the Morley Wood housing estate, has previously been quoted as saying, 'I was not surprised when she didn't come home.'

What an odd thing to print, I think, scrolling through the rest of the articles. They all have the same tone – brief and factual, almost hectoring. One of them mentions Edie's habit of roaming the streets till almost midnight. Another describes her as 'no angel'. The last one, printed in January 1998, just three months after Edie was first reported missing, details how the police were winding the investigation down. A detective named Tony Marston was quoted: 'While we will no longer be actively involved in this case, the file will remain open.'

I find a picture of Peter Liverly in an old archive of pictures on the St Mary's church website. He was short and balding, with broad shoulders and a rosy face that hung in soft folds like rubber. He'd been released without charge, of course, but it had cost him his job. I know the way rumours germinate. They spread like a stain, like pollution. They taint you.

Samantha – Then

In the last few days I'd been getting a lot of calls. At first I spoke with everyone who asked me questions, until Tony Marston told me to stop. I'd been quoted in the newspaper, but whatever I said seemed to come out wrong. Sometimes the caller hung up as I answered; other times there was nothing but the sound of their breathing, a cough, distant traffic. Sometimes the breathing was wet and flabby, lungs full of catarrh, or muddy water. Other times it was dry like a desert wind.

Sometimes they said things.

'I have her. I keep her locked away. She doesn't like the dark.'

'The Africans got her. They keep her as a slave in a caravan. I saw her at the window, begging to be let out.'

'Your daughter wouldn't stop screaming so I cut off her tongue.'

After a while I learned not to answer at all.

Then there were the psychics. One elderly woman called regularly, sometimes giving me contradicting information. She had visions, she told me, of my daughter with an older man, in a black car, heading north. Another caller was a man with a lisp who claimed to have an untainted Romany bloodline. He told me she was buried in a shallow grave in a field near Reading. Another, that she had eloped to marry an immigrant from a war-torn country. Another to tell me she was pregnant. Another, lying wounded in hospital. Another, lying at the bottom of a reservoir. Another. Another.

I was afraid to change my number because it was the only one Edie knew, so the calls kept coming, and the machine filtered them for me.

One night I heard the sound of the phone ringing. I woke slowly, chemically submerged, brain buzzing pleasantly. At some point during the night I'd kicked off the duvet and my skin was puckered with goosebumps. I reached for the phone by the bed just a moment too late and listened as the answer machine kicked in. Silence. The crackle of wind on the line. My mouth was dry. I needed a drink of water, to change out of my clothes. I sat up, head swimming, and then I heard it. A female voice, slightly watery, as if she'd been crying.

'I'm sorry, Mum.'

I waited, entirely poised and still. *It's her*, I told myself, and the line cut out. I picked up the receiver, frantic, saying her name over and over, *Edie, Edie, talk to me*, but it was just the single note of the dial tone.

I played that message over and over through the night, sleeping curled around the answer machine with the receiver hanging off the edge of the bed. I didn't want any more calls to come through and wipe out the sound of her voice. The next morning, as the sky brightened, I called Tony Marston on his home number.

'She phoned me.'

'Who? Edie?'

'Yes!'

'What did she say?'

'That she was sorry.'

'What else?'

Something chipped away at the edge of my excitement. I paced the room, smoking. 'Just that, that she was sorry.'

'Huh, okay. Keep hold of it. I'll have a listen later on.'

'Is that it?'

'Samantha.' I didn't like the way he said my name. I wished I'd never called him. His underwhelming reaction was like a dash of cold water. 'How do you know it's her?'

'Who else would it be?'

'Well—' He broke off to cough thickly. 'I don't mean to dampen your enthu—'

'I know her voice, Tony! I know my own daughter!'

'Samantha, calm down. What do you want me to do?'

'Can't you trace the call? We could track her down inside ten minutes!' I pitched my cigarette out the window. There was a hardness in my chest, like a stone dropping through water. 'What about getting someone on to that?'

'It's not that simple, love. Not like the movies. You need the tracking device in the house before the call comes through.'

I stared at the handset for nearly a full minute, even as I could hear Tony's voice bleating my name over and over again: *Samantha, are you still there, Sam, Samantha*, and then I slammed it into the wall, denting the plaster. I was sobbing as I sank on to the bed, hands over my eyes. *It was her*, I told myself, choking on my tears, *I know it was her.*

I called my brother Rupert that afternoon. Danny had died twelve years ago of pneumonia. I'd held his hand and watched his chest slowly rise and fall and rise and fall and stop. The same strong hands that had once lifted me out of the water had gone slack and cold in my own.

'I need you here, Rupert. I'm going mad.'

When I opened the front door to him and his small suitcase he looked at me as though he had a bad smell under his nose. 'Bloody hell, Pot, you look awful. Listen, will my car be all right out there? This is a dodgy area and I don't want my premiums to go up.'

Over the next two days Rupert was galvanised by a roar of nervous energy – he cleaned and tidied and arranged, wiping down all the surfaces around me as if I were a typhoid carrier. He made a lot of soup – the freezer was full of the stuff, and when we couldn't fit more in he started stockpiling it in the shed. Within the first hour of his arrival he pressed a bottle of vodka into my hand and said, 'You need your strength.'

'You sound like Mum,' I replied, and then we both laughed until I realised one of us was crying. *This is my life now*, I thought. *Get used to your emotional landscape shifting like time-lapse erosion, Sam. Everything is fluid, you have no constant. Except soup*, I reminded myself. *You constantly have fucking soup.*

◆ ◆ ◆

I was upstairs when I heard the phone start ringing. I'd been folding laundry and staring blankly at the wall, my mind purring gently, cocooned by Valium. What was it they called it? Mother's Little Helper? I blinked slowly.

'You want me to get that?'

'No,' I answered. 'Let the machine get it.'

I heard the machine pick it up, but then heard Rupert lift the receiver, talking urgently. Next thing I knew he was calling to me up the stairs. 'Pot, it's a detective. Says he wants to talk to you. He's got some news.'

I can't describe the feeling I got then. A coldness, an apprehension. Dread, like a tidal wave building and building and me beneath it, small and insignificant, waiting to get washed away. I walked slowly downstairs and took the phone from Rupert. He was looking at me with concern and barely disguised horror. *This is it*, I thought.

'Tony,' I said.

'Sam. We're bringing someone in.'

'What do you mean?'

'You know who Peter Liverly is?'

'No. No, I don't think so.'

'He's the – I suppose you'd call him the caretaker up at the church, St Mary's. He looks after the grounds mostly, and helps out at the youth club up there.'

Something jogged my memory then. The night I'd gone to my women's group and caught Edie and her boyfriend on the sofa. The group had been cancelled and the church hall locked. That man, the one with the twisted rope of scar tissue on his neck and the keyring of the cartoon bird in bright pink. He'd had dead rabbits in a bag, swinging it like a pendulum.

Told 'em to stop coming here, all of 'em, but it don't make a difference.

'I think I've met him once. Odd sort,' I said.

'We've had a tip about him. Anonymous. I thought we'd check it out. When we arrived there this morning we found some photos.'

A chill spread through my chest, my lungs. I couldn't breathe. Rupert put his hand on my arm.

'What kind of photos?'

Somewhere far away, as distant as another planet, I heard Rupert mutter *Oh my God* under his breath. I turned away from him.

'Pictures of your daughter and her friends. Some of them are candid, taken in the youth centre. We're not too concerned about those. But the others we found are obviously taken without their permission. It looks like he's been hiding himself and watching them for a little while now.'

'What do you mean, "hiding"? Why was he doing that?'

'That's what we're trying to find out. There's nothing sexual about the photos, they're terrible quality – the man can't take a picture to save his life – but the fact he has them at all is concerning to us, especially considering Edie's disappearance. We just want to see what he knows.'

'Is he under arrest?'

'No, but you'll be first to know if anything turns up. We're searching the rest of the church hall now.'

'Thanks, Tony. Have you spoken with her boyfriend? William?'

'That's not how he described himself.'

A memory then, like a camera flash. William on top of Edie, one hand sliding into her underwear, the look on his face when I walked in, his eyes wide and dark.

'I see. You don't find that suspicious? That he's trying to distance himself?'

'No. They're teenagers, Sam. Fickle. He's not suggesting he had nothing to do with her, it just wasn't a serious relationship.'

'I want to talk to him.'

'Absolutely not.'

'Tony—'

'Listen. We've spoken with William and when we get a chance we'll speak to his father as well, okay?'

I heard the click of a lighter as he lit a cigarette. I could imagine him behind his desk, the surface littered with paperwork and wires and framed pictures of his kids. There would be one of those little plastic signs they sell in joke shops: *Just file it in my bin.* There would be coffee cups and chewing gum wrappers and an overflowing ashtray. And somewhere in there, among all that, would be a file with my daughter's name on the top. *Don't count on it*, I thought, sarcastically.

'What do you mean, his father? Why? Who is he?'

'Edward Thorn. His car was seen by the church the night Edie ran off, but that's not unusual – he had some dealings at the church and in the park nearby. He was a custodian for some of the land there. They named the duck pond after him.'

Edward Thorn. I'd heard of him, of course. He was what someone would describe as 'very active in the community'. Tony coughed into the handset before saying, 'Sit tight, okay, Sam? Look after yourself.'

Sit tight. Huh. He might as well have told me to stop breathing. I stood with my head lowered to my chest after I'd hung up the phone, silent even as Rupert asked me over and over what was going on, had they found her?

'I need to get out of here,' I said. 'I need to do something.'

Rupert looked exasperated. He wanted to stop me, but there was a hesitation there, an expression I'd seen on his face since childhood. 'Why did you let Samantha do that?' our mother would cry, after I'd ridden my trike off the shed roof, after I'd poured all her Rémy Martin brandy down the drain, after I'd scraped my elbows trying to fit all the way up inside the chimney. 'Why did you let her do it?' Exasperated. Rupert would look at her dumbly and reply, 'I just wanted to see what would happen.'

◆ ◆ ◆

I left the house and turned left towards Malling Fields, crossing the large park at an angle towards the bridge. I used to bring Edie to play here when she was little, pushing her on the swings as she'd sat stone-faced and unmoved.

One day she'd asked me why I kept on bringing her back to the park when she hated it, and I'd turned to her and said sweetly, 'Because if we don't get out the house your mother will lose her fucking mind, darling.'

Over the bridge, past the lido; shimmering in the summer like polished turquoise but now, deep into the autumn, the untreated water had turned malachite green beneath the heavy grey sky. On the corner of St Mary de Castro there was a single police car parked, but no officers anywhere to be seen. I pulled my hood up, hoping not to draw attention to myself. I didn't want them to know what I was doing. I walked quickly past, angling right and down Hillman Terrace towards the school.

◆　◆　◆

It was nearly three. They'd be coming out soon. There were other parents at the gates, but only a handful. Our kids were grown up now, didn't need us the way they used to.

As the bell rang I stood across the road and craned my neck towards the entrance. I was still feeling the effects of the Valium I'd taken at lunchtime, but there was a rawness to it; my thin resolve had been stripped away. My hands in my pockets, I itched for a cigarette.

Then I saw them. Just two Rattlesnakes arm in arm. Moya and Charlie, moving through the crowd like eels, glossy and sinuous in their tight dark clothes. Moya was a lot shorter than Charlie, with wild curly hair and glossy doe eyes. Charlie was tall and angular and noble-looking, like royalty. She was cover-girl pretty, with a wave of thick black hair over her shoulder. I watched them go through the school gates, heads close together, talking as if in a secret language. Something made them both laugh, Moya with her head thrown back, Charlie as if she was imparting a great secret, looking askance at her friend, one hand over her mouth to hide her secretive smile. I followed them for a while until the crowd thinned out and we were nearing the railway bridge, a tunnel of metal girders criss-crossing overhead, flaking grey paint and rust and graffiti.

I waited till they were on the covered bridge, empty except for the litter blown into the corners, and called out, 'Hey!'

They both looked back at me, turning slowly. I saw, very clearly, Moya mouth *Oh shit*. Charlie, of course, was unfazed. She put a hand on her hip and jutted it out, tilting her head and smiling sweetly.

'Mrs Hudson. We were just talking about you.' She looked at Moya from beneath her long eyelashes. 'Weird!'

'You know something,' I said abruptly. 'About Edie. You know something happened to her, and I know that you know that Peter Liverly had something to do with it.'

'Who?' Moya said. She looked frightened, but I was too overwrought to be gratified by it. I kept my eye on Charlie, who was still smiling and looking at me with her head on one side. It was like that day back at the beginning, in those numb, strange hours after Edie had disappeared and I'd tried to talk to them in the headmaster's office – tried to talk to them like an adult would a child, cajoling, patient. I wasn't going to do that any more. They didn't deserve my consideration.

'You mean the old guy from the church? That *pervert*?' She said the word 'pervert' like a cat purring, rolling her 'r's. 'It wouldn't surprise me if he's kidnapped her. You should ask Moya, she's been *inside* his house.'

Moya looked from Charlie to me and back again. She was wearing a tight skirt of a rubbery material, like PVC, and torn fishnets. Her ears were pierced in neat little rows following the curve all the way to the top.

She pouted crossly. 'Don't tell her that, Charlie, you dick.'

'When? When were you in his house?'

Moya shifted uncomfortably.

Charlie gave her a nudge with her sharp, pointed elbow. 'Tell her, Moya. She won't tell on you. Will you, Mrs Hudson?'

'No,' I said immediately, unsure if that was true or not. 'Of course not.'

Moya considered, and when she did finally answer she wouldn't look me in the eye. 'Everyone dared me to.'

'Dared you to what?'

'Go into his house. There's a window. I was the only one small enough to go through. I used to bring things out to show them.'

'Things? What things?'

'You can see if you like,' Charlie said brightly, and held out her hand for me to take.

◆ ◆ ◆

They took me to the back of the churchyard. It was the first time I'd been there since Edie disappeared. My blood roared in my ears. My baby. My little girl. She had been here. Right here.

'Come on then,' Charlie said, laughing now. She turned towards me and pressed her face against mine. It was so intimate I could smell her perfume, the powder on her skin. When she spoke her breath fluttered along my cheekbones. 'We'll show you our treasures.'

Then she was walking away, swinging her schoolbag by the handle. Moya hustled to catch up with her. I'm drawn to trouble. That's what my mum always said. So of course I went with them, through the large wrought-iron gates, veering off the overgrown path, which had narrowed to a single line. The air was scented with pine and muddy water and something else, rotten and ripe-smelling, almost sweet. I pulled the collar of my coat up over my mouth. Charlie looked back at me and laughed.

'It's the rabbits,' she told me. 'See?'

I looked down to where she was pointing and saw a small, furred corpse lying in the grass, leaking a black ichor from its mouth. Another lay not far away, thick with flies. The eye sockets were black and empty, sightless voids. I gagged, feeling the contents of my stomach rise, burning the back of my throat. I remembered the day I'd met Peter Liverly at the back door of the church, the way he'd held the bloodied bag in his meat-like fist. *Why has he stopped picking them up?* I thought, following the girls with my hands pressed deep into my pockets. *The place is full of them.* I wove through crumbling headstones and sunken graves, wrong-footing myself into a pothole and nearly stepping on a small pile of rabbit bones, picked clean. I had a single, terrifying image of Peter Liverly sitting here in the moonlight, squatting on his haunches and gnawing the meat from these bones with his yellowing teeth, his sunken, witless eyes glittering in the dark. *Jesus Christ, listen to yourself,* I thought. *He's a caretaker, not the Wolfman.*

Back in the summer Peter Liverly had told me that the graves would flood and sink right into the ground. He'd been right about that. Days of rain had left the churchyard waterlogged and swampy, thick with mosquitoes and mayflies. Puddles had formed in the cradle graves on which floated brown leaves like small, rudderless boats. As we headed further in, the headstones grew smaller, less stately, becoming grey and blotchy with algae. One or two had crumbled away entirely, leaving unadorned humps of grass. Up ahead was the deep grove of trees, swimming with shadows: the yews, black against the sky and studded with waxy berries, a clutch of holly trees, gospel oaks wrapped in ivy. I could hear crows calling to each other from the branches.

'In here,' Moya said, and pointed through the treeline. I squinted into the gloom. Up ahead there was an elm tree, the trunk thick and gnarled with age. Its leaves were a burned amber colour, mottled with decay. I peered closer. There was something hanging on the low branches. It looked like a face.

'Go on,' Charlie said. 'Go in.'

I turned and looked at them both. Moya was chewing her sleeve, round eyes watching me closely. Charlie gave me a flash of teeth, the tip of her tongue just brushing her upper lip. I suddenly realised that I was afraid of these girls and told myself not to be ridiculous. I had nearly twenty years on them. I'd survived birth and death and divorce. I was older and wiser and uglier, so why did I feel so afraid of following them into this dark, shaded copse? Why did I feel that ripple of unease? Is this what Edie felt the night she disappeared? I ducked my head and walked slowly behind them across the grass. *My head will be caved in with a stone*, I thought, unable to help myself, *and the hand that holds it will wear chipped black nail varnish.*

'Slow *down*,' Charlie snapped at Moya as she stumbled across the damp ground in her heeled boots. She tugged at the hem of her skirt, swearing. Moya put on a baby voice, pretended to suck her thumb: 'I'm sew sowwy.'

Under the canopy the light was grey and diffuse, like old film. There was a hush under here that was almost unnatural, the *drip-drip-drip* of rainwater from the leaves. Something caught my eye as I turned my head. A little to the left, through the trees. Movement, something caught there and blowing in the breeze. Police tape.

Edie.

I took a step or two forward and then hesitated. The tape had obviously been there a while – it had come untethered from its mooring at one end, sagging limply to the ground. I remembered Tony saying they had cordoned off an area of the churchyard where Edie had gone missing so as to preserve any evidence that might be found there. 'What *did* you find?' I'd asked him, and he'd shaken his head. 'Nothing. Not a button,' he'd replied.

I lifted the end of the tape up and tied it back around the tree. There was a squirrel in there, a grey one – my little brother Danny had always called them pirates because they'd seen off all the reds – and it sat on its haunches, quivering at my approach. It was even darker over here, where the yews pressed thickly together. What little light fell through was milky and cold. The squirrel stared at me with round black eyes. He was sitting on a cantered gravestone, old and weathered. I peered a little closer, careful not to cross the tape, and read the inscription there: *Mary Sayers. Departed this life 1897, Eighteen years old. Lost to the Waters, She will Return.*

'Mrs Hudson.'

The voice was breathy, muffled-sounding. Right behind me. I spun on my heel and there was a monster there, something with round insectile eyes and a horrifying black proboscis. It was leering towards me, gasping for breath like something birthed from a nightmare. I screamed, flinching away, my hand reaching for the back pocket of my jeans without thinking, a smooth, practised motion. The creature reared up, shrieking. I'd got my teeth bared like an animal; I could see myself reflected in those strange round eyes.

'Jesus, Mrs Hudson! No!'

I saw Charlie standing off to one side with her hands stretched out, pleading. Her face looked pale and sick. The monster had stumbled backward and landed on its behind. Now it scooted away from me until it backed up against the tree. I gasped, couldn't seem to get any oxygen. Adrenaline is a strangler, a robber of breath.

'What the fuck! Is that a *knife?*' a muffled voice said. I looked down at my hand. Back up again. It wasn't a monster, I saw now. It was Moya, her face sheened with sweat. She tossed something to me over the grass. I looked down at it.

'A gas mask?'

'Mrs Hudson,' Moya said, her voice watery. 'Please, we're sorry. We were just kidding around.'

'Huh?'

She pointed at my hand. Her fingers were shaking.

'The knife,' she said. 'Please put the knife down.'

I looked down at my hand holding the stiletto knife. It was Italian, belonged to my father, the man Edie called Nonno. He used to slice apples with it, spearing the flesh with the needle-sharp tip and eating them right off the blade. 'Oh. You scared me.' I felt embarrassed now.

'Why do you carry that thing round with you?' Charlie asked. Some of the nervousness had left her voice. Now she just sounded curious, her voice soft. It was nice. It was like being stroked by a cat. Despite myself, I found that I wanted her to like me.

'Protection.' I snapped it away and slid it back into my pocket. 'I don't like people creeping up on me.'

'It was just a *joke*,' Moya protested, and she looked at Charlie for help.

Charlie ignored her. 'That's cool. I wish I had a knife like that.'

'You wouldn't know what to do with one,' Moya snapped. Charlie stared at her before rolling up the sleeve on her right arm and turning the wrist there outward to face us. Even in the dusk I could see the white stippling there, the scars that embroidered her skin. She poked her tongue out at Moya, who was getting to her feet.

'Is this what you found in his house?' I asked her, lifting up the gas mask with the tips of my fingers. This was what I had seen hanging from the tree in the dusk. I didn't like to touch it. It was heavy and the blank eyes made my skin crawl.

Moya nodded. 'Yeah.'

'Anything else?'

They'd hidden all the things Moya had stolen from Peter Liverly's bungalow in the hollows at the roots of the big oak: old playing cards, a silver teaspoon, a matchbox. There was even an old snuff tin down there.

I dusted the earth from it carefully. 'You know Edie used to do this. Bury things. When she was a little girl. I'd find them all over the garden.'

The two girls looked at me mutely. Charlie came over and kneeled across from me, taking my cold hands in her own. She didn't seem to mind the damp and the dirt beneath her. At this angle her skirt rode up over her pearly thighs to reveal the delicate pink of her underwear. She looked at me, her tongue trembling, the tip of it touching her upper lip. It was delicious, like we were about to share a secret.

'You must miss her, Mrs Hudson.'

'Call me Samantha, Charlie.'

'You know, Samantha—' She looked at Moya as if for approval. 'Maybe there is something we can try.'

'What do you mean? What thing?'

She and Moya exchanged glances again.

'The night Edie went missing was a full moon. I know this because we were playing Quiet Mary. If you go under the police tape right now you'd find the stubs of our candles on her grave.'

'So?' I stared at her. It was now getting so dark she was just luminous eyes, a snarl of white teeth.

'Imagine. If we spirited her away, maybe we can spirit her back.' She patted my hands gently, still smiling. 'Think about it. We'll do it if you want. We're good at rituals.'

She stood up carefully, unfolding her long limbs like a mantis. *She's so beautiful*, I thought. *No wonder all these girls are in awe of her.*

'You can bring your knife, too, if you like, Mrs Hudson,' she said, and blew me a kiss before walking over to where Moya was standing and looping an arm around her waist.

I found I couldn't stand. My legs wouldn't lift me. I watched the two girls flit off into the gathering dusk, all blue and violet shadows cradled in the hollows of the trees. A magpie barked from somewhere behind me, *chk! chk! chk!* That smell again, rolling on the slow-moving breeze, beneath the fragrant wood and moss and old stone, of ripe decay.

What are you doing, Samantha? I asked myself, creaking slowly upright like a woman twice my age. *Sitting out here in the dark with teenagers? And why are you even considering this? A spell won't bring her back.*

Hope shatters you. It does it with great care, so slowly you barely notice it. It carves you hollow, leaving nothing but the seed of itself, and of course you plant it and nurture it because even though it is destroying you, without it you are a shell.

So no, it might not bring her back.

But what if it does?

◆ ◆ ◆

When I got home that evening Rupert fussed over me, rubbing my damp hair with a towel, pressing a cup of tea into my numb hands.

'Your detective called. Tony.'

'Okay.' I lit a cigarette. 'Any news?'

'Nothing to report, he said. The man is worried about you. *I'm* worried about you.' Rupert looked at me suspiciously. 'Where did you go?'

'I went to the school to talk to those friends of hers.'

'Those goth girls?'

'That's them. They want me to join them in a ritual.'

He scoffed. 'A what?'

'A ritual. Like a spell. They said they were doing one in the graveyard when Edie went missing.'

Rupert was silent, anticipatory. He was waiting for me to tell him the punchline. I shrugged and turned away from him, jettisoning my cigarette into the sink, where it hissed and died.

'Come on, Pot, really? *Really?*'

'Yes, really.'

He put his hand to my forehead dramatically. 'Are you feeling all right, Pot? Think we should call a doctor? How about a witch doctor?'

'Stop it.' I brushed him off more angrily than I intended. 'I'm the only one left looking for Edie. I'm all she has, Rupert. Don't fucking patronise me.'

'Oh, Sam—'

'Besides. What if it works? What then?'

'If the spell works, you mean?'

'It's not a spell, it's a ritual. What if it could bring her back and I haven't at least tried it?'

'Pot, you're not thinking straight. Edie will come back when she's good and ready. I've never met a more headstrong girl. Not even all the combined forces of hell could budge her. You must know that. This is madness. It's madness. Let the police do their job.'

I snorted derisively. 'And where's that got me? Here. To a point where all I have left is watching some girls do parlour tricks in a graveyard. That's where it's got me. You know I walked into town the other day? Most of the posters I've hung up are gone, either blown away or ripped down. I went into the school and the headmaster couldn't even look me in the eye. Did you see the piece on her in the *Argus*? They called her "Ellie". "Missing: Ellie Hudson". No one *cares*, Rupert. I'm all she's got. So I have to try.'

'Sam, I have to go back to Devon tomorrow. I can't leave like this. What'll happen to you?'

'I'll be fine,' I told him. The Valium had made my tongue thick and it came out *Uhllbefine*.

He stared at me and I held his gaze until he huffed a noisy sigh and I reached for the phone, dialling Tony's number.

'Samantha. Thanks for getting back to me.'

'What news have you got for me?'

'Nothing much. We've let Liverly go.'

'What? Why?'

'We can't keep him past twenty-four hours unless we charge him and we've got nothing to charge him with.'

'Well, what about the photos?'

'He said they were for security purposes. Those girls have been causing a lot of mischief in the churchyards. He's convinced they've been coming into his house at night. Talking about getting a guard dog. He's built up quite a file on them.'

'What about Edie? You asked him about her?'

'Well, the problem there, Samantha, is that I can't prove anything. We deal in evidence and as far as Edie's concerned, there is none.'

'But you searched his house, didn't you?'

'We're doing everything we can with everything we have.'

'I don't – I don't know what that means. Have you searched the house?'

'You know, you need to get some sleep. Let me get on with my job.'

'I'm sick of people telling me that!'

I could feel the weight of Rupert's gaze on my back, a heat building between my shoulder blades. Tony was right, though – I couldn't remember the last time I'd had a full night's sleep. I ached all over, and my head pounded like a muffled drum. I should have told him I went to see the girls at the school – the Rattlesnakes, as they called themselves – but I had a feeling low in my gut that Tony would disapprove of it so I kept quiet, holding the phone so tightly to my ear the skin there started to burn.

'What about that boy she was seeing? William? You going to bring him in?'

There was a rustle of paper. 'William Thorn was at school all that day. That's been confirmed by his teachers. In the evening he and his brother had a takeaway pizza. That's confirmed by his mother.'

'And Edward Thorn? His father? Didn't you say something about his car being parked nearby?'

'Yes, but—'

'But what?'

He sighed again. I knew he was looking at his watch, hoping to wind this conversation up. 'I went to school with Edward Thorn. Did you know that? He taught me how to fish. He works hard and he's built up a lot of goodwill in this community. It's a currency, Sam.'

'What do you mean?'

'Just—' Another sigh. I knew I wouldn't like what was coming. 'Just don't go around using his name in connection with Edie's. People won't like you for it, and you need people on your side.'

'On my *side*? Is this a competition?'

'You know what I mean.' He sounded irritated, worn out. *Join the club, pal.* 'I'll talk to Edward and as soon as I do I'll let you know. As soon as *anything* happens I'll let you know. But you need to rest, Sam. You sound like shit. Please. I know this is hard for you but you have to let me do my job.'

I didn't remember dropping the handset, but I must have done because Rupert was staring at me strangely and the phone was swinging from its cord, *tick, tock, tick, tock*, like the pendulum of a clock. For a moment I heard Tony's muffled voice at the end of the line saying my name over and over again and black wings fluttered at the edges of my vision and maybe I was going to pass out; in a way I hoped I would. What was it Tony had said? *I would welcome a coma right now*, but no, hands were gripping me firmly under my arms, my big brother. I couldn't think clearly. He was saying *Oh, Pot* under his breath and I wanted to answer him but I couldn't, I couldn't.

Rupert must have put me to bed but I don't remember, I only know I woke late and it was dark and the room was cold, I was cold. My head ached as if my skull had been caved in. There was a glass of water beside the bed and I sipped it, holding it in my mouth for a moment before swallowing. Outside, the night sky bristled with stars and the slender curve of the moon, white as bone. For the first time since she went missing I had a feeling that Edie would not be coming home. A shard of ice lodged in my chest, piercing my lungs. I struggled to take a breath.

Admit it.

I levered myself off the bed on legs that felt shaky and weak, using the wall to lean against as I made my way out into the hallway and down to the bathroom. I sank on to the cold toilet seat and rested my elbows on my knees as I urinated, my head in my hands.

Admit it.

I washed my hands in the sink, glancing at myself in the mirror that hung there. I saw a woman ageing badly, genetically, like her mother did, all jowls and crows' feet, fissures of grey in her hair. Pale bloodshot eyes that couldn't look at themselves too long. They skipped, stones on a lake, away from the woman in the glass.

It's a relief, isn't it?

I walked downstairs in the dark and filled the kettle, opening the kitchen drawer and rummaging inside for the cigarettes I kept there, the ones I'd hidden from Edie because she used to steal them, just one or two at first and then whole packs. When I started hiding the packs she used to steal the money to buy them. I found the carton pushed right up against the back of the drawer and lit one from the cooker, making myself a cup of tea with the cigarette clamped between my teeth.

You did your best for her, Sam, the voice said, the one I'd been blocking out ever since that first night when she didn't come home. I didn't like it much, that voice. It sounded cold and impersonal, not like myself at all. I dragged on my cigarette and let the cool blue smoke fill my lungs. *Anyone else would have broken under the strain.*

I walked over to the small patch of lawn, letting my feet sink into the damp grass. *He knows,* the voice continued, *that policeman. His gaze will turn on you soon, Sam. The shouting, the fighting, the fear. He'll find out. He'll find out that you hurt her when you got angry. Then what?*

'Stop it,' I said out loud, eyes tightly closed. 'I didn't hurt her. She hurt herself.'

You think he'll believe that? You know what they do to women who beat up their kids in prison, Sam? An echo of Edie's words that morning in the bathroom, the day she left the house and never came back. I clenched my fist so tightly I could feel the sharp pain of my nails slicing into my palm. *But it's a relief, isn't it? That's the worst thing. You can breathe again. You can walk around the house without fear of what mood she's in, or how she'll look at you with that expression she has, the flare of her nostrils, the way her eyes used to seek you out like floodlights. Waiting for her to snap, to push, to bite. Admit it. Admit it.*

'Yes,' I said quietly. The word was small but it filled the air, the space around me, like rubber expanding.

'Yes.'

That Monday I decided to go back to work. My smoking was getting out of control, for one thing. I'd find myself lighting a cigarette and then craving another even as I smoked it. Also, I'd run out of Valium and the doctor had refused to give me any more.

'It's addictive,' she told me briskly, shaking her head. 'It'll make you feel worse in the end.'

Worse? I wanted to scream. *Worse than lifting the rock of my daughter's life and finding all the horrible things down there, squirming in the dark? Worse than that, you mean?*

I didn't, of course. I smiled and thanked her and left the surgery just as a brief, hectic rainstorm had begun, drenching me through my clothes to my underwear.

On my first day back at work a woman I'd never met before from the human resources department held a fifteen-minute meeting with me and gave me a leaflet titled *Dealing with Grief in the Workplace*.

I handed it back to her, smiling grimly. 'I'm not grieving,' I told her. 'Edie's missing, not dead.'

'I know how you must feel. Last year our cat disappeared for three months and I was out of my mind.'

I stared at her until she squirmed uncomfortably and told me to speak to her about anything I needed. As I left I turned back and asked her if she'd ever found her lost cat.

She looked at me, struggling to formulate a reply. Finally, she smiled sadly. 'He got hit by a car. We only found out when his collar was found in a hedge. It's a sad world.'

I went back to my desk with a strange, sick feeling in my stomach. Worst of all was the way my heart hurt; it *ached* as though it was infected. If you cut my chest open, my heart would be shrivelled, dark and sticky, and crawling with flies.

I was due to meet a counsellor on Friday afternoon but instead I drove past her offices and straight on towards Brighton, parking up at the back of London Road. It's a long stretch of neglected grimy concrete, lined with a handful of high street shops and fast-food restaurants. The squall of bus brakes and the throb of engines choke the air; pigeons throng the gutters, searching for food. It had been raining, and the pavements were glossy mirrors stippled with rings of blackened chewing gum and cigarette butts. What I'd come here for were the pawn-brokers and cash converters, the ones who will take in a valuable object – a solid silver dragonfly necklace, for instance – and trade it for cash. If Edie had sold it – the same way she'd sold my other items, the ones I'd found in the second-hand place in Lewes – she would have come out of town to do it. She'd been burned by that before, of course. Brighton was my guess; Eastbourne maybe, if she'd been able to find the train fare. If she had come here to sell it, someone might remember her, or better still, know where she was heading. At the very least it would give me a time frame of her movements. Something solid. Something good.

It took me over two hours to walk the length of both sides of the street and by the time I got back to my car I was frustrated and tired and feeling despondent. I'd visited nineteen pawn shops and none of them had seen a necklace or a pendant fitting that description. I'd even shown a photograph of it – a picture of my mother in 1964, her hair coiled and pinned to the sides of her head, wearing an evening gown of pale blue satin and standing in the doorway of our old house on Mortimer Road. Her head is turned slightly, chin tilted upward, and the necklace rests just below her exposed clavicle. I've always thought my mother looks beautiful in this picture, like a movie star, one of the ones from old Hollywood, Bette Davis or Lauren Bacall maybe.

I sat in my car, smoking, thinking. Tuesday night was the ritual. There was a flutter of nerves in my stomach when I thought about it, a feeling like a rising crescendo, birds taking flight. Rupert had called me earlier and asked me if I was still intending to 'go through with it', as if I were contemplating hiring a hitman instead of meeting teenagers in a churchyard. He didn't get it, and that was okay. 'I just have to know,' I told him. 'I just have to slip into her skin. It might give me a clue. It might save her. It might even bring her home.'

◆ ◆ ◆

As I drove back towards Lewes, I hesitated, just for a fraction of a second, before turning left on to the road that would take me up past the prison. I knew where Thorn House was, just outside town, over the humpback bridge. I'd driven past it before, on the days when I used to take Edie out to look at the horses in the nearby fields. She was much, much younger then, of course. Dewy-eyed but not frightened, not even with her small hand outstretched with a fistful of grass in it.

'Keep your hand flat, honey, so it doesn't bite,' I'd told her. She had seemed so small as the horse bent its giant head to her, and I'd almost snatched her away. Edie had laughed, though, as that soft velvety muzzle had pressed against her skin. 'It tickles, Mummy!' she'd crowed. We must have passed Thorn House a number of times, but we hadn't even noticed it then. There was a gate, of course, separating the big Georgian property from the road, and at first I drove right past it, making a turn on the right so I could drive around again and park a little way away, with the front of the house in view.

It was a quiet street, all the houses grand and imposing and concealed behind high hedges and gates and old stone walls. Behind them the woodland stretched out towards the hem of the South Downs and the soaring cliffs beyond. I leaned my car seat back a little and lit a cigarette, rolling down the window a few inches. By now the sky was turning a pale lavender colour, dusk-stained. I turned on the radio and watched and waited.

Edward Thorn's car pulled up on the drive at four thirty, just as the streetlights were coming on. The car was one of those big ones, a proper family car, an old, well-used four-door, spattered with mud. I watched as the brake lights flared red and winked out before opening my own car door. I didn't climb out just yet. I wanted to surprise him. I saw a man climbing stiffly from the driver's seat wearing a wax jacket with the collar turned up, a pair of scruffy-looking jeans. He moved to the rear of the car and opened the boot and started to rummage inside. I slid silently out of my car and crossed the road quickly, hands in my pockets, face set in a grim, hard line. There was what felt like an electrical pulse running through me, crackling with charge.

Edward was pulling something from the boot, a large white object, a rectangle. As he turned it towards the road I could make out the writing on it: *Private Property – NO Entry!* written in thick black strokes.

'Hey!' I called out, starting to jog towards him, unable to keep myself from moving; it was a propulsion. I wanted to grab him, throw him against the car. But, of course, I didn't. He turned and for a moment I saw the expression on his face change. Eyes widening, mouth opening in a slack zero. It was just a second and then he was blinking and smiling hesitantly, eyebrows raised.

'Yes?'

'Do you know me?'

'I think I do, yes.' Up close his face was heavily lined, like the gnarled trunk of a tree. His deep-set eyes were very dark, glittering like buried jewels. 'You're Mrs Hudson. The missing girl's mother.'

I wasn't expecting that.

He nodded, placing a large hand on my shoulder, his voice softening. 'Of course I know who you are. I was sorry to read about your daughter in the paper. Edie, is it?'

'That's right.'

'So. How can I help?'

'I want to know what your car was doing at the churchyard the night Edie disappeared.'

His face fell but his expression was hard to read. Disappointment? Fear? He crossed his arms in front of his chest. 'You know I've already spoken to Tony about this.'

'Well, now you can talk to me.'

'I don't think that's wise.'

'I'm not giving you a fucking choice!' I shouted, my voice shaking with the force of it. I was suddenly furious with him, his calmness, that reasonable tilt of the head, the sympathy in his voice, oversweet. I was furious with Tony for telling me that goodwill is a currency and that Edward Thorn had a surfeit of it. I was angry with Edie and myself and with this stupid town for swallowing her up. My fists were tight, arms stiff and thrumming with tension. Edward didn't raise his voice or step away from me. He simply lowered the lid of the boot so I could see there was someone standing behind it, car door open. He must have climbed out while we were talking. William Thorn, the boy I'd found on the couch with Edie. His eyes were wide in the gathering dark. His school uniform hung off his skinny frame, his bag slung over one shoulder giving him a strange, lopsided look. His mouth was hanging open in shock.

'Dad?'

'It's all right, William,' Edward told him without taking his eyes off me. 'Go inside and help your brother.'

He didn't move.

'What's going on? Why is she here?' His voice cracked as if he might be about to cry. *Good*, I thought.

'She's upset, William. As she should be.'

Was that a slight? I couldn't tell. I took a big, deliberate step closer to Edward, head tilted so I could look him in the eye. I heard William behind him, saying, *Dad, Dad*, again and again, but Edward stood very still, watching me.

'Why were you there at the churchyard? That's all I want to know. You can tell me, and I'll leave you alone.'

'I've already spoken to the police and I don't have anything further to say to you.' His voice was still gentle, as if he was talking me down from a ledge. 'Please, Mrs Hudson, go home. Get some rest.'

A door at the front of the house opened and an oblong of warm orange light spilt out on to the drive. I saw a woman emerge holding something in her hands. She wasn't looking at us, not really, and it was only as she drew closer that I realised what she was carrying. It was a carved pumpkin, lit from the inside with a candle. She looked up, smile fading as she took in the scene, her words falling away as if cut by a blade.

'Look at what we did this aftern— Edward? What's going on?'

'It's all right, Mimi love. Mrs Hudson just came to ask me about Edie. Take William inside.'

Mimi didn't look as if she knew what to do with herself. She lowered the pumpkin to the ground and stared at me with large, worried eyes. She looked almost leporine in the half-light. A prey animal. There was something else too, wasn't there? She was afraid. But of who? Me? Or Edward?

'Mimi – now, please!' Edward said shortly, and I saw her taking William by the arm and moving him towards the house, the two of them looking back at us over their shoulders until they were safely inside. The pumpkin sat on the drive, casting a strange, strobing aura.

'I understand the worry and upset this has caused you. But as I said, I've spoken with my friends at the station and if they have any concerns with any part of my statement I trust they will get back to me. They seem to be of the mind that your daughter ran away. I must say, from what I've heard about Edie, I agree with them.'

I was wrong-footed. I reached out and gripped his arm. 'What do you mean? What have you heard about her? Edward?'

He peeled my hand away firmly, taking a deliberate step away from me.

'You should go,' he said, lifting the sign he'd pulled from the boot and tucking it under his arm. 'This place will be overrun with kids in a minute. You're in no state to see them.'

I stared after him as he walked away, his shadow long in the light coming through the open doorway. Inside I could imagine the warmth of their comfortable home, the security of it, the way love can knit a family together, and something inside me worked itself loose. I felt like I might start to cry and never stop so I turned and ran back to my car, standing beside it with my head bowed and my shoulders shaking, taking big, whooping breaths.

'Trick or treat!' a voice shouted behind me.

I turned around and there was a little vampire there, dressed in a frilly shirt with his hair parted to the side, slick with gel. He was smiling, his little round face pressed with talc to give it a chalky, post-death whiteness. Two runnels of blood dripped down from the corners of his mouth, which was lifted in a grin. I stared at him until someone – his mother, presumably, dressed in regular clothes but with a witch's hat on in a nod to the season – scooped him up and walked him away towards a bigger group of kids gathering at the top of the road, looking back at me over her shoulder with a furrowed brow. There were already a few groups milling about as the darkness crowded in, a lot of shrieking and laughter, a bright high howl as a werewolf ran past, little bucket dangling at its side. Halloween. Nearly a whole month without Edie. My knees felt watery. I managed to open the car door and sit on the seat before I fell down. She'd called me. I'd heard her voice. She was out there somewhere. I looked through the windscreen as a clatter of noisy children ran past, witches and warlocks and dread vampires, all in their black finery like miniature versions of the Rattlesnakes. I watched as they approached the house to my left, the one with pumpkins cut out from orange crêpe paper strung in the trees. I heard the chorus of their voices, almost singsong, 'Trick or Tre-eat!', and I had an idea.

I pulled all the junk from my car boot on to the ground before I found what I was searching for. An old dust sheet, put inside when I was decorating back in February. Edie had kicked a hole in the wall of the stairs as big as a fist and I'd filled it in that same weekend. I couldn't even remember what she'd been mad about now. It was just one of those things, those moods, fraught with violence. I pulled it out and gave it a shake, using my lit cigarette to burn two small holes into the white fabric. When I pulled it over my head I had to adjust it carefully so I could see. I could smell my own ragged breath blasted back at me; nicotine and something sour, like spoiled milk. Maybe Edward was right; maybe I was in no fit state.

I watched as the groups wove among each other along the street, joining and detaching like shoals. I hung at the back of the biggest one, trying to shrink myself beneath the sheet, hoping no-one would turn around and say, 'Who the hell are you?' But nobody did. I felt a tug as some little girl grabbed my dust sheet and pulled at it, but she laughed and spirited herself away and I managed to gather it back over myself before I was revealed. As we approached Thorn House, I experienced a moment of apprehension. *What if Edward doesn't answer the door? What will you do then? Take a hostage? You'll get yourself arrested. Think, Samantha. Go home. Don't do this. Don't.*

A little zombie stood on tiptoe to ring the bell but the door was already opening. They'd seen us coming. I hesitated, trying to stand behind one of the men at the back of the group despite the fact that my face was covered. Edward stood there beaming, a bowl of sweets held in one of his large, flat hands. I felt for my knife in my pocket. I had to be careful. I didn't want to scare these kids.

'Well, look at this!' he exclaimed. 'I see a Dracula and a mermaid and a scary-looking monster and, hello, who's this?'

'Frankenstein,' a small voice said, dipping a hand in the bowl.

Edward's smile broadened even more. 'Well, of course, Frankenstein was the name of the Genevan student but we'll overlook that for now, shall we?'

There was a ripple of laughter as he handed out more sweets. Some of the children were already running off. One of the fathers called out, 'Mind the road!'

There was a soft click as I released the blade from the handle. 'Happy Halloween!' the little zombie yelled, taking his mother's hand. They were starting to disperse. I moved forward, slowly, the dust sheet trailing on the ground behind. Edward looked up, slightly puzzled but smiling.

'And who are you? The ghost of Christmas past? Here you go then. Even the adults need a sweet from time to t—'

His voice dropped off as I grabbed his hand, jerking him towards me. Startled, he dropped the bowl and it clattered to the ground, sweets spilling everywhere. My adrenaline had sharpened my focus and I pressed the tip of the blade into the webbing of skin between the thumb and forefinger. He yelped.

'You're coming over the road to my car,' I said. 'And you're going to do it quickly.'

'Edward?' That was Mimi, walking into the hallway. She took in the scene, her husband standing too close to a ghost in a dirty white sheet with cigarette burns for eyes. She saw the spilled sweets, the bowl broken neatly into two halves. Her face flickered with worry.

'It's all right, love,' Edward said, his voice slightly strangled. 'You need to get another bowl before the next lot arrive. I'm just going to sort something out. Go on. Go on, dear.'

'Alex wants another hot dog,' she said flatly.

'Tell him it's fine. It's fine, Mimi. Tell him he can hold the fort till I get back.'

I increased the pressure on the blade so that the tip pressed into his skin and pulled him towards me so that we could stumble together like two drunks, out the driveway and over the road. When we reached my car I opened the passenger door first and ushered him in. He still looked pale but had regained some of his composure and did so gracefully, even leaning over to unlock the driver's-side door for me. I pulled off the dust sheet and slid in, snapping off the radio.

He looked down at the knife in my hand. 'Carrying something like that around is going to get you in trouble one day,' he said.

I'd never really thought about it like that. I'd always thought of it as protection. 'Just tell me. Just tell me and I'll go. Why were you at the churchyard on the night of the ninth?'

He sighed, long and loud. 'I'll tell you what I told the police. It isn't unusual to see my car down at St Mary's. I do a lot of work there, both for the youth group and the preservation of the woodland on the church ground. I raised a lot of money to get the roof of that church repaired just last year. I'm there a lot. But I wasn't doing any of that on that particular night. I parked there, yes. But I was visiting an address nearby.'

'Go on.'

He looked out through the windscreen. 'Mimi and I, we've been together a long time. Like most people our age we married young and kids came not long after. So sometimes it's difficult to . . . keep the momentum going. We haven't told the boys that we've been having marriage counselling because it's not for them to know, but that's how things are and that's what we're doing. Once a fortnight we visit a woman down there who has a studio in her home and she talks us through our problems. Is that enough information for you? Or would you like all the gory details?'

'I thought—'

'I know what you thought. You thought someone took your girl, maybe by force. But if you think that, you don't know her at all, do you?' He leaned closer. 'Mimi liked her a lot, your daughter. Said being headstrong and stubborn were qualities that would stand her in good stead as a woman. She never had a problem with Edie in class. So maybe the problem wasn't Edie, have you thought about that?' His eyes dropped down to my hand again, the one still holding the knife. 'Maybe the problem was you, Samantha.'

He climbed out the car and walked over the road without looking back, a tall stooped man with grey in his hair and a smile for everyone. A man who championed good causes. I closed my eyes, the shock of his words rippling through me like a soundwave.

By the time the Rattlesnakes emerged through the gate on Monday afternoon it was gone four, and the light was already fading from the sky. All three girls were present this time, crossing the road hand in hand like children. I noticed Charlie had a black beret on her head, slanted sideways over one eye. Everything about her was matt black, deep as a shadow. Next to her, tiny Moya and skinny ghost-girl Nancy just seemed to fade away. Charlie smiled when she saw me, one hand reaching into the pocket of her leather jacket to pull out a packet of cigarettes. Her lips were a deep, vampish red.

'You want one, Mrs Hudson?' She extended a cigarette towards me. The girls crowded round. It was like being mugged by shadows.

'No,' I told her flatly. 'I want to do the ritual. Tomorrow. Full moon, right? I want to do it exactly the way you did it when Edie disappeared. Everything the same.'

She arched an eyebrow, inhaling deeply on her cigarette. 'Well, I don't know about that. We'll need to buy some stuff.'

'Like what?' The answer didn't matter. I was already reaching for my purse.

Charlie pretended to think, rolling her eyes. 'Uh, we'll need to buy some Thunderbird.'

'That's alcohol,' Moya chimed.

Charlie flashed her a look. 'She knows that, dumbass. We'll need money for candles too. And a little bit of dope.'

I stared at her. She stared back. Flat, confrontational. She wanted me to say *no*. She wanted me to fight her, to fight for dominance. *Not going to happen, honey*, I thought as I handed over twenty pounds.

'What time?' I said. My heart was racing. Hope, the flame sparking in the cave. A pale light, distant and wavering as though in a breeze.

Charlie looked at the others and then turned back to me, making my money disappear into the pocket of her shirt.

'Eight o'clock. When the church bells toll, come through the gate. You'll find us round the grave.'

'Which one?'

'Quiet Mary. You'll see it. We'll lead you there.'

She turned away and I noticed her leather jacket had an emblem drawn on it, an ouroboros with the word *Rattlesnakes* printed round it in a circle. The other girls chimed their goodbyes, turning away from me in a sooty flare of chiffon and leather, black winged birds from a fairy tale. I caught Nancy's eye – they were such a pale blue they were almost transparent – and she immediately dropped her gaze. She was wearing a satin ribbon choker round her neck and had a crucifix drawn in felt-tip on the back of her hand, the ink slightly smudged.

'Nancy,' I said, but she hurried away from me, head down. *She knows something*, I thought. I made a note to try to talk to her the next night, to get her away from the group. I'd shake it out of her if I had to.

'You must be mad, doing this,' I said, not caring that I was talking aloud, that people were looking at me and sniggering, hands over their mouths.

What if it could bring her back? I'd said to Rupert and that was my hope, that was my flame in the dark. But that's the thing about hope: it doesn't vanish. Not ever, not quite. It swells and shrinks like a tumour, turning the blood black in the process, ruining you. Even when I told people that I'd lost hope, I knew it was there somewhere, glimmering with the bright intensity of a comet. It filled me with excitement or despair or dread and yet even when I knew it was no good, I wanted it. Hope is a vice. It refuses to be snuffed out. I hate it. I love it.

At two minutes to eight the next evening I arrived at St Mary de Castro feeling sick and anxious. The ground was gilded with an early frost, glittering in the moonlight. The moon itself was fat and waxy and ringed with colour. We'd inched into November and the air was singed with the scent of bonfires and ice. I breathed in, let the cold sharpen my lungs. I couldn't stop thinking about Edie's winter coat hanging on the hook at home where she left it. *She'll be cold*, I thought, and suddenly there was a stone in my throat, a rock, and it was difficult to breathe. *She'll be cold.*

The bells chimed and I walked through the iron gate without hesitation. Since he'd been taken in for questioning, Peter Liverly hadn't been up to the job of caretaking, and now the gates were left open most nights. His house, the little bungalow just beyond the old stone wall of the churchyard, had been empty since his release.

Someone said he'd had hate mail. Another that masked gangs had been knocking on his windows at night, frightening him. We'd all seen the words that had been printed in thick black letters across his living room windows where the curtains hung drawn and still: *pedo scum*. I hadn't seen the photos the police had found when they'd searched the church hall, the ones he'd taken of Edie and the other Rattlesnakes. Were they evidence? Would he be given them back? I'd have liked to find out where he'd gone. He didn't deserve comfort. He didn't deserve shelter. He killed rabbits and he stalked teenage girls.

It was dark here, round the back of the church, despite the full moon. The street lights didn't penetrate the trees and the frost gave everything a pale blue glow that crunched underfoot. In the darkness beside me, something rustled. I told myself it was the wind sifting through the dead leaves. There was still that wretched smell of rot and blight and I was walking carefully to avoid stepping on any rabbit remains. Up ahead I could see movement, the dim glow of candles in glass jars, the glowing orange heads of handfuls of incense sticks jammed into the soft ground. I headed towards it, drawing my collar up against the chill. There was the police tape, fallen into disarray. The night air was still and brittle as the ice beneath my feet. In my back pocket, the reassuring weight of my knife.

As I drew closer, I saw Nancy sitting cross-legged on the ground. She was wearing gloves with the fingers cut off and holding a bottle in her hands. She was laughing too loud, her cheeks and eyes bright. She was drunk. Half the bottle was already gone. *It'll make her sick, drinking so fast. A rookie mistake.* I saw Charlie encircled in a violet haze of smoke, the resinous smell of dope scenting the air. She was wearing a lace veil over her face, black of course, like a Victorian spiritualist. She motioned to me with a wave of her hand. I caught the glint of her smile through the darkness.

'Where's Moya?' I said, looking around.

Nancy looked up at me, her lips wet. 'She's not coming.'

'Oh, shush,' Charlie purred. 'She'll be here.' Her head turned towards me. 'She has very strict parents. They wouldn't let her within ten feet of us.'

'She lies,' Nancy laughed, digging furrows into the earth with her heels. 'She tells them she's coming to the youth club.' She hiccupped, burying her chin into the fur collar of her coat. 'I tell my parents I'm at Charlie's.'

'And I tell my parents I'm working at the pizza place in Brighton,' Charlie said. She was a little unsteady on her feet, dancing a slow waltz. She exhaled smoke towards the stars. 'They think I'm employee of the month.'

Nancy burst out laughing. The bottle fell from her hands and Charlie called her a clumsy bitch, which made her laugh even harder. There was something desperate about the sound of it, as if at any moment it could dissolve into tears.

I turned to Charlie. 'So teenagers lie to their parents? You think that's new?'

Charlie lifted the veil slowly from her face, casting it in elegant shadow.

'I think it's appropriate,' she says. 'You want one of these?'

I looked down at her outstretched hand. Pills. Small and diamond-shaped. I reached out my hand and then hesitated. *What would Edie have done? That's an easy answer*, I told myself almost immediately. She'd have taken one, no question.

'What are they?'

Charlie smiled, her head tilted to one side. 'My little brother's got ADHD. This is what he takes for it.' She lowered her voice and leaned closer. 'It'll just help you focus, that's all. You did say you wanted the ritual done right.'

I took one from her and held my hand out for the wine. It was warm and sweet and cheap-tasting, but it washed the pill down. Charlie laid a tablet on her tongue and grinned at me.

'That's my girl,' she purred.

I looked down and saw the candles in jam jars at the compass points of Mary Sayers's grave.

'What's so special about this grave?' I asked, squinting at the headstone. *Lost to the Waters, She will Return.*

'It's Quiet Mary,' Nancy said, passing the bottle to Charlie, who wiped the neck with her sleeve. 'We've been trying to summon her.'

'We *have* summoned her. I've seen her,' Charlie said. 'One time I even spoke to her.'

'What did she say?' I asked, lighting a cigarette. I wanted some more of that awful wine.

'She said, "The water's so cold, Charlie, I can't breathe. Help me. It's so dark down here. Help me."'

I wished she'd lift the veil again. I didn't like not being able to see her face.

'Tell her what she looked like!' Nancy hissed, her eyes round with awe. She swigged from the bottle again.

Charlie stepped closer to me, pale hands swimming before her. 'Like the fish had been eating her. She had pondweed coming out of her eyes.'

Nancy was leaning back against the grave, listening with the rapt attention of a child to a bedtime story. I had a feeling this was one she'd heard before.

'Quiet Mary found a way back,' Charlie said into the darkness. 'She found a path into our world and we can open the gateway just enough for her to come through.'

'Where's the gateway?'

'Behind you.'

The dope made my head swim a little as I turned slowly, aware suddenly of how fast my heart was beating, my fingers twitching with my pulse. I was nervous but there was also a flash of excitement that ran through me like a shiver. I wanted to see what would happen. I wanted to feel how Edie must have felt. The way the night had stretched out for her.

'It's just a tree.'

'That's right. The tree is the gateway.'

I stamped my feet, urged my hands to be still. 'Shall we get on with it?'

'What about Moya?' Nancy said.

'We have to wait. It has to be four. An even number.' Charlie again. I wondered how she knew so much about rituals and spell-casting and then I remembered someone telling me that all magic relied upon was the strength of your belief in it. Everything else was window-dressing.

Charlie suddenly sighed dramatically, hunching her shoulders as if in pain. She stretched out a hand to me, black-tipped nails over the cold stone.

'She's waiting for us,' she whispered. 'I can feel her presence drawing closer.'

'Who is it?'

Charlie didn't answer. Behind her I saw movement and for a moment my heart rose into my mouth, my vision blurred. It was her! But no, it was just Moya, walking at a brisk pace, long coat dwarfing her small frame.

'I'm sorry!' she said breathlessly. 'My dad's a miserable bastard. Am I too late?'

Everyone looked to Charlie, even me. *It's a pantomime*, I told myself, but I couldn't help feeling swept along with it – the candles, the graveside, the smell of old stones and frost as sharp as blades. The Rattlesnakes themselves looked like psychopomps, black shrouded creatures taking the newly deceased into the afterlife. I shuddered again. *It's the cold*, I told myself. I took another sip of the wine.

I helped Nancy to her feet and we wordlessly drew closer to the large yew. Moya took my hand on one side, Nancy on the other. We formed a loose circle in the darkness, the candlelight making our faces stutter and seize. *What would Rupert think if he could see me now?* I wondered, and immediately dismissed the thought from my mind. I had to do this right. I had to get into Edie's frame of mind. I had to find some trace of her, anything. Rupert had told me it was desperation, and I'd answered simply, 'Yes, it is.'

'Mrs Hudson? Samantha?'

The girls were all looking at me expectantly, except of course for Charlie with the veil obscuring her face. Her head was turned towards me, though, and her voice was as smooth as antique silks.

'We need your knife. Hand it over, please.'

I hesitated. Moya squeezed my hand. *Go ahead, it's okay.* As I passed it to Charlie I couldn't help saying, 'Be careful with that, it's sharp.'

'I should hope so,' she whispered, and took it from me, expertly flicking it out and turning it so the blade caught the candlelight. She extended her other arm and slowly carved a line in the skin of her palm. Blood welled to the surface, deep and rich and slow-moving. I stared at her in horror as she passed the knife to Nancy and said, 'Your turn.'

Nancy gingerly took the knife and quickly sliced into her own palm, drawing a shallow, hair-thin scratch before hurriedly passing the knife to me and closing her fist.

Charlie lifted her voice. 'Quiet Mary, can you hear us?'

I could see blood smeared on the knife handle and absent-mindedly wiped it clean on my jeans. Is this what Edie did with them that night? A blood bond between friends? Perhaps they were just pushing me to see how far I'd go. *This is madness*, I thought, but I held my palm out anyway, feeling the blade open the skin there just above the mount of Venus. The pain was sharp and exhilarating, making me gasp. A silver cloud of my breath rose like a ghost. Blood seeped through the tear in my skin. Nancy took my bloodied hand in hers. It felt slippery and warm. A wave of dizziness, a warm tide, swept over me. I closed my eyes, feeling heady. *What was in that pill?*

'The veil is thinning. Let our blood command you to rise, rise!'

I opened my eyes to see Charlie with her bloodied hand spread against the bark of the old yew. Moya did the same, and Nancy next, urging me on. The trunk was sheened almost lilac-coloured and satin-soft with age. Huge, sombre-looking, like something primordial, the bark so thick we couldn't comfortably fit in a circle around it. Instead we stood in a line, all four of us, heads bowed, hearts racing, palms pressed flat against the tree. When I heard the tapping at first I thought it was coming from somewhere beyond the tree. My mind turned to the gateway Charlie had spoken about, the one that led to worlds beyond this one. A jolt of fear rushed through me, brief and bright as a spark.

> *One, two, three, four,*
> *Rattlesnake hunters knocking at your door.*
> *Give them meat and give them bone,*
> *And pray that they leave you alone.*

The air was cold against my teeth. I felt that wave again, building, building beneath me. It was like too much caffeine, a warm rush, sharp and anxious at the edges. When I opened my eyes it looked like there were shimmering auras around the Rattlesnakes, like the one I could see around the moon. I smiled at them, these funereal girls with their ebony plumage.

'Now what?' I heard myself say.

'Quiet,' Charlie said, her hand held up. In that moment, stiff and tall and regal in her black fur collar and silk slip, she looked like a murderous queen. 'Do you hear it? Samantha, do you hear that?'

I strained to listen but the blood was rushing in my ears so fast it sounded like a high wind. I looked over at Moya, her eyes white and round in the darkness. Then I heard it. A rattling, like stones being shaken in a hand. Old bones knitting together. My temples pounded. I itched all over. My muscles tensed, like fight or flight.

'I hear it,' I said.

Something sailed out of the darkness, a small white object, striking the ground near our feet. It was a pebble. Water-washed smooth. Then another, from out there in the dark. It rolled to a stop in the grass.

'Who's there?' Nancy called out in a quavering voice, and at the same time Charlie intoned, 'It's her. Quiet Mary. She's coming.'

I listened, straining to see into the blackness, where the frost had laced everything an icy blue. Then the cracking sound of branches broken underfoot. Someone was back there, in the shadows. I saw a movement, a shadow detaching from the black trunks of the trees, receding further into the dark. I didn't even think about it. I peeled my sticky palm from the trunk and called out her name.

'Edie!'

My heart was instantly racing, my pupils were wide black moons. *God, what was in that pill?* I dashed into the shadows under the trees, moonlight speckling the ground like scattered silver pennies. It took a moment for my eyes to adjust but when they did I caught sight of a hooded figure a little way ahead of me.

'Edie!'

Nothing. I forced myself to stop running, to catch my hoarse breath. My lungs burned but I was still jittery with energy. I turned and turned again, feeling as if I was being circled. Eyes in the gloom, watching me. I heard the telltale rustling of her pushing through thicket and I rushed ahead towards the sound, heels drumming up clods of earth.

'Hey!' I shouted, as branches tangled themselves in my hair. 'Hey, Edie, wait! It's Mum! Don't run, Edie!'

There, to my left. She'd feinted, swerving away from me. I turned sharply, feeling a branch whip across my cheek. The drumming of my feet was a cadence, her name, over and over, *Ee-dee, Ee-dee, Ee-dee.* I must be catching her up. My arms pistoned at my sides. I wanted to tell her to stop running, I just wanted to talk to her, I just wanted to explai— *whumph!* Something slammed into my shoulder with a flat whacking sound, knocking me off balance. I fell with an ugly grunt, tasting mud and dirt. A stitch roared in my side like boiling oil. For a moment I wondered if I'd been shot. Then I saw that hooded figure – *Edie?* – standing a little way off with something in its hand. A stick? A bat? I propped myself up, reaching out to her. There was so much I wanted to tell her. About how I'd missed her, how things would be different now, how she could have all the freedom and boyfriends she wanted if she'd just come home. *I don't mind*, I wanted to tell her, but my voice snagged in my throat. *I don't mind the pain, Edie.*

'Please don't hurt me,' she said.

I blinked. Her voice was deep and gluey with fear. *No*, I told myself, *not her voice. Not Edie.* My breathing was returning to normal but my right side was numb all the way to the shoulder blades. Whatever she'd hit me with was going to leave bruises like night-blooming flowers on my skin. My feet scrambled in the dirt, suddenly cold and stiff.

'I'm not going to hurt you,' I told her.

The figure moved forward a little, into a space where I could see her more clearly. She was cautious, almost hopping from foot to foot as if she would take off if I made any sudden moves, like a startled rabbit. 'We've got a rabbit problem,' Peter Liverly had said to me, and the rabbits in his bag had been bloody and stripped down to the raw meat. The smell of their tiny deaths was everywhere.

'Why'd you hit me?' I said, struggling to get to my feet. 'I think you've broken my collarbone.'

The hood slipped down to reveal an angular, bony face beneath a scrawl of dark curls. I saw fear etched on to its male features, drawn with a quick, sure hand. Disappointment settled in my stomach, plummeting like lead. I told him again I wouldn't hurt him. He didn't reply, simply pointed to me with a shaking finger. I looked down in wonder at the stiletto knife, clutched in my hand. I hadn't even been aware I'd pulled it out. For a moment neither of us spoke.

'I wouldn't have hurt you, William,' I said, although I didn't know if that was true. Why had I drawn it if I hadn't been prepared to use it? *More to the point*, a suspicious little voice in my head asked, *why did you draw it if you thought it was Edie you were chasing?*

'You come near me with that, you'll get done for GBH,' he said. He had his breath back now, the fear replaced with a hostile expression I was more familiar with.

'I'm sorry – I – I don't know—' I stood up, still holding the knife, my other hand reaching for my shoulder, which felt as though it was embedded with hot splinters.

'Carrying a fucking knife,' he muttered, shaking his head as if he couldn't believe it. He hawked a mouthful of phlegm and spat on the ground between us. 'No one told me you'd be fucking tooled up.'

He was tall and slight, like a stick of hazel. I didn't know how I could have thought it was Edie. Rupert would say, 'The mind sees what it wants to see.' I laughed when I saw what he'd hit me with: his skateboard, gripped tightly beneath his arm. I bet if I went for him he'd have used it again.

'You're bleeding,' he said.

I looked at my other hand, the maroon stain it had left on my grey sweater.

I laughed, shrill. 'It's fine. It's nothing. I cut my palm open. God.' I ran my hand over my sweaty face. He was looking at me, concerned. I must have looked like a crazy woman. Maybe

I was. Maybe this was it, the slow burn of insanity. It started in the dark with the frost and the rabbits, the candles guttering on graves. 'William—' I said. I thought about reaching out to him, but which hand to use? The one smeared with blood or the one holding the knife? I settled for taking a step towards him. He was looking away, past me, into the dark, somewhere distant and cold and underwater.

'They're not nice, those girls. Rattlesnakes. You shouldn't hang around with them, Mrs Hudson. They don't want to help you.'

'You sound like my brother.' I laughed. It hurt my chest, my shoulder. 'I could say the same to you, of course. Besides, I have to try to find Edie. The police aren't doing their job, so I have to.'

'Is that why you came to our house and made my mum cry?'

'I didn't mean to do that, William. That wasn't my intention. I just wanted to talk to your dad.'

'Why?'

I sighed. I'd no reason to keep Edward Thorn's secrets but William was just a kid, and he looked as scared as I was. 'Because your dad knows a lot of people. Important people. I thought he might be able to help me.'

He scuffed his foot on the ground. His head dipped. 'I wish she'd come back,' he said. 'Edie, I mean. We weren't serious, me and her. But I still wish she hadn't gone, you know?'

'Did Edie know that?'

'Know what?'

'That it wasn't serious?'

'Huh?' He sounded genuinely confused. I felt a ripple of that old familiar anger, as sleek and sinuous as a cat coiling about my legs. I tightened my grip on the knife. The buzzing in my head was making it hard to think straight. I stepped forward.

'Did my daughter know you weren't serious about her? Or did you lead her on, the way all the others did?'

'Mrs Hudson, listen – I'm – I'm not here to—'

'Why *are* you here, William? It's a cold, dark night in a grave-yard. What are you doing here?'

'Ch-Charlie.'

'Charlie?'

'Yeah. She told me it would be funny if I hid in the dark and threw those stones. To frighten you. She wanted to make you believe in Quiet Mary the same way they all do.'

William swallowed noisily. He flattened himself against the tree behind him, his fear of me real and almost comical; large round eyes, slack jaw. It came from him in waves. I'd forgotten that he was just a kid, that he was just as scared and confused as I was. I took another step forward. I looked down at the knife in my hand. *I should put it away*, I thought, but I didn't. I could feel my fast pulse in the tips of my fingers, the cushion of my palm. The pearl handle felt cool to the touch, the blade a delicious weight, smooth and clean. I liked the way light ran along it like water.

'I swear on my mother's life, Mrs Hudson, I don't know any-thing about your daughter!'

'Shh,' I told him, pressing the knife against his skinny throat. He whimpered. I pressed the tip in the soft spot behind his earlobe, nicking the skin there in a series of little cuts, like stitches. I was numb, amputated. It was like I'd stepped outside my body.

'Please!' he whispered frantically. 'Please don't do this . . .'

Suddenly I heard voices, moving through the trees. Low rustling sounds, the scuffle of leaves, someone calling my name. William slumped a little and I looked at the blood on the tip of my knife with mounting horror. *Had I done that to him?* Turning round, I could see torchlight slicing through the dark, hear Tony Marston's familiar, dense tone saying, *Come on, Samantha, come on out of there.* William shook his head, muttering, *Oh my God*, and all the while I felt hollow, scooped out on the inside and left like a cave, dark and wet and empty. The frost would creep over me in the night like white lace. In the morning I'd shatter as the sun rose, my frozen body blown to the wind like flakes of snow.

◆　◆　◆

Later, in the back of the police car, I felt the first warmth creeping back into my fingers and toes. Tony turned down the radio, which had already begun to play Christmas songs. He rubbed his forehead, flicking the indicator on as he made a right turn.

'What's going on, Sam?'

I stared at him in the rear-view mirror, unsmiling.

He sighed again. 'You pull a weapon on a minor, you've been taking God knows what, you're covered in blood – just help me out here, please.'

'He said she made him do it. Charlie.'

'I know, he told me. Poor kid's terrified. Some girl put him up to coming into the graveyard to give you a fright. I don't know what's wrong with people. The world's gone to hell.'

The rumble of the engine, the drone of the heaters. I tipped my head backward and leaned into the seat, suddenly sleepy.

'I mean, you're lucky you're not under arrest for that knife.'

'It's an antique,' I mumbled.

'Yeah? Well, so am I.'

'How did you know I was there?'

'Your brother Rupert called me. He's worried about you. Said you were going off to do some sort of voodoo with Edie's friends.'

'Ah.'

We let a minute or two pass. He cleared his throat. 'Those girls aren't going to help you find her, Sam. They're as bad as the psychics that keep calling. You stay away from people like that. And you stay away from the Thorn family. All of them.'

The click of a lighter. He passed me a lit cigarette. 'Smoke that and stay awake. I don't want you burning the car down.'

'He was frightened of me.'

'I'm not fucking surprised. You had a knife on him.'

'He smelled bad.'

'Yup. The whole place smelled bad. We've had complaints. Dead rabbits everywhere. That man, Liverly, he's gone to stay with his son. Indefinitely.' His eyes flicked to me in the mirror again. 'There's been a bit of a backlash since he was taken in for questioning.'

'Good.'

'Sam, listen. I know how much you're hurting. I know it's hard for you to feel like you're doing nothing, but this – this isn't helping find your daughter.'

'How would you know what's helping? You've given up.'

Tony looked pained but said nothing as he pulled up outside my house. He switched the engine off and the two of us sat quietly in the dark for a minute, smoking. I saw the curtains of the house twitch over the road. I felt like waving at them. Fuck, I felt like flashing them. Top up, tits out. *Come and see this, Graham, that woman over the road has finally lost her mind. Samantha Hudson, brought home in a police car.* It wasn't the first time a police car had drawn up outside our house but usually it was Edie inside, clothes ripped from fighting or banned from whichever shop she'd stolen from. 'Can't you keep her?' I'd joked as the officer had brought her in, except, like every good joke, there was a hint of truth to it, wasn't there? Pleading, almost.

Finally, Tony said, 'Samantha, do you remember what it was like to be fifteen?'

I nodded. I was crying again; I didn't know where these tears had sprung from. I was like a leaky tap these days, crying in jarring fits and starts until my eyes were red and sore.

'Me too. It's confusing. All those hormones. All that Brylcreem. I used so much of that stuff my mother would put sheets on the backs of the armchairs to stop me staining them. I was out of school, working in a factory, crazy with lust. You remember how it was?'

'I remember.' I'd been sixteen years old when I lost my virginity to a young man named Alfie Burrows who lived next door. We did it in his treehouse at the height of summer and played Alice Cooper records when his parents weren't home. I told him when I grew up I wanted to be a botanist. He said he would be a famous footballer. That autumn he moved away and never wrote to me again. One year later I would meet a man called Mark Hudson at the bus stop outside the greyhound racing who would later breathlessly promise not to ejaculate inside me but do so anyway, rolling a cigarette on his hairy stomach afterwards and saying, 'Women never get pregnant if they're on top anyway, don't worry.'

'Teenagers are stupid,' Tony said, interrupting my memory. 'They're dickheads. They make shitty decisions and think they know it all. I know she was a handful, Sam. I know she made your life hard sometimes. But at the heart of it that's all Edie is, a typical teenager. She's made a bad choice and she's probably somewhere regretting it right now and trying to figure out how to come home. All right?'

'I don't know if I believe that any more, Tony.'

Over the road, the neighbours had come out on their door-steps, arms folded. Peering into the street. I lifted my hand and waved imperiously, like the Queen herself.

Frances – Now

St Mary de Castro is just outside the centre of town, ten minutes from the high street. The building itself is tall and imposing, looking more like a red-brick castle than a church. It's modern, too, tall and airy and spacious, without that perfume of old churches: damp stone, old books, mildew. The churchyard itself is around the back, through a pair of rusted iron gates. As you step inside, a little sign has been erected to show you what wildlife you might see. Slow worms, finches, rabbits and mice. The sky is hazy and dull with a prickle of heat in it that suggests a summer storm. There is no one else around as I make my way down the churchyard path. I'd expected it to be hard work, but I find the grave after a few minutes' searching. It's by a large holly tree that's ringed off by an old metal fence. *Edward Thorn, 1935–1997. Steadfast husband and father. 'I am nearer God's heart in the garden than anywhere else on earth.'*

There's a tangle of ivy over his grave, and flowers, long dead, tied to the headstone. The cellophane crinkles noisily in the breeze. Alex must have been here, or Mimi maybe. Whoever it was, they haven't visited for a while. By the looks of things, no one has. I straighten up, knees popping, wondering idly if William will come and visit the grave before we head back to Swindon. I doubt it. William rarely mentions his father, except to suggest he was weak and somehow contemptible. My mind keeps circling back to the crow that flew into the greenhouse roof yesterday afternoon, cracking its skull wide open on the glass. 'A bad omen,' Alex had said. 'It foretells a death.' Of course I'd laughed, but now, standing here in this churchyard, surrounded by the headstones of people who once lived and breathed and loved, their remains feeding back into the earth – *bonemeal*, I think, my stomach queasy – it's harder to dismiss the omen of a death, even one heralded by a bird.

I hope it's not Mimi, I think, brushing leaves from my knees. I don't know how William will cope if anything happens to her. He loves his mother with the sort of deliberateness with which he approaches paperwork; a focus that is almost entirely singular. She refers to him as her 'precious first-born' and tells me that he was the only thing that kept her alive when she suffered bleak postnatal depression.

'Just to look at his face, those beautiful eyes, so innocent – as if he was just telling me to hold on.'

I had to get out of the house this morning. Mimi's taken another turn. She had her meds as usual at eight o'clock, but by half past her eyes were darting to the window, growing agitated.

'Where's that robin?' she was saying, over and over. 'He's got a message for me.' She gripped my hand with her own, fingers digging into my skin hard enough to leave marks. 'Who are you?'

'It's me, Mimi. Frances. William's wife.'

Mimi turned towards me, her bony elbow knocking over the glass of water that stood on the nesting tables beside her bed. I cried out in dismay as it soaked into her sheets and lap, but she barely noticed. She looked at me curiously, her pale eyes searching my face.

'Who's William?'

'Come on, let's sit you up, get you out of that wet bed.'

'He boiled the bones in pots on the stove.'

I froze then, in the act of helping her out of the bed. That image, of bones boiling in pots on the stove, made my blood turn cold and fast-moving, like a river of melting snow. Mimi's thin legs hung over the edge of the mattress like sticks. I could see the blue tinge of her skin, burst blood vessels beneath the surface like tangled threads. Mimi was looking straight ahead, past me, out the window into the garden. Her voice trembled.

'We return to the earth. That's why the tomatoes taste so good. Where's that robin?'

Mimi fell silent as I helped her into the armchair, smoothing back the wisps of grey hair that floated about her face. Her teeth chattered, although she wasn't cold.

I pressed on, stripping the bed quickly. 'Did you ever see him making the bonemeal, Mimi?'

Silence. Outside, the empty bird feeder swung gently in the breeze.

'Alex said he kept the bones in the cellar. That must have been horrible. I'd say it wa—'

Mimi turned her head towards me so slowly I could almost hear the creak of her vertebrae. Her eyes fixed on me, as pale as winter. They were no longer vague, but as precise and keen as a knife blade. Her voice was lower, denser somehow. It was like another person was speaking right through her.

'*You want to watch where you're poking your nose, Mimi,* he said. *Someone might snip it right off!*'

She made a gesture with her fingers of scissors cutting and laughed girlishly, drawing her legs up off the floor. I stood motionless, unblinking. Who was she talking about? Edward? Is that what he said to her? My mind returned to those bones in pots on the stove, filling the air in the shed with a rich odour, leaving long grease marks down the wall. Alex had told me Edward had taken the bones from roadkill and the old meat factory, because you fed the soil, not the plant. *Old bones make strong plants*, I thought, watching Mimi's scrawny hands settle into her lap as slow and delicate as feathers. Her face fell still, her eyes shifting to the right, back to the window.

'There he is,' she said quietly, and when I looked outside I saw the robin on the bird feeder, scarlet feathers ruffled by the wind.

◆ ◆ ◆

I walk slowly with my hands in my pockets. It's so peaceful here, with birdsong high in the trees. I'm heading towards the small, contained woodland at the back of the churchyard, past the out-building painted a municipal green. The breeze stirs the grass. It feels good to be out of the house, out of that room where Mimi sits with her newspaper folded and untouched on her knees. William has told me not to mind the things she says, but she frightened me this morning, the way her voice seemed to deepen and rasp at me, so unlike her normal softness. Head injuries will do that to you, the doctor said, and then it brings my thinking round again to Mimi slipping and falling down the stairs alone and in the dark. *Not quite alone*, I remind myself. *Alex was there.* There's something unsettling in that too, isn't there? I take a deep breath, and then another. It's good to be out of that house.

The path is narrowing, bordered by nettles, long whispering grasses and choking weeds. I suppose back here are the older graves, the ones left untended as family trees and bloodlines branched away. The headstones are smaller and rougher, like hewn lumps of stone. I'm looking at the inscriptions more carefully now, looking for the one in particular that both Alex and Nancy mentioned to me. Quiet Mary, the drowned girl. It was at her grave that Edie Hudson had been standing when she walked away for the last time and disappeared into the trees. Had someone been waiting in the darkness back there for her? Peter Liverly, the caretaker? How about Quiet Mary herself, wrapped in a water-stained burial shroud, hooded and silent, floating an inch or so from the ground?

I shudder. The wind picks up. The trees sigh and press together, conspiring, whispering their perennial secrets. I don't see the figure kneeling among them until I have almost tripped over her. In her dark coat and jeans she is barely visible in the gloom. A cap has been pulled down over her head, obscuring her face and her ashy grey hair.

'Jesus!' I jump back, heart pounding.

She looks up at me, unfazed. 'Watch where you're going.'

'I'm sorry! I didn't – it's hard to see you in the dark.'

She turns away from me, back towards the ground. She is kneeling near the roots of a tree, carving out a little hole in the earth with a trowel.

'Whatever you're planting there is going to struggle,' I tell her. 'There's not nearly enough light in here for a young plant.'

She doesn't turn around. 'Are you a botanist?'

'No. I'm a – a therapist.'

'Pass me that bag, would you?'

I hesitate. There's a strange feeling in the air, like the approach of a monsoon. Anticipation and a sense of unease. Still, I lift the bag she points at and hand it to her. She rummages inside with dirt-streaked hands, finally pulling an item out. It's a stained-glass suncatcher in the shape of a bluebird, about the size of her palm. It twists in the breeze as she holds it towards the light.

'That's lovely,' I say.

'It is, isn't it? It's so hard to buy for someone you don't know.'

Even with the brim of the cap pulled low I can see this woman is older than I'd first thought. Although her face isn't lined, it has a weathered quality, abrasive, like her voice. She has crystal pendulum earrings and silver rings stacked on her fingers. *I bet she does tarot cards*, I think, *and burns incense in wooden holders until the air is smoky and thick.* I am about to say goodbye and turn away – hey, nice to meet you here in this dark and hallowed ground, you mad old lady scrabbling around in the dirt – but then she does something strange. She takes the suncatcher and gently, reverentially, places it in the hole she has dug. Then she lifts the trowel and begins to heap the earth back over it.

I can't help myself. I've always been nosy. Ask William. Ask Kim. 'I can't help but think that suncatcher would be better placed in a window somewhere,' I say, forcing myself to laugh.

She doesn't look up. She pats the earth with her hands as if she is building a sandcastle, firming it. When she sits back on her heels, her knees crack like pistols. 'It's her birthday today. She'd be thirty-three.' She pulls a pack of cigarettes from her bag and puts one between her teeth. 'You have any kids?'

'No. We haven't – we haven't got round to it yet.'

'Huh. Edie wasn't planned. I had her young. You look like a good age for a child, and you seem nice. You'd be a great mum.'

I stand very still as she pulls herself to her feet and asks me if I want a cigarette. I shake my head, tell her no, I'm sorry, I don't smoke. I'm thinking, *Edie.* That name again. The disappearing girl on everyone's lips.

When the woman removes her cap a spill of long grey hair falls over one eye. Her face is familiar to me, and it takes me a moment in my shock to place her. Then, 'You were in the cafe,' I tell her. 'You saw me talking to Nancy Renard.'

'Oh yeah? Nancy Renard. You know what the girls at her school used to call her? Nancy *Retard.* She was a late developer, you know? Very shy. Then she started hanging out with my daughter and her friends. It brought Nancy out of her shell a little bit, I suppose you could say. She's a different woman now.'

'Kids can be mean.'

She looks at me with eyes narrowed against the smoke. My mother always told me I was a terrible judge of character ('That's the problem with you, Frances,' she'd say to me, leaning in too close, her breath heavy with alcohol, cheeks flushed. 'You're not smart enough. You get fooled by everyone.'). Well, joke's on you, Ma, because I got wise to people very fast. Leaving home at sixteen will do that to you.

I'm sizing up this woman, Edie's *mother*, I remind myself, right now. Tough and uncompromising, unruffled. With her wild, wiry hair and the sullen jut of her jaw, she looks like a good person to get into trouble with. Then I remember Alex telling me she'd once held a knife to William's throat and my mouth dries up a little.

'What did you say your name was?' she asks, and immediately I lie, out of habit. It's a legacy of being in trouble with the wrong people most of your adult life – bailiffs, dealers, nasty exes.

I stick out my hand with a smile on my face. 'It's Kim.'

'I won't shake.' She holds up her dirty hands. 'You new to Lewes, Kim?'

'Sort of. I'm here with my husband. His mother's sick.'

'That's too bad. Is that why you're here? Looking for a plot to put her in?' She laughs, which immediately turns into a barking cough.

I smile. 'No, no. Nothing like that. I was just looking.'

'You want to walk this way with me? I feel like I want to get out into the sunshine a bit. It's so heavy in here. Oppressive.'

'Sure.'

She introduces herself as Samantha Hudson and I have to bite my tongue to stop myself telling her I already know her name. I've read the papers. I'm already half regretting lying to her about who I am, but I don't want her to know about my connection to William. How did Alex describe it? 'It was a bad time for him.' Instead I follow her through the trees towards the churchyard, where benches sit in sheaves of sunlight. I ask why she was burying the suncatcher.

Samantha looks back at me. 'I've been doing it every year since Edie went missing. When she was a little kid she would bury things in the back garden – cotton reels, bars of soap, my fucking house keys – she was obsessed with it. Used to drive me crazy. I bought her a sand pit – you know, the kind you get in a big plastic clam shell – and told her to bury stuff in there if that's what she wanted to do. But no, she went right on putting things in the dirt. I think she liked the way it felt in her hands.' Samantha crushes her cigarette out underfoot. 'In the beginning I think I went a bit mad, you know? I didn't hold it together very well. I suppose it was a way to stay connected to her. Now, I think it's just habit.'

We're out in the churchyard again, and immediately I feel my spirits lift. She was right, it was oppressive in there, the melancholy weighing down on you. Out here the sky is pale blue and endless, stretching out towards the distant Downs. Samantha hoists her bag on to her shoulder, smiling wearily. Her jaw is square and angular, the cords in her neck tight. There is a tension about her, a hyper-vigilance I've only ever seen in military victims of post-traumatic stress disorder. I recall one veteran I treated who'd been the victim of a roadside bomb in Basra. He'd seen his friend crawling away from the explosion with his intestines trailing after him in the dust. This woman, Samantha, has the same set in her shoulders; the way she carries herself is as though she is braced against an ambush, the world turning on her.

We leave the main path and follow a smaller one, no more than a single rut worn smooth by the passage of feet. The two of us are lost in thought, contemplative. The ground rises and falls like a tide. We pass an area sectioned off by a bamboo trellis that crawls with honeysuckle and clematis. Just beyond it I can hear the low, somnolent drone of bees and see the little hives that have been built there. A metre or so further on is an old wooden bench. Samantha sits down on it with a sigh, opening her bag at her feet. I join her, the two of us looking out over the sprawling graveyard, the dense woodland, the steep hills beyond that rise and fall like music.

'Here.' She's pulling something out of her bag. A bottle of beer. She opens it with the edge of her lighter, flipping the cap high into the air. Foam bubbles up the neck and she passes it to me hurriedly, saying, 'Quick, quick, before it escapes', and laughing. I take it and suck at the froth. It's malty and good, dark-tasting like honey and old casks. She produces another bottle and opens it the same way. She clinks hers against mine and then leans across and pours a little out on to the grave in front of us.

I frown at the headstone. 'Who's Tony Marston?' I ask, peering at the inscription. It gives the year of his death as 2001 and below that, in looping cursive, *May he find peace.*

I read it aloud and Samantha snorts derisively. 'You know what he wanted on his headstone? *Here lies the last fuck I ever gave.* His wife said no, so now he's stuck with that.' She kisses her two dirty fingers and leans forward, pressing them briefly against the marble. It's genuinely touching, without affectation, and I find myself looking away as tears threaten. Samantha gulps her beer.

'Was he a friend of yours?'

'Yes.'

'How did he die?'

'Heart attack. He smoked a pack a day. He was the detective in charge of Edie's case back in the beginning.'

'I'm sorry.'

'What for?' She looks at me with her keen blue eyes.

I sip the beer again. 'For your loss. Both your losses.'

'You know, after Edie went missing Tony convinced me to go to a local group for bereaved parents. They ran it in Brighton. This would have been about 1999, I think, a couple of years after she first disappeared. As soon as I walked in, this man asked me to help make the teas. He said he'd read Edie's story in some of the papers. As I was washing the cups, he said something that has always stayed with me. He said, "It's all right for you, isn't it? You still have hope. You don't know what it's like for us. You can't even begin to imagine.""

'That seems harsh.'

'The point is, she's not dead. She's missing. The loss is a limbo. It's fucking purgatory.'

I take another sip of beer. A plane crosses the sky, trailing white vapour. I wonder where it's going.

'You know, I might be able to help you,' I say. 'I'm a therapist. I mainly deal with anxiety disorders, OCD, stuff like that. If I can—'

'Aw, that's nice of you, pet. But you're about twenty years too late. I've had psychologists and psychoanalysts and forty-pound-an-hour hypnotists look inside my brain and all of them have said the same thing. *There's nothing wrong with you, you just need to move on.* Okay, I'd say, sure. Tell me how I'm meant to do that. You know what happens next?'

'Nope.'

Samantha makes her face go slack, her mouth fall open, aping stupidity. She lowers her voice and says, 'Uh, gee, Mrs Hudson, uh, we can't really help you with that part. That'll be nine hundred pounds, please.' She smiles, breaking the charade. It doesn't soften her face, that smile. It simply changes it without emotion, like arithmetic.

'I get it,' I tell her, draining my bottle of beer. 'Trauma freezes you. It makes you a rock in a river. The water flows around it, sometimes fast, sometimes slow, but the rock doesn't move. It can't. It's stuck in one particular point in time, just getting worn down by the constant pressure.'

She looks at me carefully. I know that look. It's cautious, but not hopeful. Kindred.

'That's exactly it,' she says. 'Fuck.'

'That'll be nine hundred pounds, please,' I say, imitating her, and we both laugh throatily.

'You want another, Kim?' she asks me, pulling a bottle from her bag. I hesitate, but only for a moment. I can smell the alcohol coming off her, her eyes slightly glazed-looking. She's already on her way to being drunk. Still, who can blame her? I take the bottle. She watches me uncap it the same way she did, against the edge of a lighter.

She laughs. 'That's a wasted childhood right there.'

'Yeah,' I tell her. 'By the time I was fifteen I could roll a joint blindfolded and had six types of fake ID. I wasn't a good kid.'

'Well, you seem to have turned out okay.' She smiles at me again. Her narrow eyes are faded, washed-out sea glass. 'I saw Edie going down a similar path. I always wonder how she would have turned out. Oh, don't get me wrong. She was a good kid—'

There's a hesitation there. I hear it a lot. It's pre-emptive, a 'but' you forget to swallow. *He hit me but I provoked it. I want to but I'm frightened. She was a good kid, but she made bad choices.*

'But what?'

'Nothing. Just that. She was a good kid.'

The silence settles softly between us again. She lights another cigarette and points it towards the church wall running opposite. Just visible beyond it is a low roof. 'See that house? This man' – she jerks her cigarette in the direction of Tony Marston's grave – 'thought the man who lived there had something to do with Edie's disappearance. He was convinced of it.'

I think I know his name but I ask her the question anyway, because after all I am 'Kim', just a stranger in a churchyard with no prior knowledge of Edie Hudson's disappearance. I have to keep up the pretence. Another thing I've got good at. 'Oh yeah? Who was he?'

'Peter Liverly. He was the groundskeeper here, among other things. He helped at the youth club Edie and her friends went to from time to time. I only met him once. He invited me into the empty church with a dead rabbit in his hands.'

'Wow.'

'Yeah. I just thought he was a bit strange, like most people did. When the police took him in for questioning they searched that house and found a stash of photographs he'd taken of Edie and her friends over here in the churchyard and the hall. He'd been hiding in his bedroom and taking pictures through a gap in the curtains.'

I shiver. What a creep.

'Heard a rumour that one of Edie's friends once saw him in the bushes with his camera in one hand and his dick in the other.'

'Urgh. Is that true?'

'Who knows? When he was released it caused so much trouble that after a while he went to live with his son. He's still there, as far as I know. The house kept getting trashed so in the end his son boarded it up and left it, and now no one wants to live there because it needs so much work. Besides, mud sticks, right?'

I nod. Second time I've heard that phrase recently. How true it is.

'They never charged him?'

'Taking photos without consent isn't illegal, even of minors. They had no evidence that he had anything to do with Edie's disappearance, although I don't know what that was based on.'

I wonder how hard the police looked for her, really. I searched the slim volume of press cuttings from Edie's disappearance, noted the way they'd spoken about her and her mother. The insinuation had been that she was a neglected, uncontrollable child without boundaries. 'No angel', they'd said. I look at Samantha, who is still staring at the house over the wall, thumb absent-mindedly rubbing at a slim scar running diagonally across the palm of her hand.

'You know, I sometimes think – what if he had kept her in there? Like that guy in Austria?'

'Josef Fritzl? You mean, like, in a basement?'

She shrugs. 'Maybe. I mean, who would know, right?'

'But the police searched the house.'

'But they were only looking for photos. What if they missed something? A trapdoor in the floorboards? Or – or what if they didn't look in the loft? You think they checked those places out? The garage or the shed?'

'I don't know.'

'Listen, Kim. One thing I am very sure of is that when girls like Edie disappear, they don't funnel money into a big search operation. They see it as one less troublemaker on the streets. Sure, there'll be a nod towards good police work – I mean, they took the local creep in for questioning – but the reality is you get the occasional phone call and a detective with a weak heart.'

She nods towards Tony's grave and turns to me. She is smiling tightly. Her wavy hair is grey and wild as steel wool.

I consider her for a moment before saying, 'You think he hid your daughter in there?'

'I said *might* have.' She's slurring, but only a little. She drains her drink and slumps in her seat. 'I nearly broke in once, but I bottled it. That was years ago, when you could climb in through the back windows. The son put up better security after that. He was concerned someone would burn it down.'

'Why didn't you?'

'Go in there?' Samantha looks at me glassily, unsmiling. 'I used to have a recurring dream about it. It was always snowing in those dreams, and my footsteps were totally silent. I could hear Edie calling me from inside the house, so I'd sneak in through the broken window. Inside, it was so dark you couldn't see. The house was a maze, like a rabbit warren. I had to just creep blindly along the walls, following the sound of her voice. But I never reached her.'

'That's awful.'

'I used to think I'd let Edie down in so many ways, but the worst of it was I always felt that I hadn't looked for her hard enough.'

I smile grimly. She looks away, back towards the house. 'The dream frightened me so much I never went in, and because I never went in I spent years feeling as if I hadn't searched properly for her. It's a – what do you call it – a self-fulfilling prophecy, right?'

'Do you still feel like that?'

Samantha lights another cigarette. Her face is lined in that harsh way that smokers carry, like carvings in the skin.

'Always,' she says.

We're both silent for a moment. I wish I could take her hand. I wish I could help her.

'So, go on then. You're a therapist. How do I move on from that?'

Something ignites inside me – a low burn, like a pilot light, a flickering blue flame. 'Well, in CBT – that is, uh, Cognitive Behavioural Therapy – we recommend exposure therapy. Facing your fears.'

'Huh. Makes sense.'

'But we do it in increments. So in your case, the first step would be walking up to the house. The next, standing beside it for a full minute. Then opening the door. Then going inside. You get the idea.'

'Sounds like a lot of work.'

'It is. It's not easy. Hardest work you'll ever do is on yourself.'

'I've never been one for hard work. Maybe that's my problem.'

'Is that right?'

'Uh-huh.'

I finish my drink. I can feel the weight of what's going to happen, the way it feels as if the two of us are on an edge, tilting forward. I look across at her, this wild-haired older woman, her face hard and set and sombre.

'I'll come with you, if you want,' I hear myself say, because I am always spoiling for trouble, like Samantha, like Edie.

She looks my way, lips curling into something resembling a smile.

'Oh yeah?' she says.

The little bungalow has been empty a long time. It's accessible only from the road, so Samantha and I leave the churchyard and find ourselves in front of the high privet hedges that have grown around it almost as high as the roof. The little wooden gate has rotted away, the wood soft and spongy beneath my fingers. Somewhere in the trees behind the house a magpie chatters.

'See how the windows are boarded up?' Samantha says, pointing. Her voice is low, whispering. There are iron sheets over the windows, riveted into place. A sign in the top-left corner of one reads: *This Private Property is Under Surveillance.* Underneath, someone has written in marker, *Didn't see this tho, did U?*

There's other graffiti too, on the brickwork and reinforced front door. Tags, mainly, or big peace signs irregularly drawn. Someone has scrawled *The Beast* in large, irregular letters along the boarded windows. There's a twinkling litter of glass in the lawn, crunching beneath our feet. Samantha explains that the windows were repeatedly smashed until they were boarded up.

She lights a cigarette, looking for all the world like a woman at peace with herself in front of faded graffiti which reads *Burn In HEll U sick FUk!*

'"Nothing gets more tarnished than a reputation." That's what my brother said.' She tests the boards with her finger. They don't budge.

'I don't think we're going to get in this way,' I tell her, and she nods in agreement.

'Let's try round the back,' she says.

I know something's wrong as soon as we turn the corner of the house. It's a tingling, like excitement. It's dark back here in the shadow of the tall hedges and oaks of the churchyard. Samantha points out the window from which he took his photographs, the one that overlooks the churchyard. Other trespassers have left a lot of litter on the ground; broken bottles and cans and fast-food wrappers bagged and swung up into the hedge, where they hang like foul fruit. I stand on the ancient, blackened remains of something set on fire and left to burn out. I can smell something rotten, as if an animal has crawled into the long grass to die. The shed roof has fallen in, the glass panes smashed and tools presumably stolen. I duck my head in through the crooked door. In the corner, a rat's nest, long empty. A strand of cobweb brushes my face softly, like a whisper.

It's only as I pull my head out that I realise Samantha is speaking to me. 'I've been calling you! Didn't you hear me? Look, over here. There's a gap in the boards. Looks like someone already managed to sneak in a while back. Come on.'

I pause, swallowing drily. I don't like how dark it is back here in the shade. I don't like the way the house seems to be waiting gravely, like a doctor about to deliver bad news. *What if she is in there? I think to myself. Have you even thought about that, Frances? What if you find her body in a freezer all wrapped in plastic, lips frozen and blue and cold? What will you say to Samantha then?*

Samantha is standing beside a window where one of the boards has been peeled away from the lower corner. She glances over at me, one hand fumbling in her pocket.

'Hey, Samantha, wait—' I begin, and then I'm quickly cut off by someone shoving against me, pinning me up against the wall. It's her. Samantha. Her forearm presses against my windpipe and I make a noise like a tea kettle when I try to scream.

'Do you think I'm fucking stupid?' she asks.

I struggle – I haven't been in a fight for a good long time, but Samantha must be nearly twenty years my senior and I once put a man in hospital after he tried to mug me. I get a grip on her arm and am about to shove her away with the heel of my hand when I see what she was reaching into her pocket for. She has a knife pressed against me. I lower my hands. To be pierced by that thin blade would be painful. Samantha sees I've noticed, and grunts.

She held a knife up to William's throat, dummy, my brain tells me. I wonder how I could have been so stupid as to think coming back here with her to this deserted place would ever have been a good idea.

'Just now I was calling you over and over again,' Samantha says, her breath on my cheek. 'And you never turned around. I know that Kim isn't your name. I knew right away. Why are you lying to me, huh?'

I slump against the wall. Her pupils are tiny pinpricks floating on the glassy ocean of her eyes.

'It's a small town, honey,' she spits, 'so tell me who you are.'

'Okay, okay!'

Samantha releases the pressure from my windpipe, but only a little. The knife stays where it is against my ribs. A pea-sized drop of blood soaks into the fabric of my T-shirt where the blade has punctured my skin.

'My name is Frances Thorn. I'm married to William.'

'Uh-huh. I know who he is. And what you said about his mother – Mimi? She's really sick?'

'Yes! Please, Samantha, just back off a bit.' My voice shimmers with fear. She looks at me warily but steps back. I exhale, hands trembling.

'William Thorn, huh? Always wondered what kind of woman he would end up with. I always thought he had a *type*.'

I think again of the photograph I've seen of Edie Hudson, the one that reminded me so much of Kim and Samira: the dark hair, the haughtiness. *Oh, he has a type*, I think.

'His dad. Edward Thorn. What do you know about him?'

'Put the knife away and I'll tell you.'

She studies me for a moment before letting the blade slide back into the handle. She keeps the knife in her hand, though. I can tell how comfortable she is with it. It must be exhausting to be on your guard all the time.

'I know he died in a car crash. I know he didn't try to get out, even as the car was sinking. The boys don't talk about him much.'

'The boys?'

'William and Alex.'

'Oh yeah, the brother. The younger one. He's an oddball, isn't he? Still at home with his mum. It's all a bit Norman Bates.'

Something catches my eye. Movement in the hedgerow behind her, a rustle of leaves. Briefly, I see the rabbit bolt for the safety of the shadows, eyes like beads of obsidian.

Samantha is still talking. 'Edward Thorn. You want to know something about him? His car was seen at the church the night

Edie went missing. I chased and chased the police to get him to give a statement, and what do you know? Not a month later he's dead. Drove right off the bridge. Then he's dead and any evidence in that car got washed away. Huh. He told me it was my fault Edie ran away, and you know, some days I think he was right.'

'You think he had something to do with her disappearance?'

'You tell me.'

'Samantha, I never met him.'

'But you're married to one of his boys. They must talk about him. What kind of man he was. A drinker, a shouter, a saint. You must know. They must have said something.'

I'm thinking. I'm thinking about the only things I know about Edward Thorn. About the well he filled in after retrieving the sheep skull from the bottom so his youngest son could display it on the shelf above his bed. About the sacks of bonemeal out in the green-house and Mimi whispering, 'He boiled the bones in pots on the stove.'

'I don't – I can't help you, Samantha.'

'So why are you here? Why have you been having cosy little chats with Nancy Renard in the cafe and asking me about Edie as if you don't already know all about her?'

'I *didn't* already know! I swear! First I ever heard about her was the day we arrived, when I found the photo. Honestly, Samantha!'

'What photo?'

I pull my phone from my bag and flick through until I find the one of the Rattlesnakes and William and Alex in the bright sunshine. When I show it to her I see the wince of pain it causes. I imagine she's never had the chance to see it before. It must hurt. I look down at the place where the knife has pricked me and try to imagine that small sharp pain over and over again, for eighteen years, slowly slicing into your heart.

'I found this at Thorn House. I've never seen William at that age. That's why I took it, because I thought he looked funny. I didn't know about Edie or Peter Liverly or any of this until then.'

She looks at me suspiciously. I can see she wants a cigarette. Just moments ago my fear was huge and vivid – a technicolour cartoon explosion – but now it is ebbing away.

I reach towards her. 'Put the knife away, Samantha. I meant it when I said I want to help you.'

'Why? You don't know me!' Aggressive again. Stepping right up close to me so I can feel her breath on my face.

I lift my hands, try to keep my voice calm. 'William's having an affair.'

That magpie, the sound it makes is rough, like a dog barking. Not like a bird at all. We stare at each other, Samantha and I. I swallow carefully. 'I found out just before his mum had a fall. He doesn't know that I know.'

'Why not?'

'I haven't had a chance to confront him with it. She's nineteen.'

'He's sleeping with a nineteen-year-old?'

'No, not – he's not sleeping with her. Not yet, at least. He's giving her money. For photos.'

A beat. Samantha nods. 'How do you feel about that?'

'She said he's paying for her to go to university. He buys her presents. Expensive ones. We're meant to be saving up for a baby.'

'That doesn't answer my question. How do you feel about that?'

'I – I don't know.' How can I articulate the feeling of betrayal? I don't have the language for it. It makes me want to scream. I feel the anger like a pressure on my chest, one I've been feeling since I found the memory stick in the box room.

'You going to leave him?'

'I don't know.'

'So you're using this, my daughter, as some sort of distraction?'

'No, no. It's not like th—'

'You know, I walked in on them once, eighteen years ago. William and Edie. He had his hands in her underwear.'

I don't know how to respond to that. Samantha grabs fistfuls of her hair and ties it up with a band, knotting it on top of her head. Her anger is palpable, coming towards me in waves.

'I asked him to show my daughter some respect. Looks like he still hasn't learned. I'm sorry to hear about Mimi, though. When Edie went missing Mimi used to come and check up on me, even after her husband died. "Us women have got to look out for each other," she said. Shame she couldn't instil her values in those boys of hers.'

A noise then, making us both jump. Our heads switch round to the house. There's a scraping sound, like a lock turning. Then, a soft thud. We exchange a glance.

'Someone's inside,' I whisper.

Samantha nods. Suddenly I am glad she has that knife. I wonder if people are squatting in there. I did it myself for a few years in my late teens. Samantha pulls her phone from her pocket and, using it as a torch, shines it through the gap in the boarding. The edges of the metal are rusty and sharp. We peer inside. The room is blue-dark and murky, like sunlight on the seabed. We can see the shrouded shapes of furniture covered in dust sheets and a doorway that appears to lead out into a hall. We both strain to listen, hearts in our throats.

Finally Samantha says, 'I'm going in.'

'I thought you were afraid.'

'I am. I'm terrified. But like you said, it's exposure therapy, right?'

'Not like this, Samantha. Jesus!'

She doesn't wait for me. She leans against the boarding, which gives a long, metallic shriek as it tears away from the window frame.

With one foot braced against the wall she hauls herself through the narrow gap, landing with a thud on the other side. I see her lit by the glow of her phone screen for just a moment, then it cuts off. The darkness swarms in. I lean through, reaching out my arm into the cold, still darkness. My hand gropes empty air.

'Samantha?'

There's no reply. No sound at all. I lean in further and the smell of the house hits me. Mould and rot, the sweetly cloying smell of rising damp. Beneath my weight the metal hoarding groans, my feet scrabbling for purchase on the brickwork. I'm thinking of Samantha's dreams buried in the soft darkness, the maze, the bloodless voice calling her name, and I'm suddenly breathless with fear.

'Samantha? Can you hear me? Samantha?'

It's cold in there. It has that strange, deserted quality that houses left empty for some time possess: a vacancy, almost a grief. There's a pattering sound in the hallway, like running water, or fast-moving feet. My blood chills.

'Samantha, for fu—'

A hand, reaching out of the blackness, circling my wrist in a sharp, snapping motion. I scream.

'Shut up, for God's sake! I'm trying to listen!' She tugs at me, hard. 'If you're not coming in, then piss off home, Frances.'

I almost do. I make it as far as the furthest corner of the house, where long arching fingers of buddleia brush against my face. What stops me is the graffiti I find written there, almost obscured by a clump of stinging nettles. The rust-coloured paint has run and faded, but the message is still legible: *Where is Edie Hudson???*

I catch the collar of my coat on the raw edge of the bent metal and hear a satisfying *rrrrip* sound as I drag myself through the gap and into the bungalow. Glass crunches as I land awkwardly, twisting my ankle beneath me. Dust settles in my throat and sinuses, making me want to sneeze. *What are you doing?* the sensible voice in my head shrieks. *All this just to spite William? All this just to dig into his past? Go home, Frances.*

As my eyes adjust to the dark I see Samantha in the doorway, her back to me. Some of the dust sheets are spattered with paint and damp, giving them an eerie Rorschach effect. It gives me a jolting memory of William and me on our holiday in Tenerife, drinking sweet red cocktails and watery pina coladas. He asked me if I ever used ink-blot tests in my work.

'Rorschach?' I said, stirring my cocktail idly. 'That's psychology. It's a different type of therapy. I don't do that.'

'Shame,' he answered. 'I always wanted to try.'

I picked up the napkin beneath my glass and, eyes fixed firmly on William's as I did so, poured a little of my cocktail in the crease, folding it carefully before opening it before him.

He studied the dark mirror image for a moment before lifting his head and looking right at me. 'I see *you*,' he said. When he took my hand I felt something blooming in my stomach, a warmth, a sticky, carnivorous love.

When I reach Samantha, I see what she is looking at. Someone has drawn a swastika on the wall. They've made a bad job of it and paint has run down into the floorboards. There is a hole in the door leading to the kitchen, like someone has put a fist through it. More scuffling in the corridor and the sound of a door creaking slowly closed. *Or open*, a little internal voice speaks up. I put my hand on Samantha's shoulder.

'Do you smell it?' she asks me.

I nod. Something has died and rotted away somewhere in this house. I'm reminded of a story I heard once about a remote asylum in Ohio. An inmate there disappeared, the body eventually found in the attic over a month later. When the decomposing corpse was removed, they found a stain beneath it; a ghostly outline of the body in chalky white, and no matter how hard workers tried to clean the floor, the stain would not come out.

'Back then, the whole graveyard smelt like this,' Samantha tells me in a low whisper. 'He was killing rabbits and just leaving them to rot.'

'What do you think it is?'

'Well, Frances, I'm no pathologist, but I think there's a dead body down there.'

'But – but you know it can't be Edie, right? She's been gone almost twenty years.'

Samantha turns towards me in the darkness. I see the flat glaze of her eyes. 'Well, then, we'd better go and see who it is, hadn't we?'

Together we sidle down the hallway, backs pressed against the wall where the flowered paper peels away in long strips to reveal grey plaster, damp to the touch. The smell of urine and rot is stronger out here. As we creep towards the kitchen I can see the units have been destroyed; cupboard doors hang from hinges and gas pipes jut through the wall, black holes like wide, unblinking eyes. I can see the place where the sink once stood, and the cooker, and the fridge: the large pale outlines against the dark walls like the ghosts of furniture past. I think of that dead woman turning to liquid in the asylum attic and the imprint that can never be cleaned away and I reach for Samantha, squeezing her hand so hard she gasps. Her skin is icy, and there is a tremor running through her. She's afraid.

Across the bumpy lino of the kitchen floor is another door, partly open, revealing a slice of black space. The rustling sound is coming from inside. We exchange a glance. Samantha pulls the knife from her pocket and together we cross the room as quietly as we can, trying to ignore the fetid smell that is rising up from the basement like something corroded and black.

It's Samantha who eases the door open carefully, allowing us room to slide through. The stairs creak ominously, and the darkness is thick and so dense that I feel I might reach out and stroke it. The smell is the worst of it, so putrid it is almost toxic. Sweet, like spoiled meat. *I want to go back*, I try to say, *I want to get out into the light and the clean air*. Something bad has happened down here, something unspeakable. This whole house is an open wound, festering. Someone should burn it to the fucking ground.

'God!' Samantha suddenly cries out, jumping in horror. I feel the panic run through her and almost turn and bolt back up the stairs.

Instead I hear my voice, high-pitched, scared, saying, 'What? What is it?'

'Something just – it got hold of my foot!'

Bile, rising in my throat. Samantha fumbles in the darkness and in that moment when she lets go of my hand the darkness and isolation feel so total I could be adrift in deep space. I resist the urge to reach out for her, panicky. Adrenaline, bright in my mouth and behind my eyes, purple pulses in the darkness. Suddenly Samantha's face is lit by her phone screen and she swivels it outward in order to see the basement better.

A litter of newspaper across the floor, a stack of mildewy boxes in the corner, collapsing in on themselves. Shelves hanging ragged on the walls, brick walls slick with condensation, and mould spots black as tar.

'See? There!'

I look where Samantha is pointing. A rat, a big one, bristly body and thick pink tail, suddenly darting for the safety of the shadows. She runs the light along the ground, picking out discarded carrier bags and stacks of yellowed magazines turning to pulp in the damp. Then, we see it.

We both recoil. Samantha makes a noise in the back of her throat, *urk!*, and for a second I think she is going to be sick. I run my hands over my face, stomach turning queasily. The dog must have been lying down here for some time, judging by the ragged remains. Partially skeletal, glimpses of bone through blackened skin. Where its stomach should be is just a cavity, torn apart by ferocious rodent teeth. There is a pool of dried blood beneath it on which flies settle and lift. Something long and purple has unspooled from the hole in its stomach. It makes me think of the sheep in the well, rotting to liquid while a young boy peered over the edge, fascinated. I look away, my hand over my mouth, the taste of the beer I've drunk rising in my throat. Samantha approaches the dog and peers at it. For a moment I wonder what the hell she is doing, and then she turns and looks at me over her shoulder.

'No collar,' she says sadly. 'Poor little guy. Must've been the rats we heard. There's probably hundreds of them eating off this thing.'

Behind Samantha, pushed against the far brick wall, is a long chest freezer. I'm flooded with a sudden dread, a brisk shiver. The image I had earlier of Edie Hudson lying wrapped in her plastic burial shroud – lips blued and dusted with frost, eyes like blank pennies – surfaces suddenly in my mind. Samantha is dusting herself down and telling me we should get out of there.

I point behind her and say, in as normal a voice as I can manage, 'Check in there.'

Samantha sees the freezer and I notice her face change, even in the weak light of the phone. There's a falling-away, like a shelf of Arctic ice. Her eyes seem to marble; it's frightening to look at. It's like something inside her has been punctured and everything that's vital is being slowly sucked away. I walk over to her and put my hand on her shoulder.

'I c-c-can't—' she stutters, shaking her head, stepping away from me, crossing her arms over her chest. 'Frances, I can't look in there, I can't.'

'Okay,' I tell her. 'I'll do it.'

I think she will stop me. I almost want her to, and then we can get out of this pit and into the sunlight. I want to shower in water so hot it leaves my skin pink and boiled. Tonight I know I will have bad dreams, of dead dogs dragging themselves towards me, muzzles foaming with decay, of dead girls with skin turned blue with cold, opening their mouths and blasting me with chips of ice that slice into my skin again and again and again.

They say what you don't know can't hurt you. How stupid, I've always thought. Knowledge is power. I get it now, though. As I put my fingers under the lid of the large freezer and lean in to lift it, I get it. Behind me, Samantha is breathing fast, almost panting. She has retreated to the foot of the stairs, where she stands hunched over herself, just the flat sheen of her eyes visible in the darkness. Just as I heave the lid open I'm almost sure that what I will find in here is not Edie but Quiet Mary, her bones rattling like dice.

I shine the phone in. The beam of light trembles. What I see makes me weak with relief. I almost laugh.

I turn to Samantha. 'It's empty,' I say.

She begins to laugh and then it abruptly changes to harsh, choking sobs, so sudden I don't know how to respond. I see her buckle, sliding down the damp wall to sit on the bottom stair, clutching herself, hair worked free of her bun and hanging in her face. I cross the room quickly, trying not to cry out when I connect with something soft and yielding underfoot, and kneel in front of her. For a little while she is crying so hard I can't make her words out. I shush her ineffectively, patting her shoulder, stroking her hair. 'It's all right,' I say. 'It's okay, Samantha. Edie wasn't in there.'

By the time she catches her breath the violent shaking has stopped and her face no longer has that dead, slack look that so unnerved me. She wipes her eyes with the heels of her hands and just as I am about to ask her if she is all right, she snaps, 'Let's get out of here.'

◆ ◆ ◆

We find a nearby pub. We must look a sight, the two of us, staggering into the Queen's Arms with dirt-streaked faces and cuts all over our hands from scrambling out through rusty metal boards. As I order a couple of pints – 'and two whisky chasers,' Samantha adds, 'doubles' – she flexes her hands and says drily, 'I hope you've had your tetanus shots.'

We take a seat in a booth with high-backed wooden pews and sit and stare at each other, draining our glasses quickly and ordering another round. The music is loud but the pub is quiet, with only a few old boys playing darts in the furthest corner. Samantha is spinning a bar mat on its corner, flipping it, sliding it around the table. She doesn't meet my eye.

'I'm sorry,' she says evenly, when she comes back inside from smoking her third cigarette. 'I went to pieces a bit. That hasn't happened for a long time. Took me by surprise.'

'Sam—'

She holds up her hand. 'I'm happy the freezer was empty. Of course I am. I want you to understand that, okay? If Edie had been in there I don't know what I would have done. Screamed the place down, probably. Set fire to it. I don't know. But at least—' She searches for the words, fiddling with her necklace, and even though I know what she's going to say, even though I can see her discomfort, I let her because she has to be able to say it. 'At least if she'd been in that freezer I would have *known*. Edie was fifteen years old the day she disappeared. I've thought about her every day since. You know how hard that is?'

I shake my head.

'When she was born I nearly handed her back to the midwife. "You take her, I don't want her. She frightens me. I made a mistake. I don't want her." God. When I think of it now—'

'But how could you have known?'

'I'm a fucking monster. No, really.' She laughs, shaking her head as I start to refute her. 'I am and it's okay. It is. That's what I think about every day. Her, a newborn, unknowing and innocent, and me, saying over and over, "I don't want her."'

She gulps for air, teary-eyed. I look at her, feeling my own tears burning in my throat. I think of the empty box room at home, the one I've been hopefully calling the 'nursery' for nearly four years. I turn thirty-four next year, just a year older than Edie would be now if she hadn't spirited herself away. I'm running out of time. I don't think of myself as maternal but sometimes I see a woman with a baby strapped to her chest or pushing a pram and something *clenches* inside me, a pain so great it is almost a bereavement. I see Samantha's pain reflected in my own, that feeling of loss and separation, and I realise that this is the root of my rage, the one that burns red-hot, scorching through my insides. It's not William's betrayal. It's the loss. The baby. Our baby. The one he's never had any intention of giving me.

I reach across the table and take Samantha's hands in mine, cocooning them. We sit that way a long time, and the sky begins to darken outside.

By the time I get back to Thorn House it is gone seven, and William has left increasingly agitated messages on my phone. *Where are you? What time will you be home? I'm getting worried, Frances, call me.* I walk calmly into the kitchen, my head a little clouded with booze, and see William sitting at the dining table. The smell of rosemary and garlic sweetens the air. I put my bag on the chair, rubbing the back of my neck.

'Smells good.'

William looks up at me, dark-eyed and serious. 'I was worried about you. You should have called.'

'I just lost track of time. Is this food left for me?'

'You've been gone for hours,' he snaps, before adding, 'Yes. Doubt it'll still be warm.'

'How's your mum?'

'Alex is in there with her now. It's been difficult today. She thinks she's back in Blackpool in 1963. Keeps asking for a go on the Ferris wheel.'

I uncover the plate left for me on the counter. It's pasta with a tomato sauce, rich and thick and glossy, but my appetite curdles at the sight of it. I don't think I could eat another of those greenhouse tomatoes, fat and red, nurtured by black dirt and bonemeal, the scraps of living things. I put the plate back over it and pour myself a glass of water instead.

'Where have you been? You stink of booze.'

He comes up behind me and clatters his dirty plate into the sink. The problem with William and Alex is that they were brought up like tiny kings, who never needed to do anything as menial as housework. When William first moved in with me I had to teach him how to hoover and iron his own clothes. Mimi still thought of them as her little boys, even after they developed chest hair and their voices dropped. I watch him do it, and say nothing. I've told him before I'm not his cleaner.

'I was in the pub.'

'You should have said. I could've done with a drink myself.' He lifts my hands, turning them over to study my palms. They are scratched and blotchy, cold to the touch. 'What have you been doing, Frances? Who were you with?'

'I need to go and have a shower, William.'

Too late. He spots the rip in the collar of my coat and lifts it with the tip of his finger. His eyes travel down my body and rest on the small bloodstain on my T-shirt.

'You're hurt,' he says flatly, lifting the material to reveal the small, star-shaped puncture wound clotted over with dried blood. 'And you're shaking.'

I'm angry. Inside, I'm a blizzard of cold, hard rage. It buckles me, twisting my organs into hard, calcified objects like crystals found under the earth. I am slowly turning to stone.

'Frances, what's going on? Please talk to me.'

I look up. His face is so linear; the long line of his nose, the sharp edges of his cheekbones flaring against his skin. He is a man of angles and mathematics, cold logic. He compartmentalises; that's always been his problem. Isolates himself. I open my mouth to tell him the truth of it – *I wanted a baby and you took my chance away and you're spending all our savings on a girl on a screen and you lied to me, you lied, you lied* – but then he says something that knocks me back on my heels.

'Do you remember when we first met, Frances?'

I stare at him. 'Yes. You took me to the cinema. We watched *Slumdog Millionaire*.'

'No. That was our first date. Before that. When we *met*.'

I stiffen. Why is he bringing this up now? I feel a cold frost creeping up my arms. 'Yes,' I say. My voice is very small.

William reaches up a hand and tucks a stray hair behind my ear very, very gently. 'It's almost like you had a twin,' he continues, in that same soft voice, 'but you killed her. Isn't it?'

I don't speak. I just look at him. There is no trace of the person I was when William and I first met. I razed her to the ground.

'You remember the old you, Frances? What do you think she would make of you now? I often wonder.'

'I don't. I don't ever think about it.' *Not true.* That bright blue paint in long, looping spatters. The way the word had been written in letters four feet high across the hallway. *Whore.* 'Why are you bringing this up, William?'

'Alex said you'd been looking through the old photos. He mentioned that you'd been asking questions about it. About me, and my old friends. About Edie. I suppose I thought if you wanted to rake over my past we may as well do yours as well.'

'That's not fair.'

'No?'

'No! I was – that wasn't me. Not who I am, not really.' *If you keep telling yourself that, one day it will be true*, I think coldly.

When I think back to the day I met William Thorn for the first time, the memory is slippery and black as an eel. It comes to me in a series of images: the big house in a small town on Osborne Road, brickwork and windows blackened by soot, the sound of the door buzzer like an angry insect, the bed that sagged in the middle, the coldness of the mattress in the winter, a pile of used tissues, waking with the taste of cocaine in the back of my throat, cold sores, the thinness of the curtains that let the light through. Tiny flats with paper-thin walls. Worn carpet. The couple next door who had grinding, panicky sex that seemed to last forever. They spoke a fast, urgent language that might have been Polish. I don't know.

A man followed me home one night. I remember blurred lights and chewing gum, my jaw clenched and aching. MDMA. No, speed. It doesn't matter. He started talking to me, the man. Telling me I looked familiar. He started off nice but it soon turned nasty. What's your name? Where do you work? We know each other, don't we? Have we fucked? We have, haven't we? Hey, hey, look at me. Look at me. We're just talking. Don't be shy. You do it for money, eh? I remember you. Sweet girl. Nice tits. Don't – don't ignore me. Come on, come on, baby. Are you still at that place – Osborne Road, yeah? You heading there now? You working there now? Fifty. Fifty. It's all I've got. It's cash. You can get something nice with that. Hey, where you going? You don't need to be rude.

Running home, inside, up the stairs. Keys in my fist, jutting out between my fingers. Imagine a world with no men in it, and you could walk at night and simply not worry. I double-lock my bedroom door. In the morning, blue paint, all the way down the hallway. A single word: *Whore.* There were handprints all over the bannisters in that same blue, the colour of lapis lazuli. Looking at it made me feel sick. The man who lived downstairs came to help me scrub it off, rubber gloves and white spirit, his terrible jokes, designed to make me smile. William means 'resolute protector'. I found that out after he'd introduced himself. I looked it up. Small towns strangle you; so many hands at your throat. I moved away, big city this time. I kept William's number, hidden away between the pages of a book. I didn't find it for another seventeen months and then I didn't call him for another three. Mud sticks. That's all I know.

'Do you know why I'm bringing this up now?' he asks me.

I shake my head.

'Because the past is the past. I know you're probably wondering why I didn't tell you about Edie, but honestly, Frances – cross my heart – I never think about her. I didn't treat her well, and when I dumped her she was mad about it. Talked about getting her mum's knife and cutting me' – when he says that I have a brief flash of Samantha holding the knife against me, the blood blooming on my T-shirt – 'having me beaten up. All kinds of stuff. We were teenagers. You must remember what that was like?'

'It was very different for me,' I remind him. 'I had to grow up very fast. I had no family.'

'No, but look how far you've come. You're a warrior, Frances Thorn.' He smiles but I'm not mollified. I can still feel the hot pulse of my fury.

'Do you love me, William?'

'More than anything.'

'What have you been spending our money on?'

'What money?' Smooth. Careful.

'The money we put aside for the baby.'

'Okay.' He presses the palms of his hands together and holds his fingertips to his lips. He's looking at me earnestly. 'I might have lost a little on the poker. I thought I'd be able to pay it back before you noticed and, you know, I'm an arsehole, I should have told yo—'

'William—'

'I know. I know. I'm a sad old man. But that money was just sitting there anyway, not doing anything.'

'But you promised me. "We'll try for a baby this year." You *swore*.'

'I did, I know. I know.'

'You'll have to pay it back. We'll need it, won't we? For when the baby comes.'

He's silent and for a moment I forget about Kim – my trump card in her pale pink bra and sheer knickers – and watch him shift uneasily in the beam of my irritation.

'William?'

'I never promised you that.'

I stare at him, tears brimming. Even though I've already figured this out it still hurts to hear it from him.

He looks away from me. 'Can't we just wait and see what happens?'

'That is what we've been doing!' I yell, piston-straight, my head pounding. 'And here we are, still doing it six years later! You lied to me then and you're lying to me now!'

'Frances, I swear to you—'

'You don't know what it's like, to feel like this,' I tell him. I'm forcing myself to be composed but it's hard, it's hard. 'To want something so much it hurts. You have no idea!' He studies me, head tilted. 'You were never going to agree, were you? You're just here waiting out the clock, right? If we wait another year I'll be giving birth at thirty-five. By the time the baby goes to school I'll be forty. By the time it goes to university I'll be sixty. Even if I leave you and I'm lucky enough to meet someone else I would have kids with, how long will that process take? Four years? Six? Longer?'

He reaches for me and I brush him aside. I can barely speak without my voice shaking. Anger, burning my throat like acid.

'Frances, I don't know what to say.'

'What you should say is what you should have said six years ago. "I don't want kids." It would have saved all of this! Why lie to me?'

'Because I had nothing else to offer you! I wasn't exciting. I didn't take risks. I hated the parties you went to and the people you hung out with. I hated the drugs you took – cocaine made you nasty, ketamine made you boring. All I had in my favour was my security. That, I could give you.'

'But it's not enough. And you knew that. And you did it anyway. You're a fucking monster.'

I pick up my drink, knocking him aside with my shoulder as I push past him. I hear Alex open the door to the dining room and ask William what the hell is going on in here, Mum's trying to sleep, but already I'm pushing open the back door and heading into the inky soft night, the grass damp under my hot, bare feet, stars glittering in the vast sky above. Tears blur my vision and my breathing, ragged, uneven, makes a rasping sound in my throat. I find the place where the hammock has been strung between two old apple trees, the ropes of it greyed with age, and sit there, head down, letting the sobs come, letting them slowly erode my defences as the moon rises between the branches of the trees.

William finds me an hour or so later. By this time I am lying on my back, one leg hanging over the side of the hammock, nudging it from side to side. I don't respond to his presence, or his questions, and I pretend not to notice the concern on his face as he squats down beside me.

'I know about Kim, William. I went to see her.'

'Who?'

'*Rattlesnake80*,' I tell him. 'She said that's the name you use.'

Oh boy, the look on his face. It's like watching a meteor impact, like a cave-in. I can almost forget my own pain.

'How long have you known?'

'Since before we came down here.'

A pause. The rasp of his breathing lifts into the air.

'It's just money, Frances. It's a transaction. We've only talked once or twice. I don't even know her real name.'

'It's Kim.'

'Is it? Huh. She doesn't look like a Kim. She was using one of those corny cam-girl names like Dallas or Cherry or something.'

'What did you know about her?'

'Not much. She said she's a student. She wouldn't tell me which university.'

I feel oddly calm. Knowledge is power, after all. William, on the other hand, looks swept away, grey-pallored, almost queasy. *Good; he deserves it.*

'What's it for, William? If it's not sex, what is it?'

'I don't know.'

'You gave away nearly three thousand pounds.'

'I know that, Frances.'

'Why?'

I let him be silent long enough, his eyes downcast.

Finally he says, 'She gave me something you didn't.'

'Oh yeah? What's that?'

'Distance. You were always so intense. Like you were on the verge of a – I don't know, a – a breakdown. Your career, your moods, even the way you had sex – it was always so intense. I just needed to get away from that.'

'Huh.' My temper is a wildfire, fast-spreading and hard to control, always changing direction. But when it burns out, as it inevitably does, I feel washed out. Numb. Fire is cleansing. It purifies. But that doesn't mean I don't want to hurt him back. To sting him like the words will come back and sting me, the sharp pain of them in the middle of the night, at home alone.

I turn my head upward, looking towards the sky. It's high and vaulted, a cathedral ceiling finely painted with silvery clouds and pockets of stars, a perfect crescent moon. I almost expect a seraphim to appear.

'I saw your dad's grave today.'

William immediately bristles. His posture changes, becomes stiffer. His arms fold across his chest. It's that subconscious behaviour again, animating him from within. How well I know it. How well I know him.

'Would you say you two were much alike?'

'Frances, whatever you think you know about my dad—'

'That's the problem, isn't it, William? You've never told me anything.'

'I just – I don't know how to make you understand. I wish I could be more helpful.'

'Then answer the question.'

He thinks for a moment. 'Okay, yes. Very much. From what I remember he was a good, practical man. He liked routine. I know he seemed boring to some, but it was just his way of getting things done.'

'Well, that *is* like you.'

'Yup. It's in the genes.' He laughs weakly.

'Would you say he was capable of keeping secrets?'

William seems to think about it. 'I would have said no. Honesty was his bedrock, really. But then I think about how he was with Alex and that bloody sheep's skull – "Don't tell your mum or she'll kill us" – and I wonder. He was obviously able to keep secrets, so maybe he did have that side to him, although it doesn't sound right. Why do you ask?'

'Just thinking. About you. About deceit.'

'Well, you know what they say. The sins of the father and all that. I like to think he was a good man, an honest one. That he wouldn't have let you down the way I have.'

Silence. All around us, the dark heart of the night.

'Are you going to leave me, Frances?'

He swallows convulsively and I am sure he is about to cry. I can't look at him. I can't answer his question either, because I don't know. I once had a patient who had been experiencing a strange pattern in their behaviour. When their anxiety peaked, as it so often did on public transport, they found themselves buttoning and unbuttoning their coat, almost obsessively. They were barely aware of it, until they looked down at themselves and noticed the movement of their hands. It's a displacement activity, usually seen in animals, a way for the brain to deflect stress or uncertainty. My mind is circling, again and again, back to Edie Hudson, as it has done since I picked up the photo in the shoebox, the one I wasn't supposed to see. My brain picks over the scant details as a way of deflecting from the way my marriage is collapsing, the way the nursery will remain empty, the money we've lost. It's displacement. I welcome it, for now. 'Right now I'd really like to just be on my own, William.'

He gets up silently, walking back towards the house with his hands in his pockets and his head down. I wonder what he's thinking about. Me, I'm thinking about Alex telling me not to mention the photo to William, but then doing so himself. Mostly I'm thinking that a man who drives his car off a bridge and into the river would at least try to remove his seat belt. But Edward Thorn let himself sink to the bottom and didn't make any attempt at escape. A man with no secrets doesn't do that.

In the middle of the night I wake up in bed, mouth dry and furred. William is gently snoring next to me, one hand pinned to his chest. I ease myself out and down the dark hallway, my head cloudy with sleep. In the kitchen I drink straight from the tap, head bent under the faucet. A dark bib of water appears on the neck of my T-shirt. When I stand upright again there is a thin face reflected next to me in the dark window. Coldness rushes through me.

'Is he seeing to those tomatoes again?'

I spin around. It's Mimi. In her long nightdress studded with pink flowers and her bare feet she looks like a Victorian ghost. Her hair is a nebula about her drawn face, her cheeks sunk, deep pools of shadow.

'He'll get cold out there. Get him in, dear.'

She's looking past me, towards the greenhouse. I put a hand on her shoulder. I'm shaking all over, my knees weak and watery.

'Come on, Mimi, back to bed. It's late.'

'He'll catch his death.'

'I'll go and get him in a minute, okay? Through here, that's right. Back into bed.'

'He told me his secret once,' she says, as I pull back the covers. I stare at her in the darkness, blood ringing in my ears. My heart thuds against my ribs. I have a very clear image then of Edward Thorn in his shed at the bottom of the garden with a bag of old bones, grinding them into powder, boiling them in huge pots, bent over the stove. *Tell me, Mimi. Tell me where they came from. Did you know about Edie Hudson?* I look over at her, so pale she is almost transparent. Her eyes are filmy.

I say, very quietly, 'What was the secret, Mimi? Can you remember?'

'He said—' She tilts her head as though listening to a distant voice. 'He said the secret was to feed the soil, not the plant.'

Tamped down by disappointment, I tuck her in, pulling the covers up to her neck. What had I been expecting? *This is madness,* I tell myself sternly. *You're chasing the ghost of an old man through his widow. Look at yourself. Edie Hudson is long gone but your marriage is falling apart right here and now. That's what you need to be looking at.*

I sit awhile as she falls easily back to sleep, her breathing sliding into a deep and regular rhythm. Her small hand lies in mine, limp and cold. Just before I leave I plant a kiss on her temple, the woman who, at our wedding, took me to one side and told me I'd made her so very, very proud.

I sleep fitfully for the next two hours and then give up, brewing strong tea and heading back out into the garden. The sky is lightening to lilac, clouds drifting like unravelling wool. The air is punctuated by the bright voices of the birds. I stand at the fork in the path that splits off towards the wood on the left and the greenhouse and allotment on the right. There is a thin mist obscuring the top of the Downs but the sun, already the colour of a warm peach, will soon burn it away. I look back at Thorn House over my shoulder. The silvery panes of the windows reflect the broad blue sky. I cross the lawn on bare feet, my cup of tea curling silvery steam into the air.

Inside the greenhouse that fertile green smell of the tomatoes hits me again. I try to avoid looking upward but a morbid curiosity compels me. The poor dead bird has been scraped from the glass but there is still a smear of gore left behind, a dark stain. The tomato plants are a lush and vibrant green, the fruits glossy-skinned and plump as if they are about to pop.

The sack of bonemeal is in the far corner, slumped like a drunk with his head on his chest. Back here, cobwebs fur the window frames and the desiccated corpses of flies crunch underfoot. I reach inside and sift the gritty powder through my fingers. I find myself thinking of the last couplet of the rhyme Alex told me: *Give them meat and give them bone, and pray that they leave you alone.*

Beyond the greenhouse is the edge of the garden where gooseberry bushes grow in neat, orderly rows. Beyond that is the woodland, dense and thick and ancient. William told me how his father campaigned to have it protected when it was in danger of being sold off to developers in the mid- nineties. He'd sourced funding from various charities and organisations, held demonstrations, circulated petitions. In the end he raised enough money to buy the two hectares of land just beyond Thorn House and fenced it off. There are still the signs he hung up there reading *Private Property* and *No Entry*. I've always found it strange that he would campaign so hard to protect the land and then not allow anyone to go in there. It was just trees, after all, wasn't it?

And the well, a voice says. *Don't forget that.* My mind circles the image of a sheep's carcass, bristling with insect and bone, lying on the cold stones at the bottom of the well, lit by the flare of the boys' torches. Edward boarded that well up in the end. It was dangerous, Mimi had said.

I've only been in the woods once. William took me on one of our first visits down here to see his mother and brother. He insisted we only use the marked path, the one that leads through the trees towards the pasture fields on the other side. It was autumn, the ground in there churned mud and marshy in places, black standing water lying glassy in ditches. Roots rising from the earth like groping white hands. Dark hollows and mossy hummocks all screened by the thick trunks of the trees. It was silent and very, very still. You could do anything in there and no one would see you.

Anything.

Samantha – Now

I call Frances a little after eleven, nursing a cup of coffee close to my chest. She answers on the third ring, husky-voiced and tired-sounding.

'I was just thinking about you,' she says, and laughs. 'How's your hangover?'

'Deceptively okay. I keep thinking it'll catch up with me later on. That's what happens when you get old.'

'I always look worse than I feel. I think in a way that's harder. I mean, I don't mind feeling like shit but when people physically recoil at the sight of you, you know it's been a rough night.'

Then we're both laughing, the two of us, bonded women who only yesterday sneaked into a long-abandoned house on a trail of breadcrumbs. The pain in my head eases a little. In my little kitchen I can stand by the sink and see the places in the garden where the cats have dug holes in the flower beds, turning over the bulbs I've planted there. I'll have to do them again. I don't mind. It's meditative, gardening. And I still hope, even now, to come across something Edie put there in the dirt nearly thirty years ago. A small plastic bracelet, a tiny rubber dinosaur, a single block of Lego.

'I couldn't sleep last night,' I tell her, pulling an errant cobweb down from the ceiling. 'I can't believe we went in there. What were we thinking? And, Frances, what if Edie *had* been in the freezer?'

'But she wasn't.'

'But she could have been. That's the point. I still don't know. After all this time, I haven't come any closer to finding her and now I just feel like I have to do something. Anything.'

'Are you still drunk?'

I laugh at that, rinsing my cup with the phone cradled against my shoulder. 'I'm going to go and talk to Nancy.'

'Is that a good idea?'

'I don't know. Honestly, I don't even care. I've always thought she knew more than she let on. Perhaps I can persuade her to tell me.'

I know where Nancy is going to be this morning. I know where she is going to be most mornings, and afternoons too. I don't think some people realise how easy it is to keep track of them on Facebook. Nancy Renard is a phenomenal Facebooker, updating her status almost hourly, checking herself in everywhere she goes. I've got a fake profile I use to keep tabs on her, but she exposes herself so often it isn't necessary. *Just meeting my girls for lunch at Café Rouge!* she'll type, marking herself on the map at Brighton Marina, or Bluewater Shopping Centre, or Gatwick Airport. *Nancy Renard checked in to the Odeon, Leicester Square. Date night with this one at Wagamamas! Nancy Renard is at the Royal Sussex County Hospital – in sooooo much pain!!!*

People think the over-forties are all digitally illiterate, unable to comprehend the advances in technology. It isn't true. In 2002 I taught myself code and built a simple website: 'Where is Edie Hudson?' A counter at the bottom racked up how many hits it had, and a primitive message function allowed me to categorise all the tips and sightings it garnered. It allowed me a worldwide reach, for the first time throwing a net out there, a lure, a beacon to Edie. *I still think of you. Come home.*

I managed to find Moya, too – not on Facebook but in a national newspaper. She's a columnist, her byline photo show-ing a pretty young woman with good skin and a wide smile. You wouldn't know it was the same person if it weren't for the tight curls of her black hair. Her surname is King now, and she's married with three beautiful children. I think about writing to her often, just to pierce the normality of her life, to take a blade to it the way we did to the palms of our hands that night in the churchyard standing around Quiet Mary's grave. *I SEE YOU*, I would write, just that, those three short words. And she'd know. She'd remember.

I looked for Charlie Roper for a long time. Beautiful Charlie, a serpent with glossy black scales, the high witch with her curled fist knocking on the tree to call the soul of a long-drowned woman. I searched through all two thousand of Nancy Renard's friends and even went through the marriage sections of the local paper as far back as the year 2000, when all three girls would have turned eighteen.

It took me a long time to find her, and when I did she was dead. She'd died in a fall from a second-storey window in the early hours of the morning, aged just twenty years old. The article said she'd been living in Brighton and had called her death a tragic accident, although later reports cast doubt on her rationality at the time. One witness, who didn't want to be named, had said of Charlie, 'She seemed like a party girl, always on the lookout for a good time.' It had sent a shiver through me. They'd used similar language to describe Edie when they'd reported on her disappearance, camouflaged words to conceal the weight of what they were trying to say. Like thinly veiled threats whispered into your ear with a smile.

I closed the paper when I'd read the short article and studied the scar on my hand, white and hair-thin, puckered tissue forming a narrow ridge you can run your finger along.

> *One, two, three, four,*
> *Rattlesnake hunters knocking at your door.*
> *Give them meat and give them bone,*
> *And pray that they leave you alone.*

Earlier this morning I switched on my computer with no intention of seeing Nancy Renard. I'd planned to spend the day wallowing in my unexpected hangover and eating the cold Chinese takeaway I must have brought home last night and promptly forgotten about. *You're too old for this*, I thought to myself as I logged in; *you're not eighteen any more. You're not a party girl, not like Charlie or Edie.*

Nancy's status was the first thing to pop up as I scrolled through the feed on my other, anonymous, account. *Looking forward to brunch with this bunch!* she'd written. There was a photograph of her with three other similar-looking women – slim, white, neat hair, gold jewellery, teeth as large and polished as marble tombstones. She's unrecognisable as the girl she once was, thin and stooped, peering out at me from under the cloak of her hair. Nancy, the baby bird with the broken wing. Logging in again now, I see she's checked in, too, of course. *Nancy Renard is at Le Petit Patisserie. 11:02 a.m.* I look at my watch. She must still be there. I can't allow myself too much time to think about what I'm doing. If I do, I worry I won't be able to go through with it.

Le Petit Patisserie is just off Lewes High Street, round the corner from the brewery that fills the air with rolling, malty steam. I make my way through town with my head down and my hands in my pockets, cap pulled low over my face. It's not a disguise, but it acts as a deterrent to anyone who wants to stop and talk to me, which happens more often than you'd think. It's a small town; we all know each other. You ever hear the expression 'familiarity breeds contempt'? There it is. That's your little market town in a nutshell. I step through the doors of the patisserie breezily, noticing Nancy's table right away. Clean pressed shirts worn with fine scarves of linen or silk. They look like colonial missionary wives with eating disorders. I move to the counter as if I am about to order so I can better listen to their conversation. I'm sweating beneath the band of my cap.

'Don't,' Nancy is saying, theatrically rolling her eyes. 'Don't get me started.'

'Oh, *do* get started. We want you to get started,' another woman coos. There is a low ripple of laughter and Nancy tucks her hair neatly behind her ear.

'I just think,' she says, urgently, 'that if you're going to charge someone that much for a service then you bloody well need to make sure you're doing what I've asked you! How long does it take to upholster a chair, really? I mean, it's staples and a glue gun, isn't it? How hard can it be?'

More cooing and nodding. Another voice, strident and high, pitches in. 'When we tiled the en suite I went to Morocco myself to source them. I can buy tiles for twenty pence a time in the souk at Marrakesh, darling, so don't try to play a player, right?'

'Absolutely.'

'It's a joke.'

I turn around so that Nancy can see me properly. I know she knows who I am, even now. I saw her that day with Frances opposite the pharmacy and I saw the way her face changed when she recognised me. Like a door, slowly closing.

'Hi, Nancy,' I say brightly. She sits up. I allow her that pause, that moment of recognition. I savour it. I like the way her baby-blue eyes widen, the way her long fingers play with the collar of her shirt. I know she got divorced last year because the news was all over her Facebook feed, and I wasn't surprised. From the pictures I'd found of him he was a boring-looking, weak-jawed man at least a foot shorter than Nancy, who wore golfing jumpers and long leather shoes. At least Charlie went out with a bang.

'Mrs Hudson?' she says, unevenly. 'Samantha, right?'

'That's right.'

All the women are looking at me with mild interest. I'm the equivalent of the mantelpiece you run your finger along for dust. My smile aches.

'I was just thinking about you the other day,' I tell her, reaching out to shake her hand. She puts hers in mine with no enthusiasm. It's like holding the hand of a corpse. 'I was hoping we could have a talk sometime. About Edie.'

'Oh?' She's reaching for her phone. 'I'll check my calendar. It's a busy time of year. The kids are heading back to school, you know?'

'I'm free any time. I've just got a few questions.' Firm. Refusing to be fobbed off. My pulse throbs in my neck. I realise I forgot to put make-up on before I left the house. I must look deranged. Nancy is scrolling through her calendar wordlessly, her cheeks bright pink as if they've been slapped. I've ordered a takeaway coffee and the waitress brings it over to me.

'Shall I get you a chair?' she asks me, and Nancy looks up sharply.

'No,' she tells her. Then she smiles at me, weakly. 'How about later in the month? After I come back from Capri?'

'How about now?'

'Now?' She laughs uneasily. I see one of her friends mouth to the other, *Oh my God.* I ignore her.

'Now.'

'I'm – you can see I'm here with my friends. I'm busy.'

'I'll wait outside. You've got to leave sometime.'

All the women exchange thrilled glances. The brunch bunch. I keep my eyes on Nancy, unblinking. She looks around at them all for help but one by one they drop their gaze. They like a drama. *Keep watching*, I think, *it's only just getting started.*

Nancy and I take a seat in the sunlit courtyard out the front, screened off from the pavement by large potted ferns and slender bamboo screens. She orders a chamomile tea, fixing a large mono-chrome sun hat to her head. Nancy has skin as creamy as alabaster. She is wearing a fringed kimono and large, oversized sunglasses which she takes off slowly.

'I burn,' she tells me, pointing to her sun hat, 'and the sun is very ageing.' She gives me a look then, a quick up-down flick of the eyes, a sly smile. *Too late for you, bitch*, that smile says. *Too late*.

'Show me your hand,' I tell her. She rolls her eyes and extends her left palm. I shake my head. 'The other one, dummy.'

'Oh my God, what is this? Theatre?' She thrusts it out towards me. There's nothing there. No line, no pink scar tissue. She didn't cut deep enough to leave a mark. 'Happy? What's all this about, Samantha?'

'What do you think?'

She shrugs. 'Honestly? Darling, don't you – don't you *ever* think, "You know what, Samantha, it was twenty years ago now. Move on." Twenty years and yet you're *still* trying to get informa-tion from me that I don't have. What do you want me to do? The way you're behaving, following me around – it's not healthy.' She leans back to allow the waitress to put the teapot on the table and then tilts her head towards me. 'Listen. As a mother, I feel for you. I can't imagine the pain of your child going missing. It's my worst nightmare. But I think, deep down, it must have been a relief. Oh, don't look at me like that, you know as well as I do what Edie was like. She was an animal.'

'Don't you talk ab—'

'Well, it's true! Jesus, you know what you suffer from? Selective blindness. Don't you remember how she was? You want to see scars? Don't look at my hand, sweetheart, look here!' She jerks the scarf away from her throat to reveal a vertical slash just below her left ear, running from her jaw to her collarbone. It's twisted like rope. I remember all the times I've seen her in her fussy, button-up Victorian blouses and thought she was just melodramatic.

She nods at me slowly.

'My parents wanted me to have plastic surgery. Said if I left it, it would make me look like Frankenstein.'

'Edie did this to you?'

'Yup. Every once in a while she would lash out without warning. It was okay when it was just pulling hair or scratching, the way she sometimes did. You could almost laugh it off. But when she started carrying around a knife the whole dynamic changed. Suddenly she was frightening. Deadly, almost. It stopped being fun to hang around her then. Danger's only attractive from far away, isn't it?'

I'm shaken. I want to smoke but instead I sip my coffee. Something warm expands inside me, a heat. Shame, maybe. I stammer out my words. 'I'm sorry. I didn't know.'

'Sure you didn't,' she says, in a tone that tells me she doesn't believe a word.

And she's right, isn't she? that sinuous little voice in my head says, the one that coils and twists. *You knew what she was like. Remember how frightened you were when she jumped out at you? It wasn't the shock. You thought she had a weapon. You thought she was going to hurt you. You were scared of her. Why can't you admit it?*

'You carried a knife of your own, didn't you? Why *was* that?' She looks at me down her thin nose and takes a bird-like sip of tea. She has such a narrow neck. You could snap it like kindling. 'You know Charlie and Moya used to think you'd killed her? After you pulled a knife on Moya in the churchyard. They thought you were crazy. I'd always argue back that it was Edie who was the crazy one, and then inevitably someone would say, "Can you imagine living in that house?"'

It is as though I've been plunged chest-deep into iced water. Like I can't draw breath. I concentrate very hard on the gold teardrop necklace nestled in the deep hollow of Nancy's throat.

'Listen. Listen to me, Samantha. No one would blame you. It must have been hard, right from the start. How old were you when you had her? Twenty?'

'Eighteen.'

'Most women now wait till they're in their thirties.'

I look across at her but beneath the wide brim of her sun hat I can't see her face, and I can't tell if it's a dig. It feels like one. Hurtful, prickling. I'd just turned eighteen when I had Edie. I once overheard someone in the supermarket say to my mother, 'You must be so disappointed.'

'They thought I might have killed her?'

'Nobody would blame you.'

'That's absurd. I was her mother. I loved her. She was all I had.'

She looks at me curiously and takes another sip of tea. I straighten up in my seat. I'm not done yet. Down, but not out, as they say. I light a cigarette and Nancy immediately fans her hand in front of her face.

'You used to smoke,' I tell her.

She rolls her eyes. 'I was fifteen. I did a lot of stupid stuff.'

'Hch. You've got that right. Remember Quiet Mary?'

Nancy nods, but I've already seen the hunch of her shoulders, the way her eyes widen just a fraction. She's still afraid of her. Even now. I curl a fist and tap it on the table, slowly and deliberately. Four times.

Her face blanches. 'Stop it.'

'*Rattlesnake hunters, knocking at your door,*' I say, letting the smoke drift out my mouth like blown silks. 'Do you think that's who snatched Edie? Quiet Mary?'

She shakes her head. 'I don't want to talk about Quiet Mary.'

'You know something. What is it?'

'Leave it, I said.' Her accent's slipping. When I arrived, it could have cut glass. Now there's that twang in it that sounds almost Cockney, home-bred. She crosses her legs, coils around herself.

'All those spells you did. All the blood and the candles and the wine. Then Edie disappeared and Charlie, well, Charlie left a good-looking corpse, didn't she? Did it frighten you? Did you think it was Quiet Mary's revenge?' I lean in, whispering, 'Do you think you're next?'

Nancy is silent for a moment but I can see her fear. It's visible, like a shiver. She runs the pads of her fingers beneath her eyes, swiping at errant make-up.

'I do know something,' she says quietly, pouring tea from the pot with hands that look unsteady. 'About Edie. She made me do a deal.'

'What kind of deal?'

'After this' – she points to the grisly scar on her neck – 'my parents wanted to press charges. I was always Daddy's little girl and Edie knew that if I wanted to, I could talk them out of it. She was frightened she'd go to prison, you see. So she told me that if I could talk my parents out of dropping the charges she would tell me a secret.'

'And did you?'

'Yes. I didn't like it, and honestly, no secret is that interesting, but when Edie wanted you to do something—'

'You did it,' I finish.

She nods. 'Yes, you did, or it was worse for you. She made me promise not to tell anyone or Quiet Mary would get me. Said she'd come for me in the night and strangle me with her burial shroud. Edie told me Quiet Mary was silent, so I wouldn't hear her coming. The first I'd know of it would be her dripping wet hands brushing against my face in the dark.'

I shudder, despite the sunshine. My cigarette tastes awful but I'm going to smoke it right down to the filter.

'So I talked my parents out of it. Made them call off the lawyers, the police. "I'm dropping charges," I told them, and they went along with it because my daddy loved me more than anything in the world. The next day I told Edie at school, near the canteen. "You're safe," I told her. "My folks'll never invite you to my birthday parties again but at least you won't end up in prison." You know what she said?'

I shake my head, heart tapping a swift percussion in my chest.

'Nothing. That's what she said. Absolutely nothing. Didn't thank me, didn't even smile. Later on, she took me into the toilets at breaktime and showed me what she had in her bag.'

'What was it?'

'A pregnancy test. She wouldn't answer any of my questions, just made me stand with my foot under the toilet door so I could hold it closed for her. All the locks were busted, you see. After about a minute she came out and even though I could see she was scared, she put the test face-up on the sink and we both watched those little blue stripes come up just as clear as anything.'

It's as if a tiny bomb has been detonated. The shock of it rings in my ears. Distantly I can hear a dog barking, a car grinding its gears.

'She wanted to keep it, she said. But it was making her sick. She was puking all the time, even at school. She told the others she had food poisoning.'

I think back to the last days I saw Edie, how she would tie up the bathroom in the mornings, the sound of the toilet flushing over and over again. Morning sickness. *Oh my God.* I have to clutch the edge of the table for support. My heart is pounding like it might give out. All these years and I never knew. I promised to take her to the doctor to get some contraception – it was the night of all that rain, the two of us sitting in the garden. But then of course she split up with Dylan and I didn't think I needed to worry about it.

'I remember.'

'Yep,' Nancy says. 'I was the only one who knew. Well, me and the father.'

'Who was the father?' I'm thinking of William with his hand in her underwear. Or Dylan? And who else was there? How many that I didn't know about?

'She wouldn't tell me. I mean, Edie wasn't a virgin. Most of us had – uh – a series of overlapping boyfriends. You know?'

'But you must have some idea.'

Nancy shakes her head, sighs. 'Honestly. She wouldn't say and I didn't push it because – well, because it was Edie. You didn't push things with Edie.'

I have a flash of memory. Shoved into the corner of a room, something spilt across the carpet. It's the table; Edie's upturned the dining table. There's spaghetti all over the floor, red sauce. I can see broken glass glittering on the rug. I'm saying, 'Edie, stop, I mean it.' I'm reaching into my back pocket for the knife. *This is stupid*, I'm thinking, even though my heart is beating at a hundred miles an hour, *this is so stupid, it's just homework. Why can't she just do her fucking homework?* Her face is so angry I don't recognise her. It contorts her from the inside out. She's a monster.

'Yeah,' I say resignedly to Nancy. 'If she didn't want to do something, she wouldn't do it.'

'Listen, I have to go. I've got Pilates,' Nancy says, breaking the spell. Her voice is more precise again and she's wrapping the scarf around her neck. This moment is over.

She stands, holding my gaze with her heavy-lidded eyes. 'You need to try to move on, Samantha. Don't lose your present to your past.'

Wow, I think. What a wise thing to say. It seems vaguely familiar and then I remember where I've seen it before. On Nancy's Facebook wall, one of those quotes set against the backdrop of a waterfall, written in calligraphic script.

I almost laugh. 'I appreciate your help, Nancy.'

'I'm lactose intolerant but if you ever want to meet for coffee, I'm here. Always here.'

'I'll bear it in mind.'

'You look after yourself, Samantha,' Nancy says, picking up her handbag, and I'm left alone again.

I walk aimlessly through the market stalls that are set up in the pedestrianised centre of town. I can't face going home. I feel weak, like I'm getting sick. Edie, pregnant. It changes everything. It means that she could be out there somewhere, living with her own son or daughter, my grandchild. It was a catalyst for her leaving, quietly and without incident, that had nothing to do with my necklace or the argument we'd had that morning. My hope soars. I wish Tony was still here. He'd know what to do. I try to picture him, his soft grey eyes, the gentle burr of his voice. The first thing he ever said to me was, 'I am here to help you find your daughter.' At the time it was soothing, like a warm compress. I believed him.

I buy a paper and sit on a bench with it folded on my lap. Pregnant. She must have been so frightened. I remember how I felt. As though my own body was turning on me. Nausea, exhaustion, pain. All that sickness. And that strange, alien feeling of a life growing inside you. Cells dividing again and again and again, bones forming and hardening beneath soft, stretched skin. I'm unnerved to find that my face is wet with tears. I didn't realise I was crying.

There's a hand on my shoulder. I twitch, swiping at the wetness on my cheeks. It's Frances, peering at me with concern.

'I thought that was you. Are you okay? Did you speak to Nancy?'

'Yes. What are you – why are you here?'

'I had to get out the house.' She sits beside me on the bench. 'I had an argument with William last night. You look like you've been crying.'

'Allergies,' I say, straight-faced.

She nods. I don't want to talk about it. Frances understands.

We sit side by side in silence, pigeons cooing softly in the eaves of the nearby buildings. The River Ouse runs beneath us, brown and tarry.

Finally, Frances speaks, without looking at me. 'I think I'm leaving him.'

'Okay.'

More silence. I reach over and awkwardly pat her hand. She smiles, closes her eyes. When she speaks again she doesn't open them, doesn't look at me. 'There's something I wanted to mention to you. There's an old well in the woods near Thorn House. It's very old and pretty much dry, from what I can tell. Edward Thorn boarded it up when the boys were kids because it was so dangerous. I think it mi—'

'No. No more.' I stand up, pressing the newspaper against my chest. When Edie first went missing the same newspaper buried her story in its pages, using the headline 'Troubled Teen Runaway: Missing Edie Hudson may have fled to capital'. *Troubled.* So polite. So generous. That scar on Nancy's neck, twisted like rope. 'No more, Frances. I don't have the energy. It's the hope. I don't know how much longer I can sustain it before I fucking sink. It's making me sick, that hope. Sometimes I can lose hours just wondering what she looks like now, how she's grown into a woman. Does she look like me or her dad? Sometimes I even think I see her; a woman who is lean and strong-looking, with dark glossy hair. I double-take when I see women with their jaws set hard like Edie when she was in a temper, or women with multiple earrings, little gold hoops and crosses. That was the kind of thing she loved, always trying on my jewellery when she was a little girl. When I see them, these phantom Edies walking their dogs or bouncing a baby on their knee, it's like walking into a cold room. I can't breathe. I try not to stare. I try not to *cry*. It's harder than it sounds. Because there's that hope, you see. *Maybe* it is her this time. It's the hope, the fucking hope. I carry it with me, all the time. I can't – I can't keep hoping. I'm sorry, Frances.'

'Don't be. Don't be sorry.'

'She was pregnant. Nancy told me. They did the test together, in the bathrooms at school. So there you go. My violent fifteen-year-old daughter was facing expulsion and an unwanted pregnancy and she hated me. Some parenting, huh?'

My voice is shaking by the end. I have to walk away quickly before Frances can reply, before she can see the fault lines in me, splitting all the way through to my hollow, worthless spine.

Frances – Now

I watch Samantha walk away from me, hunched over as if she is in pain. I too feel winded, a sucker punch to the gut, a quick one-two. Pregnant. And not just any baby. William's baby. *Not necessarily*, that nasty little voice replies.

This morning I went into Alex's bedroom. He was at his desk in front of the window, just sitting and staring out at the trees beyond the house. He didn't turn around when I knocked and opened the door, but I suppose he must have seen my reflection in the glass because he said, 'Come and see this, Frances. There's a magpie out there on the grass. I should tell Mum.'

I walked up behind him, careful to close the door behind me. I didn't want to be overheard. I put my hand on the back of his chair and peered out towards the woodland. 'Those woods look awfully dark.'

'Well, there's been no one to look after them since Dad died. It closes over you, you see, the canopy. The branches reach out towards each other, slowly shutting off the sunlight.'

'I don't like to think of it being neglected. It's a shame.'

Alex shrugged. 'Who would take the job on? You need to be a specialist.'

'Like your dad?'

He turned to look at me, face unreadable. He was wearing a button-down shirt tucked into his trousers, hair neatly parted. So tidy. Even his fingernails were close-cropped and clean, despite all that digging in the dirt.

'I suppose. He learned on the job, but hired people for the big clearance work. You volunteering yourself?'

I laughed, but he wasn't smiling. It's so hard to tell with him sometimes, where the jokes are. 'No.' I looked over at the shelf above the bed, as if my eye had just glanced upon the object that sits there and not deliberately sought it out, that it was not in fact the best part of the reason I came in here. 'Is that the sheep's skull?'

Alex looked over his shoulder, nodded.

'Can I pick it up?'

'Of course.'

I crossed the room and lifted the sheep's skull from the book-shelf. It was grey, almost dirty-looking, not polished white as I'd been expecting. There were fissures along the surface and on the left-hand side a small dent I could press my thumb into.

Alex turned to look straight at me. 'That's where it got the head injury. That's how it died.'

'Amazing.' I wanted to put it back. I didn't like it, didn't like the way the teeth jutted down into the palm of my hand. I forced myself to keep holding it, though, and to keep holding Alex's interest. 'Do you think you could still find the old well, if you had to?'

He thought for a moment. 'I suppose. Certainly the area should be easy enough. It would be entirely overgrown in there now and the boards Dad put over it will probably be rotten. It wouldn't be very safe.'

'But you'd be able to show me where it is?'

'What did you come in here for, Frances?'

My heart picked up, just a little. I put the skull back on the shelf, resisting the urge to wipe my hands on my dress.

'I just wanted to talk to you about last night.'

'Oh. The argument you two were having? Yeah. I heard it all.'

'I'm sorry. That was inconsiderate of us.'

He shrugged.

'Thing is, Alex, one of the reasons Will was cross was the photo I found in the shoebox. The one you told me not to mention. What I don't understand is why you then went and told him about it yourself.'

'He's my brother, Frances,' he said simply, as if that answered the question. 'He needs to know if you're digging around.'

'I'm not digging around,' I said. 'I just think it's an interesting story. Edie walked away from her friends and was never seen again. And your dad's car was right there. You don't think that's interesting?'

'My dad loved this family, Frances. He did a lot for us.'

I stared at him. 'I would never suggest otherwise.'

'He just wanted to help people, all the time. To do the right thing. That was his problem.'

'Okay.'

'Edie Hudson was a pest and her mother's no better. My dad knew it and William knew it and you'd be wise to stay away from that woman while you're here, otherwise she'll taint you, too. Although I suppose you won't be here much longer now, will you?'

'What do you mean?'

He turned away again to look out the window, hands flat on the empty desk in front of him. 'I suppose I just thought after last night, after what William did – I assumed you wouldn't be staying together.'

'Do you think William is like his dad?'

Alex didn't even pause. 'Absolutely.'

'Do you think your father was unfaithful?'

I didn't know what I was expecting from Alex. I didn't know if honesty was too much to ask for in this strange situation.

He thought about it for a good long time, his eyes closed. 'Yes.'

'Does your mum suspect?'

'My mum wouldn't see it. She sees what she wants to see.'

I thought about Edward Thorn. A good man. A family man. Solid, dependable. It was even on his gravestone, wasn't it? *Steadfast husband and father*. William had taken after him – William himself had told me that, and now Alex too. Like father, like son. Had Edward had his own Kim squirrelled away somewhere, like William? A younger girl – much younger, perhaps. Someone like Edie Hudson. *Don't be mad*, I told myself. *Men like Edward Thorn didn't do things like that. She was a schoolgirl; he'd have got himself arrested.*

'You know, you remind me a bit of Edie, Frances. How troubled she was. I suppose that's William's type, though, isn't it?'

I smiled, but my insides were curdling. The pain of William's betrayal was low and sharp and raw and I didn't know that I would ever get used to it. I opened my mouth to respond but then he asked me another question that froze me in my tracks.

'Were you? A whore?'

I felt my mouth drop softly open. He'd heard everything. He must have been right outside the door. I felt my knuckles crack as I curled my hands into fists. 'I have to go, Alex.'

'Sure. See you soon, Frances.'

As I closed the door I experienced a moment of vertigo so steep it was as if the floor had dropped away beneath me. I gripped hold of the bannister, sure I was going to either fall down or throw up, but neither of those things happened and after a moment I heard Mimi call for William in her small, fragile voice. I walked slowly the rest of the way downstairs to tell her about the magpie in the garden.

Sitting here on the bench overlooking the slow-moving tidal river, I think about Edie taking her pregnancy test in the toilet block at school among the smells of bleach and paint and wet toilet paper. My mind circles back to the hidden well again, how all your bones would break if you were to fall down it on to the old bricks below. What would drive a man to do that? His secrecy exposed, perhaps? An unforeseen pregnancy? Blackmail? I think of the way Samantha looked yesterday, her face lined and blotchy with tears, and I know, I *know* I can't leave yet. I can't go without finding out where Edie Hudson is, and whether or not she has Edward's baby with her.

I stare out the window as the bus judders along the road back to Thorn House. The narrow road is lined with overgrown hedgerows and snarls of brambles. My head is spinning. I keep thinking about missing girls and ghost hitchhikers and the bowlful of round, ripe tomatoes that sits by the kettle in the kitchen and makes my stomach curl every time I look at it. I'm thinking about Kim and Edie and the way poor Mimi's brain seems to be full of holes. I'm wondering about what really happened the night she fell down the stairs, alone in the house with Alex.

Don't be ridiculous, I tell myself, *you've already got his dad pinned for getting Edie pregnant and bumping her off and now you think Alex is trying to harm his mum? What for?*

I know what for. I don't even have to think about it. He's been closeted by fear of her disapproval for years. A young man having to make clandestine trips to London and Brighton to meet men, to forge relationships and just to be himself. How tortuous to carry that secret around with you for your entire life.

♦ ♦ ♦

By the time I get back to Thorn House the weather has turned. Low, ponderous clouds gather, charcoal-grey and heavy as iron. It's going to rain. I carry the bags of shopping into the kitchen and take out the fruit, putting it into the sink to be washed. I've been teaching myself how to brew the fragrant tea Mimi likes, using flowers from the garden. Rosebuds and petals of chamomile, dandelion, jasmine and pale yellow chrysanthemums. After I've tidied the shopping away I take a pot of it into her room, nudging the door carefully open with my hip.

'Rosebud and jasmine t—' I cut off.

Mimi's flushed, the colour creeping up her neck into her cheeks. Her hands grope blindly across the bedside table, knocking against the phone, which dings brightly. I rush towards her, putting the tea tray down on the bed, noticing the thin sticks of her legs beneath the covers. I catch her hands gently, surprised at the wiry strength I can feel thrumming beneath her skin, and wonder if this is delirium, passing through her like a voltage. I call for Alex and William, but by the time they come running through the doorway Mimi is calming down, glassy-eyed and a little vacant, looking around her as though she has just woken up. She says there were black spots on her bedside table, 'crawling all over it like insects'. William, Alex and I exchange concerned glances over the top of her head. Alex begins to insist on calling the doctor but Mimi abruptly shuts the idea down, telling him, 'All I need is the company of my boys and a good rest. Thank you for my tea, dear heart. Sit with me, William. I'd like to hear you read.'

'I'm busy, Mum. I've got a conference call in ten minutes. Can Frances do it?'

Of course I do it. I read her the headlines and some articles from the supplement, her horoscope. 'Use your excess energy today to get out there and do some exercise!' We both laugh at that. I quarter her some oranges and put them in a bowl on her lap. The bright smell of them fills the room, almost tropical.

'You look better now, Mimi,' I tell her.

She nods and smiles. 'I feel it. It's hard to be unhappy when you've got all this garden to look at. See those roses? Edward planted them for me. He wanted us to have a daughter called Rose but sadly, well – these things can't be planned, can they?'

'No.'

'Tell me again the story of how you and William met.' She squeezes my hand and her eyes are misty. William has always told me his mother was a born romantic, not the Barbara Cartland kind but deeper and more destructive, the kind Kenny Rogers would sing about. I swallow. She's heard the story before, of course. That's all it is, a story. Entirely fictional. It's a tall tale about a man (William) and a woman (me) sitting opposite one another on the 20:22 to Reading. Two people, catching each other's eyes, both thinking the same thing: *How can I strike up a conversation?* Alas, these two lovers seem doomed to remain silent and separate as the train pulls into the woman's station, but when she leaves the man notices – oh no! – that she's left her purse behind. He gallantly leaps out of his seat and off the train despite the fact that his own stop is another forty minutes away. As the train pulls out of the station he catches up with the woman at the turnstiles, who is getting increasingly upset and frustrated at being unable to find the purse containing her tickets. But wait, what's this? (I often pause here for dramatic effect and watch as Mimi's face is dimpled by a small, knowing smile.) It's William, purse in hand, reaching out to her through the crowd, and their hands touch and their eyes meet and that, as they say, is it.

Mimi has her eyes closed, leaning back against the pillows, hands folded on her lap. I move the bowl of oranges gently aside, so as not to disturb her, and let the silence spool out. I wonder how she would react to the real story of William and me meeting: the smell of white spirit, the dingy studio flat, the word *Whore* in bold letters that would only fade and not disappear, not even beneath three coats of paint, my pupils inky-black pools, white spittle collecting at the corners of my mouth because I'm still high. Even when we got together years down the line, it wasn't simple, our jerky, stop-start relationship characterised by reluctance and hysterical bonding, punctuated by my abrupt disappearances, sometimes for whole weekends. All the times he came to help me, all the comedowns he nursed me through, all those nights he carried me to bed after too much wine, too many cocktails. The states he found me in. My white knight.

'Your white knight,' Mimi says quietly, the way she always does when I reach the part of the fictional story where William catches me at the ticket barriers. 'Just think of all the ways it could have been different. If one of you had sat in a different seat, if you hadn't left your purse behind, if William hadn't jumped off the train in time – all these little things we don't know are actually cogs in the engine.' She leans forward, smiling tightly as if imparting a great secret. 'You know how Edward and I met?'

I've heard this one before. Sunday. At the bandstand, listening to jazz. Eighteen years old. He asked her to dance and showed her all the flowers in bloom on the village green. They never spent another night apart. Since his death, whenever she tells this story her eyes fill with tears and she has to dab at them with a hanky, even now.

'I do, Mimi. I remember.'

'Do you know how he died, Frances?'

I stiffen. In all the years I've known her, Mimi has never spoken about his death with me. Not in real detail, and certainly not without dressing it up in euphemism. Despite my interest I try to look nonchalant, reaching for the bottle of nail polish on her bedside table beside the phone. My heart skitters, my mouth dry. This man, this man. He's everywhere, still.

'I don't think so, Mimi. Shall I do your nails while you tell me? It's such a pretty colour.'

She extends a thin pale hand over the coverlet and I lift it into my own, surprised at the lightness of it. Bird bones.

'It was a car accident. Something on the road, they said. An animal maybe. He skidded off the bridge. It was autumn, and it was dark and maybe he was going too fast. That doesn't sound right, though, does it? He was always so careful. Such a careful man.'

'He was,' I say, although I never met him. I don't want to interrupt her flow. Her eyes have misted over with recollection.

'I had a knock at the door about four o'clock. When I answered, it was the police. They both removed their hats. That's when I knew something bad had happened. They said, "Are you Mrs Thorn?" Of course I said yes. I had an apron on and my fingers were shaking too much to untie it. They said, "There's been an accident, Mrs Thorn", and I said, "Not my boys, please. Not my boys." There's no worse feeling in the world.'

I think of Samantha, still searching. All these years doing it alone. No worse feeling in the world.

'He said, "It's your husband, Mrs Thorn. It's Edward." And then do you know what happened?'

I shake my head, still stroking the brush over her short square fingernails.

'Edward walked past the doorway. Right there, clear as day. He looked in at me, but he didn't say a word. I think it was his ghost just coming to say goodbye to the house and his garden. It sounds silly now, of course, but at the time it was the most normal thing in the world. It gave me strength to keep going, Frances.'

'I'm glad to hear it, Mimi.'

She falls silent and after a moment I'm starting to wonder if she's fallen asleep; then when I lift my head I see her eyes are open, but heavy. Her voice is starting to slur.

'I wonder where he is now.'

I finish her nails, blow on them gently before asking, 'How long were you together?'

'We met when I was eighteen but didn't wed until I was closer to thirty. I was beginning to think he'd never ask, but Edward was a cautious man, didn't like taking risks. Of course we thought we'd start a family right away, but we didn't have our boys for another seven years. We didn't think we could have any. That's what the doctors said. "This union will not bear fruit." But then we were blessed, weren't we? Not once, but twice.' She sighs, looking out towards the garden again. 'He died the year of our twenty-fourth anniversary. I found his present to me the day of his funeral. Pulled it right out of the drawer as if I'd always known it was going to be there. He must have bought it months in advance.' She extends her arm to show me the slender bracelet of silver.

A question occurs to me then, and it comes out of my mouth before I can hesitate. 'How do you know it was for you?'

Mimi looks up at me, face blank.

I flush, suddenly embarrassed but unable to help myself; I'm still talking. 'I mean, how can you be *sure*?'

Mimi swallows, her thin fingers going to her neck, fluttering against the thin skin that hangs there. 'He wouldn't. Not him. Not my Edward.'

There, I think, with a jolt of surprise, *you have a tell too, Mimi.* For William it is the tugging of the hair that coils at his neck; for Mimi it is playing with the loose skin below her chin. Do we all have them, these little tics that betray us? I watch her eyes begin to close, her breathing deepen. The reflection of the rain plays the shadows softly across her face.

He wouldn't. Not my Edward. Ah, Mimi. How little we know these men.

◆ ◆ ◆

In the evening I find myself in front of William's laptop. I'm meant to be looking for a divorce lawyer, something I'm keeping hidden from William for the time being, but instead I have spent the last hour on websites dedicated to missing people, reading up on those who vanished like ghosts or just drifted away from their lives, their jobs, their families. I learn that teenage runaways are overwhelmingly female, and that ninety-three per cent of missing teenagers are, like Edie, from single-parent families. I read that children with no siblings are more likely to disappear than those with. I find a website dedicated to missing children, which has age progression photos of the long-term missing. I find photographs of children disappeared from care homes and institutions and vulnerable teenage girls trafficked from Thailand and China and Vietnam. Slowly I discover that media coverage is mostly absent for teenagers who are black or of mixed ethnicity, those with foreign-sounding names or piercings or the skinny self-harmers, the streetwise repeat offenders, hooded and scowling, unphotogenic and tough-looking from a background of crime and estates and high-rises. These children are the dark undertow, drifting below the surface.

I find a site dedicated to the thousands of unidentified bodies on police files in the UK, listing clothing and tattoos and jewellery in the hope of a loved one being able to identify the deceased. I scroll through the contents of their pockets with a pain in my chest that burns as bright and singularly as a candle flame. 'Unknown male, 18, Asian: Black disposable cigarette lighter, William Hill winning slip, tobacco, phonecard (for India), orange soft drink.' 'Unknown female, 14–20: Silver ring, conch shell design worn on index finger of right hand.' I wonder if Samantha knows what Edie had in her pockets the night she walked out of the churchyard. I check my own, pooling their contents on the table. An apple sticker, thirty pence, a bus ticket stub. These are the things that would remain. I read until my eyes are dry and sore and my stomach feels heavy as concrete. *There but for the grace of God.*

I climb into bed next to William and lie very still, watching him. He lies with one hand on his chest, lifting and falling with his deep, measured breaths. Something uncurls softly inside me, a slight loosening of the tension I've been feeling since we arrived. His lips are parted and I have an urge to reach over and touch them with the pad of my thumb, feeling for the warmth of his breath. William would know what I was carrying in my pockets. He saved me. A resolute protector.

William stirs and looks at me in the half-light, frowning. 'Are you okay? You're not asleep?'

'Will you give me a cuddle?' I ask him, and allow myself to be folded against him, the warmth of his skin, the tight curls of his chest hair pressed firm against my cheek. All those stories have needled their way into my gut, acid burning a hole through the lining of my stomach. It's upsetting. So many lives in limbo; I can't sleep alone. I need the comfort of the man I married.

William falls back to sleep right away but I lie awake in the dark with my eyes wide open, listening to the night sounds: the creaking rafters, the rattle of the water pipes, the lonely, plaintive cry of a tawny owl. In the end I reach for my phone and sketch Samantha a quick text. I've been trying to imagine what it's been like for her all these years with no answers, no leads. Just that emptiness, hollow as a cave. *I don't know how much longer I can sustain the hope before I fucking sink,* she said, and I think of her, that slim knife in her hand, fighting against the world the way she has been for eighteen years. That hope, the kind you carry everywhere with you, gestating like a foetus. It nails you to the earth, because without it you would simply float away like smoke on the breeze.

Samantha – Now

The calls have started again.

About a year after Edie went missing I was getting as many as nine a night. My landline would bristle with the faintest crackle, like static from an untuned radio. I would wait, hoarse with anticipation, clutching the receiver in both hands.

'Edie?' I would whisper, my breath snagged like a fishhook. 'Is that you, baby? Say something.'

Nothing. Some nights I would hear the wind on the line like ghosts whispering into my ear. The longest call lasted seven minutes, the shortest just four seconds. The calls came as late as three o'clock in the morning, when I'd take the phone from the cradle and nestle it into the empty pillow next to me so I could hear her breathing in the dark.

Then, for a time, they stopped. The last one I had was nine months ago, just as dusk was settling into the hollows of the Downs. I had a glass of white wine in my hand as I picked up the phone, sliding a Rizla into the folds of my paperback to mark my place. That time, the last time, I was convinced she was going to speak to me. I felt so sure I'd hear her voice that my legs grew weak and I let my back slide down the wall to the floor.

'Edie?' I said gently. 'Talk to me. Please, just say hello.'

Nothing. I let the silence fill the line. I told her I loved her and missed her and that I was sorry, so sorry I hadn't been enough for her. I told her I hoped she was well. 'Well' was the word I used, but what I really meant was 'safe'. Be safe, my baby.

Since then, nothing. Until this afternoon.

Despite what I've told Frances, I am still searching for Edie, unable to resist carving my way through the scant online information about Peter Liverly. His name circles my skull, a constant orbit. I've updated the 'Where Is Edie Hudson?' website and posted the new picture of her that Frances showed me. The last few nights, sleep hasn't come so easily so I spend the long night lying and staring at the ceiling with my hands folded over my chest, a cigarette smouldering in the ashtray, the shipping forecast playing in the background. *'Westerly or southwesterly six to gale eight, occasionally severe gale nine in Southeast Iceland. Rough or very rough, occasionally moderate at first. Rain or drizzle. Good, occasionally poor.'*

The call came at four thirty, as I was hauling the wet washing out of the machine. I reached for the phone – the landline, always the landline; I've refused to change the number since the day Edie left, in case she ever needed to contact me again. It's that hope, you see, stretching its long, leathery wings about my ribs, crushing my chest.

I didn't say hello this time. I didn't say, 'Is that you?' either. I let the silence stretch out and I pressed the phone against my cheek and said, 'I know about the baby, Edie.'

Was that a gasp? A quick indrawing of breath? Or was it the wind making the lines shiver? I pressed the phone more tightly in my hand, letting the washing drop to the floor at my feet.

'Who was it, love? Was it that man from the church, the caretaker? You could have told me. I would have helped you.'

Silence. Then, a rustling. Very quick, like Edie was scrabbling for the phone. In the background I heard a voice, a woman – maybe

229

Edie herself saying something. I could only make out one of the words. It sounded like *nosebleed*.

Then, a *click*.

'Edie? Edie?' I reached out to the phone and tapped the button inside the cradle. 'Edie? Hello?'

The dial tone, flat and monotonous in my ear. I quickly hung up in case Edie was trying to call. I lay back on my elbows, thinking. That voice. It was so familiar. I *knew* it. It had to be her.

I dream about Tony Marston and wake up imagining the phone is ringing. The surface of my sleep is thin, and breaks apart easily. I'm panicking, reaching for my bedside drawer out of instinct, even before my eyes have opened. Tony told me that Mace was illegal but he didn't take it away from me. It is still there, a small metal canister featuring the silhouette of a cowed attacker being repelled beneath the words *Take Down Spray*.

I let my hand drop away from the drawer and release a shuddering breath. There's a memory lodged in my head, the way they do sometimes, like a squeaky wheel needing oil.

It was more than two years since Edie's disappearance. I called Tony on a grey February morning and asked him to come over. The smell of frost and woodsmoke filled the air, and the heavy grey clouds were threatening snow. I stood in the garden smoking cigarette after cigarette, waiting for him to arrive, and when he did he was barely out of his coat before the anger overtook me, breathless and shaking and spitting words like bullets.

'Do you know who this is?'

He looked over at me, puzzled. I was holding a newspaper out to him. Not a local; a national. A broadsheet. I'd bought it in the supermarket earlier that morning. He took it from me, studying the photograph of the girl on the front. I bit at my nails, already wishing I could light another cigarette.

'Her name's Jemima Kennedy. Middle name Avaline. She's fourteen. Blonde-haired, green-eyed. Tall, sporty. Approximately five foot two—'

'What's going on, Frances?'

'—weighs about ninety-eight pounds. It's all there, that information. In the article. She went missing on Sunday evening.'

'Okay—'

'Her father owns a chain of car dealerships. That's in there too. She went to Roedean School for girls, where she was a straight-A student with a flair for languages and music. Her parents had asked her to come straight back from a friend's house, where they were watching a video. *Austin Powers*, her friends said. Jemima left their house at nine. It's a twenty-minute walk along well-lit streets to her parents' house on Roedean Crescent. She never came home. You know they've given her a nickname?' I laughed, although it wasn't funny. I was so angry I could feel the heat of my blood through the skin. 'They're calling her the "Brighton Belle". I mean, fuck!'

I slammed my hand against the wall, hard enough that my palm rang with pain. It was satisfying to watch Tony jolt a little, his expression sharpening, becoming more watchful. I wondered if he thought I was going to attack him with the Take Down Spray. Who knew? I might.

'Read it!' I told him. 'Read the fucking article! Someone in Whitehawk has opened up the community centre – they've had hundreds of volunteers out looking for her, putting up posters. Read what the police spokesman was quoted as saying.'

'I'm getting to that; hold on.'

I snatched the paper from him. He looked at me despairingly, his coat half-shrugged from his shoulders.

'Here. Look. "We will not rest until this girl is safe and home with her family." That's pretty – that's pretty noble, right? Constant vigilance. She's been all over the news. I saw it last night, and again this morning. You know what I just heard on the radio? They found her. Alive and well, just hiding out at a friend's place.'

'Uh-huh.'

'She's only been missing thirty-six hours and look at the fuss. Look at the coverage. I can hardly get Edie's name into the local rag – don't touch me!'

His hand, which had been edging towards me, dropped.

'Why didn't you ever say that to me? Why didn't you not rest until *my* daughter was home?'

'Samantha, here. Let me make you some tea. Sit down. Come on. Please.'

I stared at him. 'I remember you saying to me that girls like Edie will always find their way home. I didn't know what you meant by that then. I do now. You mean girls like Edie aren't photogenic enough. Girls like Edie have been in trouble at school and have a bad home life. Girls like Edie don't warrant the same level of attention the Brighton Belle got. For one thing, girls like Edie can't be relied upon to make a nice story at the end of the news. Girls like Edie never do.'

Tony looked at me. He didn't tell me what I was saying wasn't fair. He didn't tell me they'd done all they could. He didn't tell me about the slashed funding, the budget cuts, the lack of resources. He didn't try to explain at all. I was sobbing, great wracking gulps that squeezed my chest like a vice. He ran his hands over his face and gestured for me to sit. He made us tea in silence, watching me smoke in quick, darting puffs.

'I let her down,' I said. 'Edie. If I'd worked harder, if I'd got her some help – she was disadvantaged from the start with her shitty father and me, desperately trying not to sink. I couldn't scrape together a search party if I fucking tried.'

Tony lowered himself into the seat opposite me. I didn't know it then, but he'd already had the first in a string of heart attacks that would eventually kill him. He was grey-faced and looked suddenly old and washed out, sun-faded.

'Sam, I don't know what to tell you. I can say, though, with one hundred per cent bloody certainty, that you did not let your daughter down. You did the best you could, just like I did with mine, just like our own parents, and everyone before them.' He took a cigarette from my pack and lit it, coughing wetly as he exhaled. Then he reached over the kitchen table and squeezed my hand. His skin felt like sun-warmed leather. Outside it started to snow, fat white flakes dusting the streets and the window frames, blanketing the roofs of parked cars.

I wish Tony were still here. I could tell him all the things I've found out about Peter Liverly – about how he tried to sue the local papers for the stories they printed about him, the gilded language they used: 'eccentric', 'unusual appearance', 'an awkward bachelor'. How he had stones thrown at his bungalow windows, how he started sleeping with a cricket bat beside him on the bed. His adult sons appeared on the local news, talking about his good work with the church, how Liverly had been a member of the Neighbourhood Watch for years and kept himself to himself.

'Mud sticks, though, doesn't it?' the elder son said, speaking directly into the microphone, pale eyes almost colourless, just like his father's. 'Mud sticks. It's ruined his life, it has. What's he going to do now, in his seventies? I feel sorry for the woman whose kid ran off but what about all the other people suffering because of it – like my dad?'

I don't check my mobile until late in the morning, the sun warm on my back. I'm hanging the washing in the back garden with the radio playing quietly through the kitchen window. The Siamese from next door is sitting on my flower bed enthusiastically washing his balls. I pull my phone out and see that there is a message from Frances, sent the previous night. I remember waking up thinking I'd dreamed the phone ringing.

I open the message cautiously, staring at the words on the screen: *I know u said no more but going to the old well today. 3 p.m. F x*

I hang up a bedsheet, clothes pegs clamped between my teeth. No more. I've had enough. I move further along the clothes line and see the cat has moved a little to the right in a patch of syrupy sunlight. He is sniffing the ground, tail in the air, quivering slightly. I pull up a towel from the basket and pin it to the line, humming softly along to the radio. When I look back the cat is digging in the flower bed with his front paws, scrabbling a small divot in the earth.

'Hey!' I snap, stepping towards him. 'There's bulbs in there, you little shit!'

He regards me with cool contemplation.

'Go on, bugger off,' I tell him, and when he moves away – slowly, tail raised – I see he has exposed something down there in the dirt. Four-year-old Edie loved the garden, and the two of us spent a lot of time squatting on the grass, pulling weeds free from the ground and making comical ripping sounds out the corners of our mouths. We dug and planted and pruned, and when I presented Edie with the stunted fruits of our first vegetable crop she glowed with excitement.

I sink down next to the flower bed, brushing the loose dirt away with my hand. She buried things all over this garden. I thought I'd found them all. I peer closer. It's a watch. Cherry-red plastic, digital face. The screen is frosted with condensation, the strap partially chewed. I pull it out of the ground with a hand that doesn't feel quite like my own. I remember this watch. It was in her stocking that Christmas. She was so wowed by it she barely looked at another present that whole day. It looks incredibly small in my hands, doll-sized. It's hard to imagine it fitting her wrist. There's a lump in my throat. The sun, pressing hot on my shoulders. Prisms of light through my closed eyelids, like needles.

I put the watch in one pocket and pull the phone out of the other. I swipe it open with that same distant feeling, as if I'm floating away from myself. *Dis-ass-o-shi-a-shun*, as my therapist had pronounced it. I know better, though. It's my mind, breaking. I've been waiting for it to happen for a long, long time. At the base of my skull I can feel myself becoming untethered, as if some internal rope is working itself loose from the mooring to which I've secured it for eighteen years. I'm getting closer. I can feel it.

Frances – Now

She's coming. I wait impatiently, one hand holding the torch against my hip. I flick it on, off, on, off. *Come on*, I think, although I've arrived at the spot early and still have a good ten minutes before the time Samantha said she'd be here. I reach for my phone and realise I have left it charging in the kitchen next to the kettle. *Shit.* Have I got time to head back to Thorn House before Samantha arrives? It's a fifteen-minute walk in the other direction, along the narrow country lane. Samantha and I have agreed to meet here, next to the stile, which will take us over the ploughed field and eventually on to the bridle path that Edward Thorn fought so hard to keep to himself. Alex said it was because of his need for privacy. I wonder if perhaps there was a secret he'd been keeping. I touch the wood of the stile. It's worn smooth by the passage of feet over the years, and warmed by the sun. I close my eyes. *Edie*, I think, *hold on, girl. We're coming for you.*

There's a car approaching. Good. I stand with one foot on the stile and my arm raised so she can see me in time to slow down. I'm nervous, excited. It sounds bad, but it's true. I was once told that the neurological responses of panic and excitement are basically the same. Heart pounding, dry mouth, shaking hands, dizziness. It's our brain's interpretation that takes them into fear or joy. I don't feel joy – I'm about to head into a dark wood on a late summer's day to look for the body of a missing girl – but there is a sense of exhilaration as I stand here, shifting from foot to foot, urging Samantha to hurry up.

The gleam of a car over the top of the winding hedgerow, then it's gone, hidden as it turns the corner. I hear the engine rattle as the driver changes gear and then I see it, a dark blue Ford, a solid, practical car for a solid, practical man, and my heart sinks. It's not her. It's William. What am I going to tell him? Now the panic rises, full-throated, and I wonder how I could ever have thought it was close to excitement.

He slows down as he drives past me and then I see the red brake lights come on as he draws to a stop in the middle of the dusty road. I hesitate before walking towards the car with legs that feel wooden and strange. I hear his window slide down. He is keeping the engine on, and I'm hopeful he's just going to ask what I'm doing here, where I'm headed, hopeful he's just caught me as he drives out towards Seaford and Eastbourne along the back roads. Just a stroke of bad luck. I smile tightly. Samantha will be here any minute and I don't want him to see her. I look back over my shoulder, straining to hear her approaching car as I bend down to the driver's window.

He is smiling. 'What're you doing, babe?' he says.

I can hear the radio playing, smell the lemon air freshener hanging from the rear-view mirror. His voice is steady, mildly surprised. Something is wrong. I can feel it. My hand instinctively goes for my phone and then I remember it's back at the house. I tense, and William's smile turns to a puzzled frown.

'Are you okay?' he asks. 'What are you doing out here? You look like you're waiting for someone.'

'No, no.' I laugh; it's too high. 'I'm going for a walk.'

'Where to?'

'Just – around.' Is that her car coming? I lift my head and look back but see nothing except the hedgerows. A bird lands in the road and pecks at something there. A black bird; a crow, maybe. I think of the bird that flew into the roof of the greenhouse, that smear of blood it left behind. *The omen.*

'You need a lift?'

'No, it's fine. I'll see you back at the house, yeah?'

'You okay, Frances? You're sweating.'

'It's hot,' I snap, feeling my pulse rocket. Why won't he leave? 'Off you go, see you in a bit.'

'Frances—'

Samantha's car; I am sure I hear it now. I can't help looking back along the road for that glint of sunlight on chrome. William moves his hand over mine and squeezes. It's painful and when I try to snatch it back, he pins it down tighter.

'Why don't you get in the car?'

'Wh-what?'

'You heard me.'

We stare at each other. Weirdly, I don't feel threatened by him. His gaze is blank and void of interest. He may as well be telling me about the weather. I look back down the road again, desperately.

He sighs, switching off the engine. 'If you're going to run, I'll catch you. I'm faster than you think. There's a lot of things about me you don't know, Frances. So come on round and get in the car.'

There is a bright, pulsing light in my vision. It's fear, manifesting itself. Rising, rising, like the panic in my chest and throat, rising to the crown of my skull. *You are not my William,* I want to say, thinking about the man who curled his arms around me in bed late last night. *He is a good man.* William's grip on my hand tightens to a shimmering pain. My heart thumps giddily, drumming out a beat, over and over, *run rabbit, run rabbit, run, run, run.* And maybe I could. Up and over the stile, through the field. How long till he catches up with me, though, me with my smoker's lungs and decades of pills and powders and cheap bottles of wine?

I walk slow and stiff to the passenger side and open the door as he watches me indifferently through the windscreen with his soft gaze. My glance drifts over the back seat as I climb in. William's car is, like the man himself, always neat and squared away. His glovebox contains only a roadmap and a torch. He keeps high-visibility vests and emergency supplies in the boot in case we should ever break down and get stranded, despite the fact that the furthest we've ever driven is to Devon. I'm always teasing him about it.

On the back seat is a large leather bag I recognise. It's Samantha's. The zip has been pulled roughly open and the contents lie scattered in the footwell and across the seat itself; lip balm, lighters, keys. It makes me think of those dead bodies again, the items that were found in their pockets and recorded for identification. I feel something twist inside me, a sharp pain followed by a wave of dizziness. I grope for the door handle because now that frantic percussion, that *run rabbit, run rabbit, run*, has amplified and grown huge, filling me with fear. My stomach is knotted and slick as William pulls away from the side of the road and turns back towards Thorn House. I turn to face him in my seat and he looks over at me, brow furrowed.

'Frances,' he says. 'Seat belt.'

I pull my seat belt across me with hands that won't keep still, feeling tears swell in my eyes. I catch sight of Samantha's bag in the back seat again and can't help thinking: *Unknown female, 50–55: lip balm, lighters, keys.* It turns me cold and silent. What has happened to her? Where is she? And how much does William know?

We drive in silence, windows rolled down. The breeze flutters my shirt sleeves and tickles my skin. The radio is playing too loudly for us to speak and I'm afraid to reach out and turn it down. My hand is still throbbing, red marks on the skin to match William's grip. I rub at it with my other hand to massage some feeling back in. About halfway back towards Thorn House, I see Samantha's car. William slows down as we pass it. It has been driven off the road and parked in front of a wooden gate, hazard lights flashing. There is a handwritten sign on the windscreen reading *Broke Down – Gone For Help*. It's William's writing.

My stomach falls. 'William? You're scaring me. What happened to Samantha? Is she okay?'

'*Me* scaring *you*?' He grins, and looks at me sidelong. 'You're Frances Thorn, you aren't scared of anything.'

'Jesus Christ, William, this isn't funny!'

'No, you're right. It's not.'

He lowers the volume on the radio with his left hand and I recoil from it when I see the dried blood on his fingers. 'What happened to your hand?'

'Huh? Oh, it's not mine.'

There is blood on the tips of his fingers and more spattered on the cuff of his sweatshirt. I twist my T-shirt in my fists, suddenly feeling violently sick.

'What's happened? Where's Samantha?'

'I said I'll show you. Calm down. You'll still get to play Girl Guides with your new little friend.'

His voice, the flat, idleness of it, as if we were rowing down a sunlit stream on a hazy day, frightens me the most. There's no urgency. He's not afraid. He's almost happy. My blood runs cold as he looks back at the road again, humming along to a song on the radio. I once lived with a Russian girl who told me someone had tried to kidnap her from the small village where she lived. 'Don't get in the car,' she told me in her slurred, heavy voice. Her lips tasted like snow. 'If they get you in the car you are dead. Better to die on the street than see what they have planned for you somewhere quiet and private where people do not hear the screaming.'

But I did it, didn't I? I got in the car. Stupid Frances. *But William wouldn't hurt me.* I look towards the blood on William's fingertips again, and I don't know any more. My heart keeps sending me the same message. *Runrabbitrunrabbit.* We're nearly at Thorn House and suddenly I feel very sure that if I go inside I won't come back out again. If you had asked me this morning, I would have told you that there was more chance of the sun falling out of the sky than of William – my William, strong and kind and humble – hurting me. But now I'm not so sure. It's that blood, you see. The spots of it on his cuffs. And his voice, so calm and distant, a flat, glassy sea. He looks over at me, still smiling as we pull into the drive. I remember the first time William brought me down here to meet his family. We'd pulled up in this exact spot outside Thorn House and he'd turned to me and said, 'My mum is going to love you.'

Now he turns the engine off and sits quietly, his hands in his lap. I can't take my eyes off the smears of blood on his fingertips. When I say his name he looks right at me.

'What have you done with Samantha?'

'Come on,' he says.

We go into Thorn House together, and I'm immediately struck by how quiet it seems. Even the tick of the hallway clock appears muffled, as though everything is holding its breath. I stand in the hallway shivering, although I am not cold. William removes his sweatshirt but not his shoes, which are crusted with dried mud and dirt.

'You left your phone behind,' he says, quietly. 'I wouldn't have known about it if Alex hadn't told me. "Oh, Frances has left her phone," he said. "Where's she gone?" I asked him. You know what he told me?'

I shake my head.

'He said you were going "up on to the Downs". But that isn't what you told me. You said you were going into town, to the library. You were quite specific. And I couldn't work out why you'd lie about where you were going. It made me wonder what you were hiding. So I picked up your phone.'

'It has a passcode.'

'It does, and of course yours is the same as your PIN. One – two – three – four. Theoretically, there are ten thousand possible four-digit combinations the numbers zero to nine can be arranged into, and you've gone right ahead and picked the most obvious. It's asking for trouble. I've been telling you that for years.'

He's right; he has. I keep saying I'll change it and not getting round to it. Now look what's happened. He's got blood on his cuffs.

'I found your messages to Samantha. I couldn't work out who she was at first. I thought maybe it was someone back in Swindon, but then I saw the one that said that you were thinking of going out to the old well. The one in the woods, right?'

I nod. My hands hang limp by my sides. That's the thing I always tell my patients about panic. There's always a crash afterwards.

'You know my father boarded that well up over twenty years ago? You *know* that because I told you the story of the sheep's skull. So I thought to myself, what's the deal, Frances? Why are you heading out there to go and look for it? What does that have to do with Samantha? And then I remembered. Edie Hudson.'

242

'You were her boyfriend.'

He snorts.

'I had a lot of girlfriends when I was a kid, if you can believe it. Edie was one of them. She was insane, so I dumped her. Edie was mad about it and ran away. Do I feel guilty? I did, for a while. Did I go and look for her? No. Did I want her to come back? Probably not, if I'm being honest. There you go, that's it. That's the story.'

His hand, the one with the gold band of his wedding ring on, lifts to his hair. He tugs at it gently, distracted. But I see it. I see it.

'I don't know how you got involved with Samantha. Seems to me like she's a lot more trouble than she's worth. I remember reading all that stuff about her in the papers after Edie went missing. Come on.'

I follow him silently down the tiled hallway. At the far end the sun slants through the large arched window that looks out on to Edward's beloved rose bushes. My stomach is full of shrinking knots, pulling themselves tighter and tighter. When William puts the flat of his hand between my shoulder blades, the skin there grows cold with gooseflesh and it takes all my restraint not to pull away from him. He opens the door to our left, the one that leads into the kitchen.

'Go on,' he says. 'In you go, Frances.'

It takes a moment for my eyes to adjust to the darkness, grainy and diffuse. The curtains have been drawn to block out the light but I can make out the bulky shapes of the dresser, the dining table, the long old-fashioned range that heats the room in the winter. Then I see her. Samantha. She is slumped in one of the dining chairs, her chin resting on her chest, wiry hair falling over her face. A rope has been bound around her chest, restraining her. I stare in mute horror.

'I intercepted her on her way to meet you,' William says in a low voice, as if she were merely asleep. 'Good job I found your phone when I did, otherwise I'd never have known where to find you.'

'What have you done to her?'

'I made her pull over and get out the car by pretending I was hurt. I flagged her down just two miles up the road. She didn't know it was me at first. I guess I've grown up a lot since the last time she saw me. You know she carries a knife? She pulled it on me once, in the graveyard.'

'You have to let her go. What is she even doing here? It's kidnap, William.'

'*Kidnap*. Listen to yourself. You're always so dramatic.'

I take a step towards her and William holds me back firmly. There is a black patch on the back of Samantha's head. From here, in the dim light, it looks like dark regrowth of roots. I don't think that's what it is, though. I think of the blood on William's sleeve and something in my chest cracks open, leaking cold, cold water.

'What did you hit her with?'

'I was careful. I only used enough force to knock her out. At worst she'll have a concussion. Just hope she can get to the hospital in time. It can be fatal if it's untreated.'

'William, you have to let me help her. I don't know what you're doing, but this isn't – it's not right!'

'Help her? You have been helping her. You've been helping her with this continuing delusion that somewhere out there her daughter is still alive. You've stirred it all up for her again. Now look what's happened.'

'How do you know?'

'How do I know what?'

'That her daughter isn't alive? You called it a delusion, which would mean you know something to the contrary.'

'All right, Miss Marple, I think we're done here.'

He's been holding me by the wrist, and now he tugs at me insistently. When I resist he pulls me so hard my shoulder seems to pop. I yell out. William just continues to look at me in that same blank way. His eyes, already dark, are almost muddy, his pupils swollen and black. He drags me down the corridor, holding my wrist so tight I can feel the bones grind together. I clamp my teeth against the pain, so sharp it is almost sweet. William motions for me to be quiet before rapping on the closed door further down the hall that leads to Mimi's recovery room.

I hear her voice, her weak-sounding 'Come in.'

William opens the door a slice, just enough to poke his head around.

I say, 'William, plea—' and he gives my wrist one hard, sharp twist. My knees buckle. I have to hang on to the wall to stop myself crumpling to the ground. Hot breath catches in my throat, silencing me. His voice when he speaks to his mother is calm and gentle, the man I recognise, the man I know the bones of.

'I'm just heading out, Mum.'

'Okay, sweetheart. Are you all right? You look a little peaky.'

'I'm fine. Just a bit of a headache.'

'It's the weather,' she says, and I gasp loudly as my wrist sends out bright spikes of pain shooting up my arm. William's hand tightens.

'What was that?' Mimi says. 'Is someone there with you?'

'Nope. Just me. I'll see you later.'

'Be good. And if you can't be good—'

'I'll be careful. I know, Mum. Love you.'

He closes the door quietly and kneels down next to me in the darkened hall. I wish someone would walk in – Alex, maybe, on his way back from the greenhouse, or Samantha, groggy from her blow to the head. Anyone. I'm so frightened of this man. I feel like I'm going to die.

'Come on, on your feet. We're going for a little walk, you and me.'

◆   ◆   ◆

We head outside into the bright sunshine. The air is very hot and still and heavy. I switch my head left and right for Alex. No sign. William has let go of my wrist now and I massage it against my chest. He opens the passenger door for me and I look at him flatly.

'I'm not getting into the car with you. You're crazy.'

'No, Frances, I'm not. I'm just tired of having to look after you, get you out of scrapes. It's like having a kid. You wonder why I've avoided having one? It's because I know who'll end up looking after it. Me. You can barely look after yourself.'

'That's not fair—'

'Look at Samantha. Look at how she fucked it up. She didn't know what her own kid was doing half the time. Edie was into all kinds of shit – drugs and black magic and she was something of a known slut, if you get my drift. You think you've got what it takes to bring up a kid? Look at what harm you can do if you don't get it right. Look at how you end up.'

I stare at him, open-mouthed.

'I'd rather bring up a lively, interesting kid than someone like you.'

His face darkens, but I can't help myself. It's always been my problem. *Spoiling for trouble.*

'Don't, Frances.'

'You're a repressed, dull man with nothing to show for all his years on earth except his bank balance and a stack of dirty photos. Your mother sh—'

Crack! I hear it before I feel the sting of the slap, right across my cheekbone. It's hard enough to make my skull shake. I look at him in horror, one hand covering my face. His lips are pressed tightly together, eyebrows drawn. He looks furious, but when he speaks his voice still has that same, flat tone.

'Get in the car, Frances. I won't ask you again.'

I stare at him. I could run, I think. Maybe I *could* outrun him. I've always thought of William as a desk slob, someone weak-muscled and unfit, but when he gripped my wrist earlier I felt a lean, wiry strength there that belied his physical appearance. But if I could – and it's a very big *if* – where would I run? William grew up here; he knows this area like the back of his hand. I've no money and my phone is still in there in the kitchen, plugged in and lying on the counter. *So what do you do, Frances?* the voice in my head asks me. *Just what are you going to do?*

'I need to pee,' I tell him.

He stares at me. I bend a little at the waist, my hands folded into my crotch. It's a lie, of course, but now I've said it the urge has suddenly become very real.

I stare at him with round eyes. 'Please. I have to go!'

'Jesus, Frances,' he says with undisguised disgust, and he drags me a little way down the drive to where the hydrangea bushes line the pathway. He points. 'Go on then. Do it on the grass. Like a dog.'

'You're going to stand here and watch me?'

'Believe me, Frances, I've seen you do a lot worse over the years.'

My cheeks flush as I unbuckle my belt. *He doesn't trust you,* that voice says again. *Can you blame him?* He watches me, unblinking, as I relieve myself into the earth, shuffling to avoid getting any on my shoes. I don't look up at him again until I'm done, and when I finally lift my gaze I'm horrified to see he is holding something in his right hand. It's a hammer. A claw-head. It's dropped down from his sleeve like a magic trick and now it swings slightly in his hand like a pendulum slowing down. I can't speak. I can't take my eyes off it. My reaction is so strong I wonder if I will be sick, bile rising in my throat.

William talks to me kindly, squatting down beside me on the grass, careful to avoid the dampness beneath me. 'It's all right, Frances. I'm not going to use it. I just need you to do as you're told. So no more diversions, okay? Come on. Let's go.'

He helps me to my feet and I walk beside him slowly back to the car. In my dreams the figure chasing me with the claw hammer always changed, but the weapon remained exactly the same: a red handle wrapped around the middle with straps of black gaffer tape. Just like the one William is holding.

Samantha – Now

There is a sound like a chainsaw, something buzzing through the ridges of my skull. A deep throbbing pain in the back of my neck. If I open my eyes everything seems to slide away, like a ride at the fairground, so I keep them closed. It hurts less that way. I'm being moved in the dark. Bumped around. Something against my chest, a weight. I don't fight. I lean into it. Tight bands restricting my breathing. God, my head. I fade in and out. A woman's voice that I recognise, but only a little.

'Put her over there so I can see her.'

Hello? My voice doesn't work. I fade out. In. Out. Like my breath. A hand against the shelf of my neck. Ow.

'There's a pulse. You think I should throw cold water over her?'

'Only if you want to clear up the mess it'll make, young man.'

That woman again, so familiar. *Who is it?* In. Out. I'm trying to repair my memory. What happened? I was driving. I had sunglasses on, because the sun was right in my eyes. So blinding that I almost missed him. *Who?* The man standing by the side of the road. *Who?* The man in the grey sweatshirt. He was clutching his chest like he was having a heart attack. His car was skewed across the road. I was driving to – to meet someone. *Who?* Frances Thorn. William's wife. *William. William.* I got out of my car, sliding my sunglasses up to the top of my head. I was saying are you hurt, should I call an ambulance? The sun was in my eyes, making it hard to see his features. I wasn't looking at the way he was holding his arm behind his back. I was only looking at the way his hand was massaging his heart.

'Help me,' I say weakly, turning my head just a little, so the pain is muted. I wait. The chair creaks as I shift position. I prise my eyes open. Everything is a blur, prisming, smeared colours without form. Then I hear a man's voice say, very quietly, 'She's awake, Mum.'

'Help me,' William said as I raced forward. Both our cars were blocking the road now. The lane was baking in the heat. Dragonflies rose and fell in the air. I was reaching for my phone, the other reaching out to steady him, when he struck. First the back of my head, producing a loud ringing noise in my ears that made my whole head shiver, then my shoulder. I heard something crunch beneath the impact of that, with a roaring pain that shot up my neck and across my skull. I looked up at him as black spots swam across my vision, pitching me into a hole, a blackness. A deep well.

In. Out. It's difficult to lift my head without discomfort but the sickening see-sawing of my vision has stopped and I can see a little better now. There is a deep, angry throbbing in my shoulder and a dark stain has spread on the fabric of my T-shirt. The floor beneath my feet is deep, cream carpet. It lifts towards me and then falls away. I tilt my head and look to my left, where there are long windows, sunlight filtered by gauzy net curtains. The agony in my head recedes a little and I want to lift a hand up to the wound and feel for the damage there. I know there is blood because I can smell it, rich and coppery, tangled in my hair.

Instead I keep my head down and slide my glance sideways. The pain in my head recedes like a low tide but my ears still buzz, my skull filled with worker bees building a hive. *Worker bees, Sam?* a voice in my head says, gently. *Honey, be careful. You were knocked out. This is a concussion. You're going to need help.*

I see the clawed feet of a bed, a day bed, one of those vintage French ones with flaking white paint and rattling supports. There is a pale paisley coverlet draped over a skinny form, like a bundle of sticks. I can hear a television playing softly, a laughter track. An old show, one I haven't heard of in years.

'*Do you mean a bloodhound, Katie Marigold?*'

'*No, sir! My daddy calls him a bloody hound, sir, 'specially when he's mad.*'

I hear a woman laugh softly, in the room with me. I risk lifting my head a little higher, hoping her attention is firmly fixed on the television where the old show is playing. I see a pale face floating above the covers, cocooned with white, wispy hair to the shoulders. Her pale eyes aren't looking at me, and she is chewing something slowly, thoughtfully.

I know her. I know her.

'Mimi?' I can't help it. It slips out my mouth. A spark of pain flares between my ears as I sit upright. For a second I see flashing white stars. The woman, Mimi Thorn, I'm sure it *is* her, lowers the apple she is eating and looks at me curiously. With her other hand she feels for the remote in the bed and mutes the television.

'Looks like we're twins,' she says finally, pointing to her own scalp. I can see a part of her hair has been clipped away to reveal a long wound criss-crossed with ugly black stitches. 'Please don't bleed all over my new carpet. I've only recently had it done.'

She takes another bite of her apple, still chewing, still staring at me. I wonder if I am dreaming. A hallucination, conjured up by my shocked brain. I twist against the ropes. They are very tight, wrapped around my chest and the back of the chair. If I could walk, maybe I could stand and limp with the chair attached to my back, tortoise-like. If I made it as far as the door, however, it's doubtful I would fit through. *If I made it that far.* My legs feel weak and shaky. I don't think they could carry me all that way. The woman in the bed places the apple core, very carefully, into a dish on the table beside her. I don't see a weapon, but she looks at me with the calm confidence of someone who is holding one.

'You're Mimi Thorn. Edie's teacher. What am I doing here?'

She continues to look at me flatly, her expression unreadable. I feel panic clutch my chest.

'You don't need to tie me up. I'm hurt. I need help.'

'There was a knife in your pocket. I think under the circum-stances tying you up was the only appropriate course of action.'

I feel a rush of anger and have to clamp my teeth together. I push against my bindings, trying to ignore the pounding in my head, the warm trickle of blood oozing down the back of my neck. She watches me with that same bland curiosity. I'm a pinned insect.

'I'm meant to meet someone,' I gasp, twisting against the ropes. 'They'll be wondering where I am.'

'If you mean Frances, she's with William.'

'She's not safe with William.'

'Oh?'

I slump into the chair, exhausted, head pounding, a metallic taste bright against my palate. The rope hasn't slackened an inch. If anything, it's burrowed deeper. I can see purple welts on my arms where it has burrowed into my skin.

'He hit me.'

'You were coming at him with a knife – and not for the first time, I might add.'

I stare at her. She is sitting upright, straight as an arrow against the pillows. The day bed has been inched away from the wall at an angle so that she can see through the French windows into the long garden. When I first noticed the bed I presumed I was in one of the bedrooms upstairs, but now I realise we are on the ground floor in a room that has been converted, just for her. There is a trolley with wheels that serves as a lap tray on which sit a bowl and a fat round teapot in olive green. There is a pile of magazines on the bedside table, next to a jug of water. A bowl of fruit sits to her other side, where a chair is positioned, drawn up right next to the bed. She is like a little empress sitting high on her plump white pillows.

'You remember that, do you? William was sixteen years old. You threatened him in a graveyard. You're lucky we didn't have you charged.'

My head throbs. The pain is sparked kindling, blown embers. I remember the sound of William's voice: *Mrs Hudson, please! Please!* The way the frost crunched under my boots, the smell of woodsmoke and snow, almost metallic.

Mimi leans over and plucks a grape from the fruit bowl. She rolls it between her thumb and forefinger thoughtfully. 'We don't blame you, you know. No one would.'

'Blame me for what?'

'For what you did to Edie.'

I have been trying to shrug the ropes up my body instead of twisting out from under them, working them over my chest in small, caterpillar movements. Now I stop, lift my aching head. Mimi is smiling.

'I didn't do anything to her.'

She slides the grape into her mouth and bites down on it hard between her teeth. It makes an audible popping sound. I wince.

'Are you sure? Are you quite, quite sure? Because William has seen you in quite a temper on more than one occasion, hasn't he? All his interactions with you were stained with your anger. That night you caught the two of them together, Edie had wanted to leave with him. She practically begged him. Maybe she was scared of what you might do to her behind closed doors?'

'That's crazy.'

'Is it? William said it doesn't take much for you to fly off the handle. It's not such a stretch to imagine you went over the top one night in a fit of rage. After all, he saw you assault her.'

'I didn't assault her – Jesus.'

'You didn't grab her arm? Push her through the door?'

I blink. Mimi takes another grape, bites it clean in half. I'm trying to think but my head is full of clanging bells. I remember finding William and Edie together on the sofa, the way she called me a bitch. The word came out of her mouth glowing hot, hateful. I grabbed her arm. I wasn't rough. I didn't hurt her. At least I hadn't meant to.

'I was angry.'

'I know. Like I said, no one blames you. She put you through a lot. It can't have been easy for you, being on your own.'

'It wasn't. It was really, really hard.'

'I know. I know that, Samantha.'

'I loved her, though. I loved her so much. I would never have hurt her.'

'But you did, didn't you? You killed her.'

Another grape. Her eyes flick back to the television, then over to me again. I think I can hear footsteps on the gravel path outside, but perhaps it is just my imagination.

'Can I ask you, Samantha, why you carry a weapon in your pocket?'

'Protection,' I say immediately. The vision in my left eye is blurred, casting everything in a shimmering aura. For the first time I wonder if this head injury is more serious than I first thought.

'From whom?'

'Edie.'

'She was violent, wasn't she?'

'Yes.'

'And you were frightened of her, weren't you?'

'Yes.'

'Samantha?'

'Mmm?' I'm falling asleep. Everything is losing shape, softening. I struggle to sit upright.

'You were saying you were frightened of your daughter.'

'Yes. Yes, I was. I kept Mace in a drawer by the bed. Some nights she'd sneak into my room and wake me up by pulling my hair. I couldn't sleep. I couldn't eat. I was nervous all the time. You don't know what it's like to live like that. Not knowing what mood she would be in. Not knowing if she was hiding somewhere to jump out at me. It used to make her laugh, my fear. That's not right, is it?'

Mimi shakes her head. Now I can definitely hear footsteps walking round the front of the house. I can hear keys jingling, the click of the front door. Fear rises in my chest. I can't think straight. Everything is falling away from me.

'Samantha, keep talking. It'll keep you awake.'

'I couldn't admit it to anyone. Imagine that. No one's going to take me seriously. "She's fifteen, for God's sake, just ground her," they'd say, but how can you explain what it's like? I couldn't ground Edie. I may as well have tried to hold back a tide.'

Mimi brushes imaginary crumbs from her lap. There is a soft knocking at the door. She says 'Come in' without taking her eyes from me. The rooms tilts suddenly. It's a nauseating, violent

255

movement, like the heaving of a ship on rough water. I close my eyes, steady myself. I need to get to the hospital. I should tell her, *I think your son has done something to my brain.*

Instead, I hear myself still talking. 'I was pleased when she started dating, going out more. It meant I didn't have to see so much of her. She was distracted. I could start getting my own life in order again.'

'You were relieved?' Mimi says.

'Yes.' I sigh, and I feel it, even now, here in this room where I'm bound to a chair while a dent in my skull seeps blood and my ears ring like Alpine bells. I remember the relief I felt, as short-lived and bright as a firework.

A movement in the corner of my eye. I turn my head carefully. In the doorway stands a short man with dark hair and eyes, clean-shaven, polite-looking. His gaze skims me before he turns to his mother.

'Do you know Alex? Alex, this is Samantha Hudson. We're just talking about what she did to her daughter.'

I open my mouth to protest – *I didn't do anything!* – but nothing comes out. My throat is shrinking, becoming a blowpipe. *You want to know what happened to Edie, don't you?* that voice in my head asks. *After all this time, maybe you should keep going. Maybe there are things about yourself you don't know.*

Alex nods, unsmiling. I can see he is nervous. His hands are in constant motion, tugging at his clothes, his hair, his lips.

'We're talking about forgiveness,' Mimi says, pointedly. 'How important it is to forgive yourself when you've done wrong. Mahatma Gandhi himself said, "Forgiveness is the attribute of the strong", after all. Do you think you're strong enough to forgive yourself, Samantha?'

'Forgive myself for what?'

'For killing her.'

I can feel myself drop like a stone into the pool of silence. I open my mouth and hear someone laughing, wetly. It sounds almost like a sob. It's me.

'I didn't kill my daughter.'

'Samantha—' Mimi says.

'What? I didn't kill her! I loved her!'

'No one here is suggesting you didn't love her.' Mimi sweeps her hand around the room as if it were full of people. 'But until you forgive yourself, you'll always be like this.'

'Like what?' I croak.

'Desperate and hollow. Always looking for someone else to blame. Edward, William, that poor man Liverly. Driven out of his home.' She leans forward in the bed, skeletal and spidery, her skin rustling like paper. 'Forgiveness is going to set you free.'

Alex's face is set like a stone, something torn from granite and rock. He is watching his mother with a faint smile. I have to get out of here. I don't want the truth. I don't want forgiveness. Let me be blind and ignorant, always.

I turn to Alex. 'Alex. Alex, I'm hurt. Please. I need to get to the hospital.'

'She doesn't want to see it, Alex,' Mimi says, sighing. She picks up the television remote again. 'There's none so blind, I suppose.'

'Alex, please untie me.'

He doesn't move. He doesn't even look at me. He's looking across the room to the French windows.

'Bird's back, Mum, look.'

'I see him. "The little red robin goes bob-bob-bobbin' along." Off he goes! He loves those seeds, doesn't he?'

Alex nods. His face is so still but his hands, in and out of his pockets, smoothing the front of his jumper, they are in almost perpetual motion.

'I didn't kill her,' I say quietly. 'She just never came home.'

257

'She was in trouble, wasn't she?' Mimi says, and it takes me a moment to understand the euphemism.

'She was pregnant, yes.'

'Dear God. You must have been in pieces.'

'I didn't know. I only found out a few days ago.'

She looks at me carefully. My throat is so dry my voice is cracking. The condensation on the glass jug is beautiful; sparkling, slow-moving crystals rolling down its fattened sides. I lick my lips. I am so thirsty. My head pounds.

'You think you know your children,' I say, trying to hold her gaze with my own slippery one. 'You grow their bones inside you, you think you know who they are, but you don't. Not really. Not ever. They keep their secrets close because it would cost you too much to look at them.'

Mimi's eyes slide towards the door, to where Alex is standing. He has jammed his jittery hands into his pockets.

'Alex,' she says, and although she is smiling I hear the frost on that word, the way it sounds so brittle it might crack. 'What do you think?'

'About what?'

'Secrets,' she says, and tilts her head to one side. 'Forgiveness. The things we keep to ourselves.'

'I don't know th—'

'It's funny,' Mimi says, turning back towards me. I am not looking at her. I am only looking at that water. I have to have a drink. My tongue is as cracked and swollen as a blister. 'When I think of my two boys it was always William I thought I'd have trouble with. When he started courting your Edie, I didn't know what to make of it. What did he see in this girl, all lipstick and ripped tights and snarling? It was a match made in hell. Then, after his father died, I thought he would go off the rails entirely. I could imagine him winding up in one of those detention centres, doing community service in the parks in Brighton. I was so afraid for him and I watched him so closely I almost missed what was happening right under my nose. Didn't I, Alex?'

He stares at her, his jaw tense. A sweat has sprung out on his brow and beneath the armpits of his grey T-shirt. A small gold chain, wire-thin, hangs around his neck. He looks at his mother with such acute discomfort I wish I could turn my back.

'Mum, please.'

'Forgiveness. That's what we're talking about. But I can't expect Samantha to forgive herself if we can't demonstrate the same. So we'll start with you. We'll start with the night you pushed me down the stairs.'

The silence is as thick and heavy as velvet. I want to scream but the inside of my mouth is rustling sandpaper.

'Mimi. Please, can I have some of that water?' I manage.

'I'll do it,' Alex says automatically. He lifts the jug with a shaking hand, making the ice cubes chatter against the glass. Mimi watches him, smiling that tight, mean little smile. He brings it over to me, using his other hand to steady it, which is trembling so violently now I'm worried the water will spill into my lap. I open my mouth, feeling as vulnerable and helpless as a baby bird. As he pours a dribble on to my tongue I can smell the outside on him; the warmth of the sun like baked clay, green shoots, damp earth like a hole dug deep. His gaze is as cold and dark as Neptune.

'You think I don't know these things, Alex, but I do,' Mimi is continuing. 'I felt your hands in the small of my back in the empty house. I heard your breath behind me on the stairs. In the dark.'

Alex says nothing. He stands, water jug in one hand, the other hanging limply by his side. He's cowed, like a scolded dog. Mimi switches her attention suddenly back to me, a sea change so abrupt I feel the room sway.

'What did you use, Samantha? Did you use the knife? Did you push her down the stairs, like Alex here, so you could tell yourself it was a misstep in the dark?'

'No, no—'

'Was it about her boyfriends? Her behaviour? Her outbursts? What was it that finally tipped you over the edge, Samantha?'

I stare at a mark on the floor, say nothing. *No comment*, I think, and that voice again, unsure now, almost whispering, speaks up in my head. *Are you sure you didn't do it, Sam? Are you positive?*

'Memory is a funny thing,' Mimi says calmly, 'because we create it ourselves. We can bend it to our whims, sometimes without even realising. Your memory can trick you.'

'I would remember hurting Edie. I know I would.'

'Would you? Are you sure? Are you remembering right?'

'Yes!'

'So what's *your* memory of the last time you saw her?'

A single bright light like a flashbulb in my head. I can almost taste the electricity, the hum of the static.

'You had an argument, didn't you?' she prompts. 'Said some terrible things to each other, maybe?'

'Yes. It was just – it was just a stupid necklace.'

'That's right. The one with the dragonfly. Did you shout at her? Did you hit her, Sam?'

'No, no,' I say, shaking my head despite the bright pops of pain it causes. People talk about the 'glimmer of doubt' but it isn't like that, it's not a fleck of gold on a riverbed. Doubt, real doubt, has teeth, long and needle-sharp, and they sink into the soft matter of your brain slowly, inch by delicious inch. *Did you hit her, Sam?*

'I loved her,' I say, simply. I look up at Mimi, who has tears in her eyes. *I'm just trying to help you*, she is saying; *you've suffered for so long.*

'I know you did. We love our children despite seeing the worst of them sometimes.' Her eyes slide over to Alex, who stiffens. 'When she left that morning, did you say goodbye to her?'

'I don't know,' I say miserably. Doubt, the predator. The carnivore. I feel my stomach rise and fall like seasickness. 'I must have done, I suppose.'

'She never made it to school, did she, Sam?'

I shake my head.

'Did she even leave the house?'

I stare at the carpet. There are drag marks in the deep pile from the doorway, clots of mud from my shoes. I wonder what I did to my little girl. The cellar below our house was old and damp and out of bounds since before we moved in, a dirt floor prone to flooding. Some nights I would hear rats scratching at the walls. There was no light. The bulb had blown and I never replaced it.

Why?

I don't know.

What have you been keeping down there in the dark?

Shut up. Shut up.

'You need a hobby, Mum,' Edie said to me that morning, the last time I ever saw her. 'You've started to imagine things.'

'Is it possible that you just wanted her to sleep?' Mimi asks. 'Just wanted some peace and quiet? Just wished for a break from it all?'

'Yes,' I sniff. 'I did want a break.'

'And how did you get one?'

I look up at her with round, glassy eyes. 'Did I do it?' I ask her, the pain in my head a cleaver. 'Did I? I don't remember any more.'

I keep seeing her, the last morning. Edie, dashing her face against the plaster, the look in her eyes mean and hungry. I didn't know she was pregnant then. She'd hidden it from me.

'I think this is going to be painful for you, Samantha, but I hope you can forgive yourself,' Mimi tells me sweetly. Her eyes shimmer with tears held back.

Edie and I on the landing, her shrieking at me, the trickle of blood from her nose, me shouting back, angry and hurt and frightened, our voices intertwined like climbing vines, up and up and up. I wish I could take it back. It was only a necklace. It was only a—

'How do you know?'

'What's that?' Mimi says.

I grit my teeth against a fresh wave of agony. 'The dragonfly on the necklace. The one my mother gave me. You mentioned Edie had it. How did you know?'

She watches me a long time. It's a thoughtful, considered gaze and it makes my skin crawl. Finally, she unwinds the scarf she is wearing and hands it to Alex. He approaches me and I shrink away as far as I am able but the ropes have pulled so tight around me that I can barely move at all. I'm shaking my head, *no, no, no.*

'Those are constrictor knots,' Mimi tells me, settling back against the pillows. 'They get tighter the more you struggle. Alex was in the Scouts. He won awards for his knot-tying.'

Alex's blank, distant face is terrifying. He doesn't even flinch when I kick him in the shin, spitting at him, pulling the ropes into my arms so deep it burns.

'Get away from me!' I scream. 'I didn't kill her! I didn't kill her! I didn't kill her!'

My head seems to split like an overripe peach; a fresh gout of blood in the newly opened wound spatters on to Mimi's fancy carpet, coin-sized drops of scarlet. The bells ring, clamour, a flock of crows lifting off from the base of my skull, circling the little bone dome; I close my eyes, breathe. In. Out. I want a memory, a real memory, fleshy and true, not fed to me piece by poisoned piece by this woman.

Something is nagging at me. I can feel it, as insistent as a flickering neon sign. *Nosebleed.* The phone calls in the night, the breathing. That one word, in a voice so familiar I can almost grasp it. *Nosebleed.*

Alex shoves the scarf into my mouth and I gag against it, tasting the bitterness of Mimi's perfume on the fabric.

I hear Mimi, to Alex. 'Pass me the phone. Sadly, I think it's time for Plan B.'

I open my eyes, making a concerted effort to see. My vision is blurred and seems to be skipping, as if on a time delay. Breathe in. Mimi has a handset pressed to her ear. Breathe out. Now she is talking calmly into it. In. She looks across the room at me. Out. Alex turns to her and says, 'I'll make you that cup of tea now, Mum.'

In. Out. In. I open my eyes. The television is back on, playing quietly in the background. Alex is no longer in the room. I look over at Mimi, who has her arms folded.

When she speaks, she doesn't look at me. 'You implode without forgiveness. That's what happens. It's what happened to Edward. He drove into an icy river. Never ever struggled. He let the car fill up with water, all the way to the top. Just sat there, hands in his lap. He couldn't forgive himself for not going to the police when he had the chance. He couldn't live with the guilt of knowing. Now the same thing will happen to you. Because you can't forgive yourself.'

I make a muffled bleating sound through the scarf. She doesn't even look at me.

'William left your car by the side of the road. Later, Alex will take it to the Kissing Bridge, where – as it happens – my Edward drove into the water. This evening, after dark, the guilt and the depression that has been building up inside you will cause you to throw yourself off the bridge and into the water, where the head injury you suffer will cause you to drown.'

No, no. I shake my head.

Mimi smiles kindly. 'I wondered if anyone would believe it. "Grief-stricken mother takes own life" is a bit – well, it's clichéd, isn't it? But then I realised. Nancy Renard will believe it. Peter Liverly's son will believe it. Your brother will believe it. They've all seen how you've been behaving. The slow chipping-away of your sanity. You'll be surprised how little impact the loss of your life will have.'

I've never been so frightened in my life, such sheer, unending panic; I can feel it crawling all over me like a swarm. Even the pain in my head is muted, suffocated by fear. I wonder what she sees when she looks at me, all bloodied face and round eyes and sweat, the shoulder of my shirt torn at the seam, the skin already mottled with purple bruising.

'I've already spoken to William. He's taking Frances now. He's going to show her something. Something awful. But she'll forgive him. Because forgiveness is strength and Frances is not strong unless William is beside her. It's what he likes best about her. And she'll forgive you, too, in time. She'll understand.'

Frances — Now

He's driving too fast. My fingers dig into the car seat until the tips turn white. A car blasts its horn at us as we speed past, missing it by a whisper. The lanes are too narrow for this. I can't look. I can't look at the road, I can't look at the hammer in his hand. Red and black and wound with tape. It makes my blood turn cold.

'Slow down. You're going to kill us,' I whisper, pleading.

He looks at me and eases off the accelerator, but only a little. Good old William, the man who could be relied on to intuit a speed limit within a ten-mile radius, who never drove fast, not even when late for our honeymoon flight. What has happened to him? This man, *my* man, usually so composed and inanimate, is suddenly full of a fierce and frightening energy, kinetic with it, laying his hand on the horn as we narrowly miss a truck coming the other way, forcing it into the side of the hedge as we pass. I catch sight of the driver's face, slack with shock, then it is gone.

'You know why I started gambling, Frances?'

I shake my head. Our trivial little life together in Swindon feels like a lifetime ago.

'You made me go to those meetings, didn't you? Gamblers Anonymous. This man there told me I was addicted to the thrill of winning. A chemical in my brain shot like ejaculate when my numbers came up. I don't know how I didn't laugh in his face. It wasn't the thrill, the winning or losing. I wasn't like the other hopeless sad sacks in there craving their little dopamine release. I liked the control.'

I jerk forward as he suddenly slows down, the back of the car fishtailing a little. Speed camera. I press my hand against the glass of the window. I wonder if they see me.

'You ever see someone lose control, baby? I mean, you know, *really* lose it? I have. Only once. It was horrifying and beautiful and I've never quite got it out of my mind. Imagine – you're stepping backward into an empty lift shaft. You descend into blackness and above you, the light of the doorway you came through is falling away from you faster and faster. You know the impact is going to break all your bones and that light is dropping away to nothing. That's what it looked like. In her eyes. The light of sanity, falling away.'

He's forced to slow down again as we approach town. I recognise the garage coming up on our right and remember that a little further up ahead there is a set of traffic lights. *If they're red*, I tell myself, *I'm going to jump from the car and start running*. I think of the Russian girl with the kisses like snow. *He can chase me, and he might catch me, but if he's going to beat me with that hammer he's going to have to do it right here on the street.* My hand reaches for the handle. I'm sweating enough to make my palms slippery. There's the lights up ahead. They're green. Green is fine. They can still change. I need to keep him talking.

'You're the most in-control person I know,' I say, knowing as soon as I say it it's the wrong thing. He wanted me to ask who he was talking about. Who she was. I have a feeling I already know.

'Of course I am,' he replies. 'I cultivate it day after day after day. You don't know what it's like to feel like that all the time. Like you can't let go because if you do, you'll fall apart. It's a state of constant vigilance and it's fucking exhausting. You want to know why I did what I did with Kim? Control. You want to know why I won't turn that box room into a nursery? Control.'

The lights are still green. There are five cars ahead of us, there's still time, there's still time. I stare as if I could will them to change colour with my mind. My hand is so tight on the handle I think it will come off. Then I remember. Seat belt! My other hand, the free one, moves slowly down to the latch that will free it at the last second when I wrench the door open. The lights suddenly switch to amber. I hold my breath.

'It's an illusion, control,' he says, moving the hammer to his other hand so he can switch on the indicator. 'My dad knew it. Even as his car filled up with water.'

Just as we reach the lights he speeds up, pushing the car over the line just as they turn to red. I sit in shock, eyes wide, heart pounding, my hand still on the door handle, the other still wrapped around the buckle of my seat belt. *I missed it. I missed my chance.* William looks at me and I am shocked by what I see in his face, the blankness in his eyes. It's like he doesn't know who I am. He licks his lips and indicates again, turning off the main road down a side street of terraced houses. I suddenly know where we are going, even before I see the spire of St Mary de Castro over the rooftops.

'William,' I say, trying to sound composed, and failing, 'please, pull over. We can talk. About anything you want.'

'Thing is, Frances, you – you're a case study in lack of control, aren't you? You just can't say no to things. Charity cases, drugs, trouble. You're just my type, apparently.'

'You make me sound like a terrible person.'

'Hardly. You're a sucker for a good cause, but now look where it's landed you.'

'What do you mean?' *Keep him talking*, I think. *You* have *to keep him talking.*

'Samantha. You couldn't resist it, could you? A boo-hoo story about a missing girl and you're getting ready to climb down an old well and wind up with a broken neck and you know what you'd have found? Nothing. Not a damn thing.'

He falls silent as we turn into the strip of wasteland at the edge of the graveyard. William pulls up alongside the crumbling wall spilling with ivy. To our right is Peter Liverly's bungalow; to our left a small, empty two-storey office block with a *To Let* sign attached. The road is quiet, and from here I can only see the backs of the terraced houses, silent and cast in shade. I don't want to get out of this car. There is no one else around.

'William?'

'Huh?'

'Where is Edie Hudson?'

'Come on,' he says. 'Out.'

We walk away from the car towards the bungalow. He's got the hammer in his hand, hanging loose by his side as if he's forgotten it's there. Every time I notice it my chest floods with a gush of hot blood and I'm thrown back into my dream, the way my breath catches in my mouth, the way my feet are sucked into the ground, slowing me down as the man swinging the hammer stands over me, his eyes pitiless black holes. The broken wooden gate to the bungalow hangs askew on its single rusted hinge, but William still stands aside and indicates for me to go ahead as if he is ushering me into a high-class restaurant. *Ever the gentleman*, I think, and then my eye is drawn to that claw-head hammer again and my guts squeeze horribly.

'I slept with Edie Hudson a handful of times,' William says suddenly as we round the corner of the bungalow, heading towards the back of the house over the crumpled litter and overgrown grass. 'One of those times was here.' He points towards the brick wall, the one that runs along the back of the Liverly property, separating it from the churchyard. 'I don't remember much about it. She was my first proper girlfriend, although I don't think our fumbling around in the dark deserves such an eloquent description, you know?' He snorts laughter, but he isn't smiling. He has that faraway look again, staring at the wall. 'When she told me she was pregnant I was sick. I mean actually, physically sick. Right into my lap. That's what losing control does to me. It infects me. Come on, I'll help you through.'

'Through where?'

He walks to the wall and stands in front of it for a moment, walking back and forth a little, staring. Then he lifts his hand and runs it along the brickwork, beneath the clutch of dark green ivy that spills over the top of the wall.

Finally he turns to me with a miserable, ghoulish smile. 'Here.'

I walk over and peer through the parting he has created in the foliage with his hands. There is a gap in the wall, no more than thirty inches at its widest point. He nods towards it.

I stare at him. 'I won't fit!'

'You will if you turn to the side. "Squeezeguts", we used to call it. Charlie Roper, one of the Rattlesnakes, found some loose bricks on the churchyard side once, and we all got to working on it. We discovered we could make a hole big enough that we could fit through. Took us all the best part of an evening.'

'What was it for?'

'To get in and out the churchyard after the gates were locked, mostly. The old man didn't like it. Liverly, he was called. Weird old thing he was, like a goblin. He used to take pictures of us out here from his bedroom window. Moya said he was a pervert. Edie wanted to burn his house down but Nancy and Alex talked her out of it. Said she'd end up in juvenile prison. One night someone

269

smashed all these back windows and they never found out who did it, but we all knew it was Edie. She hated him. Used to chase him out the graveyard with firecrackers when he was doing his rounds.'

'Jesus, that poor man.'

'Uh-huh. We must have made his life hell. I was sorry about what happened to him. He was unfairly vilified. Sometimes people are such easy targets. Come on.'

I edge through Squeezeguts with my breath held deep in my lungs. It leads out into the back of the churchyard where the old trees grow thickest; giant yews and spreading oaks, tall wavering pines. Here and there old graves spring up out of the ground, old stones smoothed away. It's dark beneath the trees and the air is hot and still and swimming with gnats. William indicates for me to move forward with a flick of his hand.

'William, you don't have to do this. We could turn around and go back home and it'll be fine, it'll all be okay.'

'Will it?' he says in that same, measured tone, looking at me sidelong as we walk through the trees over the bumpy ground.

I nod enthusiastically. *Oh God, please listen to me.* 'Yes! We'll go back to Swindon if you want and you can play golf again and see your friends and I'll – I'll go back to work and we'll eat at the Thai place at the end of the road every Friday just like before. Everything just how it was.'

'I thought you were bored of that life?'

'No!' I exclaim, although of course I mean *yes*. 'You've made me see it now. All of it. We had a good life. We had fun. We loved each other. Please don't waste it. Please.'

He looks at me then, considering. It's the first time I've seen William look like himself since I climbed in the car with him. His face, so sunken and shadowed all the way here, eyes like blank bullets. He draws a breath and it's him, it's William, my William – I almost want to put my arms around him.

'We can go back to before,' I tell him softly, stepping close enough that he can feel how fast I'm breathing, how much I'm trembling. 'All you have to do is say yes.'

The silence is so delicate I daren't breathe for fear of breaking it. I touch his arm and he looks down at my hand in wonder, as if he has never seen it before. He opens his mouth just as his phone rings in his pocket, and my heart jerks at the sound of it. I stare as he removes it and looks at the screen briefly before taking the call. It only lasts forty seconds or so, and at the end of it he speaks only three words: 'Love you, Mum.'

'William, please, just look at me. Here.' I stop and he turns to face me and I try not to let my eye be drawn to that red striped hammer in his hand but I can't help it, it's there, and for a moment I see the head of it the way it looks in my dream, furred with hair and blood and flakes of white bone. Acid rises in my throat. 'You're frightening me. Whatever this is about—'

'It's about Edie Hudson. *You* made it about Edie Hudson.'

'—we can sort it out. Please put the hammer down. Please take me home.'

'I can't do that. Not now. It's too late. Plan B. I'm so sorry, Frances.'

'What did your mum want, William? What did sh—'

'Frances—'

'Just tell me what this is ab—'

His hand swings out of nowhere. I never even see him lift his arm. He strikes me on the jaw, snapping my head back so fast spit flies from my mouth. I can hear the clack of my teeth coming together, the way my mouth fills with blood. It tastes metallic, like sucking pennies. There is a glittering pain along the shelf of my jaw and up towards my left ear. I don't fall down but I need to grab hold of the nearest tree for balance because the whole world is spinning.

William is standing very still, his expression barely changed. I lift my hand to my jaw and it comes away smeared with blood.

'Next time it'll be the hammer,' he says.

I wipe my blood-smeared palm on my jeans as William nods for me to follow him. After only a second's thought I do so. I don't know what else to do.

Samantha – Now

The pain begins at the crown of my head and travels sluggishly down my neck and the rack of my spine, bloody and feverish. My head is filled with a high-pitched note, the long, singular tone of tinnitus. Alex walks through the doorway, looking oddly incongruous wheeling an old-fashioned hostess trolley. On it is the little olive teapot, a cup, a saucer and a bowl of sparkling white sugar lumps. He doesn't look up at me and he speaks only one word to his mother: 'Tea?'

She nods briskly, and then, horribly, reaches out and strokes her fingers down the side of his face. 'I forgive you, Alex,' she says mildly. 'For all your dirty little sins. You can't hide anything from your mother.'

'Mum, I never – I would never—'

'Ah-ah,' she says softly, and slaps him gently on the face. It's a tap, a reprimand for a child. It's sickening. 'No more lying. You know what you did. You know what you are.'

He leans over and kisses her softly on her temple, the good side of her head, the one without the ugly snarling wound stitched across it.

She takes the tea from him with a slow, careful smile and says, 'You always were the apple of my eye, Alex Thorn.'

She looks over at me, smiling that same gentle smile, telling me about the tea Alex makes especially for her, using the flowers from the garden. Rosebud and chamomile, dandelion, jasmine and chrysanthemum. I let her voice fade into the background. I try not to think about Frances, about where she is and what may happen to her. I wish I could speak to her, or warn her. She's with a killer. If only I could reach my phone. Or my knife.

Alex says something and Mimi laughs. It's a nice sound, like the scales on a flute. I close my eyes dreamily. An old friend of mine, Theresa, once hand-stitched me a sampler, which I'd framed and hung over my bed. One word, beautifully cross-stitched in brightly coloured threads: *FUCK*. When I close my eyes I can see it imprinted over and over on my eyelids in glorious technicolour and shimmering neon. It's a clarion call. *FUCK*. It's an urgency I feel running through the marrow of my bones like a voltage with a high-pitched hum. It's an intensity that demands to be felt through the agony of my poor, throbbing head.

My eyes snap open.

'You've gone very pale, Samantha. I do hope you're not going to pass out.'

'I think she's fractured her skull, Mum.'

'Nonsense. You've no idea how hard it is to break bone with a hammer. Edward used to do it all the time for his bonemeal. He once struck a pork knuckle seven times and the bloody thing barely dented the surface. Took a mallet to it in the end. Talk about using a sledgehammer to crack a nut!' Again she laughs, but her face doesn't look right. It's her eyes, maybe. She takes another sip of tea, lifting her hand to point at me. 'Take the scarf out of her mouth, Alex, would you? She looks like she's got something to say.'

He does so gingerly.

I let the words fall from my mouth with a snap. 'Rosebud.'

'I'm sorry?'

That voice I heard on the phone, the call I got the other day where I heard Edie saying 'nosebleed'. *Just because you recognised the voice*, that sane, reasonable person in my head speaks up, *doesn't mean it was Edie.*

Nosebleed.

'On the phone. That was the word. Not *nosebleed*. Rosebud. It's what's in your tea.' I look from Alex to Mimi and realise I am smiling. 'It was Frances's voice I recognised. Not Edie. God. I was so sure.'

'I'm afraid I don't quite—'

'The phone calls to my house. This is where they've been coming from, isn't it? It was Frances I heard talking, not Edie. Only the phone wasn't hung up quite quickly enough, was it? I heard her. I heard her saying "rosebud".' I nod towards the phone beside the bed. 'I barely use my landline any more. I keep it because it was the only phone number Edie had for me. Other than sales calls, hers were the only ones I got. But it wasn't her, was it?' I look right at Mimi. 'Your son is a killer.'

She looks at me and to my surprise she yawns, pressing the back of her hand against her mouth. Still, her eyes settle on me, avaricious. 'Oh, really? Which one? A moment ago you thought my Edward had killed Edie. It must be very tiring to be inside your head. So go on then. Whodunnit? Poor old Steady Eddie? Alex, my plump little black sheep? We all know he's got it in him. Look at what he did to his own mother.'

'You know who I mean.'

'William? You can't prove that.'

'He got her pregnant and he got scared.' I'm thinking more clearly now, the pain a distant drum. Some part of me notices the way Mimi's head seems to loll on her neck, but I don't grasp it, not then. 'And you, your marriage was in trouble, wasn't it? You were having counselling. Edward told me about it.'

She laughs, but the edges of the sound are blurry. *Something's wrong.* 'Edward and I? Counselling? You'll believe any old rubbish, won't you? I'm afraid that was a lie, Samantha. The car wasn't there because we were having marriage counselling. The car was there because I'd driven William to the bloody youth club where he met your slut daughter. But my wonderful husband, my clever, honest Edward, he couldn't live with it. With the guilt. Especially after you showed up on Halloween. Another death on your conscience. How does *that* feel?' Mimi yawns again, her hand covering her mouth.

Slowly, a realisation is building in me. 'Edward drove off the bridge because he knew his son had killed Edie and he couldn't live with it.'

'Oh, please. My boy isn't capable of such violence. Believe me, I know. I raised him right.' She gives me an arch look, as if to say *You wouldn't know about that*, but I'm already gone, the impact of it hitting me with a jolt, a fiery obliteration that turns my insides liquid.

'Edie isn't gone. She isn't missing. She isn't unaccounted for. She's dead. And William killed her.'

Mimi suddenly yawns again, this time so long it seems her mouth is coming unhinged at the jaw. When she looks back at me her eyes are heavy-looking, doleful. I lift my chin defiantly and stare right back at her.

The teacup she is holding rattles against the saucer. 'You think a seventeen-year-old boy was able to murder your wilfully violent daughter in the dark and the cold, just feet away from a group of other people, leave no evidence and dispose of the body by himself? Is that the conclusion you've come to? I must say, I'm disappointed.'

She laughs uncomfortably but I notice something strange. Her face is growing slack: mouth lifted in a half-smile, eyelids drooping sadly. The hand holding the tea cup falls on to her chest and the empty cup rolls down the slope of her body into her lap.

'You,' I say, flooded with a cold and horrifying knowledge. 'You helped him. Not Edward, not Peter Liverly. You. Why?'

She doesn't answer for a minute or so. Her chest rises and falls softly and her glazed eyes stare out through the window to where the robin has returned to the garden, swinging on the birdfeeder.

When she finally speaks her voice is slurred and almost incomprehensible. 'She would have ruined his life.'

Alex pulls something from his pocket. It is my knife. I shrink back against the chair again. Mimi's head slumps forward.

'What are you doing?' I babble. 'Alex, what's going on?'

He approaches me silently, with a calm confidence that sets my nerves singing. Alex moves behind me and I'm convinced he is going to slit my throat. My heart gears up. I drum my feet on the floor, I gnash my teeth. It's feral, this feeling. I want to bite him. I switch my head from side to side and then try to bolt. It's useless; the chair lifts with me, strapped to my back, and I half-run, crabwise, towards the door, hair hanging in my face, breath pinched in my tight chest.

He tackles me as I reach the doorway, pulling me back towards him so roughly I cry out. He yanks the chair back and me with it, head whiplashing as he sets me back on the floor. From this angle I can see Mimi's prone body, the way her chin rests on her breastbone, eyes open and vacant.

Alex sets a firm hand on my shoulder. 'Hold still. I can't do it if you keep struggling.'

I hear the soft chink as the knife slides open. I've handled that knife often enough to be able to recall the way the mother-of-pearl handle will be cool to the touch, the satisfying sheen of the blade, the whisper of it. *I would never have hurt her*, I tell the voice in my head, and it replies, *I know.*

'Hold still, I said!' Alex presses against the chair and I slump forward, exhausted. He is cutting into the place where the ropes

277

are tight across my back. I feel the heat of his hands, the coolness of the blade on my feverish skin. I let my breath fill my lungs, close my eyes. I want to tell him to be quick.

'What are you doing?'

'I can't untie the knots. You've struggled too much and pulled them too tight. I have to cut you free.'

My arms are shrieking with pain after being pinned behind my back for so long. There is a crimson tint to my vision, as if my eye has filled with blood.

'What have you done to her?'

'Sedated her. She has a lot of medications; it's easy to get them mixed up. Can't think how they got added to her pot of tea, though,' he remarks, drily. 'I'm sure she'll wake up in an hour or so. Here.'

I hear the *fsst* sound of the knife sliding against the ropes. I'm waiting, tensed. Alex's hand grips my shoulder. His fingernails are rimed with dirt.

'Did you do it, Alex? Did you push her down the stairs?'

'Hold still.'

'Alex? Is she right? Did you do it?'

Silence. I can feel the bonds weakening, the blood flow into my arms increasing in warm waves. The ropes slither away from me, ends frayed where Alex has cut them. When I turn to look at him he is folding the knife and holding it out to me.

For a moment I just look at it blankly. 'Alex, did you push her? Yes or no?'

'We have to get to the churchyard.'

My eyes widen. 'Frances?'

'Plan B.' Alex nods. 'He's going to kill her.'

Frances — Now

The throb in my jaw has settled to a low hum, the blood drying in streaks all the way down to my neck. I am thinking about our old life. Back then I thought the worst of our problems was William's gambling and my nagging boredom. How little I knew.

It is getting dark. The shadows stretch and shiver, the sky turning from peach to pink. A small electric light, designed to look like an old Victorian gaslight, hangs outside the back of the church. Moths, drawn to the soft glow, circle and flutter beneath the bulb.

We pass the grave of Mary Sayers, also known as Quiet Mary, who went into the river and never came out, just like Edward Thorn, pale and drowned. We stop when we reach the large yew, the one known as Quiet Mary's Tree. The trunk is thick and ridged with scars, deep fractures splitting the wood. Sap has oozed and trickled and hardened. Beneath my feet the floor is soft with fallen needles.

'You know what Peter Liverly once told us?' William says, touching the trunk. 'He said, "The roots of the yew are very fine and will grow through the eyes of the dead to prevent them seeing their way back to the world of the living."'

He holds his hand out for me to take. I think about running. The shadows swell where the trees huddle close. I might be able to hide, hunkered down in one of the thickets back there. I might get all the way to the wall, find my way back to the hole they created, Squeezeguts. I might even be able to get round the church to the front gate and flag a car down. I might.

I take his hand. I don't know why, but I do. Part of me still thinks he won't hurt me. Part of me wants to see what he is going to show me. That's the worst of all. I want to see.

'Here.' He hands me a small pocket torch. 'Switch it on.'

William approaches the trunk of the tree and knocks against the wood, head cocked as though hearing a distant sound. He moves a little to the left and does so again. And again.

'One, two, three, four,' he intones, eyes glittering in the half-light. 'Rattlesnake hunters knocking at your door. Give them meat and give them bone, and pray that they leave you alone.'

He curls his fist and taps a final time, listening, and this time I hear it too. The sound is different. Not a *thud*, but a *thunk*. A dead echo. In this part, the tree is hollow. William moves forward. He lifts the hammer two-handed, his face in the torchlight a perfect carving of concentration and force; lips drawn back from his gums, brow lowered, the cords on his neck standing out like cables. The hammer hits the tree with a thud, spraying flecks of wood into the air. He brings it back up and down, again and again, succeeding in making a small, splintered hole about the size of a saucer.

Breathless, he turns, cheeks flushed, oily with sweat. 'Go on then. You wanted to know.'

'What?' I'm stalling, of course. My heart has fallen all the way to my knees. Goosepimples ridge my arms and shiver up to my neck. I know what's inside there. The ring of my torchlight quivers.

'It's where we put her. When she was really gone.'

'Who's "we", William?'

'Me and Mum. She wasn't about to let some jumped-up little goth ruin my life. I was going to university. I was going to get a good job. I had a future. Edie Hudson was about to destroy all that.'

I step forward, heart pounding, trying to take a deep enough breath to stay upright. Lights flash across my eyes. I wonder if I'm going to faint. The collar of my T-shirt is damp with blood. Another step. Another. I'll need to stand on tiptoe to see inside; use the torch with my right hand and hold myself steady with my left.

'"We'll just make her see sense, William." Those were Mum's words. I didn't wonder why Mum wasn't mad. I was just so relieved that she could solve the problem for me. Because that's what it was, Frances. A problem that I couldn't fix. I had no control over it.'

He sighs. I watch his face soften with memory, his whole body seeming to go slack. I wonder how it must feel to have held on to this secret all your life, how heavy it must be.

I look at him in quiet wonder. 'How did you do it?'

He laughs softly. 'I didn't. I couldn't, in the end. Wasn't brave enough. Mum stepped in. Thank God. She slipped one of Dad's belts around Edie's neck. She'd brought it with her. I think she must have planned it all along.'

I lean against the wood. It is dark and good and heavy. Without it I feel like I might fall down. William stares past me, seeing something I don't.

'Edie brought the whole gang with her, though. The Rattlesnakes. Jesus, those girls. You know what I did?'

I shake my head.

'I threw stones at them. You should have seen them. They lost their minds! Thought it was Quiet Mary coming out the trees. Only Edie didn't run. She walked right on in to see what was going on. She had no fear. It's what killed her, Mum said. Fear keeps you safe. Keep going, Frances.'

I'm so close to the trunk now I can smell the damp wood, the old, musty scent of rot and age. Under my fingertips the ridges are cavernous, a map to another world. A world where a young girl, long dead, is waiting for me.

'I was meant to help Mum but in the end I just watched. I was shaking too much. Her face, Edie's face, was beautiful. First time she'd ever looked that way. She reached a hand out for me and I stepped away. But I didn't stop watching. I made myself. Right to the end.'

No wonder they all thought she had disappeared, I think. There would have been no noise, no blood, no crime scene, no struggle. A silent murder. I swallow. My mouth is so dry and I am cold all over. I keep thinking of William saying to me, 'My mum is going to love you.' What if she hadn't? Would I have ended up like poor Edie Hudson, strangled in the cold and the dark until her heart stopped?

'You know the thing I remember most? How Edie was so heavy that it took both of us to lift her. I asked Mum, "How do we know she's really dead?" and Mum said, "Because she's not breathing, dummy." Then she laughed. Like it was a joke. Like it was fun, just a fun thing the two of us were doing together.'

I can barely breathe. I stare at William as if I have never seen him before, and it's true: in a way, I haven't. He is a statue with eyes as cold and hard as fossil. I think of all the times he's talked about how much he loves his mother, how she made so many sacrifices for her boys, what a good person she was, so giving. Then I think of Edward Thorn, implicated in a crime he didn't commit, and my heart sinks.

'Your poor dad,' I say.

'What else could he have done? The murder weapon was his, his car was parked nearby. He'd have taken the fall for it, too, if they had ever found Edie's body. Mum knew that. But in the end, just like all the Thorn men, he lost his nerve.' William's head turns slowly to look at me. 'What about you, Frances? Will you lose your nerve?'

I stare at the hole he has beaten into the tree. It is an empty socket, black as the devil.

'Go on, Frances,' William says.

He's right behind me. I've forgotten about the hammer in his hand. I take a deep breath, stand on the ends of my toes and shine the torchlight into the hollow.

Samantha – Now

I run. Alex won't let me drive, saying I will end up wrapped around a tree. He insists we take his car but his hands are shaking so much it takes him three tries to get the key in the lock. I can smell alcohol on his breath. By the time we get to the edge of town there is a queue of traffic that grunts and inches along; flared red brake lights and fuming exhausts.

'Why are you doing this, Alex?'

He stares wordlessly ahead, eyes red and watery. Finally he says, 'Because this is my fault. I showed Frances the photo of Edie. I made *sure* she saw it. Then I made sure William knew she was asking questions about his past. But I never meant for all this to happen.'

I put my hand gently on his arm. 'No. None of this is your fault.'

'I just wanted *him* to suffer for a change. He deserves it.'

I stare at him, head throbbing. Poor Alex. Watching as his older brother – the apple of his mother's eye, by her own admission – moves away and gets married and settles down while he's left behind meeting lovers in the dark and confined at home, too cowed by a matriarch to break free. He wipes his face with his hand, swearing as we approach yet another set of traffic lights turning red.

'It's rush hour. We're not going to make it. I'll try a different way as soon as we get past these traffic lights.'

'No. Not quick enough.' I'm opening the door. A car blasts its horn as I lurch out on to the road. I can hear Alex saying, 'Sam, Samantha, don't do this', but I stumble over to the pavement and then around the corner, down through an alleyway that will take me to the end of Eastleigh Avenue. I pinball off the walls, my woozy head clotted with dried blood. There is an urgency buzzing in my chest, those bees again, building their hives. I laugh aloud.

As I emerge through the end of the alley I realise I can see the spire of St Mary de Castro through the poplar trees. There is a sudden flare of agony in my head, white flashing lights popping in my field of vision. I bend double with my hands on my knees and wait for it to pass. I can feel the knife in my back pocket, my phone in the other, and I wonder about calling the police. But there's no time. I have to keep moving.

As I round the corner the perfume of the honeysuckle and jasmine that grow over the church walls overwhelms me. I lean against the iron railings and use them to prop me up, staggering towards the large iron gate. Thank God. I'm coming, Frances. I'm coming, Edie. I reach the gate and push against it. It doesn't move. I lean harder, straining until the muscles in my arms tremble and a fresh blast of agony detonates in my skull.

'Fucking *move*!' I yell, rattling the gate back and forth. The large padlock holding the gates closed rattles uselessly. *What now?* I think, hopeless, knees buckling, head pounding. *What now?*

I think of Peter Liverly's bungalow and the wall that runs along the back of it. Didn't Edie once say they'd got in that way, over the wall maybe? I can't scale that.

I have to.

I stumble towards the bungalow but a horrible feeling – something akin to dread, bloated and toxic – balloons inside me. *I'm too late*, I think, desperately, *I'm already too late.*

Frances – Now

The torchlight lances through the hollow like a needle, a single beam revealing cobwebs and wood slick and black with damp. A nest of woodlice, startled by the intrusion, scuttle deeper to safety. I lift myself higher on my toes, pointing the light downward. The smell in here is rich and pungent, the smell of rotting leaves and black earth. There is a rustling as something in the bowl of the hollow – a mouse, maybe, or a rat – escapes.

'I don't see her.'

'You're not looking hard enough.'

I draw the light down, down. The faint shimmer of sunlight that comes through the leaves is lacy and finely grained like an old photograph. Behind me I hear a sound – it's familiar and yet I don't place it, my concentration elsewhere, falling into this dark hole with the wavering needle of light. A whisper of leather, the clink of a belt buckle. I'm not listening, not really, and by the time he puts the belt around my neck – gently, like a caress, so I don't flinch or fight back – it's too late. I feel it draw tight about my windpipe and try to make a sound; it comes out like air from a puncture, *whiiiii.* I put my hands to my neck and it's funny because it's William I'm looking for to save me, William who I'm trying to call out for in my high, whistling gasp. *Help me, William, someone is attacking me.* It takes me a good minute to realise that the person attacking me is him. My fingers scrape uselessly for purchase against the strap and I hear him grunt as he tightens his grip, leaning against me, crushing the air from my chest.

His voice, low and thick, presses against my ear. 'I wish Mum could see me now.'

My throat burns, my heart's a fast-running drum. Stars flash in my vision.

'I'll tell her what I've done. She'll be so proud of me.'

My nails tear at the trunk of the tree and I don't feel the pain of the splinters. There's a lightness in my head as if my skull is disintegrating, all of my bones full of air, hollow, like the tree. Stars, stars. I blink and they come back. His hand on the back of my neck, holding the noose of the belt together. He sounds genuinely happy. 'I'm doing it, Mum! I'm doing it!'

There is a gurgling sound in my chest. It forces its way up the thin reed of my throat. My face is hot. Black dots swarm in front of my eyes. *This is it*, I think, *this is death*. William tightens his grip for the final gasp.

Samantha – Now

They didn't want to show me but I looked anyway, because I am dogged, because I am that bitch with a knife. 'Who stabbed you, sir?' the police had asked William, handcuffing him and helping him to his feet, and he had pointed and said, 'That bitch with the knife.' I hadn't answered, of course. I was too busy looking into the hole in the tree, using the torch I'd picked out of Frances's cold hands.

Autumn's coming. That's what the weather forecast says. Cobwebs are strung in the hedgerows glittering with dew and mist lingers over the churning water of the Ouse, the sky a softly smudged charcoal. I'm wearing a beanie hat to cover up the scar on my crown, the one William stove in with a hammer blow. The doctor says it's healing nicely but they want to look at my brain to be sure. I wonder what they'll see in there? Holes where the light escapes? A dark shadow creeping across the scan? I hope not. Despite it all, I still have a lot left to live for.

I knew it was Edie as soon as I saw her. I grew those bones inside the cage of my own. They had to cut the tree open to get inside, like a surgery. I saw the photos they'd taken of the scene. Like I said, they didn't want to show me at first, but I reminded them I'd already pictured it in my head a thousand times.

Weeds and ivy had grown through her ribs. Spiders had built nests in the cavities of her eyes. Tangled around her sternum was a silver necklace with a dragonfly pendant. That's what got me. I held that photograph in my hand so long it started shaking. The bones were old and yellowed and dirty, her clothes rotted away. Her jawbone was missing, as was her lower left foot, taken by scavenging animals slipping through the gaps in the trunk. Next to her in the dirt was a leather belt I was not able to identify. Leather, with a large bronze buckle. It was Alex who identified it as belonging to Edward Thorn.

I'm walking slowly down Eastleigh Avenue with my shadow long behind me. There is the smell of bonfires on the air; woodsmoke and charred ash, the embers of damp leaves. There's a figure waiting by the gate. I don't know if they see me. I don't know if they feel the same nervous energy I do, the feeling of ropes breaking, ballasts burning. Bottles clink in my bag. I've got four, and my trusty lighter. A pack of cigarettes in my pocket because we all know that smoking will kill us, but today is not that day.

Frances has a band of bruising around her throat, blue and purple and a yellow the colour of nicotine stains. She keeps it covered with a scarf, and even though the doctors say she will be fine she is still talking like a one-hundred-a-day smoker, her voice as thin and crushed as dry leaves underfoot. When I found her, struggling with William in front of the yew, her face was turning ashy blue and her eyes were white and bulging. I didn't think twice about planting Nonno's knife between William's shoulder blades. I had a brief flash as I did so, something sparking in my brain, Nonno using the same knife to peel an apple in a long, single coil, and then William was shouting, his hands groping to a place on his back that he couldn't reach, and Frances was on her knees and someone – Alex, it later turned out – was racing over the grass towards us saying *Oh God, oh God*, and I swung at William, hard enough that he spun on his heel as my fist connected with his jaw, hit him with such force he fell backward and drove the knife in deeper.

Alex was on his phone. I fumbled with the belt around Frances's neck and although there was a pulse she did not gasp for breath and she did not open her eyes. I said to her, hold on, and she mouthed a word at me, teeth stained with blood: *Tree.*

That's when I picked up the torch. That's when I looked inside the hole. That's when I found my daughter.

'Hello,' I say to her, and offer her my arm to go through the iron gates like we've just got married. Frances smiles at me. While in hospital she wrote a statement for the police, naming Mimi Thorn as Edie's murderer. William is still in custody. Alex is not. I've been told Mimi is unfit to stand trial. Dementia, they said. I wonder how much of Edward Thorn's banked goodwill is still working in her favour. 'I've spoken with my friends at the station,' he had told me that Halloween. The Thorn name is still in good standing, apparently.

I squeeze Frances's arm. 'You look well. Don't talk if it's painful. I shall just assume you're saying the same about me.'

Frances rolls her eyes. The graveyard has in the last few weeks been a hive of activity, with police and journalists and morbid little people with mobile phones and an appetite for tragedy coming to film and document and take grinning selfies in front of the last resting place of my fifteen-year-old daughter, but today it is quiet, just us and the birds. Missing girls don't draw a crowd like a body does.

'I brought beers,' I tell her. 'Thought we could sit on the bench for a while.'

'Sounds good,' she says huskily.

'I heard from Moya.' I pull a bramble off my jeans. 'She wrote me a very short, very polite email – "Sorry for your loss" – and then in a PS at the bottom, "Edie was one of us."'

'That's sweet.'

'I know.'

Frances takes my hand in her own and squeezes it.

In the days after she was released from hospital, she came to stay at my little house on the end of the estate. I cleared Edie's room out for her, covering the old scarred carpet with a rug and replacing the dead bulb in the bedside lamp. I threw out most of Edie's things – clothes, books, posters – and then behind her mirror I discovered the photo of us in France, the one I'd been looking for when I made the *Missing* posters: the two of us standing on a bridge, arms around each other, smiling. I'd asked a passer-by to take the picture for us in my stumbling, hesitant French, while Edie had laughed behind her hands, rolling her eyes at me. I like to think she kept it because it reminded her that sometimes things were good between us. Because among the rubble, a single plant can grow. I keep the photo in my wallet now.

Frances went back to Swindon to put the house on the market – hers and William's – and to start divorce proceedings. I told her there was no rush, but she shook her head. Smiled. Her voice was low and cracked-sounding, like something had been ripped right out of her, but she told me her plans. They are good plans. Hopeful. I don't doubt she will see them through.

After our first beer I will tell Frances what else I have in my bag. A small box, barely heavy enough to contain my girl with her loud, volatile ways and her Molotov cocktail of a brain, but she is in there all the same; a small, black box with her ashes inside, and on the bottom, beneath the word *Deceased*, it reads *Elizabeth Jane Hudson*. I'm here to ask Frances for one last favour: to walk up to the Downs with me and release my girl to the wind. Below us will be the sun-warmed grass, the river, the town. We will stand together as the wind dances her ashes against the blue sky like long, winding ribbons, a grey comet trail disappearing over the hills.

ACKNOWLEDGMENTS

This book would never have made it without the combined efforts of Jack Butler, Emily Ruston, Jane Snelgrove and all at Thomas & Mercer. Thank you for your patience and understanding. As always, thanks to the mighty Catherine Cho for championing me. I'm glad to have you in my corner.

Being a single parent is hard. You need good people around you who can lend a hand when you're struggling. So my deep and sincere thanks to Andy and Clair for being so HELPFUL and letting me and my girl crash at theirs more times than I can count. Thank you to all my friends for their support, especially Alex, Amy B, Amy M, Lisa and Tina – you are my rocks in fast-moving water.

Anne Booty, you delight, you utter delight. I love you loads, thank you for all your support.

To my mum for everything: thank you. For my sisters Simone and Johanna, for my big bro Dominic and for my dad Berwyn, all my love.

I want to mention Hannah Williams, Tracy Meade, Damilola Taylor, Hannah Deterville, Joy Morgan, Patrick Warren and David Spencer, and all the other children who were overlooked and underreported. I wish we could have done better for you.

ABOUT THE AUTHOR

Photo © 2019 A. Murrell

Daisy Pearce was born in Cornwall and grew up on a smallholding surrounded by hippies. She read Stephen King's *Cujo* and *The Hamlyn Book of Horror* far too young and has been fascinated with the macabre ever since.

She began writing short stories as a teenager and dropped out of a fashion journalism course at university when she realised it wasn't anywhere near as fun as making stuff up. After spells living in London and Brighton, Daisy had her short story 'The Black Prince' published in *One Eye Grey* magazine. Another short story, 'The Brook Witch', was performed on stage at the Small Story Cabaret in Lewes in 2016. She has also written articles about mental health online. In 2015, *The Silence* won a bursary with The Literary Consultancy, and later that year Daisy also won the

CHINDI Authors Competition with her short story 'Worm Food'. Her second novel was longlisted for the Mslexia Novel Award.

Daisy currently works in the library at the University of Sussex, where she shelves books and listens to podcasts on true crime and folklore. She lives in Lewes with a one-eyed Siamese cat and a nine-year-old daughter who occasionally needs reminding that ghosts and monsters aren't real.

Sometimes she almost believes it herself.